Wes & Toren

J.M. Colail

Published by
Dreamspinner Press
4760 Preston Road
Suite 244-149
Frisco, TX 75034
http://www.dreamspinnerpress.com/

Cover Design by Mara McKennen

ISBN: 978-1-935192-47-3

Printed in the United States of America
First Edition
January, 2009

eBook edition available
eBook ISBN: 978-1-935192-48-0

To You and You,

You know who you are.

Chapter 1

WESLEY CARROLL trudged down the hall in his ripped jeans, white T-shirt, and old, red Converse low-tops. A grin lifted the corners of his lips and I felt my stomach twitter in reaction.

"S'up?" he said, passing by me. I felt my heart skip, my stomach drop, and my mouth go dry. He stopped beside me and flashed his grin again. "Cool shoes."

I was wearing a pair of old, brown work shoes, clunky leather things with thick soles. I suddenly thought of an e-mail I'd received of ridiculous pickup lines: *Nice shoes. Wanna fuck?* I blushed deeper, like Wesley could hear my thoughts.

"Thanks," I stuttered, trying to conceal my reddening cheeks.

Wesley smiled again, said "See ya," and continued on his way. Everyone knew him because he was the troublemaker, the kid from the wrong side of the tracks, the risk-taker, the school's pot dealer. I'd watched him from afar, a middling crush, but this was the first time he had spoken to me, and he left my stomach filled with butterflies.

After English Lit, Hailey stopped me and smiled, typically pretty and a little superficial, flashing her pearl-white teeth, and asking if she could borrow my notes from class. She touched my arm when I told her that she could and she promised that she would return them by the end of the day. I suspected that she was flirting with me, but Wesley was still on my mind and I blushed all over thinking about him.

I ate lunch outside in front of the school, sitting cross-legged on a cement rectangle that served as a giant planter for a tree and evergreen shrubs. It was unseasonably warm for spring but the ground was still thoroughly cold and transmitted the chill through the concrete to my thighs and rear end. I took out a book while I picked at my ham sandwich and ate my apple. I still packed juice boxes in my lunch and slurped it while I read.

I was used to eating alone; I preferred my own company to the loud and obnoxious kids that talked about nothing. I didn't think I was better than anyone else (well, maybe just a little; I had some culture) but I was shy and often earned the epithet "nerd" for getting good grades. Solitude was better than being ridiculed any day of the week.

Before sixth hour, I went to my locker for my history book. It was a heavy tome that we mostly skimmed through, studying about every other chapter. I looked over my shoulder and Wesley was walking toward me. I quickly looked down but strained my eyes to the side to see him.

"Hey, Toren," he said and held out a green notebook. "This is yours, right? Hailey borrowed it?"

I looked at the notebook and nodded my head.

"I told her that we had History together and that I'd give it back to you."

"Oh, um, thanks."

It was like he knew he made me nervous. Suddenly, he threw his head back and snapped his fingers. "Oh yeah. Hailey wanted me to tell you 'thanks' and that you were, what did she say? Oh yeah, super cool." He laughed and I tried to laugh with him but my lips smiled crookedly. "Well, see you in class." He waved slightly and walked away.

People were walking past me and fortunately, no one knew why my face was so flush. My locker was near the classroom and I went inside, sitting in the second row. Wesley probably went to go smoke or was skipping class. Mr. Hannity was a minute late and Wesley strolled in later than that, whispering, "Sorry." He glanced at me as he passed, moving to his seat in the back row.

I went home with a strange feeling in the pit of my stomach. Alycia was at swim practice, Mom worked the mid-shift at the hospital, and I was glad to have the place to myself. I did some homework, but my mind drifted to Wesley to the point of distraction.

After an hour, and an hour before Alycia came home, I found myself in the bathroom, clutching the sink, pushed in there by my own urgings that wouldn't be sated with mere thoughts. It was the first time that I touched myself with an actual person in mind and I felt ashamed as if Wesley knew by some kind of masturbatory telepathy.

Alycia came home, kicked off her shoes and moved around the small kitchen, taking a can of tuna from the cupboard. She left the apron hanging on the hook inside the pantry and I warned her that if she spilled on her clothes that I wasn't going to wash them. She made a face at me and then shook her head.

"I just don't look good in an apron…not like you," she said. "Besides, what could happen? Crumbs could fall on me after toasting the bread?"

"That's another thing too," I said, tapping the counter with my fingers. "You always make easy stuff when it's your turn. Tuna sandwiches? C'mon, even Mom can make those."

Alycia laughed and agreed, but didn't offer to make any vegetable to accompany. I took out a can of green beans and put them over a low heat. Alycia groaned and rolled her eyes.

"I swear, you're gonna make someone a wonderful housewife someday."

I thought of Wesley and blushed; I thought of my affair in the bathroom and blushed deeper and upon realizing that I was blushing, I blushed even more. Alycia caught the guilt in my eyes and grinned from ear to ear.

"Tor? What's that look for? Got someone in mind already?"

"Give me a break," I groaned.

Chapter 2

MR. HANNITY was late to class and Wesley was later, repeating yesterday's dialogue. Wesley smiled at me as he walked to his seat and my stomach fluttered. Mr. Hannity described the semester project in detail and then allowed us to choose our own partners. I hated when teachers did that; it reminded me of gym class in grade school. I stared at my desk, waiting for everyone to partner up so that I could be paired with the other person who wasn't chosen.

"Mr. Hannity, me and Toren are gonna work together." Wesley rapped his knuckles on my desk and Mr. Hannity looked at me before nodding and writing it down in his grade book. Wesley grinned and I stared back at him blankly. "You don't mind, do ya?" he asked. I shook my head and blushed. "Cool. Wait for me after class." I nodded and hid my face.

Mr. Hannity lectured for the rest of the hour, but I was too distracted to listen. I drew pictures in the margins of my notebook, but my mind always drifted back to Wesley. My heart was thumping.

Mr. Hannity asked me to stay after class. He was quiet until the classroom cleared, and then he leaned against his desk and crossed his arms.

"Thanks for staying after, Toren. I just wanted to talk to you briefly about your project... Well, more just to give you a heads-up," Mr. Hannity explained, looking down at me over his glasses. "If you have any problems working on your project, talk to me right away. Okay? Will you do that?"

"Um…sure. Thanks, Mr. Hannity."

He patted my shoulder as I walked out of the classroom. He didn't have to say Wesley's name specifically, but the implication was there. I was glad that Mr. Hannity recognized that I might have trouble working with him and gave me some leeway with his expectations. I was a good student and worked hard to get good grades. Someone like Wesley could mess that up if he screwed off instead of working on the project, but I still felt excited that he picked me to be his partner.

"Hey. What'd Hannity wanna talk to you about?" Wesley asked after I stepped out of the classroom. He furrowed his brows and stared at me. "Did he give you a warning about me or something?"

"No. He—he didn't say anything."

"Yeah, right. He already has me pegged for disaster. But you, you get straight As, right? So, I figure I got myself an A already."

"You're gonna have to do your share of the work too," I said quietly.

"Ah, he *did* warn you about me. Seems like that guy has had it in for me all along. Look, I gotta get a good grade on this project or he'll fail me, so I need you to get me an A." Wesley leaned back against the lockers and crossed his arms on his chest. "So, you're gonna do your part and not talk to Hannity about anything. Got it?"

My heart was beating wildly. He seemed so nice when I talked to him yesterday. "I'm—I'm not gonna do your work for you. You're gonna have to study too." My voice was weak and I was trying so hard to sound confident. A smile cracked Wesley's lips. I was waiting for something; I didn't know what it was, but I knew it was coming.

"Yeah, okay," he said after a long pause.

That wasn't what I was expecting.

"So we have to present on June fifth, right? That's gives us…what, about a month? Well, we should probably start thinking about a topic then."

"I'm kinda interested in the building of the Transcontinental Railroad. Or maybe the Chinese Exclusion Acts of the 1880s," I suggested. I had already thought about the topic for this project.

"Cool. Why don't you follow me to my house and we'll figure it out there."

"Follow you?"

"Yeah. Don't you have a car?"

My cheeks reddened as I shook my head. What a stupid thing to be embarrassed about.

"Hmph. I thought I saw you driving around in an old, blue Taurus."

He noticed me? "That's my mom's car."

"Well, I'll give you a ride then."

"But...shouldn't we go to the library?"

"You wanna go to the library? C'mon, I don't wanna be in school any longer than I absolutely have to be. Let's just go to my house."

"Well, I kinda think the library might be better,"

"I'd rather go somewhere with a smoking section, ya know? C'mon," he said, starting to walk away. He stopped and waited while I got my book bag from my locker.

We drove to a ranch-style house with an unmowed lawn, a broken shutter, and a torn screen door. The driveway was cracked and weeds grew in the cleavages between concrete slabs.

"You want a beer or something?" he asked, dropping his book bag inside the door.

"No, thank you." I stood just inside the front door, gripping the straps of my bag tightly. I looked around at the mismatched furniture, the nicked-up coffee table with two overflowing ashtrays, and the gold shag carpeting from the 1970s.

"Have a seat," Wesley said, coming from the kitchen with a brown bottle in his hand. "You're so uptight." He sat down on the shaggy sofa and patted the cushion. I sat down, pulled my book bag onto my lap, and pulled out a spiral notebook and folder from our history class. He held his cigarette between his thumb and index finger and put his foot up on the coffee table while I fumbled around for a pen.

"Relax. I don't bite. Are you sure you don't want a beer or something?"

"No, thank you."

I watched him from the corner of my eye. He seemed different but I wasn't quite sure what it was. He was one of the coolest guys in school, drawing attention whether he wanted to or not. He was the type of guy that would probably end up flipping burgers when he was forty with three ex-wives and a mountain of child support.

Maybe I was a little resentful because everyone liked him and I didn't really have many friends. He seemed to have it so easy. Most teachers liked him even though he skipped class a lot and never studied. Even Mr. Hannity liked him, despite his constant interruptions and obnoxious behavior. Belittling his future was all I could do to keep my self-esteem from bottoming out.

"You really wanna get started on the project now? We just got home from school. Relax a little first," he said, taking a drink from his beer and another hit of his cigarette.

"But, I've got other stuff to do, so we might as well just get started." I stared at the textbook on my lap.

Wesley looked at me for a moment, then stood up and retrieved his book bag from near the front door. "So you wanna do the railroad thing or the Chinese-whatever-Acts?"

He sat down next to me, leaned back into the couch, and crossed his ankle on his knee. His leg pressed into mine and I jerked to the side a little, but his leg still touched mine.

"Yeah, I'm kinda interested in the building of the Transcontinental Railroad. Most people don't even know that the Chinese built most of it, and basically for nothing. They were really exploited—I guess it just shows where the values of this country come from. Slaves weren't the only ones exploited. Basically, if you weren't a white European, you were pretty much screwed. And the Chinese Exclusion Acts were part of that too. The government actually excluded Chinese from entering the U.S. But the Chinese used the courts to gain entry, basically outsmarting the government."

Wesley stared at me with a grin on his face. I suddenly realized that I was just rambling. Did that sound stupid? No wonder everyone called me a nerd.

"You really like this stuff, don't you?" Wesley asked, tilting his grin to one side.

My cheeks were hot with embarrassment. "Yeah, I do." Like I could hide it after my educational rant. "Actually, this is what I wanna study in college."

"You wanna be a teacher or something?" he asked. I nodded without looking at him. "I can totally picture you doing that. I think you'd be good at it." I tried to hide the smile that was curling my lips. "So which do you wanna do? The railroad or the Exclusion thing?"

"Let's do the Chinese Exclusion Acts. I think we'd be able to find more resources about them, anyway."

"Cool. Now that that's decided," Wesley said and leaned forward, opening the cabinet on the coffee table, "you wanna get high?"

"Huh?" I glanced at Wesley and he pulled a small pipe and a clear plastic bag from the cabinet and laid them on his lap.

"It's my way of saying thanks for doing this project with me, even though you could've had a better partner," he said, sticking his index finger in the bowl of the pipe and tapping it a few times.

"Don't—don't worry about it," I stuttered. I pulled my book bag up to the side of the couch and tried to push my notebook and folder in.

Wesley stopped fingering the bowl and looked at me. "You don't wanna? C'mon, it's my treat."

I had never smoked pot; I had never even seen it before now. Wesley felt dangerous to me, but it was also part of his charm.

"I should get going," I stammered, still trying to fit my notebook and folder in my book bag.

Wesley set the pipe and baggie down on the coffee table and sighed lightly. "You know, Toren, you might look good on paper, but you're boring as hell in person."

I looked up sharply. "What? No I'm not." I looked down into my lap again. He didn't even know me. How could he make such a quick judgment?

He rested his arm on the sofa behind my head and leaned toward me with his same grin. "Prove it then," he said, moving his face closer to mine. I could smell the tobacco and beer on his breath. "I mean, you're into boys, right?"

My eyes widened and I stared at Wesley. He smiled devilishly and leaned closer. I swallowed hard and looked down. He didn't know that I sort of had a crush on him, did he? Was he trying to make me admit it? Or was he just making a joke?

"Wh—what? Why are you even asking that?"

"'Cause you always look at me like you wanna fuck me," he answered, with a grin that was almost a sneer.

"What? I—I don't—"

"No, that's not quite right," he said calmly, looking up at the ceiling and shaking his head. "No, it's more like you wanna *be* fucked by me."

My heart stopped. I didn't know what to do. I pulled my book bag onto my lap and stood up. "I have to go," I said quickly and rushed toward the front door.

"You want a ride?" Wesley asked, lighting a cigarette and looking at me over the flame. He sank back into the couch.

"I don't live too far."

"See you at school," Wesley called as I pulled the door closed behind me.

Chapter 3

I GOT to Spanish class early, as usual, and waited for the bell to ring. Ms. Harper said hello and looked back to the papers on her desk. I looked up involuntarily each time someone came in the room, waiting for Wesley. I was nervous to see him; the things he said yesterday followed me to bed and woke up with me in the morning. How was I supposed to act around him now? Wesley rushed in late, apologized to Ms. Harper quietly and glanced at me as he took his seat. He had a whisper of a smile on his face and my stomach tingled.

"*Uds. tienen un examen mañana*," Ms. Harper began, followed by a barrage of Spanish that no one really understood. She explained that she would finish up the lesson plan and then give a review in the second half of class.

The test would cover chapters 12 and 13 and Ms. Harper warned us that the exam would be vocabulary-heavy. I made a note of it in the margin and Wesley raised his hand. He went through his usual repertoire of exam jokes, finishing with one about giving us the answers. Ms. Harper smiled and tried to conceal her rolling eyes.

"Even if I did give you the answers, I somehow doubt you would study those either, Wes," she answered flatly, then smiled.

The class laughed and Wesley laughed too. Ms. Harper was young, fresh out of college, and a little more lenient than older teachers. She was comfortable joking with students and was a popular teacher.

The bell rang and Ms. Harper told us to study hard.

Wesley called after me and I turned to see him trotting toward me. He had a grin on his face and I felt a few butterfly wings in my stomach.

"You wanna study for Spanish together?" he asked, walking next to me.

My eyes strained to the side, trying to look at Wesley without looking like I was looking at him. "Um…I don't know," I answered, remembering the things he said.

"C'mon, you gotta study too, right? So why not study together?" He held his books at the side of his head and I could see the faint outline of muscle in his upper arm.

"Well, um, sure, okay," I answered. He did have a good point.

"Sweet. Wait for me after History, all right?"

I watched him walk away from the corner of my eye; I liked the way he walked—as if he owned the world. He was so confident and I really admired that about him.

I wasn't able to concentrate for the rest of the day. My mind wandered to Wesley and what he said. Did he mean any of it? I couldn't deny the feelings that he aroused in me, but I worried that I might just be a game to him.

I waited in History class. I was always early to my classes and couldn't seem to break the habit even when I wanted to. Wesley came in and sat on the corner of the desk next to mine and smiled at me.

"Hey. What's up?"

"Nothing," I answered, looking down at the desktop. He chatted with me as the classroom began to fill up. He talked about school, how eager he was for the summer, and that between me and him, he kinda liked Spanish class.

"Ms. Harper's pretty hot, so I guess that kinda makes the class go by faster too."

I looked up at Wesley and he grinned. "Yeah…she is," I murmured. I tried to sound convincing.

Mr. Hannity came in and slapped his forehead when he saw Wesley. “Well, damn, if it isn’t Mr. Carroll. Not only on time, but actually early!”

Wesley nodded his head sarcastically and rolled his eyes. The bell rang. Wesley patted my shoulder and went to his seat. I looked around and saw Jen and Olivia watching me. It was common knowledge that Jen had a crush on Wesley; they even dated for a short time. I suddenly felt self-conscious. Did they think I was competition? Of course not; I’m a guy. I furrowed my brows and stared at my desk. Fortunately, Mr. Hannity began the lesson and I forgot about Jen and Olivia.

The bell rang and Wesley walked me to my locker and waited for me to fetch my stuff. I turned toward the library and Wesley stopped me, his hands casually pushed in his pockets.

“Where are you going? My car’s this way.”

“Um…I thought we were going to the library.”

“Well, we have to practice speaking for the oral, right? And the library isn’t exactly the best place to do that. Besides, I wanna get the hell outta here anyway.” He waited for me and then flashed a grin in my direction.

“Hey, Wes! Wait up a sec!” Benny shouted, running up to Wesley and glancing at me. “Hey, I got a question for you.” He glanced at me again and then leaned forward, next to Wesley’s ear. I heard him mumble something and I stood awkwardly to the side.

Wesley backed away from Benny and nodded. “Yeah, it’s in my car.”

“Is he cool?” Benny asked, glaring at me.

Wesley furrowed his brows. “Don’t worry about it. Toren, you comin’?”

At his car, Wesley searched under the passenger seat and pulled out a small bag. Benny gave him ten dollars and pocketed the bag. Wesley rested his arm on the open door and put his other hand on his hip.

"So…you wanna hook up later and pick up some chicas?" Benny asked, glancing over his shoulder at me. I felt strange standing there, like a tag-along or a fifth wheel.

"Nah…got stuff to do. See ya around," Wesley said. Benny sneered and walked off. Wesley stepped to the side and held the door open for me. "Get in."

I sat down and pushed my book bag down on the floor and Wesley shut the door. He got in and turned down the radio before starting the car.

"Man, that guy annoys the hell outta me. You know, don't tell anyone, but sometimes I cut in a little dill weed or oregano with his stuff," he said. "He's such a dumbass too; he's never noticed. But, caveat emptor and all that shit."

I was mostly surprised that the words "caveat emptor" came from his mouth. I laughed a little and Wesley lifted the clutch and tore out of the parking lot.

We got to his house and Wesley offered me a drink but I declined politely. I sat down and pulled out my Spanish text. I heard the refrigerator door shut and the clink of bottles. Wesley came into the living room with a brown bottle and a glass of soda.

"I didn't know what you wanted, so I brought you some pop," he said, sitting down next to me. I thanked him and leaned to my side. We were sitting shoulder to shoulder. His leg was pressed against mine.

"The—the exam'll cover chapters twelve and thirteen," I said, opening my book and flipping through the pages.

Wesley groaned quietly and retrieved his book bag from the front door. He sat close to me again and I inhaled deeply. His scent was mixed with tobacco and beer and he looked at me from the corner of his eye. I stared at my textbook and took quiet, deep breaths.

"Ms. Harper said there'll be a lot of vocab on the test, so we better go over that, and also she said to study verb tenses," I said, finally finding chapter 12 after flipping through the pages aimlessly. Wesley watched me as much as he looked at his textbook and I felt nervous under his constant gaze.

We had reviewed chapter 12 and most of 13 when Wesley yawned and suggested we take a break. He stretched his arms over his head and then sat back with his beer and lit a cigarette.

"We're—we're almost done, so let's just finish up chapter thirteen, okay?

"All right," Wesley moaned, setting down the bottle and picking up the textbook.

We went through the rest of chapter, doing some of the suggested exercises in the outline. He had a good accent, pronouncing syllables like a native speaker. I was better at reading and writing than speaking and on occasion, Wesley would correct me if I mispronounced a word. I was surprised that I was actually learning something from him.

When we had finished chapter 13, Wesley put his hands behind his head and held his cigarette between his lips. I took another sip of my soda and began putting my things in my bag.

"The test is gonna have a lot of vocab on it, so you should go over that again once or twice."

"You're leaving already?" Wesley asked. He sat up on the edge of the sofa and rested his cigarette in the ashtray.

My heart started beating faster and I swallowed hard. "Yeah. I've—I've got a lot of other homework to do." I was having trouble fitting the textbook into my book bag.

"Well, that can wait a while. We just finished studying; relax a little." He inched closer to me, leaving his cigarette burning in the ashtray. "Besides, I still have to thank you for helping me."

I felt the warmth of his body next to me and he neared his way closer to my lips, teasing me with anticipation that I desperately tried to conceal. He brought his hand to my chin, turning my face to him. He still had a grin on his face, but it was a little different. With his thumb, he pulled my chin down and kissed me. His lips were chapped but they were soft too. He caressed my cheek and I closed my eyes. His kiss radiated through my entire body.

He said he wanted to "thank" mc for helping him study. Was that why? Because he needed help with schoolwork and he thought this was how he could repay me? I pulled back and looked down into my lap.

"You…should make flashcards," I whispered absentmindedly, feeling for my book bag.

"Hunh?"

"It'll help you memorize the vocab," I said. I could feel tears welling in my eyes and I pushed them back. "I have to go. Sorry. But I have to go," I said, grabbing my book bag and rushing to the door. Wesley stared at me and said my name once but he didn't follow me.

Chapter 4

I WOKE with sticky sheets and morning wood that almost hurt. The dream faded quickly with consciousness, but I remembered the feel of Wesley's kiss and I met the throbbing ache between the sheets.

I sank back into bed. My cheeks reddened as I pulled back the covers and saw the result of my dream. I stripped the sheets, balled them up tightly, and stepped out of my bedroom, nearly bumping into Alycia. She jumped back and her small breasts jiggled beneath her white tank-top. She furrowed her brows at me.

"What the hell, Toren? I just did laundry the other day!" she complained, seeing the bundle of sheets in my arms. My cheeks turned a deeper red and she arched her eyebrows knowingly. "Nuh-uh. You gotta wash out your own DNA—new house rule," she said and disappeared into the bathroom.

I shook my head and hoped that this wasn't an indication of how the rest of the day would go. I felt nervous already; I didn't know how to act around Wesley. I didn't know if he'd told everyone about what happened, if I would be made a laughingstock. My shoulders slumped and I sighed heavily.

"Hey, move it! Or you're gonna be late!" Alycia shouted, walking past me. "Why are you just standing there?" She looked back at me and touched my forehead. "Do you feel all right?"

Maybe I could stay home; no, there was the Spanish test. "Yeah, I'm okay." I shifted the load in my arms and Alycia patted my cheek.

"All right. Well, hurry up. You want a ham sandwich for lunch again?"

I nodded and Alycia trotted off to her room. I dropped the sheets into a laundry basket and figured I'd wash them when I got home. I took a cold shower and then left for school. Nothing seemed different; everyone was just ignoring me like they always had.

Wesley was late to Spanish again. Ms. Harper was already passing out the tests and she scolded him for being late on exam day.

I couldn't bear to look at Wesley. Just seeing his face reminded me of my dream and the sticky sheets this morning. I didn't know what to do or what to say to him. I left Spanish class quickly and took my book bag with me to History so I wouldn't have to talk to him after class if he followed me to my locker.

The sunny morning had faded into a gray and murky afternoon. The pouring rain complemented my mood and, of course, I forgot my umbrella at home. I waited under the overhang at the front of the school, watching kids dash for the buses or to their cars in the parking lot.

"Boy, it's really coming down hard, isn't it?" Wesley stood behind me with his book bag over his shoulder. He had one hand in his pocket and a slight smile on his face. "You don't plan on walking home in this, do you?"

"I'm just waiting for it to let up."

"Who knows when that'll be? I'll give you a ride," he said and smiled, tilting his head toward the parking lot. I shook my head but Wesley persisted. "C'mon, what's the big deal?" He grabbed my wrist and pulled me into the rain. I tried to pull my hand away, but he held tight until I followed him willingly.

I whispered thanks, but I don't think he heard me.

He sped through the driving rain, taking corners without braking, even though I told him where to turn long before it came up. The windshield wipers slapped frantically and the sky seemed even darker.

"Thanks for the ride," I said over the plunking rain and the moan of the idling engine.

"What, you're not even gonna invite me in after I saved your butt from getting soaked?" he asked with a smile.

"Oh, um, I guess…if you want to," I stuttered, gripping the straps of my backpack.

"Cool. Where should I park?"

We ran to my building and tried to dry off a bit on the stairs to the third floor. He waited patiently while I fumbled getting the key in the lock. I opened the door and Wesley stepped in, his hands in his pockets. I dropped my book bag by the door and noticed that Wesley didn't bring his.

"So this is where you live. It's…cozy," he said.

"I know that's just a polite way of saying small," I answered with a shy laugh. "But it's just me, my mom, and my sister, so it serves the purpose."

"Just you, your mom, and your sister?" he echoed, looking around the living room and into the small kitchen that opens onto it. "Where are they?"

"My mom works the mid-shift at the hospital and my sister has swim practice after school."

"Oh. So…it's just us, then?" Wesley smiled and looked at me with his deep, brown eyes. My stomach felt hollow.

"Do—do you want something to drink? We've got soda, orange juice…. I can make some coffee, if you want," I said, looking toward the kitchen.

I was trapped between him and the door. "Let's cut through the bullshit, Toren." He grinned and put his hand flat on the door, over my shoulder.

"What do you mean?" I was trying hard to sound innocent.

Wesley lifted my chin with his hand and grinned again. "You know exactly what I mean," he said and kissed me.

His kiss was amazing, overflowing my senses, and I closed my eyes. My body tensed and I pulled back, looking down. "Why—why are you doing this?"

"Because I like you. And I think you like me too." It was just for a second, but I saw his confidence slip. "Don't you?" His grin came back.

I looked away. I knew I was blushing bright red. Wesley chuckled quietly. I looked up and his expression was sincere. My stomach tightened.

"It's okay. You don't have to say it if you don't want to. But show me. Kiss me back, Toren."

He took his hand from the door and held my chin up. It took all my courage to look into his eyes. He pulled my mouth open with his thumb and kissed me again, his tongue slipping between my lips. Hesitantly, nervously, and maybe with a twinge of embarrassment, I grasped his shirtsleeves and tilted my head to the side.

"You wanna sit down? You look like you might be a little weak in the knees," Wesley asked, smiling at me again.

I frowned, but only because it was true: I did feel a little weak in my knees. Wesley followed me to the couch and sat beside me. He put his hand on my leg and I jumped a little. I looked at my lap and bit my lip.

"Doesn't it—doesn't it bother you…because we're both guys?"

He shook his head and smiled. "No. Why should it?"

I looked away again.

He brushed the hair from my eyes and looked at me gently.

"What are you so afraid of, Toren?"

I'm afraid…that my mom will hate me.

"Are you afraid that people will talk? Or that they'll make fun of you? If that's the case, then we just won't tell anyone. We'll keep it our little secret as long as you want, okay?" He smiled reassuringly at me and ran his fingers down my cheek.

Maybe Mom would never know if we kept it a secret. He sank into me on the couch, the feel of his warm body washing over me like a crushing wave. His kiss seemed different from before; it was sweeter and heavier and it felt inevitable.

He became bolder and slid his hand underneath the hem of my shirt. His fingertips traced my stomach like he was trying to memorize every inch of it by touch. His kiss dropped to my neck and then to the dimple between my collarbones. My body tingled all over. I looked down at him and he glanced up at me from the tops of his eyes, and then met my lips hungrily.

"Hey, Tor! I'm home!" Alycia stepped in the front door and her eyes rounded when she saw Wesley and me. "Oh, wow. Major bad timing, huh? Sorry, guys," she said, giggling.

I panicked and pushed Wesley away. "Alycia? What—what are you doing here?"

"Duh. I've got a swim meet tonight, remember? I told you yesterday," Alycia said, walking past us. She stopped in mid-step and stared blankly at Wesley. "Wait a minute. You're Wesley Carroll."

Wesley smiled goofily. "Hi. How ya doin'?"

"I don't believe it! *My* brother with Wesley Carroll? This is so cool!" Alycia glanced at me and then smiled broadly. "Oh, but, don't mind me. You won't even know I'm here," she said, waving her hand. Then she disappeared down the hall and I heard her bedroom door shut.

"So…that was your sister?"

I couldn't look at him. I didn't know what to do. Wesley stared at me and then stood up.

"I get it." He took the scratch pad and pen from the coffee table and jotted something down. He ripped the top sheet off and handed it to me. "Give me a call later." He smiled again and patted my cheek, then walked out the door.

I sat on the edge of the couch with my head in my hands. I felt sick. I had to talk to Alycia. She didn't react the way I expected. She didn't seem troubled or even concerned by what she saw. How could she be okay with it?

I knocked at her door and Alycia was lying on her stomach on the bed, kicking her feet and reading a magazine.

"You guys didn't have to stop on my account," she said, resting her chin in her hand and grinning.

I balled my hands into fists at my sides. "It…it's not what you think—"

"Oh? So what was it? He tripped and accidentally stuck his tongue down your throat? Yeah, I'm sure that's what happened."

"No! It wasn't…I mean…"

Alycia sat up and scooted to the edge of the bed. She tilted her head to the side and looked at me with a serious expression. "Toren, what are you so afraid of?"

That's what Wesley had asked me. I dug my fists into my thighs. "Please…don't tell Mom. Please. Promise me that you won't tell Mom I'm—." I stopped myself and looked down.

"Say it, Toren. Say it out loud."

I glanced up at Alycia and down to the floor again. "Don't—don't tell her I'm…gay."

"At least you can say it out loud now," she said, crossing her arms.

She was taking it too lightly. "Promise me!"

"All right, all right, I promise," she said and stretched her arms over her head. "Though I don't see what the big deal is."

"Are you serious? How can you say that?" I shouted, wiping away tears with the back of my hand.

Alycia looked at me and her face softened with sympathy. "Look, Toren, what happened between Mom and Dad is *their* business. It has nothing to do with us," she said matter-of-factly and sighed with a puff of frustration. "You can't ignore your feelings for the rest of your life because you're afraid of what Mom'll think. Just be yourself. Besides, I think that if you talked to her, you'd find that she'd understand."

"I doubt it," I said, shaking my head.

"Well, I think you should be proud. I mean, you landed one of the hottest guys in school." A grin spread across her face and surprisingly, I felt better. She stood up from the bed and walked across the room. "If anything, *I'm* proud of you," she said softly and hugged me. Then she pulled away quickly. "Oh yeah. Will you come to my meet? Mike can't go and Mom has to work and I really want someone there. Please?" She batted her eyelashes and smiled wide.

"Yeah, okay."

"You're the best big brother. I'll even make dinner for you tonight," she said and walked out of the room.

"That's okay," I said, following her. "I'm not really that hungry."

Alycia stopped and turned around. "Well, just remember that I offered."

I smiled and nodded. She would do anything to get out of cooking.

Alycia left for her swim meet at 6:30. I watched TV and found something to munch on, then walked to school at 7:00. I brought a book with me and settled in for a long night. Alycia swam four events and they were all toward the end of the meet. I opened my book and eavesdropped on nearby conversations.

I thought about what Alycia had said. She made me say it out loud. She seemed so calm about it too; I didn't understand how she could be so nonchalant. I knew that if Mom found out, she wouldn't be able to handle it. Alycia didn't hear the things Mom yelled at Dad, but I did. Mom had never been the same since they divorced, as if she'd forgotten what it was like to be happy.

It was the boys' 300-meter relay and I looked up from my book. I tried to remember a distinct time when I realized that I paid more attention to boys than I did to girls. I watched their slim bodies cut through the silvery water, their heaving chests when they climbed out of the pool, and their revealing Speedos that look silly on even a perfect figure. I wondered if Alycia knew I was gay before I did. But how did she know? Even more importantly, how did Wesley know?

My row on the bleacher vibrated and I glanced up; Wesley was sidestepping his way toward me. I closed my book, keeping my place with my index finger. Wesley glanced at the cover of a near-naked Persian boy dancing with billowy colored scarves.

"Whatcha reading?"

I looked at the cover and turned it to the side. "It's about Alexander the Great, by Mary Renault. It's really good so far." I dog-eared the page and set the book down.

"What class is it for?"

"It's not for class," I answered, then looked into my lap. I really am a nerd.

"Cool. So, how ya doin'?" Wesley asked, looking down at the pool and then back to me. "You seemed kinda out of it earlier, when your sister walked in."

I looked around the bleachers self-consciously, remembering bits of conversations that I overheard. "Um, I'm okay."

"Has your sister been up yet?" I shook my head. "Let's go outside. It's too damn hot in here and I wanna have a smoke anyway."

I hesitated but then picked up my book and followed him outside. He led me to the side of the school, in a shadow between yellow streetlights. He ran his hand through his hair and smiled at me.

"I wasn't sure if you would be here or not, so I took a chance," he said, lighting a cigarette and letting it dangle between his lips. "I wanted to see if you were okay. You seemed a little freaked out when your sister walked in." He looked at me and I looked down to the ground. "But your sister didn't seem surprised. She actually seemed pretty cool about it." I nodded and Wesley took a couple hits of his cigarette.

He talked and I listened. I kept my eyes to the side, on the constant lookout for anyone. I felt so nervous around him, but it wasn't like anyone could know what had happened earlier just by looking at us.

"Well, I guess we should go back in." He took the cigarette from his lips and flicked it to the side. He kissed me quickly, then he smiled and walked toward the door. "C'mon, we don't wanna miss your sister."

I followed Wesley inside and we returned to the same place in the bleachers. I still felt nervous around him, but it was a different type of nervous, an exhilarating nervous. We talked about school, and books and music, about everything. We cheered hard for Alycia. She won both the 50- and 100-meter butterfly. After the first race, she pulled her goggles up to her forehead and searched the crowd for me. A smile brightened her face when she saw Wesley sitting beside me. Now I just had to make sure she kept her mouth shut.

Chapter 5

"HEY. Hey! Toren!" Wesley whispered loudly. He was at the end of the hall, poking his head around the corner. "Grab your bag. Let's go," he whispered as I walked over to him.

"What?" It was kind of amusing; he reminded me of a cartoon bank robber looking around to see if the coast was clear.

"C'mon, hurry up! Before Hannity sees us," Wesley urged. I looked at him blankly and he widened his eyes at me. I hesitated, then grabbed my book bag from my locker and followed Wesley to the parking lot. "I'm turning you into a delinquent, aren't I?" Wesley said proudly as we drove away from the school.

We drove for a while, taking the back roads outside of town. He turned onto a narrow dirt road, pocked with potholes, and I asked him where we were going.

"You'll see," he said with a smile.

We drove past flat cornfields and thick forests, winding around the vast maze of dirt roads that gridded the farmlands. Wesley pulled off to the side next to a small patch of trees, like a mini-forest in the middle of an open field. He led me into a ring of trees that surrounded a small pond. Cattails grew at one end and the little pool was green with algae. Beside the water, a fallen tree served as a low bench and Wesley sat down, patting the crumbling log next to him.

"It's way too nice out to be cooped up in a classroom," he said as I sat down beside him.

"Yeah, it's beautiful out today," I agreed, looking through the tree trunks at the stark field on the other side. I could hear a bullfrog and I searched the pond, but I couldn't see it.

Wesley sighed lightly. A shy smile passed his lips and he glanced at me. "You know, you're the first person I ever brought here."

"Really?" I asked stupidly. I didn't know what to say, but I felt special.

"Yeah, I guess you seemed to be the right person to share it with."

I smiled and fiddled my hands in my lap. "It's really pretty out here. How did you ever find this place?"

"I don't even know," he said, peeling off a piece of bark. "I come out here when my folks get on my case. It's just sorta…relaxing."

Wesley pulled out a pack of cigarettes and lit one. There was a silence and I felt a little awkward. But the quiet passed and we talked for almost an hour. Wesley told me a little about his family, about his brother away at college, about his job, about everything. I liked listening to him talk; he seemed different from the Wesley I saw at school: he was sensitive and smart and he could be serious. I felt like I got to see a side of him that not everyone got to see.

"So, have you decided where you're gonna go to school?" I asked after a short silence. I stretched out my legs and glanced at Wesley from the corner of my eye.

Wesley shook his head and snubbed out his cigarette. "Nah. I'm not going to school. I figure that I'll start working full-time at the body shop." He placed the cigarette butt in a neat pile beside him on the log.

"You're not going to college?" I asked, turning and looking at Wesley with surprise.

"School's never really been my thing," he answered.

I looked down and bit my lip. I had always planned on going to college; my mom would kill me if I didn't go. "But, what about your parents? Don't they want you to go?"

"Nah, they really don't care. They're pretty much counting down the days 'til I move out. They pinned all their hopes on my brother, thinking he'll give them the life they think they deserve."

"Oh," I said quietly. I felt awkward and looked at the pond, searching for the noisy bullfrog again. I could feel Wesley staring at me.

"Heh, this is depressing. Let's change the subject," he said, leaning forward and resting his elbows on his knees.

"I'm sorry."

Wesley moved closer to me. "It's not your fault. Don't worry about it. But if you wanna cheer me up," he said with a grin and turned my face toward him. I glanced at him and looked around at the ring of trees. "There's no one around for miles. So, relax."

He rested his hand on my leg and kissed me, softly at first, then with a little more force. I felt nervous kissing Wesley; I didn't want him to think I was a bad kisser but it felt so good that I would sometimes forget to breathe.

We kissed for a while with nature as our witness and I wondered how I could keep this a secret from Mom. I didn't want my mom to hate me, but I didn't want to lose this exhilarating feeling that Wesley brought out in me.

"Well, I guess we should get going," Wesley said, picking up a handful of cigarette butts from the log.

"Oh. Yeah," I answered, standing up and stretching my arms over my head. Wesley poked the crease of white between my jeans and T-shirt and I hunched over instinctively. He laughed and told me I was cute.

"My mom's been on my case about cleaning up the mess in the garage. It's kinda why I wanted to ditch sixth hour, so I could see you for a little while before I had to go."

I blushed and felt a little excitement that I was contributing to his delinquency. Wesley grinned and kissed me again before we walked back to his car. He drove me home and gave me a brief kiss in the parking lot before I could protest that people might see us. He apologized and said he would make up for it tomorrow. I watched him drive away and I let my smile broaden when I got in my apartment. I really liked the way Wesley made me feel.

Chapter 6

WE got our exams back in Spanish class. I got a 94 and was a little disappointed. I got three questions wrong that I knew the answers to. I felt better when Wesley met me at my locker after class with a beaming smile.

"Check it out. I got an eighty-six," he said, holding his test up. I looked at the lop-sided smiley face in red ink.

"Good job," I said, pulling my math book out.

"I made flashcards like you said and I think it really helped." He folded the test in half the long way and stuck it in his back pocket. "What are you doing for lunch?"

"Nothing."

"You wanna eat together?" I looked up and down the hall self-consciously and Wesley noticed my blushing cheeks with his requisite grin. He looked at my math book and frowned. "Damn. You've got third lunch, don't you?"

I nodded and the bell rang. I smiled shyly and shrugged my shoulders. "I gotta get to class."

"Yeah, yeah. I'll see you in history then," he said, patting my shoulder and waving at me.

I sighed and watched him walk toward the cafeteria. I still didn't quite know how to act around Wesley at school. I liked that he paid attention to me, but I also worried that people might suspect something.

After history class, Wesley waited for me to get my book bag. We walked out together and I paused at the front of the school, looking down the sidewalk. Wesley stopped and followed my eyes.

"You don't have to walk home, you know…I'll give you a ride from now on," he said, walking toward the student lot.

"Did you get your garage cleaned up?" I asked, dropping my book bag on the floor between my feet.

"Mostly. It took for-damn-ever too," he answered, starting the car. He drove to my apartment and parked in an open space. I didn't even have to invite him in.

I gripped the straps of my book bag as I got out of the car. "I was thinking…we should probably get an outline together for the History project."

"What? It's Friday! The weekend! You shouldn't even think about homework until Sunday. Night. Around 11," he said, stretching his arms over his head and waiting for me to catch up. I laughed and Wesley smiled warmly. "You're cute when you smile," he said, tilting his head and looking at me sideways. "So, is your mom home?" he asked when we reached the third floor.

"No, she's at work," I answered, as my heart began to thump to a faster rhythm.

"I see," he mumbled as I opened the door to the apartment. "And your sister promised me she wouldn't be home 'til at least six."

"Huh?"

"I ran into her between classes today. She's pretty cool."

"I'll tell her you said that," I said, feeling my heart in my throat. I set down my book bag at the door and looked over the messy living room. I looked around everywhere except at Wesley.

"Your sister's really protective of you, you know? She told me that if I broke your heart, she'd cut my balls off. Then she laughed and said 'see ya.' It was pretty funny…and maybe a little scary now that I think about it." Wesley stepped closer to me, smiled devilishly, and slid his hand around my waist. "She doesn't have anything to worry about though." He walked me to the sofa and I fell back onto it.

His kiss felt incredible, flowing through me like electricity, and I shyly pulled him closer. He kissed my neck and collarbones and his hands slid down my arms. He pushed my T-shirt up and his kisses followed the trail blazed by his fingertips. I pushed my head back into the sofa; it felt amazing. Then his hands dropped and he began to unhook my belt buckle.

"Wa-wait! What are you doing?" I stammered, stopping his hands.

"Man, for an honor student, you sure can be dumb sometimes. What do you think I'm doing?" he said with a smile, continuing to unbutton and unzip my pants. He hooked his fingers in the belt loops of my jeans and yanked them down. I bit my lip as I felt myself respond to his touch.

"Wait a second. Wesley!"

He grinned when he felt me stiffen beneath his hand. He pulled down my boxers, touching me gently, as he climbed down in front of me, between the sofa and the coffee table.

"Why—why are you doing this?" His fingers grew bolder, stroking me with more energy as a quiet gasp escaped my lips.

"'Cause I wanna make you feel good," he answered, pushing the hem of my shirt farther up my chest. The corners of his mouth curled and he bent his head down, tracing the contours of my stomach with his tongue. He looked up at me again and his hand worked me over with a sense of urgency, producing the most exquisite feeling within me. "So, do you? Feel good?"

I nodded my head and squeezed my eyes shut.

His tongue found the way to its target and he licked and sucked on me with a renewed vigor. The feeling was unbelievable, sending amorous shockwaves through my entire body. I moaned and gasped for air, liberating the sexual voice deep within me. I was coming up fast to the moment of crisis and tears welled in my eyes from the intense pleasure.

"Wesley! I—I can't—" I shouted, almost as a plea.

Wesley remained vigilant, keeping his mouth in place and grasping my backside with his hands, bringing me closer and deeper into his mouth. I threw my head back as I climaxed and Wesley held me tightly in his large hands.

I collapsed into the sofa, delirious and panting, and covered my face with my hands. I couldn't look at him. I was embarrassed…I came so quickly. It was the first time someone else had ever touched me and just the thought of his soft, warm mouth was almost enough to make me cum again.

"Don't hide your face," Wesley whispered, pulling my hands away. I closed my eyes and turned my face to the side. He put his hand to my cheek and I hesitantly glanced up at him. "Heh, you look adorable all out of breath and panting like that."

I felt the weight on my legs lift and I sat up, pulling up my pants. I was afraid of how he would react, how he would look at me after what we did, but he surprised me with his gentle calm. He was nothing like I expected him to be; he wasn't the loud, obnoxious Wesley that I saw at school, but a kind, funny, sensitive person. My attraction to him grew instantly and I felt more confident that he wasn't just toying with me.

"So you really wanna put an outline together?" he asked.

"Um, if you don't wanna do it now, that's okay," I mumbled.

"Cool. Are you hungry? You wanna go grab a bite to eat?" He draped his arm over my shoulders.

"I can make something here," I offered shyly. "Do you want a sandwich or something more like dinner?"

"Doesn't matter. I'll have whatever you feel like."

I stood up and Wesley followed me into the kitchen. I made dinner for two, a quick chicken stir-fry that Wesley complimented over and over. We sat on the sofa watching TV, and I remembered Alycia commenting on how I would "make someone a wonderful housewife someday." I glanced at Wesley and blushed.

Chapter 7

"TOR, me and Mike are gonna go see a movie tonight. Wanna come?" Alycia asked, walking past me toward the bathroom.

"Actually, um, I have plans tonight."

"Oh! Are you going out with Wes?" she squealed, popping her head out from the bathroom.

"Who's Wes?" Mom asked, walking into the living room from the kitchen.

"He's a friend from school," I said, catching a glimpse of Alycia from the corner of my eye. Fortunately, Mom couldn't see her rolling her eyes and nodding her head sarcastically. She stepped into the hall, made quotation marks in the air with her fingers and mouthed the word "friend." I grimaced at her and Mom looked at me funny.

"What are you gonna do?" Alycia asked. She was leaning against the wall pulling a brush through her hair.

"I don't know."

"Why don't you come see the movie with us?"

"Nah, I'm not in the mood for some chick flick," I said, shaking my head.

"C'mon, you love sappy love stories like this!"

There was a knock at the door. Alycia ran past me and answered it before I even got off the sofa.

"Hi, Wes!"

"Hi. How ya doin'?"

"Pretty good. Come on in." Alycia opened the door wider and Wesley walked in. His hair was damp and he wore a white T-shirt and blue jeans. He looked at me and smiled.

"So you must be Wes," Mom said, wiping her hands on a dish towel.

Wesley looked up and smiled awkwardly. "Yeah. Hello."

"I'm Amanda. I'm the brats' mom," she said with a grin. Alycia rolled her eyes and I groaned.

"It's nice to meet you," Wesley said and bowed his head slightly. It was kind of amusing to see him so awkward. He glanced to the side and scratched the back of his head. I walked over to him and he smiled a little nervously.

"Are you ready to go?" I asked and Wesley nodded.

"Have fun, guys. And Toren, not too late," Mom said as we left.

"So what do you wanna do? Wanna go shoot some pool?" Wesley asked, turning over the engine and putting his hand on the back of my headrest as he pulled out of the parking lot.

"Okay, but I'm not very good."

"That's all right. I'll teach you." He ruffled my hair with his fingers.

We went to a pool hall called Cue. It was small and dark, with ten or twelve pool tables and a small bar against the back wall. Wesley exchanged his license for a set of pool balls and I followed him to a table in the back. He took the triangle from beneath the table and began to rack the balls.

"Do you know how to play?"

"Yeah, I used to play with my dad when I was little," I explained. "But I haven't really played since my parents got divorced."

Wesley gazed at me for a moment and then said "oh." He looked back at the table and lifted the triangle from the felt. "You wanna break?"

I shook my head and Wesley lined up his shot. He sank a solid and then two more before he missed. I looked over the table and found an easy shot. I lined it up and Wesley corrected my aim.

"Why don't you just figure out the angles? Sine and cosine and shit?" he said with a laugh.

"I'm not too good in math. Algebra is okay, but trig and calc are pretty much a mystery to me," I said and took my shot. It went wide.

"I'm okay in math. If I study. Hey, maybe there's something I can help you with." I smiled and Wesley stepped closer to me. "Wanna make this interesting? If I win, I get a kiss in the parking lot. A good kiss."

He stepped back and took his shot; a solid dropped in the corner pocket. I didn't stand a chance. I looked around at people at other pool tables. I hoped that it would be dark out before we left, because I was sure Wesley intended to collect on his bet.

I lost the first game with four balls still on the table. "Best two out of three?"

Wesley moved close to me and leaned in. "All right, but I get two kisses then."

Wesley racked the balls with a grin on his face. Some kids called out to him and waved. He lifted his chin in greeting and waved back. I figured he came here a lot from the number of people that waved to him or stopped to say hi. The man at the counter knew him by name. Wesley was leaning over the table when a blonde girl came running up and hugged him.

"Wes! Where have you been? I haven't seen you in so long! What's going on, lover?"

Wesley hugged her briefly and looked at me over her shoulder. He stepped back and flashed his smile. A shorthaired brunette girl stood behind her blonde friend and looked at me.

"Hey, Kate. How ya doin'?" he asked casually and then looked at the other girl. "Hey, Lissa."

Kate put her hands on her hips and furrowed her perfectly plucked eyebrows. "Seriously, I haven't seen you in forever. Where have you been?"

"I've been around," Wesley answered, glancing at me. Kate followed his eyes to me.

"Who's this cutie?" she asked, spreading her crimson lips into a smile. I looked around shyly and Wesley chuckled.

"This is Toren. Toren, this is Kate and Lissa." He pointed at each girl as he said her name.

"Hi. It's nice to meet you."

"Ooh! He's so polite too!" Kate squealed with a hand over her mouth. I looked to the side and resisted rolling my eyes. I hated it when people were condescending. Lissa looked at me and smiled, but it was an understanding smile—an "I get it" smile. Kate returned her attentions to Wesley and looked at the pool table. "So, can we join you?"

"Uh—"

"Me and Wes against Lissa and Toren. Can I break?" she said quickly, taking the cue stick from Wesley's hand. Wesley looked at me again and shrugged his shoulders.

We played four games; Wesley and Kate won all but one. Lissa was pretty good but she had to pick up my slack. After an hour or so, we turned in the pool balls and Kate and Lissa followed us into the parking lot. I hoped Wesley had forgotten our bet on the first game.

"Well, we gotta take off. It was good seeing you," Wesley said as we neared his car.

"Yeah. We should do this again soon," Kate answered, stepping up and hugging Wesley. She looked at me and smiled. "You too."

"It…it was nice meeting you," I said. Wesley already had the driver-side door open.

"Yeah, we'll see ya around, Toren. Bye, Wes," Lissa said, making eye contact with me.

Wesley started the car and we watched Kate and Lissa walk back into Cue. He peeled out of the parking lot and drove me home. He idled in front of my building and I started to say good night, but he interrupted me.

"Wait a sec. You didn't forget about our bet, did you? Good thing I didn't specify which parking lot."

He leaned in and kissed me, pushing his tongue between my lips and ruffling my hair with his fingers. It was dark out and the car's interior lights weren't on, so I felt pretty safe that we wouldn't be seen.

"See you later," Wesley said, pulling back and sinking into the driver's seat.

"Good night."

I waved before I got to the stairs and Wesley waited until I was up to the third floor before he drove away. I couldn't help but let a shy smile steal across my face. It kinda felt like we were on a date, and it was a good feeling.

Chapter 8

WESLEY was waiting for me at my locker before history class. He looked really cute in his ripped jeans and an unbuttoned plaid, short-sleeved shirt over a white T-shirt. My stomach tingled a little when I saw him and I immediately blushed.

"What's going on?" he asked, leaning against the lockers with his book bag over his shoulder.

"Nothing. How are you?" I asked, pulling out my History book.

He complained about not being able to eat lunch with me because our lunch hours were consecutive. He talked and I listened, nodding my head and smiling, until class started.

Mr. Hannity told us about the exam on Friday and that we should catch up on any reading since the test would cover chapters 13, 14, and 17. He glanced at Wesley a few times during the announcement, enough that even I noticed.

After class, Wesley waited for me to pack up my things. He glared at Mr. Hannity and frowned. He was ticked off because Mr. Hannity always seemed to single him out. There was no doubt that Wesley was upset, but I thought Mr. Hannity did it because he knew Wesley could do better if he applied himself.

"We should go to the library today, to get stuff for our project," I said, stuffing papers into my folder.

Wesley groaned. "No way. It's Monday. Besides, the project isn't due for, like, ever."

I shook my head and tried to convince him otherwise, but Wesley was adamant.

"Hey, Wes. What's up?" Jen asked, surprising him from behind. "I was wondering; you wanna grab a bite to eat? I'm starving."

Wesley turned around and smiled nicely. "Oh, sorry. I can't. Toren here is dragging me to the library. Maybe another time," he said cordially.

Jen's face fell but she smiled quickly. "Oh, that's okay. Yeah, maybe another time." She smiled again and then looked down at me, narrowing her eyes. It was like a black cloud circled her head and I actually felt a chill.

I got my things together and Wesley followed me out of the classroom. He waited while I got my book bag and closed my locker.

"Where are you going? My car's this way," he said, pointing down the hall.

"You said I was dragging you to the library."

"Yeah, but I didn't mean it. It was just so Jen would leave me alone."

"Well, that's not fair," I said with a smile. "You can't use me as an alibi."

Wesley stared at me a moment and then dragged his feet like they were made of lead. "All right, all right. But only for a little while," he conceded.

We found two books on the Chinese Exclusion Acts and I checked them out on my library card. We weren't there long, but Wesley complained the whole time. When we left, he drove me to his house and I gave him one of the books. He complained more, but agreed to read it if I let him kiss me. I agreed with blushing cheeks and leaned into him.

We worked on our homework, doing Spanish together and then working separately for other classes. After an hour, Wesley pulled out his small pipe and bag of marijuana. He packed the bowl and reached into his pocket for his lighter.

"Wanna smoke this with me?" he asked, tilting the lighter and inhaling.

I shook my head and gripped the textbook in my lap. "No…that's okay."

"C'mon, what's the big deal? You might not even get high since it's your first time," he coaxed, raising his eyebrows and grinning.

"No, I don't think so," I said, looking down.

"All right. Fine." He sighed, sounding defeated, then took another hit and scooted closer to me. "The least you can do is give me a kiss then."

He kissed me and my lungs filled with smoke. I started coughing and had to hold onto my book to keep it from sliding off my lap. Wesley snickered and I furrowed my brows at him.

"That—that wasn't fair!" I shouted between coughs.

"I know, I know. I couldn't help it." He held out the pipe again. "C'mon, just a puff."

I looked at him a moment and then down to the pipe again. "I don't know how."

"It's easy," he said and I took the pipe from him. "Just suck it in and breathe. Like normal."

I looked down at the glowing bowl and lifted it to my lips. The tip was wet with Wesley's saliva and I breathed in. I tried to breathe again but I started coughing instantly. Wesley patted my back and took the pipe.

"It's okay, it just takes a little practice," he said and sucked on the small pipe.

I wiped away the tears in my eyes from my coughing fit and Wesley handed me the pipe. I tried again, bringing the pipe to my lips and exhaling a plume of smoke without coughing. My eyes brightened and I was strangely proud of myself.

"Yeah, just like that," Wesley said with a smile. "Go ahead, take another."

I tried to do the same as before, but I inhaled too much and my throat became raw from coughing. Wesley laughed and took the pipe, patting my back again. He smoked what was left in the bowl and then put everything back in the cabinet in the coffee table. He closed the book in my lap and put his arm around me.

"So, you feeling anything? Are you high?"

"I—I don't know."

"Then probably not. You would know if you were. Oh well, maybe next time."

He turned my face toward him and lowered my chin with his thumb. It always surprised me by how good his kiss felt. He ran his hand across my stomach and kissed my neck and collarbones. I was entranced and thought this was much better than getting high.

A low rumbling noise stopped Wesley's lips and tongue and he frowned at me. He leaned back into the sofa and pouted. "Damn. My mom's home." He looked at me with a smile at the corner of his mouth. "And things were just gettin' good."

I looked around the room and straightened my shirt. Wesley stood up and stretched his arms over his head. I could see a swatch of his white stomach and a few sparse hairs leading downward. I swallowed hard.

"Hi, Mom," Wesley greeted, meeting his mom in the kitchen.

I sat on the edge of the couch and stuffed my textbook into my book bag. I stood up as his mom stepped into the living room.

"Hello," she said with a smile. She closed her eyes when she smiled.

"Mom, this is Toren. Toren, this is my mom," Wesley said.

I was suddenly very glad that I didn't get high. I gripped the strap of my book bag and felt really nervous.

"Um, hello. It's nice to meet you," I said, bowing slightly.

"Oh, yes, Toren. Wes's told me about you. You're partners for a class project, right? I'm Cindy. It's nice to meet you too." She had a crooked smile and a perm that was too tight. She was thin, maybe on the skinny side, and wore lots of eye makeup. "Wes, there're some groceries in the car. Bring them in, all right?"

Wesley rolled his eyes, but obeyed and left me standing in the smoky living room with his mother. I looked around nervously while Mrs. Carroll took a pack of cigarettes from her purse. They were ultra slim and about six inches long.

"What class is your project for?" she asked, the cigarette bouncing up and down as she spoke.

"It's for History. We're doing it on the Chinese Exclusion Acts," I answered.

"The what?"

"The Chinese Exclusion Acts of the 1880s," I repeated quietly.

Wesley returned with four plastic bags of groceries draped on his arms. He and Mrs. Carroll talked in the kitchen while I stood awkwardly in the living room. Wesley came back and sat down on the sofa, patting the cushion next to him. I sat down and Wesley picked up his Math book and smiled at me.

Mrs. Carroll stepped into the living room and gasped. "Holy shit. Wes, are you doing homework?" Wesley rolled his eyes and nodded his head sarcastically. "Well, I'll be damned," she laughed and then coughed into her fist. She took a hit on her cigarette and coughed again. "Toren, you wanna stay for dinner?"

"Um, thank you, but I don't think I—"

"Oh, come on. I'm just making chicken and green beans. Why don't you stay? I won't take no for an answer."

"All—all right. Thank you," I conceded. Mrs. Carroll smiled triumphantly and returned to the kitchen. Wesley smiled at me and I already began to feel nervous.

Wesley's dad came home while his mom was setting the table. He was a tall man, thick with muscle. He was wearing custodial blues and had dirty hands. He stared at me and I smiled awkwardly. Wesley introduced us and then Mrs. Carroll called us to the table to eat.

The conversation was typical of a family meal. I ate politely though the chicken was burned and the green beans were bland. I realized I made better dinners than this and then felt guilty for not appreciating her effort.

"What was your project on again, Toren?" Mrs. Carroll asked, picking at her chicken.

Everyone's focus turned to me and I felt my cheeks get hot. Wesley tapped my shin with his foot under the table and smiled. I looked down at my plate and swallowed hard.

"Um, the Chinese Exclusion Acts of the 1880s," I answered quietly, cutting through a tough piece of chicken.

"Oh, Frank! You won't believe it," Mrs. Carroll said, slapping the table. "Wes was actually doing *homework* when I came home!"

Mr. Carroll laughed hoarsely and when he smiled, it seemed crooked and strange, like he had trouble doing it. "Now that's rare," he murmured, looking at Wesley. His smile was gone.

"Yeah, about as rare as Mom actually cooking," Wesley chided.

Mrs. Carroll laughed, Wesley smiled, and Mr. Carroll dropped his fork on his plate. His face turned sour again, an expression that looked more natural on him.

"Watch your mouth," Mr. Carroll warned, narrowing his eyes at Wesley.

"Frank—" Mrs. Carroll began, but stopped and glanced at me.

"Apologize to your mother," Mr. Carroll said.

"I was just joking around."

"Didn't you hear me? I said, apologize—"

"All right. Sorry, Mom," Wesley said quietly, lowering his eyes.

It was awkwardly quiet and I stared at my plate. Mr. Carroll continued eating as if nothing had happened. Wesley glanced at me and Mrs. Carroll sighed. She asked if anyone wanted seconds and the unanimous answer was no.

"You wanna go shoot some pool?" Wesley asked, finally breaking the silence.

I looked up at him. "But, it's a school night."

Wesley laughed and Mrs. Carroll chuckled quietly. My cheeks grew red.

"So? Let's go. I'll make sure you get home at a reasonable time," Wesley said and I eventually nodded.

"Help your mom with the dishes first," Mr. Carroll said and then retired to the living room.

Mrs. Carroll told Wesley that it was okay, that we could go. I said goodbye and retrieved my book bag from the living room. Mr. Carroll stared at me in his rigid way and I felt really uncomfortable. Wesley pushed me forward and followed me outside. I took a deep breath in the warm air and sighed with relief.

We went to Cue again and found a table in the back. We played a few games, Wesley winning all of them. He made me bet again, a kiss in the parking lot being the prize.

"Sorry about my folks. They're a little weird," Wesley said, leaning over the table.

"They seem nice."

Wesley looked at me from the top of his eyes and grinned. "You're too nice sometimes."

I laughed and conceded in my mind that I didn't really like Mr. Carroll. I didn't like the way he treated Wesley. I didn't like the way he looked at me. I felt inadequate; one of the first times that I felt…girly. I tried to push it out of my mind and Wesley's hand on my rear end quickly made me forget all about it.

"Hey! What are you doing?" I asked, looking around. The place was pretty empty, but there were still some people at other tables.

"I doubt anyone saw. But I just couldn't help myself," he said with a smile. "You've got a cute ass."

I rolled my eyes and Wesley apologized sarcastically. I excused myself to use the bathroom and took a deep breath. His touch was intoxicating and I had to concentrate to keep myself calm. When I returned to the table, Wesley was talking to two girls. They didn't look like Kate or Lissa and when I neared, I realized that it was Jen and Olivia. I shyly walked up to the table.

"Oh, Toren," Jen said. Wesley rolled his eyes at me. "I didn't know you were here."

"Um, hi," I said quietly.

"Well, we'll see you at school tomorrow," Wesley said, twirling his cue in his hands.

Jen looked at him and then glanced at me. Her eyes narrowed during the short second she looked at me. "C'mon, how about a game?" she asked, stepping toward Wesley.

"Sorry. We're actually gonna get going. Right, Toren?" Wesley said, smiling at me.

Jen pouted at Wesley and frowned at me. She tried to urge Wesley into staying, but he was collecting the balls and putting them in the tray. When he was done, he waved slightly and said "see ya." I followed him with an inner feeling of satisfaction.

I got into the car in case Wesley intended to collect on his bet. He got in and turned over the engine, grabbed the back of my head and kissed me so hard that I could feel it in my toes.

"Guess I should get you home," he said, brushing my cheek with his fingertips.

I wanted another kiss. I waited 'til he stopped in front of my building then I leaned into him and kissed him. The car jumped forward and Wesley whispered “oops.” He pulled up the parking brake and kissed me some more.

I went to bed early and closed the door. Wesley’s scent was still in my nose and I jerked off as I imagined the feel of his hands, lips, tongue…even his….

I blushed, came quickly, and fell asleep.

Chapter 9

I YAWNED and rested my chin in my hand as I waited for class to begin and tried to finish up the Math homework that was due today.

"So, Toren. What's going on?"

Jen and Olivia stood next to my desk. Olivia had a slight grin on her face but Jen glared at me. They were both pretty popular; drawing leers and looks from half the school's population and sneers and scoffs from the other half. I didn't have a clue why they were talking to me.

"Nothing," I answered nonchalantly, trying to sound cool and aloof, like I talked to girls like them all the time.

"You've been hanging out with Wes a lot lately. Seems like he doesn't have time for us anymore," Olivia said, crossing her arms.

My heart skipped and my stomach dropped. Wesley didn't say anything to them, did he? I hoped they didn't notice how flustered I became at the mere mention of his name.

Jen snickered wickedly and raised her brows. "We were just curious, you know? Have you been taking care of *all* his needs?"

"What the hell are you talking about?" I said, balling my hands into fists. "We're just partners for the History project." I looked down at the desk and stared at the "I hate school" etched in the top corner.

"Whoa. Sorry. We weren't suggesting anything like that," Olivia said through a hushed laugh. "We were just wondering, you know?"

Olivia turned and pushed Jen forward. Their laughter was quiet but their shoulders were shaking. They left me blushing and angry. Why didn't they ask Wesley? Was it okay for him to be gay because he was popular and everyone liked him, but I'm fair game? Besides, he was the one who'd been taking care of my needs. What would they think about that? Would they believe that Wesley came on to me?

I closed my eyes and sighed. The rules were different for him and me. I rested my chin in my hand. He was on an entirely different social plane than I was. If he started wearing dresses, he'd start a trend. If I did it, they would beat me up and call me names.

ON the way home from school, I asked Wesley if he had told anyone about…us. It was strange to say "us," because it felt more advanced than where we were in our…relationship. That was something else completely. Wesley told me that he liked me but I didn't know if he was serious, if I was more than just a way to quench his curiosity.

"No. You were the one who wanted to keep it a secret, so I haven't told anyone. Why?"

I looked out the window and frowned. He seemed to know what I was thinking a lot of the time. Wesley kept one hand on the steering wheel and tapped my leg with his other hand. I glanced at him and then back out the window.

"You know Jen and Olivia, right?" I asked. Wesley nodded and glanced at the road. "They said…they asked why you were hanging out with me. Or something like that. They said that you didn't have time for them anymore."

Wesley exhaled through his nose in an exasperated way. "What do they mean by that? Like I ever had time for them before." He looked at Jen and Olivia in a different light: they weren't popular; they were annoying. "What'd you say?"

"I told them that we were just partners for our History project." I didn't tell him about Jen and Olivia asking if I "took care of his needs." I didn't want to know if either of them had ever done anything with him. I wanted to be his first, like he was for me, though I realized how foolish that was. If Wesley weren't the oversexed high school teenager, he wouldn't be Wesley anymore.

"Heh, imagine if they really knew," Wesley said with a smirk. I managed a laugh but felt a twinge of panic. "But I hadn't thought about that. We did start hanging out rather suddenly. I guess people would talk." He looked at me again and stretched his arm behind my head. "Don't worry about it. I'll talk to them if you want me to."

"No, that's okay."

We pulled into the apartment complex and Wesley parked in a spot a short walk from my building. I told him to bring his book bag and he groaned. He waited for me to come around the car and I saw how handsome he looked today. He was wearing his trademark ripped jeans, and an open button-down shirt with a white T-shirt underneath. His hair resisted a warm breeze and he smiled at me. I liked it best when he smiled.

As we climbed the steps to the third floor, Wesley put his arm around my shoulders. I felt nervous and giddy at the same time. I tried not to worry about people seeing us. It wasn't even a big deal; he just had his arm around my shoulders. I fumbled getting my key into the lock and Wesley dropped his hand to my backside and squeezed. I protested, but he told me to hurry up.

Inside, Wesley dropped his book bag like it was full of bricks and slid mine off my shoulder. He kissed me and walked me back to the sofa. I dropped onto the cushion and Wesley dropped to his knees. He pushed my shirt up and kissed and licked my stomach while his hands nimbly unbuckled my belt and unzipped my pants. He noticed that I was already stiff with anticipation and he chuckled softly.

"You're so sensitive," he whispered, yanking down my jeans and boxers.

"I—I can't help it…. You…." His warm mouth surrounded me. I gripped his shoulders and slid down on the couch, wiggling and spasming beneath him. He ran his hand up my chest, circling a nipple and pinching it. My body quaked with ecstasy, overflowing my senses and making me twitch with the most exquisitely pleasurable sensation.

His mouth, his tongue, the back of his throat, his nimble fingers were all in a chorus to bring me to crisis. "Wes… Wesley…."

Wesley held fast to me until I slumped into the couch, my life drained from my body. He smiled triumphantly and stood up. I was still trying to catch my breath and Wesley stepped to the side. I could see a bulge in his pants and I blushed, looking away.

"I gotta go to the bathroom," he said and patted my head.

I tried not to look at him as I pulled up my pants. I heard the door close and I sighed. Wesley didn't ask me to reciprocate the pleasure he gave and I was a little relieved. I was nervous and embarrassed and I felt a little guilty, but I didn't know what to do. I wanted to show him that I cared about him, but I was afraid. I was afraid that I might be falling in love with him and that he might not think of me as anything more than a way to pass the time.

Wesley came back from the bathroom, his cheeks rosy, and kissed my forehead. I asked him if he wanted something to drink and I brought back two sodas from the kitchen. Wesley helped me with my Math homework, his hand rubbing my thigh while I worked out the problems under his tutelage. He would kiss me and nibble on my ear when I answered a problem correctly. I bit my lip and persevered without giving in to his insinuating gestures. We worked on Spanish next and then moved onto some History homework. Wesley moved his hand from my thigh to my shoulder with a sigh when he realized that I wasn't giving in to his unspoken persuasion.

"Hey. I'm home and I'm starving. Tor, get your butt in the kitchen and start making dinner," Alycia announced, swinging the door open to its limit. She blushed a little when she saw Wesley, embarrassed by her own pushiness. She liked others to think she was sweet and kind, not a bossy loudmouth. "Hi, Wes. How ya doin'?" she asked. Wesley smiled, closing the textbook on his lap. I stood up and gave Alycia an eyeful and she shrugged her shoulders. I guess she didn't care to keep up appearances in front of Wesley and she barked at me again. "C'mon, I'm hungry," she whined. Then her eyes sparkled and she smiled broadly at Wesley. "Wanna stay for dinner? Tor's a great cook."

"Yeah, I know," Wesley answered with a smile in my direction.

"Then you'll stay?" Alycia asked, stretching her arms over her head and grinning at me.

"If it's all right," Wesley said, tilting his head back to look at me. I stood behind the sofa and nodded my head.

I went to the kitchen and looked in the refrigerator and the pantry, finally deciding to make tacos for dinner. I grabbed the apron from the hook in the pantry and began to brown some ground turkey in a frying pan.

"He looks cute in an apron, doesn't he?" Alycia said, raising an eyebrow.

Wesley looked me up and down with a telling grin and nodded. I told them to get out of my kitchen and they laughed, staying where they were. We talked while I made dinner and I realized how comfortable I felt while we were eating. We sat three in a row on the sofa and watched TV as we ate, talking and laughing. I liked this feeling, this comfort that Alycia gave me: acceptance, but perhaps it was her indifference, that nothing had changed, that my being with Wes was the most normal thing in the world.

Chapter 10

WESLEY skipped fourth hour to eat lunch with me. We sat in front of the school on the giant cement planter where I always ate. He sat cross-legged, his knee touching mine, and ate the apple from my lunch.

"What the fuck? We've been looking all over for you, Carroll."

Alan Dunne and Jeremy Read walked toward us and I leaned to the side so that Wesley and I weren't touching. "You ditched us 'cause you said you had something to do and here you are dickin' around with him?" Alan said, glancing at me.

"So? I said I had stuff to do. What do you want?" Wesley said, after a low, quiet sigh.

Jeremy looked at me and then at Wesley. I worried that Jen and Olivia might've spread rumors.

"I got a blunt ready to go and I wondered if you wanted to partake," Alan said, looking down his nose at me. I felt out of place.

"Can't. But thanks for the invite," Wesley answered, shaking his head.

"C'mon, Wes. You've been hanging out with him every damn day. What's your fuckin' deal?"

I felt a twinge of panic and my cheeks flushed.

"What the hell does it matter to you? I said I got things to do."

Alan furrowed his brows and turned on his heel. "Whatever, man." Jeremy followed him and they went back inside the school.

I breathed a little easier, but I started to get a little angry. They talked as if I wasn't even there. Maybe Wesley and I did start hanging out rather suddenly, but it didn't mean we couldn't be friends. I sighed and Wesley poked my arm.

"Sorry about that," he said, looking at me sideways.

"It…it's okay," I mumbled. "But if you wanna hang out with them, that's okay." I fidgeted my hands in my lap, nervous about his answer.

"Why would I want to hang out with them?" Wesley asked rhetorically, rolling his eyes. "You're much cuter." I glanced around and, fortunately, no one was near. "Don't worry. No one's around and, besides, who cares what others think? After we graduate, we'll probably never see these people again. Let them think what they wanna think."

Wesley's smile was reassuring, but I shook my head. "I just…I don't want anyone to make fun of me."

"Then there's nothing to worry about, 'cause I'll beat them up," Wesley said, leaning back on his hands.

He was so carefree. It seemed that nothing in the world bothered him, that nothing could touch him. I was really attracted to this side of his personality, because I knew it was something I lacked. I felt more confident just being near him.

The bell rang and lunch was over. Wesley and I parted for fifth hour and then met again before history class. Mr. Hannity gave a short review for the exam the next day. Since our projects were considered the final, it would be our last test.

Wesley came over after school to study for History. He kissed me and then I sat down on the sofa and opened my textbook. Wesley groaned and fell back on the couch, pulling his book bag onto his lap. We began to review the chapter and notes detailed in the outline Mr. Hannity provided. After fifteen minutes, Wesley yawned and let his textbook slide off his lap.

"Man, I can't do this now. I can't concentrate. I need to kiss you for at least an hour before I can even begin to think about anything else."

"An hour?" I asked with wide eyes.

"At least," he said and inched closer to me. He put his hand behind my head and ruffled my hair.

"C'mon, we gotta study," I urged, though I knew my voice was shaky.

"Nope. I need an hour."

"Fifteen minutes," I offered.

"Forty-five minutes."

"Ten minutes."

"Thirty minutes."

"No minutes."

Wesley sighed and tickled the nape of my neck with his fingertips. "All right; ten minutes," he conceded.

He leaned close and kissed me, taking the book from my lap and dropping it on the floor. His kiss curved around my chin to my neck and I clung to the sleeves of his shirt. I opened my eyes and glanced at the time on the VCR.

"Are you timing me?" Wesley asked. It was inadvertent; I wasn't actually going to time him, but I was beginning to recognize his mischievous smile. "Okay, I bet I can make you cum twice in ten minutes. So clock me. Ready, set, go!"

He wasn't joking; his kisses traveled across my stomach and chest, detouring at each nipple while his hands unbuckled my belt and unzipped my pants. It was like he was possessed or a man on a mission. He took me in his mouth and sucked on me with a zealous fervor that made me cum very quickly. He paused long enough to kiss me but then dropped to my waist again, pulling me to the edge of the cushion. His fingers worked me over, then his soft mouth surrounded me and I bit my lip and pushed my head back. He gripped my rear end and I felt the back of his throat. I came hard in his mouth and he swallowed with a grin on his lips. He rocked back on his heels, leaving me spinning in a fog of delirious exhaustion, panting and gasping for air. Sweat dripped from my brow and my shirt clung to my chest, dampened by humidity and exertion. He sat back on his heels and smiled at me, a telltale smile, an "I told you so" smile. My heart was beating furiously and my hands trembled. I pulled up my boxers while Wesley got to his feet.

"I'll be right back," he said, stepping to the side.

"Um, but, what about you?"

"Hunh?"

"I mean, you always do, um, stuff for me," I said, finding it hard to look into his eyes. "But, you never make me do anything for you. It makes me feel…kinda selfish."

His smile was sincere, not a smirk or a grin, and he sat down beside me. His touch was so gentle and I was sure that I wanted to do this for him. He leaned back on the sofa and took my hands, laying them in his lap as he spread his legs apart. My fingers were shaking as I unbuckled his belt and pulled down the zipper. He stared at me with the same soft look.

"It might be easier if you were on your knees in front of me, rather than on my side."

"Oh," I whispered and climbed over his outstretched leg to the floor between his knees. He moved my hands to his sides and I hooked my fingers inside his blue jeans and boxers. A bulge was pushing out and my eyes widened as I imagined its actual size. Wesley smiled and lifted himself up slightly as I tugged on his pants.

He chuckled softly as my eyes widened when he was fully exposed. My cheeks turned bright red as I looked over it at the smirk on Wesley's face.

"I…I don't…." I stammered, blushing deeply.

"Just do what you think would make me feel good," he said, patting my head before leaning down and kissing me. "Maybe you would feel better if I introduced you. Toren, I want you to meet…."

"Stop it! This is embarrassing enough," I told him, furrowing my brows. He smiled and laughed.

"Just give him a kiss; he's very friendly."

I took him in my hands and the shaft seemed to swell instantly with my touch. I didn't look up at Wesley again. I clenched my eyes shut and dropped my mouth around him. I tried to take him deep, but I nearly gagged as he touched the back of my throat and I covered my mouth and coughed.

"You don't have to take it all in one gulp," Wesley said. "Just do it slowly at first, get yourself comfortable," he coached, patting my head again.

I followed his instructions and eased my mouth around him, holding onto the base with my fingers. I moved up and down gently, careful not to swallow too much of him.

"Use your tongue."

I kept my eyes shut and pressed my tongue against him while I kept the rhythm of my bobbing head. I tried to remember what Wesley did for me and I began to stroke the base gently and let the tip of my tongue roam. Wesley gripped the cushion on either side and moaned my name. The way he said it sounded so sweet and I instantly felt more confident, slurping, sucking, and licking. Wesley threw his head back and moaned louder, panting my name and stroking his fingers through my hair.

"Tor, that…that's enough," he gasped, but I remained in place, dutifully finishing what I started. "Toren! I said, that's enough…."

He had done the same for me before and I wanted to return the favor. I looked up at him from the tops of my eyes and when he glanced down at me, he exploded like a volcano in my mouth. He sank back into the sofa and sighed between panting breaths.

"Damn."

I was elated by his deadpan exclamation. He looked happy and sated and I was glad that I was finally able to show Wesley how much he meant to me.

"You want some water?" he asked, pulling up his boxers and jeans. He was still a little stiff.

"What? No, I'll get it…."

"Don't worry about it," he said, standing up and zipping his pants. "I know where the glasses are. You just have a seat."

I sat down on the edge of the sofa and wiped my mouth with the back of my hand. I smiled shyly. It really felt like I was in love.

Wesley returned with two glasses of water and handed one to me. He sat on the edge of the couch right next to me and watched me take a gulp of water.

"So, does this mean you'll let me be your boyfriend?"

I looked up at Wesley with round eyes. He wanted to be my boyfriend? The shy smile returned to my face and I nodded my head. "Yeah, I guess so."

"You're cute when you smile," he said, looking at me sideways. My cheeks blushed and I couldn't stop smiling. "C'mon, give your boyfriend a kiss, then."

Wesley leaned into me and I accepted his lips like they were water in the desert. He really wanted to be with me. His kiss was indescribable; he was so good at it. Then I remembered that we had to study for History. Hesitantly and regrettably, I pulled away from him and picked up my textbook from the floor. Wesley made a face and sighed.

"Aw, you can't really expect me to study now," he complained, resting his arm around my shoulders.

I chuckled and urged him to focus. He picked up his book and we studied until Alycia came home. I made dinner again, even though it was Alycia's turn, and the three of us watched TV and talked.

As nine o'clock neared, Wesley said that he should head home. He packed up his book bag and I walked him to the door. He looked at me with a familiar expression and I shook my head. Alycia was sitting on the couch.

"Go on, give him a kiss. I don't care," Alycia said, glancing over her shoulder at us.

I shot her a look, then felt Wesley's hand behind my neck. He pulled me in and kissed me, without sparing tongue for the sake of Alycia. He grinned when he saw how red my cheeks were and I furrowed my brows at him.

"Hey, she said I could," Wesley said with his palm open in the air, shrugging his shoulders. He said good night and left and I stared at the door.

Alycia was still watching when I turned around and she smiled largely, closing her eyes. "You guys are so cute together."

Chapter 11

WESLEY and I reviewed for the History exam while passing time before sixth hour. He sat on top of the desk next to me with his notebook in his lap. He seemed to have a pretty good handle on the material and I told him so.

"That's 'cause I got such a good tutor," he said, sliding off the desk and leaning over me. I could feel his breath on my neck and my cheeks flushed. "So what do I get if I ace this test?" he asked, his fingers crawling to the nape of my neck.

"D-don't, Wesley," I whispered, taking a deep breath.

"What's the big deal? It's not like we're doing anything wrong."

My ears felt hot and I glanced around the classroom. "It's just…I don't…." How could I explain it? He doesn't know what it's like to have people laugh at him or tease him. He didn't understand that I would be ridiculed while he would escape direct mockery.

"You're my boyfriend. Or did you forget that I had your dick in my mouth yesterday?"

"Wesley!" I whispered forcefully, gripping my hands into fists. His voice was low and throaty, sexy, and I squeezed my eyes shut. "I-I just don't want anyone to know…."

"Sheesh. Maybe I should just go sit at my desk. I mean, I don't wanna *embarrass* you or anything," he said, straightening up and taking his notebook.

He was being unreasonable. "C'mon, Wesley," I quietly urged. He looked down at me and the expression on his face was indiscernible. He actually seemed a little hurt.

Mr. Hannity walked in just before the bell rang and Wesley went to his seat without another word. I glanced over my shoulder at him while the exams were being passed out and he was whispering with the person next to him. He didn't even look at me.

I couldn't concentrate on the test. It took me the full hour to finish it. Wesley waited while I got my things together and he looked relieved. He told me that the test wasn't as hard as he expected it to be.

He drove me home and idled in front of my building. "I gotta do some stuff for my mom, so I gotta get going. But I'll come by later. You wanna do something tonight?" he asked, his hand resting on the stick shift.

"Yeah, okay," I answered, opening the door. He didn't even try to stop me for a kiss. He smiled casually and waved. "See you later," I said timidly and closed the door. He waited until I got to the stairwell and then drove off.

Wesley returned later, around nine o'clock. He was wearing different clothes from what he had worn to school and he smelled like he'd just stepped out of the shower. Alycia had left with Mike an hour before and Mom was still at work. The kiss he gave me was brief—and platonic. We left and went to Cue to play pool.

"Hey, Wes! Toren! Over here, guys!" Kate shouted when we walked into the smoky pool hall. She was wearing a pair of tight, hip-hugging jeans and a low-cut T-shirt. Lissa smiled and said hi. "Let's pick up where we left off, okay?"

Wesley pulled a cue from the rack and Kate wound her arm around his waist. We played a couple games and Wesley catered to Kate's flirtations. She asked for help lining up shots and Wesley would lean behind her, his hand on her hip, correcting her aim. He didn't step away from her embraces either, and I felt a knot tightening in my stomach.

After the second game, Lissa began to rack up the balls again. "Are we up for another game?" she asked.

Wesley and Kate agreed but I shook my head. "I think I'm gonna get going. I'm pretty tired," I said, putting a five-dollar bill down on the table. I said good night and began to walk toward the front.

"Toren, wait a sec," Wesley called, but I pretended not to hear him. Tears were welling in my eyes. "Toren, c'mon!" he shouted again. "I gotta go. I'm his ride. Here's ten for the table," he said and followed me.

I slowed my pace after I was outside. The sun had set and the sky was dark except for the waning light in the west. I could hear Wesley behind me.

"Toren! Wait up. What's the matter?" he asked, closing in on me.

"Nothing. I'm just tired," I said without turning around.

"Yeah, right. Now, come on, what's wrong?"

"Nothing. I said I was fine. Why don't you just go back inside? I'm sure Kate's waiting for you."

Wesley circled around in front of me. "Is that what this is about? Toren, are you jealous?" he asked with a grin.

"No. Of course not," I said and narrowed my eyes. "I don't care what you do or with who."

Wesley's face dropped and his grin disappeared. "You don't mean that, do you?" I couldn't bear to look at his wounded face. "I'm only acting like this because of you. You're the one who's so afraid of people finding out about us. What am I supposed to do?" His voice was forceful; he believed every word he said. He tilted his head to the side and his expression softened. "Don't you trust me?"

I glanced up and tears rimmed my eyes. "I-I just…." I didn't know what to say. I did trust him, but I didn't know what to do either.

"You're the person I want to be with. It's just…frustrating that I can't act the way I want to around you. I want to be able to hold your hand and kiss you. It doesn't matter what other people think because you're the one I want."

"I-I'm sorry."

Wesley stepped closer to me. "There's nothing to be sorry for," he said, brushing my arm with his fingertips. "I guess I just have to learn to be patient."

He laughed quietly and closed his eyes. I felt relief seeing his smile again. He drove me home and parked in an empty spot. Alycia was out with Mike and Mom was still at work.

Wesley led me to the couch and pulled down the zipper on my blue jeans. My body was already on fire and Wesley fanned the flames. He stopped and looked in my eyes with a simple smile on his face.

"You know, it kinda made me happy that you got jealous. Because it means you really are into me," he said, the dim light shadowing his handsome face. I acknowledged the jealousy I felt and kissed him lightly. "But, just so you know, you don't have any reason to be jealous. You're the one I want." He slid his hand under the elastic band of my boxers and frigged me slowly with nimble fingers. I shuddered and pulled him closer. "Do you want me to use my hand or my mouth?" he whispered in my ear.

I blushed and looked into his eyes. "I want…to kiss you." Wesley moved his hand back and forth and I bit my lip. "That way, I can too."

"Wanna go to your room then? So it doesn't get…messy out here?"

I swallowed hard then nodded. I led him down the hall to my bedroom and he pulled me close. I could feel how hard he was and I shyly traced his stomach to the top of his blue jeans. He helped me unfasten them and he lowered me to my bed. His kiss was warm and hungry and he took me in one hand while he guided my hand with his other. He climbed atop me, keeping his hand in place, then leaned down and kissed me. My body listened to his every whim, my mind was hazy, and I didn't even know if I was still breathing. I moved my hand in time with his strokes and I bit my lower lip as I reached the edge of climax.

"Wait…just a sec," Wesley murmured, slowing his hand.

I opened my eyes and looked at Wesley's flushed face. I increased the pressure and speed and Wesley squeezed his eyes shut. He pulled me into him and we came together, our laboring bodies pressed close.

The feeling was incredible, the intimacy of climaxing in unison. He rested his head on my chest and I stroked my fingers through his hair. He looked up at me and smiled shyly, an unusual expression for him, and I kissed him softly.

We lay on my bed for a long while. I could feel my heart thumping and I knew Wesley could hear it. His head on my chest rose and fell with my breathing and I smiled; I was really falling in love with him.

Chapter 12

WESLEY called as he was leaving work and told me he was coming over. I hung up the phone and Alycia ran out in a panic. Her hair was uncombed and ratty and she was wearing her pink, fluffy slippers.

“Was that Mike?” she asked.

“No, it was Wesley,” I answered, setting down the phone and trying to contain my laughter. Alycia threw her hands up and marched down the hall, stomping her feet. She was cussing under her breath.

“What’s with her?” Mom asked, looking into the living room from the kitchen.

“Not sure. Mike’s probably gonna get it though,” I answered, stretching my arms out. I stood up and went to the kitchen. Mom was licking her fingers after stirring a bowl of chocolate pudding.

“You said that was Wesley? He’s been around a lot lately,” she said, washing off the spoon.

I fought the redness in my cheeks. “Yeah, we’re doing our History project together.”

“On a Saturday night?” Mom asked.

“No,” I groaned, rolling my eyes. I followed her back into the living room and we watched TV. Mom didn’t say anything more.

After a couple minutes, I went to the bathroom. I looked in the mirror and ran a hand through my hair. Alycia poked her head in the room and smiled.

"Going out with Wes again?"

"Yeah. We'll probably go play pool. Wanna come?" I asked, turning around and leaning against the sink.

"Nah, Mike's gonna stop by. He had to work late and he works with this really cute chick and I just know he…." Alycia folded her arms on her chest and pouted. "She better be a blonde bimbo with a huge rack and no personality if he's gonna cheat on me."

I sighed. "He's not gonna cheat on you. But I like your stipulations if he were going to," I added with a laugh.

Alycia smiled and nodded, then grinned deviously. She stepped into the bathroom and leaned toward me. "You're going out with Wes tonight? So, Tor, just how far have you gone with him?"

"A-Alycia!" I scolded, turning bright red.

"C'mon, tell me!" she whined, nudging me with her elbow.

"Nothing! We've just…um…."

"Uh-huh, yeah. That look totally gave you away. You've already done it? Toren, you little slut!"

"Quiet!" I looked at the open door and prayed that Mom didn't hear anything. "And no! Like it's any of your business anyway!"

"I got a feeling that you'll be giving it up soon, won't you? Still, I'm pretty impressed. I'm surprised Wes hasn't pushed you down and had his way with you. He's got the patience of a saint!" She turned around and walked out of the bathroom.

My shoulders slumped and I sighed. Wesley *was* patient with me, especially after what happened at Cue last night. I didn't trust him fully because of my own insecurities. It was my own fault.

Mom answered the door and Wesley greeted her politely. He wore grease-stained blue jeans and a navy work shirt.

"What are you guys doing tonight?" Mom asked, collapsing on the sofa and yawning. "Oh, excuse me," she said and wiped away the tears that collected from her giant yawn.

"Dunno," I answered, leaning down and kissing the top of Mom's head.

"Hiya, Wes," Alycia said, stepping out from the hall and brushing her hair. Wesley smiled and waved.

"Have fun," Mom said, putting her feet up on the coffee table and changing channels on the TV.

Wesley and I went to Cue, predictably, and Kate and Lissa were already there playing a game, also predictably. Lissa saw us and called us over. Kate hugged Wesley and he stepped back after a moment and I felt silly. Wesley grinned at me knowingly.

We played a few games, laughing and talking and having fun. I felt comfortable with Kate and Lissa, maybe more Lissa than Kate, but I couldn't explain it; I felt like I wasn't being judged.

"Want something to drink?" Wesley asked, leaning the cue stick against the table.

"I'm okay, thanks."

"Are you sure?" he asked, taking a step backward. I nodded and smiled.

"I'll come with you," Kate announced, handing her cue to Lissa and hooking her arm around Wesley's. I laughed to myself and watched them walk away, turning the cue around in my hands.

"So, how long have you guys been together?" Lissa asked, leaning against the pool table.

I looked at her with wide eyes and shook my head. "What? What are you talking about?" I tried to sound outraged.

"It's okay; I get it," Lissa said and looked down. "It's tough being gay in high school, isn't it?" She looked up and forced a smile on her lips, but her eyes weren't smiling. "At least you have someone who likes you back. I know Kate's a bit flaky, but she's really a good person. She's always there when I need her, no matter what. I keep telling myself that it'll be okay, as long as I can be close to her, even as just a friend."

Lissa looked sad with upturned eyebrows and a little pout on her lips. She was pretty with a slim figure. She didn't wear makeup and didn't need to. Her short, brown hair was pinned to the side with two barrettes, framing a sweet face.

I stared at the pool table and then glanced up at Lissa. "She doesn't know how you feel, then?" I asked. Lissa shook her head without looking up. I took a deep breath. "If…if Wesley hadn't said anything to me, we wouldn't…be together."

Lissa glanced at me with a gentle smile. "I see. You gotta learn to walk before you run. Or something like that."

I laughed lightly. "Yeah, something like that."

"You're all right, Toren," she said and smiled. This time, her eyes were smiling too. "Oh, here they come. Don't say anything, okay?"

I felt good. Lissa was the first person I told about Wesley and me and I already felt a little more confident.

"I got you a pop," Wesley said, handing me a Styrofoam cup with a lid and a straw. I thanked him and he looked at Lissa, then at me. He didn't say anything and started to rack up the balls for another game.

Chapter 13

"HEY, babe. What's going on?"

"Hi, Wesley. Nothing. What about you?"

"I'm getting outta work and I have to run a few errands for my mom, but I was wondering if you wanted to do something later."

"Um, yeah." My palms were sweaty and I felt nervous. "Do you wanna come over later? Um, my mom is working a double and my sister is sleeping over at a friend's tonight." There was a long, silent pause. "Are you still there?"

"I'll be right over."

"What? There's no rush. Just come after you've finished running your errands."

"All right. See you later."

It was gonna be just me and Wesley tonight. I was anxious and excited, so I decided to take a quick shower before he came over, hoping the warm water might help me relax.

The bathroom mirror steamed up and the small room was hot and humid. I ran my hand across the mirror, leaving streaks with my fingertips. There was a knock at the door and I heard Wesley call my name. I was surprised that he was here already. I wrapped a towel around my waist and called from the hallway.

"Hey. Come on in. I'll be out in a sec."

I pulled on a pair of boxers and slid my arms through a short-sleeve, button-down shirt. My hair was still dripping wet and I rubbed the towel over my head.

"Well, damn. If that isn't the most beautiful thing I've ever seen in my whole life."

I turned around and the towel dropped to the floor. "Wesley? What are you doing? I told you I'd be out in a minute." He leaned against the doorframe with a smug grin on his face.

"You look so good," he said, walking toward me and pulling me into his arms. He walked me back until I fell onto the bed. "You won't be needing these anymore!" he said, pulling off my boxer shorts and tossing them over his shoulder.

"Hold on! Wait a second! Wesley!" I hurriedly protested, knowing that once his lips touched me, I wouldn't be able to resist.

He was unbelievably ravenous, working me into a frenzy until I was completely ravished, panting and gasping.

"That didn't take long," he said with a triumphant smile, lying down next to me. He turned my face to his and kissed me sweetly.

"What…what are you doing here? I thought you had to run some errands."

"And let an opportunity like this slip by? No chance. Everything in the world, except you, can wait 'til tomorrow."

I rolled to my side and hid my shy smile. I loved it when he acted this way.

"Oh, damn. What a cute ass!"

Wesley pushed me onto my stomach and I felt his kisses trace down my back. His hands roamed freely, caressing my legs and thighs.

"Wait! What are you doing?" I shouted, panicking. I wasn't ready yet. His fingers became bolder, but it was his tongue that surprised me. "Stop! Wait a minute!"

I had never felt anything like it. His tongue was lapping and curling and it felt…incredible.

"Still want me to stop?"

"No!" I whimpered, surprised by the plea in my voice.

"Good boy," he whispered before delving back into his task.

I came even quicker, gripping the sheets in my tight fists and moaning louder than I ever had before. I collapsed into the bed, all my energy expended in delirious ecstasy.

"You really liked that," Wesley said, tickling the small of my back with his fingertips.

I could feel his warm breath, tinted with tobacco against my neck. He was so handsome and…manly, yet so gentle and kind with me. I loved the way he made me feel.

"What's that loopy grin for?" he asked, brushing my hair from my eyes. I didn't even realize I was smiling. I took a deep breath and closed my eyes and my stomach tightened. I wondered why he was with me.

"Wesley, do you…really like me so much? I mean, you're nice and good-looking; you can have anyone you want. I guess I'm just wondering why you settled for me."

Wesley's eyes grew big and he shook his head. "You think I settled for you? You've got it all wrong. I didn't settle for you; you were the one I wanted all along. I wonder why you settled for me?"

I looked at him blankly.

"Look, I may be cute, but that's about all I got going for me. But you, you're cute and smart. You're going places. I'll be lucky if you let me tag along."

"What are you talking about?" I asked, glancing down. "You've been leading me all along." I rolled over and rested the back of my hand on my forehead. I would follow him anywhere.

"Now what's with the grin?"

I laughed softly and looked into his eyes. "Nothing. You just make me really happy."

Wesley climbed on top of me and smiled wickedly. “Well, if I make you happy, how about I make you feel good too?” he said, planting kisses on my neck and collarbones.

“Wait. Hold on a sec. I want…I want both of us…to feel good,” I whispered, blushing to my ears. Wesley stopped kissing and licking me and looked into my eyes for a long moment.

“For real? Are you sure?”

“Yeah,” I answered timidly. Wesley stared at me and a devious smile spread across his face.

“Well, all right! Bring that sweet ass over here!” he shouted, grabbing hold of me and flipping me onto my stomach.

“Wait! Wait a second!” I shouted, floundering beneath him.

Wesley stopped, still straddling my legs, and looked at me. “Hang on; I’ll be right back,” he said quickly and jumped off the bed.

“What? Wait! Where are you going?” I asked as he ran out of the room. I sat up in bed and pulled the sheet over my lap. Where did he go? A few moments later, he returned with a brown paper bag in his hand. “What’s wrong? Where’d you go?” Then I looked at the brown bag. “What’s that?”

He took a small tube from the bag and tossed it onto the bed. “It’s lubricant. Like lotion, so it won’t hurt as much,” he said nonchalantly.

“Where did you get it?” I asked, furrowing my brows.

“I, uh, I’ve had it for a while now. You know, just in case you were ever in the mood,” he answered, scratching the back of his head with a silly grin on his face.

“Oh, gee, thanks for the premeditation,” I said, crossing my arms and looking to my side. Wesley laughed and I looked at the tube next to me. He pulled off his shirt and I looked up at him. The expression on his face was indescribable: elated, but also serious. He unbuckled his belt and pulled off his blue jeans and boxers. I guess I had forgotten his actual size and I blushed at the sight of him. This was gonna hurt.

Wesley crawled onto the bed and picked up the tube. Silently, he massaged my body and placed tender kisses on my lips and neck. He rolled me onto my side and kissed me again before turning me onto my stomach. He straddled my legs and squeezed an ample amount of lotion onto his fingers. He leaned down and nibbled my ear. "I'm gonna get you used to it first, so it'll only be my fingers," he whispered and sat back on his heels.

I was trembling with nervousness as Wesley pulled my backside toward him, bringing me up on my knees. He gently frigged me with one hand while slowly pushing his fingers inside. I squeezed my eyes shut and gritted my teeth; it didn't hurt but it felt weird. After a moment, he withdrew his fingers and leaned down on top of me again.

"Are you ready, Toren? I'll go real slow, but if it hurts too much, tell me and I'll stop," he said, kissing my cheek and then the nape of my neck. He traced the contours of my back with his tongue and then I felt the first of him.

He held steady, listening closely to my breathing. After I took a deep breath, he pressed further into me and I moaned with an edge of pain.

"Are you okay?"

"Yeah," I whispered, choking on a sob in my throat. Wesley continued and I let out a stifled cry. He hesitated and waited patiently and sympathetically for me. "Keep…keep going," I panted, gripping the sheet in my hands and burying my face in the pillow.

I felt him swell within me and he pressed on, slowly pushing his way deep inside. When he was fully within me, he stopped, holding still.

"Are you okay? Does it still hurt?"

"Ahh…" I moaned, unable to form coherent words. The pain was ebbing and with the slightest movement, an unimaginable pleasure rippled through my entire body. He moved slowly and I found myself pushing back in gentle rhythm. He rubbed my back with one hand while he held my arousal in his other. His motions grew stronger and I balled my hands into fists. Tears collected in my eyes and I moaned with a voice I didn't know I had. Wesley's hand slipped away and he grasped my hips, pulling me closer. I felt him in every inch of my body. Wesley moaned softly and I loved the sound of his voice.

"Wes-Wesley! I'm…!"

"Me too," he grunted, his voice low, labored, and sexy.

Wesley collapsed on top of me, breathing hard and kissing my neck. He was still inside me and I fought the urge to tell him that I was in love with him.

"Sorry I came inside," he whispered in my ear.

I turned to the side and saw his handsome face from the corner of my eye. He reached out his hand and laced his fingers with mine.

"It's okay…. I wanted you to."

Wesley rolled to his side and took my face in his hands. He kissed my lips tenderly and I felt like I was melting. I slid my fingers behind his head and pulled him closer, but after making love, it didn't seem nearly close enough.

I WOKE to a beam of sunlight across my eyes. Wesley slept next to me with his head on my arm and his hand resting on my stomach. He looked so innocent when he was sleeping. Memories of the night rushed to the front of my mind and I blushed looking at Wesley's smooth body thinly veiled by the bed sheet.

My arm was tired, and I tried not to move, but my body betrayed me and I twitched, stirring Wesley to consciousness. He looked up at me and smiled.

"Morning," he whispered, blinking his eyes twice.

He lifted himself to his elbow and kissed me simply. He moved his hand over my chest and stomach, lightly and slowly. He acted like waking up next to me was the most natural thing in the world.

"What time is it?" he asked, looking around the room. Our clothes were scattered on the floor. The tube of lotion was on the nightstand next to a glass of water.

"It's a little past noon."

"Really?" he yawned, finding the alarm clock on my dresser across the room. "Damn, I guess it is." He leaned down and rested his head on my chest again. "I really like waking up this way."

I smiled and ruffled his hair. I did too. Wesley looked up at me and grinned on one side of his mouth.

"Can we do it one more time?"

He pressed himself against my body and pouted with pleading eyes. I felt him against my thigh and I smirked, nodding my head as I leaned down and kissed him. I began to turn to my side, but Wesley shook his head and crawled atop me.

"No. Let's do it this way, so I can see your face," he said, moving his hands to my backside and pulling me closer. He parted my legs and pushed them up to my chest. He bent forward and kissed me, picking up the tube of lotion from the table. He popped open the top and squeezed some onto his fingers. "Did I use enough lube last night?"

I turned my head to the side and closed my eyes with blushing cheeks. "Don't…don't call it that."

"What? Lube?" he asked. I nodded and covered my mouth with my hand. He chuckled and smirked. "All right, did I use enough *stuff* last night?"

"Mm-hmm."

He was sitting back on his heels and he pulled my backside closer. He slid his fingers around; one, then two, getting me ready. He frigged me gently with his other hand, looking in my eyes with a sweet expression. He positioned himself as I drew up to accept him and he slid inside easily. He leaned forward, pushing deeper, and kissed me. He slowly rocked back and forth, staring in my eyes, and I squeezed his hands in mine. He was steady, moving slowly, until I closed my eyes with pleasure. He pushed deeper and I moaned quietly, whispering his name. His fingers tightened around mine and he bent his head down, his brown hair falling in his eyes.

"Wes-Wesley," I cried, "Oh…oh, God!"

Wesley scooped me in his arms, pulling me up, and I wrapped my arms around his neck. I clung to him for dear life, my legs wrapped around his middle. We came together, climaxing for what felt like an eternity, though not nearly long enough. He still held me in his arms, my head resting on his shoulder, his warm breath on my neck. We stayed like that for a while, until I kissed him. He smiled at me.

"You really are beautiful," he said, touching my lips.

I laid my head on his shoulder and smiled in spite of myself. My face felt flushed and Wesley hugged me.

"Do you have to work today?" I asked.

Wesley sneered and nodded. "Yeah, I gotta be in at two." He leaned in and kissed me, then climbed out of bed. I took a deep breath. His body was perfect: not too thin, not too muscular. The muscles in his arms and legs were faintly outlined and shaded by the sunlight. He had a little bit of a belly, but it wasn't noticeable unless he was naked. He got dressed, and then sat down on the bed to tie his shoes.

"Aren't you going to walk me out?" he asked, leaning down and kissing me.

"Sure," I answered, inching to the edge of the bed where I could reach my boxers on the floor. I was shy to stand naked before Wesley. He watched me dress without saying a word. I walked him to the front door and he kissed me again. His smile was happy, almost childlike.

"I'll give you a call in a little while," he said.

I closed the door after him and my heart started beating again. I looked around the living room and into the kitchen, amazed that everything looked the same. I couldn't keep myself from smiling. I was really in love with him.

Chapter 14

WE had to present our History project in less than a week. Finals were just around the corner and the pressure was really beginning to build, but Wesley and I never seemed to get any work done. I finally had to impose a ten-minute time limit on making out so that we could actually do some homework. No matter how hard I tried to enforce the time limit, Wesley always managed to double (and even triple) the time.

"C'mon, Tor, I need more than ten minutes today," Wesley pleaded as I took out my History folder and notebook. I shook my head and Wesley leaned into the sofa, crossing his arms and pouting. "You're so mean."

"We have to study," I explained, trying to focus my attention.

Wesley slid next to me, forgetting all about his sullen mood, and kissed my neck. I trembled with his touch; I knew I would end up giving in. He pushed my notebook onto the floor and leaned forward, slipping his hand under my shirt. His lips, his fingers, his pulse—it all felt so good and I couldn't stop myself. Being with Wesley was like having an addiction to some provocative drug; I gave in too easily. I pulled him closer and Wesley responded to my invitation, walking his fingers to the top of my blue jeans.

"Hey, it's me. I forgot my…."

"M-Mom?"

She stood just inside the door. Her mouth hung open and her eyes widened. I pushed Wesley away as tears welled in my eyes.

"I...I can explain. We weren't...." Mom stared at me without saying a word. "I...I'm...I'm sorry!" I cried.

Mom shook her head in disbelief. Or in fear. Or hatred. I didn't know which, or if it was all three. Wesley stood up, glanced at me, and then dared to look in Mom's eyes.

"I...should probably get going," he said awkwardly, reaching down for his book bag.

"No. You stay," Mom directed firmly. Wesley obediently sat down, his book bag at his feet. Mom shook her head and sighed deeply. She set her purse down on the kitchen table and rounded the sofa, sitting down across from me on the coffee table. I couldn't imagine what she was feeling.

"I'm sorry!" I shouted through my tears, burying my face in my hands. She hated me. I was making her go through this all over again. How could she ever forgive me?

"Toren, calm down," she said, lowering her face to look in my eyes. "Toren, I'm not angry. Or upset, or disappointed," she said, but I was barely paying attention. I squeezed my eyes shut and my body shook with my sobs. "Oh, this is all my fault," she whispered, touching her hand to her forehead.

"I'm...I'm sorry...." I whimpered pathetically. Then I felt her hand on my knee.

"Toren, listen to me. Toren?" She waited for me to look up at her, but I couldn't. "I'm sorry, Toren. I'm so sorry," she said, pressing down on my knee. "I should've talked to you sooner. I'm not upset, Toren. Are you listening?" I glanced up at her through blurry eyes and she smiled softly. "I'm not upset. I should've talked to you sooner. I knew what happened between your dad and me had an enormous effect on you and I said all those terrible things to him right in front of you. If I could, I would take them all back. But I never meant to hurt you. I never wanted you to be afraid to be yourself because of what I might think. I love you more than anything and I just want you to be happy. And to be honest, I'm *proud* of you. You did something your father couldn't do until he was thirty-five. I'm proud that you were able to discover the truth about yourself while you're still young. You won't have to suffer the way he did for so many years." I glanced up at Mom and her face was soft and kind, accepting, and my tears rolled freely down my cheeks. Mom lifted my chin, our eyes met, and she smiled. "And I think you have Wes, in part, to thank for that."

I blushed and looked down. I could feel Mom and Wesley staring at me. Mom smiled at Wesley and my heart felt lighter. I rubbed at the tears in my eyes with the back of my hand and Mom tapped my knee with her index finger.

"I just want you to be happy, sweetheart. I never want you to feel like you have to hide because you're afraid of what I might think." She looked around the living room and scooted closer to me. "I hate to drop all this on you and then leave, but I gotta get back to work. I forgot my wallet and I gotta go," she said, pushing down on her knees to stand up. She patted my head and trotted off down the hall.

I didn't look at Wesley yet, just stared at the empty space where Mom had sat on the coffee table. A moment later, Mom returned with a large, brown wallet and stuffed it in her purse on the kitchen table. She kissed the top of my head and walked to the front door.

"I love you, sweetheart. I'll see you later. You boys be good," she said and then left.

After a long moment, when the whirlwind finally died down, Wesley leaned back into the sofa and put his feet up on the table. He laced his fingers behind his head and sighed noisily. He glanced at me sideways and then looked toward the ceiling.

"That was…pretty cool," he said. "Your mom is really amazing."

I nodded; my voice wasn't settled yet. The tears receded a bit and I breathed in air as if I had been holding my breath for a long time. She didn't hate me. She wasn't disgusted. I was so afraid that she would never want to see me again. She said she was proud of me. *She didn't hate me.*

"What exactly happened between your folks?" Wesley asked, rolling his head on the back of the sofa to look at me.

"They…." I cleared my throat and sniffled. "They got divorced when I was about twelve. My dad left her for…another man. She said all these horrible things to Dad, screamed them at him. We lived in kind of a small town, so everyone found out and eventually he moved away. Me and Alycia were teased about it and everyone kinda looked at Mom in a different way. Like it was her fault or something."

"That must've been really hard…for both of them," Wesley murmured, putting his arm around my shoulders.

He was right. It must've been so hard to find out that the person you love wasn't in love with you. I couldn't even imagine what that might feel like.

"But I guess I can understand how your dad felt. I mean, I struggled with my feelings for a while too," Wesley considered aloud.

I looked down to my lap and my eyes welled up. I had always blamed my dad for what happened, but I guess it must've been hard for him too. To find the strength, the courage, to tell Mom the truth, to accept it himself, after so many years…after marriage and two kids.

I glanced at Wesley, his words echoing in my head. "You…you had trouble too?" It was hard to imagine; he was always so confident.

"Yeah," he answered awkwardly, looking away. "I went out with girls because I was supposed to. But I didn't feel anything. I mean, I would catch myself watching other guys, but I just ignored the feeling. Then…then I saw you. I guess you were the first crush I ever really acknowledged. I wanted to talk to you, get to know you. I wanted to do more than that," he said, blushing lightly. Then he looked up at me and a devilish grin replaced his awkward expression. "Heh, I mean, seriously, I can't tell you how many times I jerked off thinking about you."

My cheeks reddened, even my ears felt hot. He did it too?

Wesley stared at me and a smirk curled the corners of his mouth. "Hey, did you do it too? While thinking about me?"

"Wesley!" I scolded, my cheeks on fire. I couldn't look at him and I was sure he figured out the truth.

"C'mon, I'm being honest. Just tell me. I won't be mad if you didn't think about me."

He was really asking and I could see that his pride was on the line. Mortified, I confessed without words, nodding my head.

"I knew it!" he shouted delightfully, his pride in check. He inched closer to me, resting his hand on my knee. "But, seriously, I was always watching you. When I finally admitted that I had a crush on you, I couldn't keep my eyes off you, but you were too dense to notice," he said with a laugh, looking at me from the corner of his eye. "God, I was so nervous. The first time I talked to you, when you came over to my house…."

"What? You didn't act like that at all!" I shouted and then I looked down bashfully. "Especially because of what you said."

"What? What did I say?"

"You…you said that I looked at you…like I wanted you to…you know," I stuttered. My heart was beating through my chest. Just remembering some of our first conversations excited me.

"I…what? Did I really?" he asked. Then he slapped his knee and looked up gleefully. "Oh yeah! I said that you looked at me like you wanted me to fuck you! I can't believe I actually said that! I can't believe you didn't punch me in the face!" Wesley laughed heartily, enjoying my embarrassment, and I punched him in the arm, even if it was a little late.

Chapter 15

IT was finally the last day of school. The last day I would have to spend in the joyless halls of high school. It was a milestone, but it was a damn long day. My stomach tightened with anxiety and I went over my note cards for History again, but it didn't help. I hated public speaking.

"Hey, whatcha doin'?" Wesley asked, sidling up beside me and dropping his book bag.

"What?" I asked absentmindedly, looking up at him. He took the note cards from my hands and fanned through them.

"Man, I just had my English final and it totally sucked. I don't know why I even bothered studying," he said, thudding back against the lockers.

I furrowed my brows at him. He didn't actually study for English very much; he was more interested in getting my pants off. I looked down from the corners of my eyes and blushed. Wesley handed back the note cards.

"You ready for the presentation?" he asked.

"Yeah, I guess so. I just really hate public speaking."

"I know. You're so cute. You turn all red and stutter," Wesley said with a grin.

"I…yeah, I know. I can't help it," I conceded.

"Well, don't worry about it. I'll be right next to you. And when we're done, we'll just start making out, okay? Our presentation will also be our coming out."

"Wesley!" I snapped, glancing up and down the hall.

"You know, I heard on the news that sex before public speaking is supposed to be relaxing. So you want a quickie in the boys' room before we're up?"

"Wesley!" I scolded again. "You're not helping!"

Wesley laughed and picked up his book bag just before the bell rang. He smiled warmly and patted my shoulder. "C'mon, you know this stuff inside-out. You'll be fine."

"WHERE are we going?" I asked. Wesley seemed to be driving aimlessly.

"I thought we'd go to our secret hiding place," Wesley said, glancing at me, and then taking a hit of his cigarette. "I figured it'd be a good place to go to celebrate our first moments of freedom from the oppressive education machine."

"Oppressive education machine?" I laughingly repeated. "Hmm, I'll have to remember that one."

The windows were rolled all the way down and the fresh air felt good. I finally closed the high school chapter of my life and I vowed never to set foot in that school again. High school sucked and I was glad to leave it behind. It was warm and sunny without a cloud in the sky and I took that as a confirmation: an end to the oppressive education machine.

Wesley pulled onto the shoulder of the road and we walked to the small alcove of trees hiding the algae-green pond, leaving our book bags in the car. We sat down on the fallen log and Wesley kissed me. I tasted the tobacco on his breath and realized how used to it I had gotten. He lit another cigarette and leaned back on his hands, looking up at the sky overhead. We talked about the summer and all the things we were going to do together. I wanted to take a trip to the beach, but it would have to be an overnight excursion since there were no beaches nearby.

Wesley interrupted my daydream when he pulled a joint out of his pack of cigarettes. He slid it underneath his nose then put it in his mouth. He leaned back as he searched for his lighter in his pocket.

"Smoke this with me," he said.

"I don't know…."

"Oh, c'mon. You already did it once, so what's the big deal? Besides, you'll probably get high this time, so it won't be a waste," he urged, burning the tip then inhaling deeply. He held it out to me and I took it hesitantly. "You remember how, don't you?"

I nodded and brought the joint to my lips, breathing in cautiously and then breathing in again. The smoke filled my lungs and I exhaled fully, watching the stream of smoke from my mouth. I smiled shyly and Wesley congratulated me, patting my back and taking the joint. We passed it back and forth and I experienced only one coughing fit. When we got to the roach, Wesley put it out and dropped it in his cigarette pack. I looked at the pond and rubbed the tops of my legs with my palms.

"I feel kinda funny," I said, starting to swing my legs back and forth.

"Funny good? Or funny bad?" Wesley asked, smiling with an arched eyebrow.

"Funny good," I said with a giggle.

"Yup, you're definitely stoned, Mr. Grey," he announced and slapped my back. Mr. Grey sounded funny to me. "You've been smiling since your third toke."

"I have?" I asked, touching my face with my fingertips. I giggled again.

Wesley laughed softly and rested his hand on my leg. "Kiss me."

"Okay," I agreed and leaned into him. He slid his tongue between my lips and when I closed my eyes, the sensation rippled through my body. I kissed him with every sense escalated and it felt so good. Before I knew it, Wesley unbuttoned my blue jeans and pulled down the zipper. I jumped back and looked around cautiously. "Wait! Wh-what are you doing?"

"Relax. There's no one around for miles," Wesley assured me, continuing to push his hand down my pants.

I responded to his touch, the mere hint of it. Wesley grinned at me and I finally admitted to myself that I was really horny. I wondered if this was how Wesley felt all the time.

"Wesley!" I protested, remembering how out in the open we were.

"Oh, come on," Wesley urged. "On the off chance that someone comes by, I'll just tell them that you…were bit by a snake and I'm just…sucking out the poison."

"What?"

Wesley yanked down my pants and gasped. "Oh no! It's swelling up! And rigor mortis has already set in! I've got to hurry!"

"What?"

Wesley laughed and then licked the tip tenderly. He moved his hands to the base and then dropped his mouth around me. He sucked and licked feverishly. I moaned quietly and he pulled me closer and deeper into his mouth, moving his hand to my backside. My legs trembled and I grasped his shoulders.

"Oh, wow…."

Wesley stopped and looked up at me with a grin at the corner of his mouth. "Did you just say wow?"

I looked down at him in my lap, his brown hair falling in his eyes, the grin on his lips. My whole body felt warm and tingly. "Don't stop!" I pleaded, forgetting about the joint we just smoked, the fresh open air, the fear of being caught. Wesley was the only real thing in this world.

"Yes, sir," Wesley said, and then sucked hard on me until I came in his mouth and down his throat, which didn't actually take too long.

I panted and gasped for air, Wesley bracing me and keeping me from toppling over. I held to his arms and sighed, the world slowly coming back to me.

"Oh God…I thought I was gonna die," I whispered. I took deep breaths, remembering the fevered sensations, and reached my hand out to the top of Wesley's blue jeans and the bulge pushing out just beneath. Wesley held my hand steady and shook his head.

He pulled me to my feet and kissed me deeply. "Let's go back to your place."

Chapter 16

IT was unseasonably warm for mid-June and the auditorium wasn't air-conditioned. The ceremony was needlessly long and rather boring. By the end, everyone in the audience used their programs as fans and from the stage, it looked like a whole bunch of giant, white butterflies. I felt dizzy from the heat, but I managed to walk all the way across the stage without tripping. I fingered the rolled sheet of paper with the red ribbon tied around it while the closing remarks were being made.

Outside, students gathered with their families, but the warm, summer breeze didn't offer much relief. Mom took nearly a whole roll of film before she even let me take off the polyester cap and gown. Alycia flitted around, chatting with her friends in the graduating class until she found Wesley.

I blushed at the sight of him. He wore gray dress pants and a white, short-sleeve, button-down shirt with a black and gray striped tie. He looked really cute, even though his shoes didn't match and his hair was all over the place. He seemed a little awkward in that kind of outfit, which made him all the cuter.

He smiled and walked over to me, giving me a brief, platonic hug. He laughed and whispered in my ear, "Finally, the end of the oppressive education machine." Then, he leaned a little closer. "You look really cute today."

I smiled and patted his back the way a friend would, then greeted Mr. and Mrs. Carroll. Wesley introduced his parents to Mom and Alycia and then he introduced his brother, who drove in from Pennsylvania just to surprise him. I was excited to meet him; Wesley mentioned that he had a brother, but he didn't talk about his family much.

Scott was taller than Wesley was and thicker with muscle; he had a football player's physique and a cute, boyish face. He looked every bit the three years older than Wesley that he was, but I may have mistaken that for maturity. He seemed genuinely excited to see his brother, but Wesley seemed rather indifferent.

Mom pushed me next to Wesley and pulled out her camera again. She made us put our caps and gowns back on and then took another dozen pictures. Wesley put his arm around my shoulders and when his parents weren't looking, he slid his hand around my waist.

"Oh! We're going out for dinner to celebrate. Wanna come with us?" Alycia asked giddily. She tried to make it sound like she just thought of it, but I could tell by her smile that she had planned on asking.

Mom didn't miss a beat either. "Oh, what a good idea! Yes, we'd love if you'd join us," she chimed in, smiling broadly.

"That sounds like fun," Mrs. Carroll answered, clapping her hands together. "Sure, we'd love to!" She looked at Mr. Carroll, who remained solemn but agreed.

While our parents were discussing restaurant options, Jen and Olivia ran toward us, calling Wesley's name. Jen bumped into me as she put her arm around Wesley. She glared at me briefly then whispered "sorry" with an edge of sarcasm. I stepped to the side as Olivia focused her camera on Wesley and Jen. Wesley glanced over at me and rolled his eyes and I felt a pang of jealousy as Jen wound her arm around Wesley's waist.

Alycia nudged me with her elbow, then crossed her arms and furrowed her brows. "Just who the hell does she think she is?" She tossed me a look from the corner of her eye and I couldn't help but smile at her vicarious jealousy. "Hey, Wes! We're leaving for dinner now!" Alycia called, staring directly at Jen.

Wesley smiled and with a flick of his hand dismissed Jen and Olivia. Jen called out after him, telling him that they should get together soon. Wesley waved over his shoulder without looking back. Alycia pushed me into Wesley and he laid his hand on my shoulder. Alycia grinned at Jen and, with a sense of satisfaction, we left for dinner.

The restaurant was a fancy, Italian place with real cloth napkins, water goblets, and tons of silverware. Two tables were pushed together to accommodate the seven of us and Wesley sat next to me. He took my hand under the table and I couldn't pull away without everyone noticing, so I accepted it and rested our hands in my lap. Mom and Alycia sat next to Wesley and me and Mr. and Mrs. Carroll and Scott sat across the table. Mrs. Carroll ordered an appetizer for all of us and we chatted awkwardly while waiting for our food. Fortunately, Mom and Alycia realized that Wesley's parents didn't know about us and so were on their best behavior.

"So, Toren, where are you gonna go to school?" Mrs. Carroll asked, breaking a long silence.

"I've been accepted at the University," I answered quietly. Wesley squeezed my hand proudly under the table.

"Good for you! Have you thought about a major then?" she followed up.

"I…I'm thinking about History. Or education. I'd like to be a History teacher," I said.

"That sounds interesting. You know, the project the two of you worked on for History class was really good. It was pretty interesting," she complimented, glancing and smiling at Mom who nodded appreciatively. "Now that I think about it, Wes's grades have gotten better since you became friends. If only you'd met as freshmen!" she said, lighting one of her ultra-slim cigarettes. Wesley's hand tightened around mine and I looked down self-consciously. "I saw that you graduated with honors. That means you had at least a 3.5 GPA, right?"

I nodded my head, but Mom piped up proudly. "3.6, right?" she asked, looking at me. I nodded again.

"You know, Scott graduated with a 3.8 and now he's in a big engineering program at a university in Pennsylvania. He tried for lots of scholarships and grants and won a few of them. His education is basically paid for. If you want, I'm sure he'll help you find scholarships and stuff. Right, Scott? We tried with Wes, but with a 2.5, there's only so much open."

"2.8. Not that it matters," Wesley interrupted quietly, looking down at his lap.

"What?"

"I have a 2.8, not a 2.5," he said. His grip on my hand slackened and he stared into his lap. I squeezed his hand and he looked up at me.

"Well, anyway, Scott, you should write down some of the scholarships for Toren, and then he can look them up."

The rest of the dinner passed slowly. The food was good but I didn't really taste it. I was concerned about Wesley; he didn't say much for the rest of the meal. Mrs. Carroll extolled Scott's achievements proudly and Scott modestly brushed it off as no big deal.

After the bill was paid, we said good night and went our separate ways. Wesley told me that he'd come over after he changed his clothes.

"Boy, that Cindy Carroll is kind of a handful," Mom commented on the way home.

"Yeah, what was her deal? She kept harping on Wes about everything," Alycia agreed, turning around in the front seat to look at me in the back.

I felt a little better, hearing Mom and Alycia, because I realized that I wasn't just being oversensitive about Wesley. I stared out the window, watching the old, blue Taurus's fleeting reflections in storefront windows. I didn't really like Mr. Carroll, but I thought Mrs. Carroll was nice. Now my opinion was changing and I didn't like it. Was this what Wesley always went through at home?

"If I ever compare the two of you like that, tell me right away," Mom demanded.

WESLEY came over at a little past eight. When I ran to the car, I saw Scott sitting in the front seat. I was kind of excited; I wanted to talk to him. Like Wesley, he seemed reserved in front of his parents. But I was also a little disappointed; it meant I wouldn't be able to kiss Wesley tonight.

"Hey, Toren. Congrats on graduating. I figured that since I'm the only one old enough to buy beer, I should come along. Hope you don't mind," Scott said casually. I smiled; he just said more than he had all during dinner.

"No, that's okay," I answered. Wesley glanced back at me from the driver's seat.

We decided to go to Cue again because there wasn't much else to do. Scott walked in the front door and whistled.

"Man, same shithole I remember from when I was in high school," he said with a laugh. "You go get a table and I'll get us a pitcher," he said, walking toward the bar.

As expected, Kate and Lissa called to us and we went over to say hi. They congratulated us on graduating and complained that they still had a year to go. A moment later, Scott came up with a pitcher and three glasses.

"No way! Are you tryin' for a three-way?" Kate asked with a loud laugh. Scott looked at Wesley with a raised eyebrow and grinned. Kate smiled and introduced Lissa and herself to Scott. "Hey, you didn't bring enough glasses for us!" she whined.

"Well, there's nothing I like better than buying drinks for underage girls, but…I'll let you share with me," Scott compromised flirtatiously. I realized then just how similar Scott and Wesley were.

"You're barkin' up the wrong tree there, chief," Wesley said nonchalantly, leaning over the table and lining up his break.

Scott smiled and laughed, raising his hands up in an "I surrender" motion and stepped back. "Sorry, man. Didn't know I was stepping on your toes."

Lissa stepped forward and I grinned. "Actually, it's *my* toes that you're stepping on," she said with a smile, sliding her hand around Kate's waist.

Kate grinned and actually blushed a little. “Yeah, I’m spoken for.”

“Oh. *Oh*,” Scott said laughing, turning his beer around in his hands.

“Don’t you have a girlfriend anyway?” Wesley asked.

Scott nodded happily. He looked puzzled and leaned toward Wesley with his hand shielding his mouth. “Then, what’d she mean by the three-way thing?”

Wesley looked at Scott with a serious expression. My stomach tightened. “She meant us,” he said, nodding his head toward me. “Toren’s my boyfriend.”

“Wh-what?” Scott stuttered, his eyes wide. Then his face broke into a smile. “You gotta be kidding. You’ve got one weird sense of humor, man.”

“I’m not joking,” Wesley said, his expression still serious. He twirled the pool cue in his hand. “We’re gay. He’s my boyfriend.”

Scott looked at me and my face was bright red. I couldn’t discern the look on his face. I said Wesley’s name quietly and felt my heart thumping fiercely.

“Oh, come on! Your sister knows, so I should be able to tell my brother,” Wesley said comically, trying to calm my nervousness.

Scott stared at us and I wasn’t sure if I felt like running away or going up and kissing Wesley just to prove it. Scott crossed his arms and smiled triumphantly. “All right. Then, kiss him.”

I stared at Scott blankly. Wesley grinned. Scott waited. I shook my head.

Wesley laughed defeatedly and closed his eyes. “Toren’s not exactly out yet, so how about later?”

“Yeah, whatever,” Scott said, pouring another glass of beer. “Let’s just shoot some pool.”

We played a couple of games and Scott drank nearly two pitchers by himself, with a little help from Kate and Wesley. When he couldn’t line up a shot anymore, Wesley decided it was time to call it quits. Scott finished off the pitcher and Lissa and Kate walked us out.

When we got to the car, Wesley spun around, pulled me into his arms, and kissed me so hard I felt it in my toes. He held me steady and grinned at Scott who stared at us with wide eyes.

"Shit. You really weren't kidding," he slurred, opening the side door and dropping into the passenger seat.

Wesley smiled at me and kissed me again, gently, before opening the door for me.

"Wow. That was kinda hot," Kate whispered, loudly enough for us to hear. Lissa nodded in agreement. I guess that was the first time they actually saw us kiss. I smiled lightly; it felt like another milestone in our relationship. At least a half-milestone.

We started out for home, but somewhere along the way, Scott complained that he was hungry and needed coffee. We ended up at a 24-hour restaurant, sitting in the smoking section, and being stared at by Scott who sat across the table from us.

"You know, seriously, I half-expected to come home and find out that you knocked up some poor chick. I really wasn't expecting this," Scott said, sipping his coffee and eating french fries by the handful. "But, hey, at least you don't have to worry about that!" he added, staring at me. He leaned in close and lowered his voice. "I'm assuming that you're the "girl," right?"

My whole body blushed and I couldn't think of anything to say. Wesley shook his head. "That's enough, Scott. But, yeah, and he's great in bed," Wesley said, looking at me sideways with a devilish grin.

"Wesley!" I shouted, holding my chin in my palm and looking away from the table. They laughed the same way, and I thought, *They really are brothers.*

"I take it that Mom and Dad don't know?" Scott asked, suddenly serious.

Wesley shook his head. "Nah. It doesn't matter though. Like anything I do will ever be good enough."

Scott looked sad and stared into his cup of coffee. He rested his chin in his palm and stared at Wesley, who was tapping his fork on the table. "I'm really sorry about what happened at dinner. I didn't think Mom would still be riding you like that once I was gone." Scott stared at the table again and Wesley shrugged his shoulders before looking out the window. It was an awkward, yet intimate, silence. "Seriously, Wes, I'm really sorry. I wish there was something I could do."

"Don't worry about it," Wesley snapped. Then his face softened a bit. "It's not like it's your fault. I don't expect you to go out and fail just so I rise a little in rank in Mom's eyes. I just gotta be patient. When I move out, I won't have to worry about it anymore."

I listened quietly. This was the most I'd heard Wesley say about his family. He was sad and angry and treated unfairly, but he didn't let it get the best of him. I didn't feel pity for him; maybe some sympathy, but he was strong. He could handle anything.

"This is exactly what I admire about you," Scott said quietly. "You don't let anyone get you down. You're happy no matter what you do and it doesn't matter what other people think. I mean, you got a good job doing what you love, a cute boyfriend that makes you happy. You've got it all."

"What the hell are you talking about? You're the one that has a great job and goes to some prestigious university. You've got the ideal life!" Wesley countered, perhaps a little jealously. Scott stared at his younger brother, basking in his admiration, but he shook his head.

"You got it wrong. Yeah, I look like I'm successful, but it doesn't mean I'm happy. I'm doing this stuff to make Mom and Dad happy, not for myself. The truth is, you've got the balls to stand up to them. And your relationship with Toren is just another example. You know Dad's gonna flip, but you're all like 'what the fuck do I care? I'm happy.'"

Wesley looked up and laughed. He had a slight grin on his face and he turned and looked at me. "Yeah, I guess you're right. I am happy."

"See what I mean?" Scott said, finishing his coffee. He looked at me but pointed at Wesley. "He's been like this since he was a kid too. If he liked something, he went after it. If he didn't like it, he didn't bother. Even with school, he hated school, even in, like, first grade. He just did what he wanted to. Like math: he liked math. But, I don't know, spelling? He doesn't know shit—hell, he probably can't even *spell* 'shit'! He just wasn't interested. And he's still like that! Am I right?" Scott asked me, looking for support.

I laughed in spite of myself and nodded. It was true. I ran into that problem when we were studying for final exams. Wesley laughed too, probably because Scott's characterization was so accurate.

The tension between the brothers seemed to disintegrate and we left a little while thereafter. Scott gave me shotgun on the way home and Wesley kissed me good night. I waved from the third floor of my building and watched them drive away. I was glad that Scott came out with us. I felt like I knew Wesley a little better than I did before. And, I still got to kiss him before the night was over.

Chapter 17

"I NEED to find a job," I said, holding my chin in my palm and taking a french fry from Wesley's tray. "Do you know of any places that are hiring?"

"Not off the top of my head," he answered and took a bite of his quarter-pounder with cheese.

"I just want something where I can work close to full-time now, and then work part-time when school starts," I explained, taking another fry.

"I told you to get something and you said you weren't hungry, but you're eating all my fries," Wesley complained with a smirk.

I hadn't even realized I was taking his french fries. I looked around; it had been a long time since I was actually inside a McDonald's. There was a deluxe play area that was twice the size of the seating area. I remembered a plastic, talking tree and tables with mushroom stools from when I was little. Kids sure had it nice these days.

"So you wanna do retail? You could try the bookstore or a coffee shop or something like that. Or maybe that World Store place. You could do stock or work as a cashier."

"Yeah," I agreed, smiling sheepishly and taking another fry.

"Just remember, if you suddenly get hired, you can't work this weekend. 'Cause it's the Fourth of July. Okay?"

"I doubt I'd get hired that fast."

"Just promise me," Wesley urged, shoving the last piece of hamburger in his mouth. I nodded and he slurped his soda. He took a few fries and pushed the tray toward me. "You can finish those."

"No, it's okay. I told you; I'm not hungry," I answered, pushing the tray back. Wesley laughed and rolled his eyes at me.

"Thanks for meeting me for lunch. But next time, I want something home-cooked and made with love," he said, finishing off the fries and picking up the tray. "I gotta get back to work."

I nodded and watched him empty the tray into the garbage. He was wearing a navy work shirt that actually had his name embroidered on it. I smiled to myself; I thought that was pretty cool. He wore matching navy pants, streaked with grease. Even though he washed his hands thoroughly, they were still dirty, especially around his fingernails. There was always something about his hands that I liked; they were big and rough, but they always held me so gently.

Wesley waited for me and we left together. He looked around and then rumpled my hair with his hand. I could tell he wanted a kiss, but there were too many people around. He said that he'd call or come over after work and we went our separate ways.

I stopped at a couple different stores on my way home and filled out applications. I went to the World Store place, like Wesley suggested, and looked around a bit. They sold furniture, home décor, food, spices, beer, wine—a little bit of everything. I filled out an application and turned it in to the manager. I went home with a little hope that maybe I could work there.

On Wednesday, the manager from World Store called and we scheduled an interview for Friday morning. Mom helped me prepare for the interview and we picked out an outfit to wear. I was glad that she didn't think I needed to wear a tie. I felt pretty confident and when Friday morning came, I went to the interview full of hope. After an hour, I came home with a job.

Mom and Alycia were excited, but mostly because I got a 20 percent discount that extended to family. I couldn't wait to call Wesley. I hadn't told him anything about the interview because I wanted to surprise him if I got the job.

I changed into a pair of shorts and a T-shirt and heard a knock at the door. By the time I came out of my room, Wesley was sitting on the sofa, chatting with Mom and Alycia. I was surprised to see him; on his days off, he usually slept 'til noon.

"Hey, Tor!" Wesley greeted enthusiastically.

I was a little put off; Mom and Alycia must have already told him about my job. "Hi. So, they already told you?"

"Told me what?" he asked.

Mom and Alycia shook their heads and a smile returned to my face. "Then, guess what? I got a job!"

"You did? That's great! Where at?"

"World Store, like you said."

"All right! Let's celebrate! Go pack your bags; we're going on a trip!"

I stared at Wesley blankly. Mom and Alycia were grinning from ear-to-ear and nodding their heads.

"What?" I asked, looking back at Wesley.

"Haven't you figured out why I've been nagging you about keeping these next three days free? Man, you are such an airhead sometimes. Don't you remember? You said you wanted to go to the beach, so we're going."

"R-really?" I asked. A smile dawned on my face and Wesley nodded his head. I looked at Mom, who was smiling impishly. "Is it all right? Can I go?"

"Yup. Wes gave me all the details," she said.

"C'mon, let's go pack," Wesley said, taking my hand and leading me back to my room.

I packed an overnight bag in a hurry, grabbing clothes randomly, getting my toothbrush, toothpaste, and hairbrush. I was ready in about fifteen minutes. Mom gave me some money to take and began to ask if I had everything, like she had a checklist in her head. When she was satisfied that I had everything I needed, she gave me a hug and kissed me goodbye.

"Okay, now, be safe and have fun. Give me a call when you get there, just so I know you guys are okay. Oh, but I'll be at work. Well, call anyway and leave a message if Alycia's not here, okay?" Mom rambled, kissing me again. "And drive safely!"

WE drove for about five hours before we got to a quaint, little town that had an old Main Street, huge oak trees, and bed-and-breakfasts all over the place. We arrived at our motel close to the water and I could smell the sea in the air. It was a beautiful day already and it just kept getting better.

"Hi. I have a reservation under Carroll," Wesley said to the desk clerk.

The young man typed at the computer and then smiled and nodded. "Yes, we have you right here. A single with a king and a smoking room," he announced, then glanced at me. He typed something more and then smiled again. "If you prefer, we have a room with two singles available," he offered, looking back at Wesley.

"No, that's all right," Wesley answered. He took one of the mints from a bowl on the counter, pushed it out of the wrapper, and popped it into his mouth.

"It's the same rate," the clerk added, glancing at the computer.

"Nah, one bed is fine." Wesley grinned and leaned against the counter.

"Wesley!" I said quietly, my cheeks flaring. I looked at the clerk and then back to Wesley.

"What? You don't wanna sleep with me?" Wesley asked calmly, still grinning. He looked at my bright red cheeks and laughed loudly. My body tensed and I stared at the floor.

"All right, you're all set. Here are your key cards. You're in room 216 at the back of the building. Thank you very much and enjoy your stay," the clerk said, pushing two cards across the counter. Wesley thanked him and we went back to the car.

"I can't believe you said that!" I shouted when we got in the car.

"Oh, c'mon! What's the big deal? We're gonna be here for three days. We don't know anyone and we'll never see them again. So, let them think what they wanna think," he said, driving around to the back of the building. We pulled into a parking spot and began to take our stuff from the trunk.

He was right. We didn't know anybody here and we'd never see them again. It would be nice to be able to act like lovers. I was on a trip with my boyfriend and I decided I wasn't going to worry about what other people thought.

"Is that everything?" I asked, setting my bag down on the large bed. I looked around the room; it was decorated in an ugly teal and pink paisley and I chuckled at the horrible décor. "I can't believe we're really here," I said, turning to Wesley who locked the door.

"I know. It's amazing, isn't it? Gimme sex."

"Huh? C'mon, Wesley," I said, but he hooked his hand in the top of my shorts and pulled me toward him. He unbuttoned my pants and I stopped his hands.

"Uh-uh. Take your pants off," he said, shaking his head. He buried his face in the crook of my neck and pulled at my zipper.

"Wesley, we just got here," I said, though I wasn't resisting anymore. He took his lips from my neck and pouted at me.

"C'mon. I've been so good this whole week," he pleaded, touching my cheek with his fingertips. He smiled boyishly and I stepped into him, clutching the back of his shirt in my hands.

"I know, you have been," I said quietly and kissed him.

Wesley wrapped his arms around me and his hands roamed down to my backside. He kissed me deeply and my knees felt weak. He slid his hands under my shirt and pulled it up, kissing me until the cloth forced our lips apart. He dropped the T-shirt on the floor and started walking me backward to the bed. I sat down on the edge and Wesley pulled his shirt over his head. I took a deep breath as I looked at him. There was something about the way he took his shirt off that I always found unbelievably sexy.

Wesley dropped to his knees in front of me and yanked my shorts and boxers off. He slowly slid his hands up my thighs and my body tingled from his touch. When his fingers reached me, I was already responding to him, and he gently stroked back and forth. My legs began to shake and he bent his head down, leading his tongue from tip to base. I squeezed my eyes shut and spread my legs further apart when Wesley took me in his mouth. My sensitivity heightened and I moaned his name quietly, bringing my hand to my mouth to keep quiet. Wesley sucked harder and I lost time and space in the experience.

Wesley straightened up on his knees and kissed me, rejuvenating the passion and bringing me back to reality. I reached down, unbuttoned his shorts, and slid my hand inside his boxers, frigging him gently. He stepped out of his pants and I scooted back on the bed, pulling him down on top of me. He rested on my stomach, between my legs, and kissed me. I wrapped my arms around his neck and nibbled on his ear.

"Fuck me, Wesley."

Wesley pulled back and looked into my eyes with a grin at the corner of his mouth. "I love it when you talk dirty with that cute, innocent face."

He leaned back and pulled my backside up, my thighs resting on his. He leaned over and took a tube of lotion from the side pocket of my bag. He dribbled some on his hands and some directly on me. He positioned himself and pressed into me, gently yet persistently. My body reacted, accepting him, and soon he was deep inside and I felt every molecule respond to his presence. He moved slowly and grasped onto me, staring into my eyes as he made love to me. His movements became deeper and I bit my finger to keep from screaming.

"Go ahead. Be as loud as you want," Wesley urged, taking my hand from my mouth. He smiled then gritted his teeth as his thrusts became stronger.

"Ahh! Oh, God!" I cried, finally letting my voice free. "Please…Wesley!"

Wesley leaned down and kissed me, then with a final thrust, came inside me until I was overflowing. My life was drained from my body but I wrapped my arms around him and held him as close as I could. I stared at the ceiling and a smile came across my lips. I was on a romantic getaway with my boyfriend and I couldn't be happier.

WESLEY had thought of everything. He brought a blanket, beach towels, a radio that used batteries, and a cooler that we filled with ice from the motel. We stopped at a deli and bought sandwiches and cans of soda for later. The sun was out and the sky was cloudless. It was a perfect day.

The beach was really crowded when we got there. It was a little disappointing that there were so many people, but it was the Fourth of July weekend after all. We found a little spot between two groups of girls around our age. Wesley laid out the blanket and then took his shirt off while the girls ogled him obscenely. It made me proud that they thought he was cute, but it made me a little uneasy too.

I sat down on the blanket and took off my sandals. Wesley stretched his arms over his head and I looked up at him. There was a small, red mark on his stomach, above and to the left of his belly button. I felt the blood rush to my cheeks as I realized exactly what it was. I told Wesley to sit down and I whispered to him about the mark. He looked down and laughed, but it was a little too high up for his swim trunks to cover it.

"You were just marking your territory," he said and laughed. He pulled at my T-shirt and I stopped his hands quickly. "C'mon, I'll put some suntan lotion on you."

"That's okay, I can do it myself," I said, shyly pulling my shirt over my head. I noticed that the girls didn't look at me like they looked at Wesley.

"C'mon, I'll just do your back. And your inner thighs," he whispered, squeezing some lotion into his hand.

I shot him a look, but turned my back to him. He gently rubbed the sunscreen on my back and I had to concentrate to keep my body calm. Wesley then handed me the lotion and turned around.

The water was cold even though it was such a hot day and it felt really good. Wesley and I swam far from shore until our feet didn't touch the sand anymore. We floated on our backs and splashed each other and then back on the shore we jumped over incoming waves like little kids. We had so much fun: running into the water to cool off, looking for seashells. We even built a sandcastle. We ate our lunch and then I went and got us some ice cream as a treat.

"Hey, if you wanted ice cream, you should've told me. I would've went and got us some," he said, licking at the soft serve that was quickly melting.

"I wanted to do it," I said, leaning back on one hand. I knew Wesley meant well, but at times, I felt like he forgot that I was a boy too. I didn't want to be taken care of all the time; I wanted to take care of him too. I had already decided that I was buying dinner tonight, even though Wesley would argue with me about it. But that didn't feel quite right either. It was money that Mom gave me. I wanted to take him out for a night with money that I earned. Then, I felt, we might be equals.

"What's the matter?" he asked, brushing my chin then licking the ice cream off his finger.

"Wesley! Don't do that here!" I said, looking around. Some of the girls on the blanket next to us saw the whole thing. I blushed down to my toes.

"Then don't stare off into space like that," he teased.

It was getting late and a lot of people had packed up their things and gone home. The sun was still above the horizon and I wanted to watch it set over the water, but I was getting really hungry. At last, we decided there would be plenty of other chances for us to see the sunset over the water. We went back to our room to change, then went to a little Chinese restaurant for a late dinner.

We stayed up late into the night even though we were both exhausted from such a full day at the beach. It was the last night of our trip and Wesley was suddenly very ambitious. He didn't feel like just staying in bed. I couldn't keep up with his unending supply of energy until I got a second wind around midnight. I thought my legs were going to give out while we were in the shower, but Wesley supported me until we both came. After that, we decided it was definitely time to sleep.

We woke about ten minutes before checkout time. We gathered our things together and hurried to the front desk. We left so fast that I didn't even have time to be embarrassed about the evidence of our weekend together that we left behind.

Chapter 18

I DECIDED to surprise Wesley by coming over instead of just calling and I walked over to his house around three o'clock. It was a hot day but the sun was shining and there was a nice breeze from the north. When I turned down his street, I saw him out front starting the lawn mower. He smiled and waved when he saw me and cut the engine.

"Hey! What are you doing here?" he asked, meeting me halfway.

"I just thought I'd stop by," I told him, smiling timidly. It had been a couple of weeks since our trip to the beach and the time we spent together was limited now. I was working four days a week at World Store and our days off were usually spent doing chores. Not to mention, the time we had alone was virtually nonexistent and my body ached for the freedom we enjoyed while on our trip.

"I was gonna call you after I finished cutting the grass. I gotta do it today or my mom'll kill me," he complained.

"That's one of the nice things about living in an apartment," I teased.

"Yeah, yeah. Hey, if you don't wanna wait around for me to finish the lawn, I can come by after," he offered, wiping sweat from his brow.

"That's okay. I'll keep you company." I didn't mind waiting for Wesley. I didn't mind watching him mow the lawn either.

Wesley looked at me and took hold of my wrist. Even though there was no one on the street, I shook my head. Wesley led me back to the detached garage and kissed me. I closed my eyes and accepted him; this was what my body was yearning for.

A car pulled into the driveway and underneath the shine of the windshield, I could see Mrs. Carroll. I stepped back from Wesley as he turned and faced the car. Mrs. Carroll got out and stared at us with wide eyes that soon narrowed in anger.

"What the hell are you doing?" she shouted, slamming the car door.

Wesley looked at her with surprise and I turned my eyes to the ground. My stomach tightened and I had a hard time catching my breath.

"I said, what the hell do you think you're doing?" she demanded, stopping in front of Wesley and glancing at me.

"Mom, calm down," Wesley said. His voice was surprisingly steady.

"I will not calm down! I didn't raise you to be like this!" Her face was hard and she gritted her teeth. She took a step forward and glared at me. "You. Get out of here! Don't you ever come near my son again!"

Wesley stepped in front of me. "Don't talk to him like that," he said firmly. He looked down and took a deep breath. His voice wavered for a moment as he looked back up to his mother's angry face. "Mom, I'm gay."

"Don't say that! Don't you ever say that!" she shouted. Then she looked at me. "This is all your fault! If it weren't for you…."

"I told you, don't talk to him like that," Wesley warned. He lifted his hands, palms up, trying to explain. "Mom, I'm gay. It has nothing to do with you."

"Get out! You leave my son alone!" she yelled.

"Mom. I'm in love with him. Why can't you just be happy for me?"

Mrs. Carroll's eyes widened and she slapped Wesley across the face in one fluid motion. She was breathing heavily and her nostrils flared. She stared at the ground, her eyes darting back and forth, as she shook her hand limply. Wesley touched his cheek tenderly and stared at his mother, and then he took my hand and pulled me past her without a glance in her direction. He walked fast and pulled me along with him. My arm hurt at my shoulder but I tried to keep up. "Fucking…goddamn it," he seethed under his breath.

We turned the corner onto the main street and Wesley still kept his pace. We passed several storefronts before he slowed down to a normal walk. He was still holding my hand.

"Fuck! I'm sorry," he said. "I knew my dad would flip, but I thought my mom would be different. I'm so sorry." I squeezed his hand and Wesley glanced at me. He had tears in his eyes and then he laughed pathetically. "Heh, you can't choose your family, can you? But, just so you know, I choose you," he said, looking forward again. "No matter what, I choose you."

I stopped, letting his hand slip from mine. I looked at the ground and took a deep breath.

"What? What's wrong?" Wesley asked, stopping and turning to face me.

"You…you said…that you were in love with me."

Wesley's eyes widened and he looked to the side. He blushed and scratched the back of his head. "Yeah, I guess I did."

I walked up to him, looking into his eyes, and kissed him, in front of everyone on the street. It didn't matter. He was in love with me.

"What…what are you doing? People can see us."

"I don't care. I'm in love with you too."

Wesley stared into my eyes and then laughed with a sense of relief. I was glad to see his smile. "You just turned the worst day of my life into the best day ever."

I looked around and noticed people staring at us. My face turned red and I looked at the ground. Of course they were staring; two boys were kissing in the middle of the street at three o'clock in the afternoon. My posture shrank with embarrassment and I couldn't bear to look at

Wesley. I felt his fingers lace with mine and I knew he had a defiant smile on his face.

"Mommy? Those two men were kissing," a little girl said. She was staring at us and I felt my heart sink. I tried to pull my hand from Wesley's, but he held tight.

The mother looked down at her daughter and smiled. "That's what two people do when they love each other," she explained. She smiled warmly at us as they passed us on the sidewalk.

My heart instantly felt lighter and I gripped Wesley's hand tighter. It was exactly what I needed to hear at that time. This insurmountable barrier I erected between me and "normalness" didn't seem as large or as forbidding anymore.

We hurried to my apartment and Wesley grabbed my rear end with both hands while I was trying to get the key in the lock. I jumped a little and Wesley licked my ear.

"You better hurry up. My zipper's about to break," he whispered, lowering his lips to the cradle of my neck and shoulder. He leaned into me and I could feel him against my backside. I swallowed hard and told him to stop, but he pushed his hand down the front of my pants and began to grope. "I told you to hurry up. See? You're almost as hard as I am."

I moaned and finally the door opened. We stepped over the threshold, slammed the door shut, and kissed inside for a couple minutes. He pulled my shirt up, but I stopped him.

"Wait. Let's go to my room," I said, out of breath. Wesley smiled and led the way back, holding my hand. He unbuttoned and unzipped my shorts and sat me down on the edge of the bed. He dropped to his knees and rubbed my thighs before taking me in his mouth. He bobbed his head slowly and let his fingers roam all over. My head was spinning and I was panting when Wesley moved his mouth to my balls and frigged me with his hand. My legs trembled and I was on the verge of climax, calling his name as I came in three short torrents onto his face and neck. Wesley slowly let me go and leaned back, wiping his hand across his cheek.

Despite gasping for air, I quickly grabbed some tissues and wiped his face and neck.

"I'm sorry," I whispered shyly, feeling embarrassed.

Wesley smiled at me and licked the cum off his fingers. I took a deep breath. He never looked so unbelievably sexy before. I stepped out of my shorts and boxers and pulled my shirt off. I crawled onto the bed and rested the side of my face and shoulders on the mattress with my ass high in the air. Wesley's eyes seemed to glaze over and it actually looked like there was a little drool at the corner of his mouth. I giggled, blushed, and asked what he was waiting for.

Wesley shed his clothes and grabbed the tube of lotion from the drawer in my nightstand. He drizzled some on my backside and rubbed some on himself. I looked back at him as I felt the first of him.

"God, you're so fucking hot," he said, pushing his way inside with slow, short thrusts. He grasped my hips as he plunged in deeper and I rocked against him. When he was fully within me, he stopped. "I love you," he whispered and began to pump again. "I love you," he repeated, grunting each time he said it.

"I…love you. God! I love you," I whimpered, gripping the sheet with balled fists. Of all the times we had sex, this was the best. It never felt so good. We were really making love.

Wesley came first, which triggered my intense orgasm. I exhaled completely and Wesley collapsed, pushing me down into the mattress. He was breathing heavily in my ear and I bit my lip; even that was sexy. He rolled to his back and slid his hands under his head. I remained on my stomach and propped myself up on my elbows.

"Wow," I sighed quietly, happily.

Wesley looked at me with a grin. "I take it you're satisfied?"

"Of course, but it's just so amazing to be able to say I love you," I explained, staring at the sheet with a shy smile. Wesley brushed the hair from my eyes, then touched my lips with his finger and nodded. "You know, I've wanted to say it for a while now," I confided, casting my eyes downward.

Wesley slid his hand behind his head again. “Why didn’t you?”

I looked at Wesley and blushed. He was incredibly handsome. He made my heart beat faster just by looking at him. I rested my head on his chest and breathed in deeply. It was the smell of Wesley, not the smell of soap or shampoo, but the smell of Wesley himself.

“I was afraid to,” I said at last, taking another deep breath. “I thought maybe it was too soon. And because I was scared you might not say it back.”

Wesley’s chest muscles tightened and I could hear his heartbeat speed up. “Why would you think that? I fell in love with you the moment I saw you.”

I lifted myself up on my elbows again and looked at Wesley with a whisper of a smile. “I don’t believe in love at first sight,” I said flatly.

“Okay. Well, then, I *lusted* after you the moment I saw you. Then, I watched you closely. You were so cute and shy and…I fell in love. But, Tor, you really should have more confidence. You’ve got a ton to offer. And I don’t just mean your cute ass,” he said, trying to lighten the weight of his words.

I laughed and smiled, closing my eyes. I felt so lucky to be with him, that he would choose to be with me. It never escaped my thoughts that Wesley could have anyone he wanted. He said he loved me, but I was still insecure that one day he might change his mind.

“I love you,” I whispered.

“What? I didn’t hear you,” he answered.

“I love you,” I said again, a little louder.

“One more time?” he said, furrowing his brows and pointing to his ear.

I crawled on top of him, straddling his thighs, and leaned down close to his face. “I said, I love you. I love you I love you I love you.”

He ran his hands up and down my arms. “Just hearing you say that, with that face, we’re gonna have to do it again,” he said, turning his smile into a grin.

I looked down and felt Wesley against my thigh. I pushed into him, rubbing against his groin, and smiled. "Tell me about it."

Wesley looked down and then grasped my hips. "Well, hop on. I'll give you the ride of your life."

I raised my hips and scooted up. I sat back on his thighs and brought my knees up. I tried to position myself as Wesley watched me with a sweet look. My face flushed and I looked to the side. "Help…me," I whispered shyly.

Wesley slid his fingers from my backside, over my thighs, and between my legs. He held himself steady with one hand and felt for the entrance with his other hand. He told me to push down and I did, taking him in millimeters at a time.

My face and ears were hot and I felt embarrassed. I was on top before, but not like this. Wesley always did the moving and now he was waiting for me. It felt incredible as I slowly began to move up and down. Wesley watched me closely, his face intense and unbelievably sexy. My embarrassment ebbed as I moved with more confidence. Wesley brought his hand up and pulled on me gently. I squeezed my eyes shut as I was coming to climax and Wesley rubbed the tip with the palm of his hand, smearing pre-cum all over me and his hand.

"Oh God, Wesley!" I came hard into his hand and soon after, he erupted within me. I slumped down, depending on Wesley to keep me from falling over. He was still inside me and I heaved in breath as he held my head to his chest.

"You had one hell of an orgasm," he said happily. I couldn't even respond. Wesley lay back on the pillow and smiled. "Let's stay like this forever."

WE lay in bed for hours, Wesley resting his head on my chest. He picked up my hand and held it to his. His fingers were a little longer than mine were and thicker with large knuckles. He examined my fingers and wrist, my arm to my elbow, then looked at my chin, lips, nose, and eyes. "You're incredibly beautiful. Did you know that?" he asked. He kissed me and then sat up. "I should probably get home."

I sat up quickly and looked at his calm, handsome face. I told him that he didn't have to go, that my mom would let him stay over.

"I'm gonna have to go home sooner or later," he said. "I might as well get it over with."

I watched him closely as he got out of bed and got dressed. He always found new ways to amaze me. If I was in his shoes, I would never be brave enough to go home. Wesley leaned down and kissed the top of my head.

"Don't worry. It's gonna be okay. I'll make my parents understand, and if they don't, well, *you* don't have anything to worry about. I already told you; I'll choose you no matter what," Wesley said, patting my head as if I was a child. I didn't mind though. I needed to hear his reassurance and to feel his large hands protecting me.

Wesley left me at the door with a long kiss good night. I watched him walk down the stairs and out to the sidewalk. I noticed that his shoulders slumped under the yellow streetlight as he started walking home. My shoulders slumped too. I couldn't imagine what Wesley was feeling. He was facing all the fears I had in my heart and he did so with courage and pride. I thought about Mrs. Carroll and my stomach dropped when I thought of Mr. Carroll. How could I ever face them again? What face did I have to show?

I cleaned up in the bathroom and then stripped the sheets from my bed. I put on a fresh set and balled up the dirty ones. I hesitated, and then held the rumpled ball to my nose. It smelled like Wesley. It smelled like sex. It smelled like love. I grimaced. Would Wesley's parents ever understand? Would they force him to break up with me? I fell on my bed and sobbed, hugging the lump of sheets like a teddy bear.

Alycia was spending the night at a friend's house and Mom had to work until at least two. I felt alone, utterly alone with my fears, the way I felt every day before I met Wesley. His parents hated me now. Wesley was gonna dump me now. He said he loved me, but how could he choose me over his family? What choice was there?

My eyes were tender from crying and I just wanted to sleep. I tossed and turned in bed, but my mind wouldn't rest. Eventually, I got up and watched TV, hoping anything would occupy my mind.

"Tor? What are you doing up?" Mom asked, walking in the front door. Her scrubs were dirty and she dropped her purse on the kitchen table. "Don't you have work tomorrow?" She came around the sofa and sat down when she saw my red, puffy eyes. "Sweetheart, what's wrong? Are you okay?" She pulled me close and hugged me tightly, holding my head to her shoulder.

I couldn't say anything and tears began to fall again. I slid my arms around her thin shoulders and clung to her like a child with a skinned knee. As I gasped for air and choked on my sobs, I began to hiccup and she held me tighter. I told her what happened while she rubbed my back.

"Oh, baby, I'm sorry. I'm so sorry," she whispered.

"They hate me now. Wesley's parents think I'm disgusting, and I know they'll make Wesley break up with me."

"Sweetheart, listen, as much as I want to punch Wesley's mom in the face, you have to understand that his mom was probably surprised and didn't know how to react. Once she calms down, maybe she'll understand. But, the world is full of different ideas and, I guess, this is just another lesson. But right now, Wesley needs *you*; not his parents, but the boy that he loves. Talk to him tomorrow and I'm sure he'll put all your fears to rest. And, I don't know if Wesley's parents will ever understand, but it's not up to them; it's not their choice."

Wesley said he'd choose me. I was almost scared to allow this little glimmer of hope into my heart.

"You know, the person you should talk to is your father. I'm sure he knows exactly how you feel," Mom said, looking to the side with an indiscernible, yet pained expression. She kissed my forehead and smiled weakly. "You should get some sleep. Go to bed, sweetheart, and if you need me, come get me. Okay?"

I nodded, wiping at my tears. She hugged me tightly, hesitant to let go, and kissed my cheek again. I smiled and felt like I was telling her that it would be okay.

I crawled into bed and hugged the bundle of sheets in my arms. I breathed in deeply and remembered Wesley's face as he told me he loved me.

Chapter 19

I WENT to work with a strange feeling in the pit of my stomach. My senses seemed fuzzy, like I wasn't totally awake. I worked at the register, but I didn't find extra things to do to fill in slow times like I usually did. I wondered what Wesley was doing. As time passed, I called his cell phone, but it went directly to voice mail each time. I wanted to talk to him, but I didn't want to call his house in case one of his parents answered the phone. I took a lunch break around noon and Wesley still hadn't called.

"Hey, are you all right, Toren? You seem a little off today," my co-worker Jeanine asked, fixing me with her sharp eyes from the floor where she was pricing imported chocolate bars. Over her khaki pants and white collared shirt, she wore a navy smock with the World Store logo in white just like mine. She was really nice and funny and cute, with her long blonde hair and petite figure; I liked working with her.

"Yeah, I'm okay, thanks," I answered, sighing and letting my shoulders sag.

"Are you sure? It's just that, you're usually so…chipper. You're on your own plane of niceness—it's like there's normal-nice and then there's Toren-nice," she said, leaning back on her heels and resting the price gun on the floor.

I laughed quietly, embarrassed. She placed the chocolate bars on a sloped rack in front of the checkout and came around the register. Leaning against the counter, she folded her arms. I stared at the ground for a long moment and fidgeted with my hands.

"Well, it's the person I'm seeing. The parents don't like me very much," I confided nervously, carefully avoiding pronouns.

"What? Are they crazy? You're like every parent's wet dream! You're smart, cute, funny, nice, polite. Should I keep going?"

I laughed self-consciously and glanced at the floor again. "It's, well, sorta complicated."

"Well, she likes you, right? That's all that matters. Besides, if you just be yourself, her parents'll warm up to you in no time," she advised, bumping into me with her hip. She smiled warmly, and then furrowed her brows. "Do you know why they don't like you, or at least, why you *think* they don't like you?"

I took a deep breath. Just yesterday, I kissed Wesley on the street in the middle of the day. People were gonna find out about us now, one way or another. Maybe it was better if I told people at work, rather than having them hear it secondhand. Besides, I liked Jeanine; I trusted her.

"They, um, they don't like me 'cause I'm a boy," I said, squeezing my hands together. "I mean, his parents don't like me 'cause I'm a boy."

"Oh," she said, nodding her head. She unfolded her arms and placed her hands on her hips. She knitted her brows and shook her head side-to-side. "Do people actually still think shit like that? You've gotta be kidding! But seriously, Toren," she said, touching my arm, "if he likes you, who the hell cares what his parents think?"

I chuckled lightly at her immediate conclusion. But, maybe she was right. Wesley, my mom, Alycia, they'd all told me that other people's opinions didn't matter. It was true; I should only care about what people close to me thought. Wesley loved me; he said so. I sighed heavily though, because I cared about what people close to Wesley thought too. I didn't want to cause trouble between him and his family.

Jeanine seemed to sense my inner thoughts and smiled impishly. "So, who's your boyfriend? Anyone I know?"

"Umm," I hesitated; Jeanine was a junior, so she might not even know Wesley. "His name's Wesley," I said. I felt my cheeks burn at the mere mention of his name.

"Hmm. Wesley? Oh! Wesley Carroll?" she said loudly, and strangely, proudly. My eyes widened and I looked around the store, and then nodded. "Wow! You've got great taste! I'd been crushing on him for a while. How about that? Wes and Toren.... I bet you guys make a cute couple!"

I TRIED calling Wesley's cell after I got off work, but it still went to voice mail and I began to worry. He usually called by now. What if something happened after he left last night? My chest felt tight and I was hot, like I had a fever. I called his cell again, but he still didn't answer. Tears began to fill my eyes and I fell back on the sofa. I sucked in breath, but I was still gasping for air.

I looked at the clock on the cable box and rubbed the tears from my eyes. It was a little past six and Mom and Alycia were still at work. Where was Wesley?

There was a knock at the door and I almost tripped running to answer it. Wesley stood on the other side with a smile on his face and I wanted to hit him, kiss him, and yell at him.

"Hey, what's goin' on?" he asked, walking in and brushing my shoulder with his hand.

"What? Where have you been? What's going on? Why didn't you call me? Why didn't you answer your phone?" I shouted, unable to keep the tears from rolling down my cheeks.

"Whoa. What? Are you okay?" I leaned into him and rubbed my face on his shoulder, wiping away my tears. "What's the matter?"

"I...you.... Where have you been? I tried calling you a million times but I only got voice mail and I didn't want to call your house because I was afraid your parents would answer and I've been worried sick. Why didn't you call me?" I rambled, hugging Wesley like he would disappear if I let go.

"I thought you had to work today. I didn't want to bother you there. Plus, I was running around this afternoon and well, I'm sorry. I should've called you."

“Damn right you should’ve!” I shouted, stepping back and looking up at Wesley. He smiled at my red eyes and flushed cheeks.

“I know, I know. I’m sorry. Forgive me?”

I looked down and grimaced. But he was right here, with me.

“All right. Give me a kiss and I’ll forgive you.”

“Just a kiss?” Wesley pouted, sticking out his bottom lip.

“We can negotiate after you tell me what happened last night.”

Wesley kissed me sweetly and I smiled before Wesley licked my lips and kissed me again. He walked to the sofa and then pulled me down on his lap. I stayed on his lap, and looked at him, waiting.

“Well, nothing happened last night. My folks were already in bed, so I went to bed too. But this morning, they woke me up at, like, seven and my mom just started in on me. Obviously, she told my dad. And she went on about how they didn’t raise me to be like this and how could I do this to them. Then she started on how this was just a phase and that I’d outgrow it. Can you believe that? I actually laughed at her. I didn’t mean to. I just…did. Then my dad yelled at me and told me to shut up. He said that I had to stop seeing you and I told him that wasn’t an option. I told them that I was in love with you and that they just needed to accept it and get over it. Then, Dad said that if I was living under his roof, blah, blah, blah, so I told him I wouldn’t live under his roof. Then, he punched me and called me a fucking faggot.”

“He punched you?” I asked. I turned his face to the side and saw the red mark left by his father’s fist. “Are you okay? How could he? I’m so sorry!”

“It’s okay. I’ll be all right,” he reassured me, brushing the hair from my eyes with a gentle smile on his face. “It was the first time my dad ever hit me,” he added, looking down, his smile gone. “So, I left right after that. I didn’t know what to do, so I went to get a bite to eat and then….”

“Why didn’t you call me or come over?”

"It was early and I didn't want to bother you. Plus I knew you had to work today."

"So? You still should've…."

"I know. I'm sorry. But after that, I started looking for an apartment. I went to a lot of places, but I found one I liked, and I actually signed a lease. I can move in this weekend."

I stared at Wesley with wide eyes. His own place? "But how can you afford it?"

"Well, I'm working full-time and I've actually been saving up for this for a while. I've got enough for the security deposit and a few months rent, but, Toren." He paused and looked at me for a long moment. "Toren, I want you to think about this carefully and I don't need an answer right now. I just want you to really think about it. I…I want us to live together. I want you to move in with me."

I didn't know what to say. What could I say? It wasn't that I didn't want to live with him; it just seemed like it was too soon. Everything was happening so fast. I loved him, I didn't have any doubt about that, but we'd only been going out for a few months. I didn't say anything.

Wesley watched my reaction and he seemed a little disappointed. "So, just think about it, okay?"

I nodded my head and Wesley touched my face with his fingertips. I took a deep breath and Wesley kissed me gently. He stared into my eyes and for some reason, my tears began to collect again. He wiped them away with his thumb and then tilted my chin up.

"Let's go to bed," he whispered.

I closed my eyes and blushed. "Wesley."

"We don't have to do it. I just wanna be close to you. I wanna hold you in my arms right now." He buried his face in my chest and he was breathing hard. He wasn't crying, but he felt the weight of the world on his shoulders. "I know that sounded lame, but that's all I want right now. I just want to be as close to you as I can."

I held his head to my chest. That was all I wanted too. I stood up and held my hand out to him. I led him to my room and we lay in my bed, pressed close, with all our clothes on. We didn't talk; we just felt each other's warmth and closeness. We stayed there until Alycia came home around nine-thirty. We told her what happened as I made a late dinner for the three of us.

"Do you have a place to stay 'til you can move in?" Alycia asked. Wesley shook his head as he slurped up a strand of spaghetti. "Oh, why don't you stay here 'til then? I'm sure Mom won't mind."

I called Mom at work and asked if Wesley could sleep over. She said it was okay and I laid out a comforter and pillows on the floor. My bed was too small, but we could sleep next to each other on the floor. I told him that my mom checked in on me each night when she got home and I made him promise that we would innocently sleep side-by-side. Wesley grudgingly agreed and after Mom checked in on us, he pulled me into his arms, our bodies tangled, and we fell asleep again.

Chapter 20

I WOKE with Wesley's lips pressed against mine. I blinked groggily and smiled. I really liked waking up to Wesley. He was leaning down over me, wearing the T-shirt and shorts he wore yesterday. He had some coarse whiskers on his chin and he kissed me again, tickling my cheek.

"I gotta go to work, but I'll be back around six tonight," he whispered.

"You're leaving already? Did you eat breakfast?" I asked, rubbing my eyes. Wesley shook his head. "I'll make you something," I said, sitting up.

Wesley pushed me back down with his lips. "Nah, I gotta get going. Besides, it's your day off, so sleep in," he said, sitting back on his heels.

"Okay," I agreed easily. "Have a good day."

"I will. I love you," he said, standing up.

"I love you too," I answered, turning to my side and falling asleep.

When I woke up again, it was after eleven. I yawned loudly and looked around my room, up at my bed, then at the T-shirt Wesley borrowed. I remembered waking up when he left, but my mind was fuzzy.

Mom was making breakfast in her pajamas. I poured her a cup of coffee and told her to sit down while I put on the apron that was still hanging in the pantry. Mom kissed my forehead and sat down at the kitchen table, resting her head in her hands. She had bags under her eyes and her skin was pale. She looked as exhausted as I felt. I set down a plate of pancakes and scrambled eggs in front of her and returned to the kitchen to fix my own.

"How's Wes doing?" she asked, after a long, loud yawn. "Did he have work today?"

"Yeah. He's doing okay, I think. Actually, I'm not sure. His dad kicked him out of the house yesterday."

"What? That's ridiculous!" Mom said, furrowing her eyebrows in disbelief.

"Well, he found an apartment. He signed the lease yesterday. So, I guess he's kinda okay with it. He said he'd been saving up money to move out for a long time," I explained, sitting down next to Mom at the kitchen table. It was kinda funny; we never ate at the table except at holidays. "I'm not sure if everything has really sunk in yet, though. He's really angry with his parents, but he didn't really get along with them anyway."

Mom studied my face quietly for a moment. "He's probably putting on the tough act for you," she said.

She was right. He kept telling me that it would be okay. He was comforting me. But his parents threw him out; they abandoned him. He needed someone to tell him that it would be okay. I felt terribly guilty. He needed me to be strong for him and I was selfishly concerned with my own fears.

"When's he moving in?"

"This weekend. But, he doesn't have a place to stay 'til then, so…is it okay if he stays here?"

"Of course. He's welcome here." Mom said. Her motherly instinct asserted itself, taking Wesley in as one of her own. "Still, I can't believe his parents threw him out. That's just…. It doesn't make any sense!"

I smiled. Mom was defensive for Wesley. It made me feel good that he was so easily accepted into our family. Even if his parents did turn their backs on him, he had somewhere he could come home to.

Alycia woke up just as Mom left for work. Alycia kissed Mom goodbye, then sat down on the sofa and turned the TV on.

"Tor, make me some breakfast," she ordered with a raspy voice.

"Sorry, too late," I said. The dishes were done and the pans were clean. "Besides, it's after lunch. Have a bowl of cereal or wait for dinner."

Alycia grunted in response and switched channels. She always had trouble waking up and wasn't the most pleasant person in the morning. She was bossy and loud, but kind and caring. It was easy to forget that she was my little sister. She seemed so mature and knowledgeable about some things that I just didn't have a clue about. I was lucky to have her, even if she was a slave driver.

"Hey, Alycia? Can I talk to you?"

"Oh my God, you're pregnant," she mocked, feigning astonishment and glancing at me over her shoulder.

I rolled my eyes and sat down on the couch. "C'mon, I'm being serious."

"All right, all right," she conceded, turning toward me and resting her arm on the top of the sofa. I swallowed hard and she looked at me with upturned brows. "Is something wrong? Are you all right?"

"Oh, yeah. Everything's okay," I reassured her. "It's just that Wesley asked me to move in with him."

Alycia stared at me, as if waiting for something more. She held her hands up, palms open. "And? What, you need help moving in?"

"No. I…. Well, don't you think it's kinda soon? I mean, we've only been going out about four months and the apartment is only one bedroom, so don't you think people'll think it's strange? For two guys to be living in a one-bedroom apartment? It's not that…."

"So that's what this is all about," Alycia said, shaking her head. "I thought you came out already. It's not living with Wes; it's what people think about it. Didn't we go over this before? Tor, who gives a damn what other people think? The question is: do you want to live with him?"

I looked at the floor and squeezed my hands together. Was she right? Is that why I felt so nervous?

"Okay, let's figure this out," Alycia continued, placing her hands on her knees and looking at me with a serious expression. "You like being with Wes, don't you?" I nodded. "And you like having dinner with him and watching TV and doing stuff together, right?" I nodded again. "You like waking up with him in the morning, don't you?" I blushed, but nodded. "And you love him, right?"

"With all my heart."

"Then, you've already got your answer," Alycia said conclusively with a smile on her face. "Besides, you have to think about Wes. This isn't a choice for him. He has to do this because of his stupid parents. And even though he acts tough, he's probably scared. He needs you, by his side, reminding him why he's doing this and why everything'll be okay."

She was right. Of course, she was right. I'd been worried about what other people would think and if we were moving too fast, when Wesley's whole world was just turned upside-down. I was embarrassed by how selfish I was being.

"So, you need help packing?" she asked, grinning.

"Yeah, I guess I do," I said, leaning forward and hugging her. She was my little sister and she knew more about life than I did.

"But, you still have one more obstacle," she said ominously. "Trying to convince Mom."

I DECIDED to make something special for dinner and I ran to the store to buy some salmon filets. I placed them in a two-hour marinade and went to my room. I looked around and decided that I needed to take everything with me. Except my bed. But Wesley only had a single bed too. Maybe I would have to take my bed. But would there be enough room? The apartment was just down the street, a block or two away, but I didn't know anyone who lived there, so I didn't have any idea how big the rooms were.

As I looked around my room, I realized how much stuff we would need to buy. There was an old sofa and two end tables in the storage unit in the basement that Mom saved for me, so that was a start. But, we would need a kitchen table, chairs, pots and pans, dishes…. There was so much. I had about seven hundred dollars in my bank account, but that wouldn't be enough for all the stuff we needed. I was working full-time now, but I would have to cut my hours when school started. How was this going to work out?

Wesley came back a little after six. He knocked before he let himself in and I ran out to greet him, drying my hands on a dishcloth. He was wearing his navy work shirt and pants, streaked with grease, and he had his book bag over his shoulder. He looked really cute in his work clothes. There was just something about a man in uniform that turned me on. But, it wasn't really a uniform. Maybe it was the grease-monkey look? Then again, it was probably just Wesley.

"Hi! Welcome back! You know, you didn't have to knock," I said, smiling shyly.

Wesley stood just inside the door, smiling and blushing lightly. "I kinda felt like I should."

"Don't be silly. Did you have a good day? Oh, dinner'll be ready in about half an hour," I said, walking toward him, but he still stood just inside the door with a silly grin on his face. I stopped and felt my cheeks redden under his gaze. "What? What's wrong?"

"No, nothing. This is just…really nice," he said, scratching the back of his head and looking down and to the side.

"Well, get used to it," Alycia said, walking out of her room carrying a full laundry basket.

"What?" Wesley asked with raised eyebrows, looking at Alycia, then at me. "Is she serious?"

"Yeah," I murmured, nodding my head timidly.

"That means…. Really?" A smile brightened his face and he exhaled like he had been holding his breath. "I can't believe it," he said, dropping his book bag and walking toward me. "I'm so happy."

"Hey, don't get all lovey-dovey yet, you two. You still have to convince Mom," Alycia warned, then looked Wesley up and down. "I'm gonna do some wash. Want me to throw those in?" she asked, looking at his grease-stained clothes.

"Yeah, if you don't mind," he agreed, picking up his book bag.

"Well? What are you waiting for?" Alycia asked playfully.

I knew the look on Wesley's face and my cheeks flared.

"Oh, sorry," he answered, accepting the challenge. He pulled his shirt forward over his head and dropped it in the laundry basket. He then took off his pants and dropped them on top. "Thanks," he said with a voice certain of victory.

Wesley stood at the door, wearing his boxers, white socks, and a grin. Alycia and I both blushed, Wesley chuckled, and then Alycia glanced at me, laughed, and went on her way to the laundry room. Wesley picked up his book bag again and started down the hall to my room.

"I can't believe you did that!" I shouted, chasing after him.

In my room, Wesley turned to me and drew the waistband of his boxers away from his stomach. "Don't worry, this is just for you." Then he stepped close and wrapped his arms around me. "Is it true? Are you really gonna move in with me?"

I brought my hands around his back and brushed my fingertips over his shoulder blades. "I love you. So I wanna live with you."

Wesley hugged me tight and kissed me deeply. My knees felt weak and my body responded to his closeness. I squeezed my eyes shut and tried to calm myself, but Wesley already had his hand down my pants. I bit my lip as I clung to him.

"No, Wesley. Don't. Alycia is…." Wesley leaned hard into me and I felt him against my lower belly. He moved his hand slowly and thumbed the tip expertly, quickly melting my resistance.

"You already got pre-cum. Wanna do it?" he asked, slowing his hand and nibbling my lower lip. The sensation rippled through my body and it was hard to say no.

"Wesley, we can't. Just this." I pulled his waistband away and took him in my hand. "Kiss me," I whispered, hoping his lips could stifle the moan in my throat.

Wesley came before me, just by a few seconds, and my confidence swelled. We had done stuff like this plenty of times, and even though I knew the sounds of Wesley's pleasure, I always felt a little nervous that I wasn't doing it right or good enough. But the proof was on my T-shirt and I smiled triumphantly at him.

"Oh man, now I gotta change my shirt," I said, holding the hem out. In the back of my mind, I was embarrassed because Alycia would know we did something because I had to change my clothes.

"Sorry," Wesley breathed heavily, satisfactorily. He put his book bag on the bed and pulled out a pair of shorts and a shirt. "I went home before work," he said, stepping into the shorts. "I just hoped that my parents both left for work before I got there, and fortunately, they did. Oh, and don't worry about helping me move my stuff. I know you probably don't wanna go to my house, and honestly, I don't know what my parents would do. I'll get a buddy of mine to help me out."

"Oh, okay," I answered. I hadn't actually thought about it, but I was glad that Wesley did. I didn't know what to do about his parents. Just thinking about it made me nervous. Wesley was watching me and I smiled shyly. "Thanks."

"Don't worry about it," he said, stepping close again. "But, just so you're warned…. You're gonna get fucked raw that first night."

I blushed, but Wesley had this uncanny ability to bring out the salacious devil in me. "Promise?"

Chapter 21

I WOKE up around eleven and I sat in bed, going over what I was going to say to Mom. Wesley left for work early and Alycia worked the morning shift. I got out of bed, poured a bowl of cereal, and waited for Mom to get up.

I put the TV on and I rehearsed the conversation with Mom again. She had been so understanding and supportive, but I was nervous about this. Moving in with Wesley was a huge step forward in our relationship.

Mom got up around noon, yawning as she poured a cup of coffee. I put my cereal bowl and spoon in the sink and leaned against the counter.

"Want some breakfast?" I asked.

"No, I'll just have some cereal or something," she said, sipping her coffee and looking in the pantry.

"It's no problem. I can make pancakes again, or maybe French toast?"

"It's okay, sweetheart, I'm fine," she answered, walking into the living room. She fell back on the sofa and closed her eyes for a moment.

I sat down beside her and handed her the remote. She put on one of the news stations and we sat silently for a couple minutes. My hands were clammy and my heart was beating furiously.

"Mom? I, um, I want to move in with Wesley."

Mom looked at me over the rim of her coffee cup. "Are you asking me or telling me?"

"I…don't know. Both, I guess." I couldn't look at her though I felt her staring at me.

"I knew this was coming," she said quietly, as if to herself. She set her mug down on the coffee table.

"We figured it all out. Even though I can only work part-time when I'm in school, we can still make it. I've got about seven hundred dollars saved up and Wesley is working full-time, so…."

"But, doesn't it seem…a little too soon?" she asked, folding her hands in her lap.

"I know, but it's okay," I countered unsuccessfully. She was right. It did seem too soon, but I knew I wanted to live with him.

"Do you want to, Toren?" she asked solemnly.

I furrowed my brows and looked down. I took a deep breath. "I love him, Mom. So, yeah, I want to."

Mom's eyes widened and she stared at me, and then her face softened into a smile. "I probably shouldn't tell you this. Wes asked me not to. But, he came to see me at work yesterday. It was so cute; he was so nervous. He wanted my permission to let you two live together," she said with a soft laugh.

"He did? He went to see you?" I was surprised, and wondered why he didn't want me to know.

Mom nodded, and then bowed her head. I could hear her soft laugh and quiet sigh. "It's funny. You two remind me so much of your father and me at your age," she said. I looked up at her and her eyes were glassy. She stared at her lap and squeezed her hands together. I wasn't exactly sure what to do or say; this wasn't in the dialogue I rehearsed.

"Mom, are you still in love with Dad?" She looked up at me startled, then knitted her brows and forced a smile.

"Of course I love him. He gave me you and Alycia. I'll always love him for that," she said, smiling, though her eyes were sad.

"That's not what I meant. I mean, are you still in love with him?"

Mom's eyes teared up and I wasn't sure what to do next. She closed her eyes and buried her face in her hands. My stomach tightened; I wasn't used to seeing Mom so vulnerable.

"Oh, Tor. I don't know," she said at last, dropping her hands into her lap like they were made of lead. "I guess I… I was just so angry. I tried to so hard to figure out what I did wrong. When we first met, in high school, I knew he was the one, the one I wanted to spend the rest of my life with. People thought we were moving too fast, but it didn't matter, because he was everything I wanted. But, when that day came, fourteen years later…. *Fourteen years!* I thought we were happy! We had two wonderful children. We had a nice house. I thought we had everything! I thought…we were happy."

Mom's whimpers became sobs and I scooted closer to her. She seemed so frail and I just wanted to protect her. This was why I hated Dad. "Mom, I'm sorry," I whispered pathetically. I didn't know what to say. I didn't know how to comfort her.

"No, that's not right," she said, wiping the tears from her eyes. "I did know something was wrong. I just convinced myself that there wasn't. I mean, we were more like roommates than a married couple. And when he finally told me, I was just so angry! It hurt so much that I couldn't make him happy and that there was someone else who could. And then I said all those horrible things to him. I didn't even mean them. I just wanted to hurt him," she said, bowing her head ashamedly. I bit my lip; I could understand why she said what she did. I hugged her tighter and she looked at me, squeezing my hand. "God, Tor, I'm so sorry. I must've made things so hard for you." She let go of my hand and brushed the hair from my eyes. "But that's why I'm so proud of you. Despite everything, you were honest with yourself. You were strong enough to know who you are. You were honest with yourself, and with me. And that's why I trust you. Only you know if you're ready to take the next step with Wesley and I trust your judgment. And when Wesley came to see me at work yesterday, I knew I could trust him too. With you. So, that's why I'm going to let you move in with him."

I stared at Mom with wide eyes. I hadn't realized it, but I was holding my breath. Mom smiled at me and I wrapped my arms around her. My eyes were already red with tears and I brushed them away, but I kept crying.

Mom took a deep breath and patted my head. "I'm sorry I made you listen to all that. I guess I'm not completely over him yet. I wonder if I ever will be," she said, drying her eyes again. "Just be honest with yourself and with each other and I know you two will live happily ever after," she said with a laugh. This time her voice was cheerful and back to normal.

I was glad she told me everything. I hoped that maybe it helped her too. I didn't think she would ever get over Dad. But I understood why she said the things she did and I think I understood how hard it was for Dad too.

"You want some French toast?"

Mom laughed and nodded her head. She followed me into the kitchen and poured another cup of coffee.

"Oh! I'll let you move in with Wes on one condition," she premised with a grin. "You have to come over and make dinner every once in a while."

"All right. I can do that," I said, breaking an egg in a pie tin.

"Seriously, I don't know how you became such a great cook. You certainly didn't get it from me," she wondered aloud, leaning against the counter.

I broke another egg in the tin and added some milk, vanilla, and cinnamon. Mom and I talked about what I would need to move out as I made breakfast. Then we sat down at the table and wrote up a list of what Wesley and I had and what we needed. As two o'clock neared, I was disappointed that she had to leave for work. I hugged her goodbye and then got ready for work myself.

Chapter 22

MY dresser, bookshelf, and nightstand were empty. Laundry baskets were filled with my clothes and cardboard boxes held books, CDs, and other stuff. I wrapped the cord around the clip lamp, put it in one of the boxes, and taped up the top. I only had the closet left to pack. I looked around my room; it seemed smaller now with all my things removed.

Mom and I went down to the storage unit and found two matching, fake gold table lamps and a coffeemaker along with the sofa and end tables. Mom forgot that she had the lamps and wondered at her past taste in décor. The lamps were kinda ugly, but in a cool, retro sort of way.

Alycia and I packed as much as we could fit into the Taurus and drove to my new apartment complex. As we were unloading the car, a red F-150 pulled up. The truck bed was low with boxes, a round table, four chairs, and a small chest of drawers. Wesley got out and Jeremy Read came around the side of the truck. Wesley greeted me without a kiss and I was grateful; I felt awkward around Jeremy. Alycia ran down the stairs from the second floor, ready to take up another load. I noticed Jeremy's eyes lingered on her a little too long.

"Hi! I'm Alycia, Toren's little sister," she said, extending her hand to Jeremy.

"It's nice to meet you," Jeremy said with a smile.

Wesley and I looked at each other. Alycia blushed and I wondered if she temporarily forgot about Mike. She wiped her brow with the hem of her shirt and smiled at Jeremy again. It took a moment for Jeremy to tear his eyes from her tanned stomach and sapphire belly ring. Wesley and I glanced at each other again.

Wesley and Jeremy carried the table, chest of drawers, and boxes to apartment 204. Alycia and I took the chairs and the rest of the stuff from the Taurus. We put the boxes in the appropriate rooms and then sat down at the table in the kitchen nook to rest for a moment. I glanced around at the white, empty apartment. It was amazing to think that this was my new home. My home with Wesley. I grinned stupidly until Alycia kicked me under the table.

After a short break, Alycia and I went home to load up the car again. Wesley and Jeremy followed us to get the sofa and end tables. Then we returned and sorted the boxes according to room. Alycia left again to get the last of my things, letting me stay behind to start unpacking. I sat in the bedroom and started to put away clothes in the dresser and closet.

The doorbell rang and Wesley was already at the door, talking to two men in light blue shirts and blue jeans. He looked over some papers on a clipboard then signed at the bottom. The two men walked away and Wesley looked at me and smiled.

"Who was that?" I asked, brushing my hand across my forehead.

"It's your present to me," Wesley answered, moving boxes and stuff away from the door.

"Wait. What?" I asked, following him into the bedroom where he pushed boxes and laundry baskets against the wall.

A moment later, the two men reappeared carrying a large bed frame. Wesley told them where to put it and I stood by with wide eyes while they assembled the metal frame. Then they left and returned with a queen-size mattress wrapped in plastic. They stripped the plastic, positioned the mattress on the frame, and then left.

I stared at the large bed that took up two-thirds of the wall it was placed against. Wesley slapped my behind and I jumped, looking up at him. Jeremy stood at the bedroom door and I blushed.

"What…what is this?" I asked.

"It's a bed, dummy," Wesley teased. Then he leaned closer. "I already told you, it's your present to me."

"But…what? My present to you?

"Yeah," Wesley said, "for all the stuff you're gonna let me do to you on it."

I felt hot and blushed head to toe, then glanced at Jeremy who still stood at the door. I stepped back from Wesley, my mouth flapping though no words came out.

"But…but…my mom's coming over in a little while!" I said, all flustered and unable to think of anything else to say.

"Don't worry. It's not like I'm gonna throw you down right now," Wesley answered with a laugh.

I glanced at Jeremy from the corner of my eyes. He was grinning and leaning against the doorframe with his arms folded. "But…there's only one bed and…what's she gonna think?"

"She knew you weren't taking your bed. She obviously knew this was part of the deal when she agreed to let you move in with me," he said calmly.

"You didn't say that to her when you asked her, did you?" I asked, still frazzled and embarrassed.

"What? She told you I…?" Wesley asked with wide eyes. "Oh man," he groaned and slapped his forehead.

"You guys are too funny," Jeremy commented, then straightened up and walked into the living room.

Wesley and I both looked at Jeremy and then at each other. He stepped close, wrapping his arms around me and pushing my head to his shoulder. I slid my hands up his back and hid my face.

"He knows?" I asked in a muffled voice.

"Yeah, I told him," Wesley said with a chuckle, ruffling my hair. "God, you're so cute."

Wesley and Jeremy continued unpacking boxes while I fitted the bed with sheets that Wesley had bought. Not long after, Mom and Alycia arrived with the rest of my stuff. Mom came up carrying a large box and put it down on the kitchen counter with a grunt.

"What's that?" I asked.

Mom turned to me with a large smile. "It's a housewarming gift."

I stepped closer and looked at the box. Inside was a set of stainless-steel cookware. I looked up at Mom with an open mouth.

"It's 'cause you're such a good cook. You deserve only the best," she said and patted my back. She walked toward the door and smiled again. "C'mon, this stuff's not gonna move itself."

The five of us emptied the car quickly and we spent the rest of the afternoon and evening unpacking. Alycia and Jeremy worked side-by-side, flirting blatantly, while Mom and I worked in the bedroom. When she saw the bed, my face flared, but she didn't say a word about it.

Around eight, we ordered a pizza and sat in the living room watching the 25-inch TV Wesley brought. We talked and laughed while Wesley and Jeremy yawned. They had moved all of Wesley's stuff out by noon, to be certain it was done before his parents came home from work. After half an hour, Alycia announced that she was tired and she and Mom got ready to leave. Jeremy seemed disappointed and then decided that he should head home too. We thanked everyone for their help and I gave Mom a hug, a kiss, and a giant, grateful "thank you." Alycia gave me a hug and a wink, and they left. Jeremy said goodbye after commenting on how cute Alycia was. I smiled proudly, but I didn't tell him that she had a boyfriend.

Wesley and I turned back to our apartment and looked around with smiles. It was an amazing feeling. The furniture didn't exactly match, we didn't have cable yet, we ate off paper plates, and the walls were still blindingly white and plain, but it was our place.

At long last, Wesley pulled me close with a hand around my waist and kissed me for a long time. He looked into my eyes with a smile on his lips and whispered "Welcome home." He was unbelievably sexy when he said that.

"Ready for bed?" he asked and yawned.

I smiled devilishly. "You didn't forget your promise, did you?"

"Why do you think I wanna go to bed at nine-thirty?" he answered, taking me by the hand and leading me to the bedroom.

We stood at the door, staring at the enormous bed, and I took a deep breath. I felt really nervous all of a sudden. Wesley felt it in my hand and pulled me into the room. He stood next to the bed and faced me. He looked really handsome and I swallowed away a lump in my throat. It was our first night in our bed, in our bedroom, in our apartment. My heart thumped when Wesley began to pull off his shirt.

"Wait. Stop," I said, stepping toward him.

Wesley stopped in mid-motion with his shirt up to his neck. "Huh? Why?"

"'Cause…I wanna undress you," I said timidly, walking up to him and pulling his shirt back down.

Wesley smiled and stood still. I kissed him and slid my hands under his shirt. I bent down and kissed his exposed flesh inch-by-inch until I held the shirt under his chin. I licked at his nipple and suckled it for a moment before lifting his shirt over his head. He raised his arms as I tugged at his shirt and I had to stand on my tiptoes to pull it over his hands. I ran my fingers down his muscled arms and kissed him again. I sucked his bottom lip as my hands traveled down to the top of his shorts. He was already hard as I drew down the zipper. I took the top of his shorts in both hands, yanked them down, and pushed him back on the bed. His eyes widened and he grinned as I dropped to my knees in front of him.

"Heh, I kinda like it when you're aggressive," he said, lifting himself up on his elbows.

I glanced up at him, rubbing his thighs, and lapped at the tip hungrily. I massaged his balls and my fingers found their way further back as I dropped my mouth around him. I licked and sucked feverishly, grasping his balls with one hand and rimming the hole behind with my finger. Wesley's legs trembled and if my mouth weren't full, I would've grinned proudly. I took him as deep as my throat would allow and he came violently, his body shaking. I licked my lips and lay down atop him, giving him a long, salty kiss.

"Goddamn," Wesley panted, draping his forearm over his eyes. He breathed deeply for a moment then moved his arm and looked at me. "Wanna try doing me tonight?" he asked with a smirk.

My whole face blushed and I glanced to the side. I couldn't say that the thought never crossed my mind, but I felt embarrassed. I was worried that I could never live up to Wesley's skill.

"Um, I don't know," I whispered shyly, crawling back and standing up.

"C'mon, I wanna know what I've been missing," he said, lying in place completely naked. He then turned over and crawled across the bed on all fours, taking the tube of lotion from the nightstand.

I couldn't help myself. He was so unbelievably hot and I felt myself harden to the point that it almost hurt. He crawled back to me and tugged at my shirt, pulling it over my head, and kissing me.

"You're so ready for it," he grinned, unzipping my shorts. He pulled my pants and boxers down and looked at me with round eyes. "Oh man. We're gonna need lotsa lube. Oh sorry, I mean 'stuff.'"

Wesley pulled me onto the bed, handed me the tube, and turned around. He pushed himself against me and as I looked at his beautiful backside, I was overcome with desire. I glanced at the tube in my hand, and then screwed off the cap.

"Put some on your fingers first," he coached, glancing back at me. "Remember, my ass is virgin."

I almost passed out with lust. This was extra special to me. Just as he was my first for everything, I was going to be his first in this. I did as he instructed and laying one hand on the small of his back, I pressed my finger into him. He moaned and I was seduced by the sound of his voice. I pulled my hand back and slid two fingers in. Wesley wiggled his ass against my hand and I worried that if I didn't do it soon, I was gonna come. Wesley sensed my eager desire and told me to pull my fingers out.

"Slather your dick and go to it," Wesley said, less than seductively, and I couldn't help but laugh. Wesley glanced at me with a smile and laughed too. Then he looked at me again and began to stroke himself.

I grabbed his rear with both hands and positioned myself. I was met with resistance, but as Wesley relaxed his muscles, I pushed forward gently. He moaned with an edge of pain and I stopped.

"Does it hurt?"

"No, I'm okay," he answered, letting himself go and grabbing the sheet in both hands.

I pressed on with his assurance and gently, slowly, I found myself deep inside him. It was an indescribable feeling: my whole body was afire, and I pumped back and forth in this heightened state of awareness. I watched Wesley's back, the way his muscles flexed, and his sighs and moans tickled my ears erotically. I had never experienced a feeling like this before and I thought I would die from the extravagant pleasure. I came hard into Wesley and I gasped for air, my laboring body trembling with sweet exhaustion. I collapsed on top of him, the place of our union tingling and warm.

"Damn," Wesley panted beneath me.

I smiled and kissed the nape of his neck.

I pulled out and I felt like something had changed, something was different. I always worried that, sometimes, Wesley forgot that I was a guy too. I felt equal to him now. I felt stronger and even more connected to him. I was inside him, like I staked my claim or something. I smiled at the silly thought and flopped down beside Wesley. He turned to his side, facing me, and rested his head on his hand. He looked down and groaned.

"Geez, maybe we should start using condoms so we won't have to wash the sheets every day," he said with a laugh.

My face reddened with the mention of the word. I knew I was naïve and everyone preached about protection, but somehow, it never really dawned on me. I was a virgin when I met Wesley and he was the only person I'd ever been with, but I didn't know how many girls he'd been with. I swallowed hard and balled my hands into fists for courage.

"Wesley? Um, how…how many girls have you slept with?" I didn't look at him.

"Does it matter?" He rolled back onto his stomach and stared at the wrinkles in the sheet.

I took a deep breath. With that answer, I knew it had to be a lot. "C'mon, I wanna know."

"I told you, it doesn't matter," he said, furrowing his brows. His voice wasn't angry, just frustrated.

"Is it more than five? Or ten?" I asked.

Wesley looked at me briefly and then bowed his head. "Just one."

I didn't think I heard him right. "What?"

"Just one, all right?" His cheeks were red and he seemed embarrassed. He held his head in his hands and closed his eyes, though his brows were still furrowed.

"One?" I asked.

"Yeah. Okay? I mean, I knew the reputation I had and yeah, I fooled around a lot, but I never went all the way. I just wasn't interested in girls. The one I did sleep with, well, she sorta pressured me, and hell, she opened her legs. Besides, I was going through stuff at that time and I thought that if I actually did it, I'd prove to myself that I wasn't really gay. But…." His words broke off and he took a few audible breaths.

I stared at his handsome profile that suddenly seemed so vulnerable. I didn't care how many girls he'd been with, but my mind had been preparing for the worst. I never would've thought it was just one, though. This man, this boy I loved, was just as confused, and worried, and uncertain as I was—which only made him more attractive.

"I'm so uncool," he murmured with a pathetic laugh.

"No way," I said, slipping my hand over his shoulders. "You're the coolest person I know. And somehow, you're even hotter now," I told him, turning his face to mine.

Wesley smiled at me and kissed me gently. He turned to his side to free his hands. He gripped my wrists and flipped me onto my back. With my hands pinned above my head, he crawled on top of me and kissed me hard. He released my hands and sat back between my legs, pushing them up against my chest.

"Now it's my turn," he said with a grin at the corner of his mouth.

He pushed teasingly at my backside, driving me crazy with anticipation. He pressed into me and I accepted him eagerly, rocking into him to pull him closer. He pushed forward, then scooped me up in his arms so that I was sitting on his lap with my legs wrapped tightly around his middle. Despite how good it felt to be inside him, I liked this way the best.

I spent deliriously and felt soggy inside when Wesley was done. I remained on his lap, his arms holding me tightly, and I felt so happy that I thought I was dreaming. Eventually, I leaned back and stared into Wesley's dark eyes, running my finger over his lips. I kissed him sweetly, deeply, lovingly, and whispered, "Welcome home."

Chapter 23

MY lower back hurt and my rear end was a little sore. I felt like I was walking kinda funny, but Wesley assured me I wasn't. I made a pot of coffee for him and we watched TV for a while. We had a lot of shopping to do and I wrote out a list of things we needed.

Our first stop was at a discount furniture store. We needed another chair for the living room and Wesley had his heart set on a recliner. After we browsed a little, he found one he liked. I talked him into getting the neutral, brown leather model so that it wasn't too mismatched with the sofa. We asked to have it delivered the next day since I didn't have to work and after a little begging, the clerk made room for us on the schedule.

We went to a bed, bath, and kitchen store next. There were so many things we needed, it was a little overwhelming. So we decided to shop by room, starting with the bathroom. Wesley let me pick out the color of towels, the soap dispenser, toothbrush holder, and shower caddy. I looked at shower curtains, but we decided we didn't need one since there was a curtain liner.

We needed the most items for the kitchen. We got dishes for four settings—the cheap ones that come in one box for about thirty dollars. We also bought silverware, mixing bowls, cookie sheets, a casserole dish, mixing spoons, an electric can opener, measuring cups and spoons, and an off-brand toaster.

I looked in the shopping cart and I knew we were spending a lot of money. Wesley didn't seem to mind though. He teased me about being so excited to go shopping. But I couldn't help myself; this was my first apartment with Wesley and we started out with next to nothing.

"Oh, we should get another set of sheets too," Wesley said, steering the cart toward the bedding department. "Or maybe two, so we don't have to wash them every day."

I slapped his hand playfully but I agreed. I walked up and down the aisle, trying to decide on a color and pattern. There were a lot more choices than I expected and I asked Wesley for his opinion, but he would just nod and say "sure." I finally decided on a solid navy set and a white set. It was funny; I never had white sheets, but I always wanted some.

"Well, let's get going before we spend any more money," I said, leading the cart down the aisle. "Oh shoot! We forgot to get washcloths." We had the bath and hand towels, but I completely forgot the washcloths. "I'll run and get them and you can head up front."

Of course, the towels were in the back of the store. On the opposite side of the same aisle were shower curtains and I paused after grabbing four washcloths. There was one curtain that I really liked. It was a dark royal blue with a square pattern woven into the fabric. I hemmed and hawed for a moment, then grabbed the curtain and shower hooks and ran to the front of the store.

Wesley had most of the stuff out of the basket and as I got closer, I recognized the cashier. My stomach tightened; I didn't know Jen worked here. I slowed my pace as I neared the register and Wesley noticed me with a peculiar smile.

"Oh. Hi, Toren," Jen said coldly, glancing back at Wesley.

I set the washcloths down on the counter and then the shower curtain and hooks.

"You went back for washcloths and came back with a shower curtain? I thought we—nevermind." Wesley gave in with an honest smile.

"All right. Four seventy-six sixty-three," Jen announced, putting the last of the things in a bag.

Wesley took his credit card from his wallet and I pulled out my debit card too. I wasn't going to let Wesley pay for all of this.

"What are you doing? Put that away," Wesley said predictably.

I shook my head. "At least let me pay for half."

"No," Wesley answered decidedly.

"Put three hundred dollars on mine and the rest on his," I told Jen, handing her my card.

"Toren…."

"It's okay. Go ahead," I said to Jen and she swiped my card through, glancing at Wesley and me suspiciously.

"God, you're stubborn," Wesley said. I smiled and took it as a compliment.

Jen slid Wesley's card through the reader while I signed a copy of the receipt. "So, are you…roommates or something?" she asked.

I figured that she and Wesley chatted while I was getting the washcloths. He must have told her about the apartment, but didn't mention me. Wesley hesitated with the question, but I didn't.

"Oh no, we're more than that. He's my boyfriend," I said with a satisfied grin.

Jen's eyes widened and she stared at Wesley, but Wesley looked at me with a slow grin taking over his face. He put the bags in the cart and took my hand. I blushed and bit my lip. Jen stared at us with a disconcerted look.

"See you around," Wesley said without looking back. I had to though; the look on her face was priceless.

We filled the trunk of Wesley's car with bags. I couldn't lose the small smile I had on my lips. Wesley closed the trunk and looked at me.

"That was so cool," he said with a laugh. "I didn't say anything 'cause I wasn't sure if you wanted her to know, but…that was great."

The last stop was at the grocery store. We already spent a lot of money and I knew this was going to be at least another $150 or $200 dollars. The only thing we had was coffee, so we really needed everything. We shopped according to my list, buying the basics like bread, milk, eggs, cereal, as well as toothpaste, dish soap, and laundry soap, and also what I would need to make dinner and lunch for the next few days. In the end, we spent $150 on groceries.

We got home a little after six and we were pretty tired carrying all the bags up the stairs, but mostly because we didn't actually fall asleep until five that morning. I let Wesley rest while I put the groceries away and I decided I'd put away all the other stuff tomorrow. I put in a kung fu movie and Wesley lay on the sofa with his head in my lap. I never thought I could be this happy, but there was one tiny, nagging thought in the back of my mind.

Wesley fell asleep during the movie and I watched him more than the TV. He looked so sweet and innocent when he was asleep. As I watched him, the little thought in my head kept growing bigger and bigger. He woke up after the movie was over and smiled at me. My mind whirled and my heart thumped; that little thought was all I could think about.

"Wesley?"

"Hmn?"

"Um, the girl you slept with—" I said hesitantly, taking a deep breath.

"Hunh?" Wesley looked up at me from my lap.

"Was it Jen?" I finally asked.

Wesley sat up quickly. He leaned forward, resting his elbows on his knees, and stared at the floor. "Does it matter who it was?" He seemed aggravated.

I furrowed my brows; his response told me everything. My stomach felt hollow. "It was her, wasn't it?"

Wesley clenched his hands together. "Why do you wanna know?"

"I don't know. I just do." It was because I wanted him to say it wasn't her. Anyone but her.

Wesley sighed like he was defeated. I was wrong. He wasn't aggravated; he was ashamed. "It was when I was in tenth grade. She kept asking me out and I just finally gave in. I was over at her house one night and…it just happened."

"What do you mean?" I asked in a small voice.

"Why? You want details? Fine. She was sucking me off and next thing I knew, she was on top of me. I told her to stop, but she wouldn't. And it just sorta happened. It wasn't like I wanted it to. Hell, I had to think about someone else just to get it up for her," he said, dropping his head into his hands. "Fuck. Fuck!"

"She…she forced you? Then—"

"No! It wasn't…. I mean, I could've pushed her off if I really wanted to. I just thought that if I did a chick, then I wouldn't be gay. It didn't matter who it was." He still wouldn't look at me. I scooted closer to him and rubbed my hand on his back. "Hell, I couldn't even cum!" he said with a pathetic laugh. "Of course, she told everyone the next day and it wasn't like I could deny it. She just pissed me off so much, and I broke it off with her a couple days later. She went crazy, saying I took what I wanted and then dumped her. But what could I say? That she forced me? That I could only get it up for guys? God, I was just so pissed off."

I leaned into him and hugged him. "I'm sorry," I whispered. "I'm so sorry." Tears rolled down my cheeks. He struggled so much more than I thought. When I met him, he was so confident and carefree. It seemed like nothing got to him. Was he just hiding it all this time? How did I not notice?

Wesley glanced at me, at the tears in my eyes, and his face softened. He turned to me and wiped away the tears. "Tor, it's okay. It's in the past. I got over it, so you have to also," he said, bringing my head to his chest and hugging me tightly.

How could he be so strong? All this happened to him, and I was the one crying like a baby. I rubbed my face against his shirt. "I don't like her," I whispered, my voice muffled. "I don't like the way she looks at you, like she owns you or something. I can't stand her."

"But that's the thing: it doesn't matter anymore. She doesn't matter. Because I have you. Everything's okay because I have you," he said, ruffling my hair. I glanced up at him and he smiled gently at me. "To be honest, I did struggle with everything that happened, with being gay, all that, until I met you. You were the first person I really wanted, not just to fuck you, but that I really cared about. The first time I kissed you, it was like my head was suddenly clear. I realized that everything that happened didn't matter. I didn't care that I was gay. I knew that everything would be okay if I could be with you. It was like I hadn't been born until I met you. I know this probably doesn't make any sense, but it was honestly how I felt."

"No," I whispered, shaking my head. "I understand completely. Because I felt the same way. I was so scared of what my mom would think, that she would hate me. But I was willing to take that risk, because I wanted to be with you. And I knew, somehow, that everything would work out, if I just got to be with you."

Wesley kissed me and pulled my hand to his lap. I felt him stiffen and I looked up at him and shook my head.

"I can't help it," he said. "When you talk that way, it makes me hard."

His kisses became longer and deeper and I lay back as he unzipped my shorts. His mouth was warm and soft and my legs trembled with his movements. I came and he swallowed, running his thumb across his lips. I leaned down and kissed him, then led him to the bedroom. Fortunately, I hadn't changed the sheets yet and I knew that I would have to do at least one load of laundry each day.

"We should've bought a sperm towel," Wesley said, pulling me close. "Then we wouldn't have to change the sheets so often." I knew exactly what he was talking about. Every teenage boy has one. I agreed with blushing cheeks and noted that I would go out and buy one tomorrow. "Heh, I forgot to put one in the laundry for a couple weeks once, and that thing was so hard and crusty.... It was disgusting." I reconsidered and figured I should buy two or three. "There were a lot of potential babies in that thing," he mused with a grin.

I rolled my eyes and climbed atop his stomach. “One more time?” I asked, leaning down, inches from his lips.

“How could I say no? But remember, I gotta go to work tomorrow.”

Chapter 24

WESLEY left for work at seven, leaving me with a kiss and an "I love you." I slept until eight, then got up and took a shower. I had to work ten to five so I made a cold pasta salad for lunch. I put enough for my dinner into a plastic tub and then thought Wesley might like some for lunch too. I packed another plastic container and put the rest in the fridge.

I went to Gus's Auto Shop. It was a small building with a lot of cars in the parking lot in various stages of repair. I opened the door and a bell jingled. An older man with a large beer belly sat behind the counter. He was wearing a navy outfit with "Gus" embroidered on the left breast pocket. He had gray-streaked hair combed over a shiny, bald head and crooked teeth set in a warm, friendly smile.

"Hi. Is, um, Wesley here?"

"Yeah, hang on a sec," he answered, leaning back on his chair and looking through a panel of glass to his left. "Wes! Come up here!"

Wesley's head popped up from behind a car and he walked to the front, wiping his hands on a pinkish-red rag. He smiled when he saw me. "Hey. What are you doing here?"

"Hi. Um, I made some pasta salad for lunch and I thought you might like some too," I said, glancing at the large man behind the counter. I bit my lip; it felt like we were newlyweds and I was delivering my husband's lunch.

"Oh! So, this must be the princess then?" the man asked, looking up at me then to Wesley who was slicing at his throat with his fingers and shaking his head.

"Ah, um…yeah," Wesley answered with a crooked grin. "Gus, this is Toren. Toren, this is my boss, Gus," he said, smiling and scratching the back of his head.

"Hey, it's nice to finally meet you. Wes's told me all about you. I can finally put a face with the name," he said, standing up behind the counter.

I smiled and nodded and extended my hand. "It's nice to meet you too."

"So, can I take my lunch now?" Wesley asked.

Gus nodded, but I interrupted. "I actually have to go to work now," I said, wishing I had given myself enough time to eat with Wesley.

"Aww. All right, fine. You work 'til five, right?" he asked as I took the plastic container of salad from the plastic bag on my arm. I nodded and handed him the tub and a fork. "This looks great! Thanks so much! I'll see you later, okay?"

Wesley stepped toward me and I backed up. I wasn't sure if he wanted a kiss, but I decided against it. I was honestly surprised by Gus's amicability toward us; he didn't look like the open-minded type. But that was unfair of me to stereotype him too. I smiled again at Gus and bowed my head slightly.

"It was very nice meeting you," I said and Wesley walked past, pulling me along with him.

"I'll be back in a sec," Wesley said, grinning at Gus over his shoulder.

Outside, Wesley pushed me against the building. He kissed me, then patted the top of my head and looked around. When he looked at me again, he had a devilish smirk on his lips.

"What?" I asked, knowing that look all too well.

"C'mon, the bathroom's around back," Wesley said, taking my hand and pulling me along.

"What? No! Wesley!" I protested, stopping and pulling my hand away. I narrowed my eyes at him and shook my head. "I can't believe you sometimes."

"Aw, c'mon. Real quick, please?"

I folded my arms across my chest and shook my head. "You're the horniest bastard I know…."

Wesley laughed and smiled. "All right, all right. I had to try."

"No, you didn't," I said, finally laughing. "I gotta go, so I'll see you later."

"Okay. But you gotta kiss me."

I pecked his cheek and ran from his reach. I stuck my tongue out at him and Wesley laughed. "See ya!" I shouted and walked to work.

I WAS excited to tell Jeanine that I moved in with Wesley. She seemed as excited as I was and congratulated me. We walked around the store, deciding how we would decorate the apartment if we had a limitless budget. There were some decorations that I really liked and I decided to save up my money for them. Our apartment was so plain and I wanted to give it some life, even if it was only one piece at a time.

The store was pretty slow, so I was able to leave right at five. Then I remembered that I had to fill out a change-of-address form, so I left around ten after. When I got home, I put some chicken and potatoes in the oven and sat down to watch TV.

"Honey, I'm home!" Wesley shouted with a giant smile on his face. I laughed and met him at the front door. He kissed me and I smiled, leading the way back to the kitchen. "I almost couldn't wait to go to work just so I could come home and say that," he said, washing his hands at the kitchen sink.

"You're so silly. How was work? Did you have a good day?" I asked, emptying a can of corn into the small saucepot.

"Yeah, it was all right. I'm glad I don't usually work Mondays though. We were busy as hell," he answered, opening the refrigerator and stooping to look inside. "Oh, thanks for the pasta salad for lunch! It was great!"

"Good, I'm glad. And, dinner'll be ready in about fifteen minutes."

"Cool. I'm starving. What are you making?" Wesley opened a can of soda and placed his hand on my back.

"Just chicken and baked potatoes." Wesley leaned in and kissed me, then went to the living room.

"I was glad you came up to work today. I'm glad you met Gus," he said, flipping channels.

"Me too. He seemed really nice."

"He's a really great guy. I used to bug him all the time when I was a kid. He has all those great old cars on the lot and he let me get my hands dirty with some of them. He taught me everything I know. Hell, he helped me bring my Mustang back to life. I bought it off of him for a hundred bucks, so basically, he gave it to me. He's always sorta been…like a dad to me. When I told him about you, he was surprised, but he said that if I was happy, then he was happy. It really meant a lot to me, for him to just accept it like that." Wesley stared into his lap, pensive and serious. Then he looked up at me and laughed.

"It means a lot to me too," I said, handing him a plate. "But, didn't I tell you not to call me 'princess'?" I said, sitting next to him on the sofa. Wesley smiled goofily and I shook my head.

We ate dinner on the sofa and watched TV. Wesley took my plate and did the dishes, leaving the casserole dish in the sink to soak. We watched TV and talked and I reminded him that I had orientation for school on Wednesday.

"Do you want me to go with you? I might be able to go in late to work," Wesley asked, resting his hand on the sofa behind my head.

"No, that's okay. My mom's going with me. Thanks though." I pushed my head back against his hand. "Oh yeah, my mom is coming back for dinner too."

"Okay, cool." He seemed genuinely happy that Mom was visiting and the pit of my stomach felt warm. Wesley stood up and patted my head. "I'm gonna go hop in the shower."

Wesley took his showers at night since he got so dirty at work and the auto grease would transfer to our sheets. I watched him walk to the bedroom and then disappear into the bathroom. I went to the kitchen and stared at the pan in the sink. I heard the shower start and I clenched my hands on the counter. I took a deep breath, smiled shyly, went to the bedroom, and took off all my clothes.

The bathroom door stuck and I had to push with a little force to open it. I was trying so hard to be quiet. I tiptoed to the shower and pulled back the curtain a little. Wesley had his back to me and was rinsing the shampoo out of his hair. I stepped over the side of the tub and Wesley turned around quickly.

"What—what are you doing?" he asked with a desirable grin.

I opened my mouth, but nothing came out. I wanted to give him a cool line but I couldn't think of anything to say. "I…I wanted to take a shower too," I answered pathetically, my whole body blushing.

Wesley took my hand and looked me over amorously. I closed my eyes and allowed my hands to wander all over his body. His skin was smooth; fleshy in some places and hard and angled in others. My body responded to the topographical exploration of all the corners and crevices of his figure. My fingers wandered downward and I began to frig him gently with both hands.

"That's…gonna be really clean," he whispered with a laugh, then grunted quietly. He took me in his hands and rubbed softly. I stepped closer to him, under the spray of water, and rested my forehead on his shoulder. Wesley kissed me, licked my lips, and pulled on me harder and faster. We stared into each other's eyes silently, kissing intermittently, nearing climax. Wesley pulled me close, pressed against his stomach, and we came together, clinging to each other, exhausted.

"Aw man, that was the best shower ever!" Wesley said, walking around the bedroom completely naked while rubbing the towel over his head.

I climbed into bed and waited for Wesley. He jumped in and crawled on top of me. He touched and licked me all over and I clung to him for dear life. We were in bed by nine, exhausted by ten, and asleep by eleven.

Chapter 25

MOM came over around noon. She wore blue jeans and a T-shirt and had her hair pulled back in a ponytail. She planned to drive to campus, but I told her that I was usually going to ride the bus to school, so she wanted to take the bus too. She was really excited and I couldn't help but tease her.

"Oh, this brings back so many memories! Tor, you're gonna love college. This is so much fun!"

"Mom, calm down," I said quietly, glancing around. No one was looking at us, but I felt self-conscious. Mom always was kind of a spaz when she got excited, but it was also why we had so much fun together.

The orientation was boring and Mom and I skipped out of the campus tour. We sat outside and watched people and talked. I scheduled my classes and we went to the bookstore and got my books. I was surprised by how much the books cost and fortunate that Mom put the bill on her credit card. We got home a little after four and we sat and talked, waiting for Wesley to come home.

"You should join some clubs too. That's a great way to make friends. I'm sure they have a history club or something. It'll be good too because you can talk to others and see if you wanna major in education or if you wanna do straight history. I was in a nursing club at school and also the anthro club. Oh! Maybe you could join the newspaper too. I worked at the paper and it was so much fun!"

"You wish you were still in college, don't you?" I asked, after listening to Mom's suggestions. She was outgoing and popular; she liked to be involved in everything.

"Maybe, a little bit," she agreed. "College was just so much fun! Your dad and I went to the same school and he was on the newspaper too. I had the time of my life then, so it's all happy memories for me. And now, my little boy is all grown up and going off to college! I can't help but be excited for you."

I laughed and Mom patted my head. It was getting close to six and Wesley would be coming home soon. I stood up and Mom followed me to the kitchen, where I took the salmon filets and fresh broccoli from the refrigerator. Mom kept talking as I pulled out a box of rice from the pantry and measured two cups into a saucepan.

"Oh baby, you don't know how much I've missed your cooking," Mom said, watching as I cut up the broccoli. "Well, you too. I guess I've missed you too," she corrected with a laugh. "Wes doesn't know how good he has it…eating like a king every day!"

"Yeah, he actually does. And he appreciates it," I teased, giving Mom a broccoli stalk to nibble on.

"Oh yeah, I was thinking, you should join the…. What do they call it? It's letters, but…um, I don't know, it's like a 'gay club' or something."

I stopped and looked up at Mom. Her eyes narrowed, as if she was trying to remember something. "The *gay club*?" I asked, trying to keep a deadpan expression. "You want me to join the *gay club*?" I said, unable to keep my laughter in any longer.

"Well, no, I mean…. You know what I mean!" Mom shouted over my laughter. She shook her head and smiled. "Okay, so it's not the 'gay club,' but what is it called? It's letters."

"LGBC?"

"Yeah!" Mom said, her face brightening with recognition. "What's it mean again?"

"Lesbian, Gay, and Bisexual Community," I answered, still chuckling.

"Yeah, that's it. Well, I'm sure there's something like that on campus and you should join."

"I'll think about it," I answered, mixing lemon rind, garlic, and dill in a bowl with olive oil. I brushed the filets with the mixture and put them in the oven to bake. I turned on the heat under the rice and put the broccoli in the large saucepot to steam.

Wesley came home at six. He looked cute, as usual, and he greeted me with a simple kiss. Mom watched with a smile on her face and I blushed; I couldn't help myself. It really felt like we were married and I giggled timidly.

"Ms. Grey, it's nice to see you."

"What'd you just call me?"

Wesley glanced at me and then smiled awkwardly at Mom. "M—Ms. Grey?"

"No no no. Not Ms. Grey. Never Ms. Grey. It's Amanda. Got it?"

Wesley smiled and laughed with relief. "All right, got it."

"No, come on. Say it with me, Ah-man-dah," Mom said slowly.

Wesley nodded with a grin. "All right, all right…Amanda."

"See? That wasn't so hard," Mom said, folding her arms on her chest.

"Dinner'll be ready in about ten," I said, looking over my shoulder as I stirred the rice.

Wesley went to wash up and change his clothes while I fixed three plates. I set them down at the table, but we ended up eating on the sofa in front of the TV. Wesley told us about work; a girl had ripped off her back bumper backing over a concrete parking berm by getting stuck, and then flooring it to get unstuck. Then he asked how my orientation went.

"It was boring, but it was okay. I got all my classes scheduled though. I can't believe school starts a week from today," I said, picking at the broccoli. I had steamed it too long.

"What classes are you taking?" Wesley asked. I didn't think he even noticed that the broccoli was mushy.

I counted off my fingers. "History 105, Psych 101, Bio 103, English Comp, and…." I glanced at Mom and she was trying to remember my fifth class too. "Oh yeah, Pre-Calc. Which I'm gonna need your help with."

"Cool. Are you excited?" he asked.

"Yeah, I am. I'm a little nervous too, but more excited. Oh, and, my mom thinks I should join the 'gay club'."

Wesley looked up at me and I grinned then glanced at Mom.

"The what?" Wesley asked.

"You know, the gay club," I said, erupting into laughter.

"Oh, shut up!" Mom teased. "I couldn't remember LGBC and now Toren won't let me live it down." She closed her eyes and shook her head. Her body trembled with laughter but no sound came out.

We finished eating and sat and talked and watched TV for a little while. Mom decided to leave around eight. I took her on a final tour of the apartment, showing her the improvements we had made since she was last there. She gave me a long hug at the door and her eyes began to tear up.

"Baby, I can't tell you how much I miss you already. You're just growing up so fast," she said, wiping at her eyes. I hugged her again and she told me that I would always be her little boy. I knew Wesley was going to tease me about it too.

"Thanks for going to orientation with me. Sorry you had to skip work," I said, letting her go. She sniffled and smiled at me.

"My little boy is a college man now." She looked at Wesley and wiggled her finger at him. "Get over here," she said and threw her arms around his shoulders.

"Thanks for coming…Amanda," Wesley said and grinned.

Mom looked at him and smiled. Then she left and Wesley and I watched her walk out to her car. I shut the door and Wesley grinned at me.

"Your mom is so cool," he said, then went to the kitchen and started washing the dishes.

I smiled proudly. Mom really was amazing. I followed Wesley into the kitchen, turned the water off, and pressed myself against his warm body. I kissed him and grabbed the top of his shorts.

"Leave the dishes for tomorrow."

Chapter 26

"WE'RE going to spend the entire day playing video games," Wesley announced, sitting up in bed. He looked over at me and grinned. It was finally Monday and Wesley's first day off in a long time. He was exhausted and deserved a day idly spent playing video games.

"You can spend half the day playing video games. Remember? Alycia and Mike are coming over tonight," I said, rolling to my side and propping my head up on my hand.

"Oh yeah, that's right. What time are they coming over?" He stretched his arms over his head and yawned. He wiggled down under the sheet and kissed the tip of my nose. His chin was coarse with stubble and I liked the way it felt against my cheek. He looked good with a clean-shaven face, but he was cute with stubble too. I touched his cheek, tickling my fingers with his prickly whiskers.

"What?" I asked, blushing lightly. I forgot he asked me a question.

"Heh. What time are they coming over?"

"About seven. Speaking of which, I gotta run to the store," I said, flipping the sheet off and sitting up.

Wesley hooked his arm around my waist and pulled me back down. He kissed me warmly and pinched my nipple playfully. I started to protest, but I knew it was pointless. It was impossible to stop him once he got started. I turned over and took his face in my hands. I lapped at his lips, stopping briefly to kiss him, and reached for the tube of lotion on the nightstand. I dribbled some on my fingers and began to frig Wesley with one hand and slid my other hand between my thighs. Wesley looked at me, seeing that I was preparing myself for him, and stiffened even more in my hand. I smiled and sucked his bottom lip. I loved that I could turn him on like that.

"Okay, you're gonna have to hurry up," Wesley whispered slowly.

I climbed onto his lap, with my back to him, and he eased his way inside. I rocked against him as he slid his hand around my hip and pulled on me quickly. I threw my head back, shuddering with the unstoppable flow of pleasure. He pressed his lips against the nape of my neck and discovered an entirely new erogenous zone. He pushed up and forward as I bounced on his lap and then without warning, he came hard into me and I came into his hand.

Wesley panted in my ear and I leaned back against him. "Sorry that was so quick," he said. "I couldn't help myself. You should come with a warning label: May cause one to…cum faster than expected."

"Heh heh, where would I put a label like that?" I asked, looking over my shoulder. Wesley poked my forehead with his finger and grinned. I slid off his lap to the edge of the bed and pulled on my boxers. "Wanna go to the store with me?"

"But we were gonna play video games today," he whined.

"We'll play video games all day tomorrow."

"You're screwing up my schedule! Today we play video games and tomorrow we fuck all day. I had it all planned out!"

"If you don't go to the store with me, I may not be open tomorrow," I countered, standing up and crossing my arms with a grin on my face.

"Let me get dressed," Wesley answered, standing up and pulling on a clean pair of boxers from the dresser.

We went to the grocery store and got the ingredients to make lasagna according to Mom's recipe. I bought some garlic bread too. We got home and Wesley watched me make the lasagna and put it in the oven to bake.

Wesley sat in the recliner and I sat between his knees on the floor. We started playing video games, but I wasn't very good. I finally talked Wesley into playing Tekken since he didn't have any of the Zelda games. I usually played Jun, but I kept beating Wesley, so I switched to Haihachi.

"You're really good at this. You sucked at Grand Theft," Wesley commented, pounding on his controller.

"I like fighting games. Tekken is my favorite. The only thing Mortal Kombat has going for it is Scorpion and Subzero. Tekken is way better!"

Wesley lost again and I giggled, secretly proud of myself.

"You gotta be someone else! This sucks."

I could tell that he was surprised that I was pretty good at video games, but frustrated that he couldn't beat me. So I switched to the samurai guy and purposely let him win. He looked at me and frowned.

"You lost on purpose."

"No, I didn't. Really!"

"Liar."

I set down my controller and crawled onto Wesley's lap. I gave him a consolation kiss, and then went to the kitchen to check on the lasagna. I turned the oven off, leaving the lasagna in, and made a salad. I told Wesley to go take a shower and he refused, unless I agreed to join him. I shook my head and sighed, and Wesley took my hands and kissed me sweetly. I realized I could never tell him "no" and followed him into the bathroom.

Alycia came over at seven and I ran to answer the door. She smiled and walked in, and I waited leaving the door open. Then Alycia turned and smiled again.

"Mike's not coming."

"What? Why?" I asked, glancing outside before closing the door. "Did he get called into work or something?"

"No. He's just an asshole."

"What?"

"Hiya, Wes! How are you?" she asked, her smile back. I stood next to her and glanced at Wesley. Alycia sat down on the sofa and looked up at me.

"What happened?" I asked.

Alycia sighed and stared at her lap. "Damn it," she said and balled her hands into fists. "I wasn't going to tell you, but the more I think about it, the more pissed off I get. Mike didn't want to come because…he didn't think it was right." Wesley and I exchanged glances. "He said it was unnatural for two boys to be in love," she clarified, looking up at me hesitantly. "God. I told him that once he saw you together, he'd see how natural it was. But, he said that he didn't agree with it, so he didn't want to be around it."

I looked at Wesley and then sat down next to Alycia. It was surprising; Mike never acted strange around me or avoided me before.

"The thing is, he never said a word about it before today! And, I mean, I talked to him about you guys all the time and he never said anything! Let alone how it must make you guys feel, he…. It was like he didn't care how I felt either. Did he really think that I'd just say okay? That it wouldn't bother me? I mean, if he doesn't think it's right, does he think there's something wrong with me because I do? And he never said anything before! I had no idea he felt that way!"

"Alycia," I said softly, touching her arm.

"I'm sorry, Tor."

"It's okay, it's not your fault."

"It's just that he never told me. And what am I supposed to do? I don't wanna be with a person who thinks that way. If he wants me, he has to accept all of me, including my family. If I stay with him, is he going to avoid you guys? I don't want that. My family is more important to me, and if he rejects them, then he's rejecting me too."

My stomach twisted and my chest tightened. I rubbed Alycia's back and stared at the floor. I couldn't look at Wesley.

"I'm sorry. I didn't mean to just dump all this on you," she said quietly, her brows furrowed. "I just didn't know what to do."

"I'm sorry too." I didn't know what else to say. She had been with Mike for over a year.

"What should I do, Tor? I love him. I mean, I really do love him. But…this is just too much." Alycia sniffled and wiped away the tears in her eyes.

I patted her back and glanced at Wesley. "Could you take the lasagna out of the oven?" I asked quietly. Wesley nodded and stood up.

"You made lasagna?" Alycia asked, her face perking up and her eyes hopeful. She blinked quickly, trying to dissipate her tears and smiled childishly.

"Yeah, using Mom's recipe with a few changes," I answered, returning her smile with a slight laugh. Her stomach never ceased to amaze me. She was small, petite really, and looked delicate and fragile, but she had a stomach made of steel. It was like there was a switch in her brain that put her in "food mode."

"Ooh, I can't wait! I haven't eaten for two days waiting for dinner tonight. I just hope you made enough 'cause I'm starving!"

"Well, dinner's ready, if you wanna eat now," I said, but she was already up and heading toward the kitchen.

Alycia set the table while I tossed the salad and Wesley cut up the lasagna. We sat down to eat and Alycia and Wesley battled to see who could eat the most.

"Hey, can I have a beer?" Alycia asked after dinner. She was hunched over in front of the refrigerator and glanced back at me with a grin.

"Sure, grab one for me too," Wesley said, heading into the living room.

"Hey!" I objected, but was ignored. Alycia passed me with two beers in her hands and I followed her into the living room. "She's my little sister!" I protested halfheartedly. "Oh, forget it." I gave up, without hearing a single word of opposition.

"C'mon, Tor. Have one too," Alycia urged, pulling her legs under her on the sofa.

"Nah, he doesn't like beer," Wesley said and took a long drink. Then he stood up quickly. "Oh, but I got something he does like!"

Wesley ran into the bedroom and Alycia and I exchanged glances. I didn't know what he was getting; I just prayed it wasn't something embarrassing. He came back with a joint between his thumb and index finger and my stomach dropped.

"Tor…ren!" Alycia scolded. "Shame on you!"

"We can't smoke it on the balcony, so can we do it in here? Or do we have to go to my car?" Wesley asked. He didn't smoke in the apartment, but it wasn't because I wouldn't let him; he decided to smoke outside of his own accord. "Oh, have you smoked before?" he asked Alycia.

"Just once," Alycia said. "Me and a friend decided to give it a try, but I don't think I got high or anything. It kinda sucked. Honestly, I was a little disappointed."

I didn't know she had ever tried it. I looked at her blankly and she smiled sheepishly at me. I guessed I shouldn't have been surprised though.

"Well, if you're anything like your brother, you will this time."

"Yeah, in here is fine," I said, resigning myself to the fact that my little sister wasn't little anymore and knew more about the world than I did. I deflated with a sigh, snatching the joint from Wesley and falling back on the sofa next to Alycia. "Lighter?"

Wesley tossed me an orange lighter and sat down on the sofa next to me. I lit one end and inhaled. Wesley watched me with a smile on his lips. He seemed impressed that I could get a good burn, but I had watched him enough times to know. I handed it to Alycia and she was cute, bringing her lips out to the joint rather than bringing the joint to her lips. She closed her eyes and inhaled, holding her breath with her cheeks puffed out. Wesley and I giggled, then he took it and we passed it back and forth until it was a tiny roach. Then Wesley got his bowl and we smoked that too, although it wasn't really necessary.

"Fuck!" Alycia shouted, surprising Wesley and me. She looked at us with a loopy grin on her face. "I definitely didn't get high before. What a rip-off!"

Wesley and I started laughing and we turned on the TV with the volume low, barely audible. We sat three abreast on the couch with silly grins plastered on our faces.

"I'm thirsty," Alycia said, smacking her lips.

I got up to get her a soda and both Alycia and Wesley followed me into the kitchen. I poured a soda for Alycia, but ended up drinking it myself because she opted to have another beer with Wesley. I took out the carton of mint chocolate chip ice cream, Wesley took the entire pan of lasagna, and Alycia grabbed the rest of the garlic bread, and we sat down at the table, sharing a very unusual post-dinner snack.

"God. What a fucking idiot," Alycia stated with a mouthful of ice cream.

"What?" I asked, taking the carton back.

"Mike. He's such an *ass*hole! I mean, really…. What did he think was gonna happen?"

"I dunno. Maybe he thought we were gonna start boning in the middle of dinner?" Wesley suggested, taking the ice cream carton away from me.

"Wesley!" I shouted, because of what he said and because he stole the ice cream.

"I mean, if that's what he was expecting, then we wouldn't wanna let him down," he continued, blocking the ice cream from me.

Alycia laughed, leaning back in her chair. "Oh, ew! Please, just not in front of me. As far as I'm concerned, Toren's asexual and…."

"Oh no, you've got it so wrong. Toren's very sexual and very, um...passionate," Wesley said, with a grin at the corner of his mouth and a lascivious look in my direction.

"Oh, my God! Look at how red you are! Toren, you look like a tomato!" Alycia squealed.

I knew I was bright red, but I couldn't help myself. Wesley laughed and pushed the ice cream toward me.

"Will you guys shut up?" I said, hiding my face behind my hands.

"Aw, you're so cute!" Alycia teased, poking my arm.

I finally got them settled down and we watched TV in the living room until about one in the morning. Alycia left a message for Mom that she was staying the night and I hoped that Mom wouldn't be able to tell she was stoned by her message. I brought out a blanket and a pillow for Alycia and set them down on the sofa. We said good night, but Alycia stopped us. She came up to me and kissed my cheek.

"Thanks for dinner. And for listening. You guys are the best."

Chapter 27

"HEY! Welcome home! How was your first day of school?"

"It was good," I answered, dropping my book bag at the door. Wesley was wearing my apron and he looked so cute. "What are you doing?" I asked, giving him a kiss and glancing into the kitchen.

"No! Don't go in. I'm making dinner and it's a surprise," he said, pushing me into the living room. I peeked as I was pushed past the kitchen and it looked like it exploded. "Dinner'll be ready soon, so just sit down and be a good boy."

"You look good in an apron," I said and grinned. I sat down on the sofa and Wesley shook his ass before returning to the kitchen. I laughed and thought he would look better if he were wearing only the apron. I sighed with a grin; Wesley's fantasies were starting to affect my own.

I turned on the TV and waited. There was a loud crash followed by a string of cuss words. I got up and asked if he needed help, but he adamantly denied it. A couple minutes later, Wesley made his appearance with two plates, two forks, and a large, proud grin.

"I know it's not much, but I can't really make anything better, unless I had meat and a grill," he prefaced and handed me a plate and a fork before sitting down beside me.

There was a stack of pancakes on the plate and on the top one, "LOVE YOU" was spelled out with chocolate chips. I smiled and looked at Wesley. He blushed and watched me eagerly.

"This is so sweet!" I said, leaning over and pecking Wesley's cheek. He smiled proudly and waited for me to take the first bite. "Yummy!"

We finished dinner and flipped through channels on the TV. I stretched my legs out and leaned into Wesley. He put his arm around my shoulders and I felt so happy that I could burst.

"I guess Alycia really broke up with Mike," I said, looking down at my lap. "I talked to my mom this morning. I still can't quite believe it. They were together more than a year. Since Alycia was a sophomore," I said, wringing my hands.

"That's too bad," Wesley answered. Then he laughed, "Well, at least Jeremy'll be happy to hear it. He's crushing on your sister pretty bad."

"Still, I can't believe they broke up. I can't help but feel bad about it."

Wesley stared at me a moment. "You're not feeling guilty, are you? 'Cause it's not your fault. Even if we weren't gay, your sister's not the type who would want to be with someone who thought that way. It was probably gonna happen sooner or later, so it's better she found out sooner rather than later." He put the remote down in his lap and tapped my leg. "Okay?"

"Yeah, I know. But, still, I can't help but feel a little bit guilty."

"Well, don't. It's not your fault and I'm sure Alycia put a lot of thought into it. So, don't worry about it, okay?"

I sighed and nodded. "Okay." Wesley always made me feel better, but did I do the same for him? I fidgeted my hands in my lap and swallowed hard. "Um, have you talked to your parents since you moved out?"

"No. Why should I? My mom'll start in on me about 'how could I do this to them?' and that they didn't 'raise me to be like this' and my dad'll just say that he doesn't want a fag for a son. So, no. I don't wanna hear it," he said, making my stomach drop. He flipped the channel on the TV.

"But, you don't know that for sure," I said. "You should talk to them, just to let them know you're all right."

"Forget it. I left my phone number and address when I moved out. If they wanna talk, they can call me."

I sighed and Wesley rubbed my shoulder. He looked at me with furrowed brows. "You're not saying this because of what happened with Alycia, are you?"

"No." He could read me so well; it was pointless to lie. "Well, maybe. I just.... I don't wanna be a burden to you. Family is important and I don't wanna be the cause of any stress." I didn't know what I'd do without Mom and Alycia. I'm not strong enough to make that kind of choice. But I knew what I wanted Wesley to say.

"Tor, listen to me. I chose you. I don't regret it and I never will. I feel bad that my parents can't be happy for me, but oh well. I chose you and I would again, every time. Besides, I got you, but I also feel like I gained a mom and a sister. So don't ever think like that. Okay?"

I felt better. I felt relief. I would always feel a little guilty over what happened with Wesley's parents, but as long as he loved me, it was a guilt I could easily live with. I turned to Wesley and kissed his lips. He tasted sweet, like syrup, and I licked him tenderly.

"I love you," I said.

"I love you too. Didn't the pancake tell you that?"

I laughed and picked up the plate from the coffee table, but Wesley took it from me.

"Sit down. I'll do the dishes. Besides, you might kick my ass for what I did to the kitchen."

Wesley went to the kitchen and I watched TV, but soon went to the bedroom to change clothes. On my side of the bed, a dozen red roses were propped up against the pillow. My stomach filled with butterfly wings and my cheeks felt hot. I ran to the kitchen, spun Wesley around, and kissed him hard on the mouth.

"I can't believe you bought me flowers!"

"Well, damn. If I knew I was gonna get that kind of reaction, I would've bought you a car."

I turned off the water in the sink and took Wesley's hand. I led him back to the bedroom and wrapped my arms around his neck. I sucked his tongue and licked his lips, then pushed my hands beneath his T-shirt. I circled his nipples with my fingertips until they were hard and then bent my head down and sucked on each in turn. I pulled his shirt over his head and kissed him lightly while I unbuttoned and unzipped his pants.

"Wait. Not yet," I whispered, pulling his hands away from my blue jeans.

I took his pants down to his ankles and drew in my breath sharply. He was wearing boxer-briefs and they looked so sexy on him. He was hard and pushing against the stretchy cotton as I pulled those down too. I felt myself stiffen as I looked him over and my heart began to flutter. He stepped out of his shorts on the floor as I led him to the bed. I got down on my knees and licked my lips. Wesley sat on the edge of the bed and I slid my hands up over his knees to the tops of his thighs and grasped him with both hands. I lapped at the florid tip, guided my tongue along the smooth, rigid shaft, then under his balls until I reached the place where his thighs met. He was warm, hot even, and he leaked pre-cum onto my sensitive tongue. His balls tightened when I dropped my mouth around him and his legs trembled on either side of my shoulders. He moaned quietly and I was enchanted by his voice. I sucked and slurped harder, feeling his orgasm draw near, and then I drank down every drop he had to offer.

Wesley panted above me and I stood up, letting my hands linger, and kissed him until I felt him harden again. I stepped back and slipped my shirt off. I took my jeans down and my boxers were sticky from anticipation. Wesley watched me closely, his eyes exploring my body wantonly as I crawled atop him, finally allowing him to touch me. I almost came from the mere sensation of his warm, hard hands. I leaned back, holding Wesley as I gently lowered myself onto him. It was a little tight without lotion, but Wesley was slick with my saliva. I accepted him gradually, feeling him swell within me and I kissed his lips and neck as if it was the only thing keeping me alive. We moved together as though every thrust was choreographed and I clung to him as my climax came early. Wesley rocked me back and forth, smearing the cum on his stomach against mine, and as he pumped, I felt my heart racing and my pulse thumping. I was hard again and as I gasped for air, I came a second time. Wesley exploded inside me and I collapsed in his arms, the strength drained from my body. I heaved in breath as if I had been underwater and my body was still trembling.

"You're the best boyfriend ever," I sighed.

Chapter 28

IT was Wesley's day off and somehow, he talked me into skipping my first class. We relaxed and fooled around, but I got ready to go around two. I couldn't miss any labs and Wesley reluctantly let me go. I got to school early and settled down in the empty bio lab and read my psychology text waiting for class to begin.

"Hey, Toren. What's going on?"

I looked up from my psychology book and Josh was smiling at me. He was a junior, kinda cute, and my lab partner for biology.

"Not much. How are you?" I said.

"Pretty good," he answered, sitting down on the stool next to me.

Josh had a handsome smile, dark brown eyes, and earrings in both ears. Friendly, outgoing, and confident, he reminded me of Wesley in some ways. On the first day of class, when we were picking our lab partners, he turned around and asked me to be his partner. I didn't know anyone in class and I accepted with a smile. I thought I was going to have to wait until the professor asked if there was anyone without a partner, the way it had always happened in high school.

"So, what are you working on?" he asked.

"Oh, um, just reading for Psych."

"Oh yeah? That's my major. It's Intro, right? Who do you have?"

"McFarlain."

"She's good. She's really good. But don't ever take Davis. That guy's a total prick. But I guess it doesn't matter for you. You're a History major, right?"

I looked up and nodded. I was surprised that he remembered. Classes started just three weeks ago and I had already failed my first math test. I really needed Wesley's help.

"So what do you wanna do with it?"

"I think I'd like to teach." I wasn't sure why, but I felt bashful all of a sudden.

"Cool. I think you'd be really good at that," he said, smiling again.

We sat and talked in the biology lab until class was about to start. I packed up my book and highlighter and took out my bio notebook and folder.

The professor started class and handed out the observation sheets along with a box of cotton swabs so we could compare plant and animal cells under the microscope.

Slides of plant material were already prepared and Josh and I took turns examining the cell structure and pattern. We wrote down our observations, and then swabbed the inside of our mouths with the swabs. We looked at Josh's first, at the irregular cell shape and the lack of structure or pattern. The professor discussed the differences between the two and the benefits of each. I prepared my slide, smearing the swab on the glass, and then clipping it under the microscope. I looked closer and saw tiny, little things moving around. Josh looked at the slide and saw them too.

"What are those things?" I asked, looking through the microscope again.

Josh shrugged. "I don't know."

"Should we ask the professor?" I said, looking around the classroom. Professor Kitner was across the room.

"Sure," he said, raising his hand. The professor nodded and walked over. "What are these things?" Josh asked as Professor Kitner leaned over the microscope.

Professor Kitner's body twitched and he stood up suddenly, looking at Josh. "Whose slide is this?" he asked.

"It's mine," I answered, concerned by his unusual reaction. Professor Kitner looked at me and stepped closer. "What is it?" I asked, starting to feel a little worried.

The professor leaned close and whispered, "It's sperm."

My body froze. My heart stopped beating. My face turned white. I was sure I was going to die of embarrassment.

"It's nothing to worry about," Professor Kitner said with a friendly smile. "When was the last time you ate? It's just enzymes breaking down residual foodstuff. That's all," he said, patting my shoulder and walking away to another lab table.

I took a deep breath and Josh was watching me. My whole face turned bright red and I didn't know what to do. Josh didn't hear what the professor said, did he?

There were fifteen minutes of class left and it was the longest fifteen minutes of my life. Professor Kitner reviewed our observations and reminded us of an exam coming up next Thursday. He dismissed the class and I gathered my things together as quickly as I could. I had to keep myself from running out of the room.

"Oh, Toren, just a minute," Professor Kitner said.

My heart sunk down into my toes. I walked up to his desk, staring at the floor, where he was leafing through the observation sheets we turned in. He didn't say anything until the classroom was empty.

"Sorry, Toren. I just wanted to talk to you real quick," Professor Kitner said, standing up and coming around the side of the table. He folded his arms and leaned back. I gripped my hands into fists at my sides and I felt tears welling that I desperately tried to keep hidden. "I wanted to tell you not to worry. These things happen and it's not like I'm going to hold it against you or anything. So, don't worry about it, okay? It's not a big deal."

His words were kind, but they did nothing to settle my embarrassment. I dug my fists into my thighs and nodded weakly. I still stared at the ground because I knew I would start crying if I looked up.

"Also, I wanted to let you know that there's an LGBT club on campus. They meet Thursdays at seven o'clock in room 212 of the U-Mall. So, if you're interested, I'd really like you to come to one of the meetings, just to see what it's all about. I'm the faculty advisor for the club and I really think you might like it," he said, uncrossing his arms and standing up straight.

I nodded again while still looking at the floor. It was the "gay club" Mom had suggested I join after going to orientation. Professor Kitner stepped closer to me and smiled warmly.

"I know this must've been embarrassing," he said, patting my shoulder lightly. "But, if it makes you feel any better, I'm gay. So, honestly, don't worry about what happened today. Okay?" I glanced up at Professor Kitner's smiling, confident face and truly, I did feel a little bit better. Since he was like me, maybe he understood it better. "Well, that's all I wanted to say. I'll see you in class, then," he said and smiled again.

I nodded, whispered, "thank you," and left as fast as I could. I did feel a little better, but it didn't ease the mortifying embarrassment of what had happened. I just wanted to get home so I could mope without interruption.

"Hey, welcome home. How was school?" Wesley said as I walked in the front door.

I was glad to see him, but I couldn't shake the feeling that this was all his fault. It was his sperm after all. I just wanted a little time to cry by myself. I dropped my book bag like it was full of lead and tears streamed down my face.

"Whoa, what's wrong? Are you okay?" Wesley asked, coming to me and wrapping his arms around my back. I sniffled and realized how glad I was that he was here.

"I.... I just had the worst day of my life," I sobbed, clinging to him and burying my face in his chest.

"What happened? Are you okay?" He led me to the sofa and sat down next to me. "Take a deep breath," he said, putting his hand on my knee. "What happened?"

I took deep breaths and my bottom lip quivered. I rubbed my eyes and stared at my lap. "I...I was in my bio lab class and we had to look at plant and animal cells under the microscope. We had to take a swab from inside our mouths and there were these...little things moving around."

Wesley watched me and rubbed my back. The look on his face was curious, but it seemed that, maybe, he knew what I was going to say. His hand slid down my back as he asked what those little things were. I narrowed my eyes as a faint grin spread across his lips.

"It was sperm, stupid! *Your* sperm! 'Cause you made me do that right before class!" I shouted, crossing my arms and pouting. Instead of taking responsibility and sharing my embarrassment, he was laughing! "It's not funny!" I yelled, pushing Wesley away.

"Oh. Oh God, yes it is!" Wesley panted, trying to calm his laughter. "I'm sorry, but it really is!"

"No it's not, stupid! Stop laughing! It's not funny!" I shouted, crossing my arms on my chest again.

"I'm sorry, really," he said, wrapping both arms around me. "Are you okay? If you want, I'll take full responsibility. I'll even go to your next class and explain that it was mine, okay?" He said it with such a serious face that I didn't realize he was making fun of me. Tears rolled down my cheeks again and Wesley wiped them away. "I'm sorry. I won't tease you anymore. I'm sorry. So what happened then?"

I wiped my nose with the back of my hand and took another deep breath. "Well, Professor Kitner whispered it to me, so I don't think anyone else heard. And then he said something about enzymes or something, so that Josh wouldn't figure it out."

"Who's Josh?"

“My lab partner. But, then, after class, Professor Kitner wanted to talk to me. He told me not to worry about it, but I can’t help it. He told me… but maybe he was just trying to help. He told me that he’s gay too and he’s also the advisor for the LGBT club on campus. He wanted me to go to one of the meetings,” I rambled.

“Well, it could’ve been a hell of a lot worse. I think he was right though, so don’t worry about it,” Wesley said. “If he told you that he was gay and about the club, I think he just wanted to make you comfortable. So, yeah, don’t worry about it.”

Wesley ruffled my hair and I leaned into him. Maybe he was right; it was really embarrassing, but Professor Kitner did cover for me and keep it secret.

“Oh yeah. Earlier, when you said it was sperm, you emphasized that it was mine. So who else’s would it be?” he asked, narrowing his eyes playfully.

“Dummy,” I muttered. “And just so you know, I’m never doing that to you again,” I said, pinching his arm and finally smiling a little.

“Aw, no! Say you don’t mean it! I’m sorry, Tor! Honest! Please, don’t say that!”

Chapter 29

I SURVIVED somehow. The humiliation and embarrassment of that day slowly became a memory. I was nervous about going to bio class, but my apprehension was laid to rest. Professor Kitner didn't say anything about what happened and he didn't act strangely or treat me differently. He reminded me of the LGBT club meetings each Thursday and I decided I would go to the next one. I thought that if I attended, I might gain more confidence in myself. I was comfortable with my sexuality—that wasn't the problem—but I worried too much about what other people thought.

"Toren? You okay?"

"What?" I looked up and Josh was closing his notebook. I was thinking so hard I hadn't even realized that class had ended. "Oh, sorry. I must've spaced out for a sec," I said, clearing my mind and closing my notebook.

Professor Kitner was collecting the observation sheets and reminded us of the test on Thursday. I quickly scribbled some notes onto my observation sheet that Josh let me copy before Professor Kitner got to our lab table.

"You wanna study for the test together?" Josh asked, shouldering his book bag and leaning against the solid black tabletop.

"Yeah, that'd be great," I said, jamming my notebook in my book bag. "Oh, but I've got a night class tomorrow."

"Oh. Damn. Well, you wanna do it tonight? If you're not busy?"

“Yeah, I can do that. Let’s go to the library then.” I liked studying with someone else; I always seemed to do better when I had someone to study with.

“Okay, but…I’m kinda hungry,” Josh said, placing his hand on his stomach.

“Oh, then let’s go to the U-Mall. The food court’s open ’til nine, right?”

“Uh…yeah. Okay, let’s do that.”

I called Wesley and left a message that I was going to be late when Josh went to the bathroom. I told him to heat up the beef stew in the fridge, but I somehow doubted he would do that. He was probably dining on beer, potato chips, and ice cream.

“So, how do you like college so far?” Josh asked, taking a bite of the sandwich he bought. He offered to buy something for me, but I declined. I would probably have the rest of the stew when I got home. “Better than high school?”

“Yeah, tons better. I was so happy when I graduated from high school. I vowed never to step foot in that place again,” I said, flipping through my notebook.

“Yeah, I hear you. I didn’t like high school either. Actually, I hated high school. I was such a nerd back then. Well, I guess I still am. But….”

“C’mon! Nerds are the new ‘cool’,” I said, especially because I could include myself in that category. Josh laughed and nodded his head.

“Did you go to school around here?” he asked.

“Yeah. I went to Lincoln. Where did you go?”

“I didn’t live around here. About three hours away.”

“Oh, do you live in the dorms then?”

“Not anymore, but I did, my first year. I have an apartment now.”

“That’s so cool! I always wanted to live in the dorms, but I’m only about ten minutes away.”

“Still live with your folks?”

"No, I live with my…roommate." I looked down at the table. "Boyfriend" was on the tip of my tongue, but I couldn't say it. I was disappointed in myself. If I had more confidence, I could've said it without caring what Josh or anyone else thought.

Josh finished his sandwich and we studied for an hour or two. I lost track of time and when I glanced at the clock, it was almost eight-thirty and I wanted to be home by nine.

"Oh! I gotta get going or I'm gonna miss the bus," I said, packing up my things quickly.

"Huh? Don't worry about it. I can give you a ride," Josh said, resting his chin in the palm of his hand.

I glanced at the clock again. I wasn't sure if I could make it to the bus stop on time. "Are you sure? I don't wanna trouble you."

"It's okay. You said you live close, so I don't mind," he said, tilting his head and smiling.

"Thanks. I really appreciate it."

We studied for another fifteen minutes, but then decided to call it a night. Josh drove a red Focus and took me home in half the time the bus ride would have taken. I thanked him for helping me study and for the ride while he smiled and shook his head.

"Oh, Toren. Wait a sec," Josh said, getting out and walking around the back of his car by the time I turned around. "I almost forgot."

Josh slipped his hand around the back of my head and kissed me. My body froze and I didn't exactly know what to do. He pushed his tongue between my lips and before I could struggle to get away, I heard Wesley's voice.

"Toren? What the hell is going on?" Wesley shouted, carrying a garbage bag in one hand.

I pushed Josh away and my stomach tightened. Wesley dropped the trash bag and I could see how angry he was. Of course he would be angry; I would be angry too if I saw Wesley kissing someone else. Just the thought made my stomach drop.

"What the hell are you doing?" he shouted.

I stared at the ground. I couldn't believe what had just happened.

"Oh. You got a boyfriend?" Josh said. I could feel him staring at me.

"Yeah. He does," Wesley answered for me. "And who the hell are you?"

"Sorry. I didn't know. I didn't know you had a boyfriend. Honest," Josh said, taking a step back with his hands up as a sign of concession. "Well, I should probably get going." He passed Wesley and lowered his voice. "Sorry about that, seriously. He's just so tempting, you know?"

"What?" Wesley yelled, watching him walk around the front of the car with narrowed eyes.

"See you in class, Toren," Josh said with a faint grin.

Wesley glared at Josh until he drove away and then he looked at me. Tears rimmed my eyes and I gripped the strap of my book bag.

"So, who the hell was that?" Wesley asked without lifting his heavy gaze.

"Wesley, it…it's not what you think."

"Then what is it? You were kissing him!" His eyes flared with anger and my heart sank. Wesley lowered his gaze and his voice became quieter, but still tinged with anger. "So, were you really just 'studying'?" he asked, glancing at me from the corners of his eyes.

"How—how can you ask that?"

"You were *kissing* him!" Wesley shouted again, his voice breaking with anger. His face was tense and he was grinding his teeth. I had never seen Wesley look like that before. His clenched fists relaxed like he had given up. He stooped and picked up the trash bag. "I have to take the garbage out."

"Wesley! Please, listen to me!"

"I said, I have to take the garbage out. Just go inside," he said, turning his back to me.

"Wesley…."

"I said, go inside!"

Tears rolled down my cheeks as he walked away from me. My shoulders slumped and my heart dropped, but I did as he said and went inside. I put my book bag down and waited by the door. Five minutes passed, then ten minutes, and Wesley still didn't come back. I wrung my hands together. He had never yelled at me like that before. The door opened after a long fifteen minutes and Wesley stepped inside. He glanced at me and looked away quickly.

"Wesley."

"There's some stew left in the fridge if you want it," he said and walked past me.

I reached out and grabbed Wesley's hand. The look on his face pained me to the point that I felt I should be punished.

"Wesley, please! It's not what you think, I swear! You have to believe me!"

Wesley stared at the floor and narrowed his eyes painfully. His voice was weak and he at once seemed so helpless. "But, you were kissing him…."

"I…. I didn't want to. He surprised me. Wesley, I'm sorry." I bit my bottom lip and looked up at Wesley. "I don't want anyone else. I don't want to do that with anyone but you," I said, stepping closer and grasping his T-shirt in my hands. "You have to believe me."

Wesley pulled my head to his chest and wrapped his strong arms around me. I heard his heart beating and his warmth on my cheek. He took a deep breath and squeezed me tighter. "I do believe you. But I just don't trust bastards like that asshole. So, don't let anything like that ever happen again," he said. I could feel his chin on the top of my head as he spoke. "You really have no idea how cute you are, how many guys check you out. I know you're with me, but I can't help but feel nervous that someone might try to steal you away."

"Now you know how I feel all the time," I said. "It makes me happy that people think you're hot and proud that you chose to be with me. But it also makes me worry that someone might take you away from me."

Wesley's embrace slackened and he took my face in his large, hot hands. He stared long into my eyes and with the slightest grin, he brushed his thumb over my lips.

"Can I kiss you?" he asked in an awkward, yet seductive voice.

"Why are you asking?"

"I'm not even sure."

"You're the only one who doesn't have to ask," I whispered, closing my eyes and feeling his lips touch mine.

It was a simple kiss and he pulled back and looked into my eyes again. He took a deep breath and neared my lips again, staying longer and sucking my tongue. The kiss became deeper and stronger and I lost my breath.

"Tor, I love you so much I don't even know what to do with myself," he said, touching his forehead to mine.

"I love you too," I murmured breathlessly. I kissed him sweetly, timidly, and wrapped my arms around his neck. "Make love to me."

Wesley bent over and lifted me up. I kept my arms around his neck and my entire body throbbed with an aching longing that only this man could ease.

Chapter 30

"I'M leaving for work," Wesley whispered, leaning down and kissing my ear. "So, I'll see you tonight. Good luck on your test. Love you," he said, brushing my shoulder blades with his fingertips.

I blinked my eyes and turned onto my back. "Wesley, wait," I said, sitting up and looking down at my lap.

"Hmm?"

Wesley stopped and looked over his shoulder. His profile was outlined by the dim morning light and his features softened handsomely. I swallowed hard; my lower body had already responded to his alluring image.

"Fuck me before you go," I said quietly, daring to look up at Wesley's face. His eyes rounded, but a mischievous grin took over his surprise.

"I hope you're serious, 'cause you just flicked the switch," Wesley said, taking a step toward the bed.

I blushed to my ears and Wesley sat down on the edge of the bed. He pulled the sheet back and smiled. His fingers crawled up my thigh and met me softly. His hand rose and fell, squeezing and rubbing, and I sucked in air sharply, closing my eyes at the intense pleasure.

"Open your thighs more," he said, sitting up on one knee and unzipping his pants.

I leaned forward and lapped at his lips. He tasted like toothpaste and I smiled. I rolled to my side and climbed up on my knees.

“But, I wanna do it the other way,” Wesley said, pouting.

“But your clothes’ll get messy,” I answered, rocking back against him.

Wesley grasped my backside and teasingly dabbed at the entrance. He leaned forward and kissed the small of my back. My voice escaped my control; I was pleading with him. I pushed back against him.

“Wes.…Wesley, don’t tease me,” I whimpered and finally, Wesley pushed his way in.

His navy pants clung to his hips and I only managed to get one button on his shirt open. He pushed forward, moving me at will, and I buried my face in the pillow to stifle the moan in my throat. Wesley’s movements became deeper and my body was awake to his every touch and breath.

“Harder,” I whispered, pushing back against him. “Please, harder!” I wasn’t sure where this insatiable passion came from, but I couldn’t get enough. I felt like I was going to overflow.

Wesley grunted, sighed, then relaxed behind me. I felt him withdraw, his hands brushing over my back and rear as he leaned back on his heels. I tried to catch my breath and slumped onto the bed, happy and exhausted. Wesley cleaned up, zipped up, and kissed the nape of my neck.

“This is the best reason I could ever come up with for being late,” Wesley said, refastening the single button I got undone. He smiled from the doorway, so handsome. “Good luck on your test.”

“I’m gonna ace it for sure!” I said, rolling to Wesley’s side of the bed and pulling the sheet up.

“Don’t I know it,” he smiled, and then slapped the doorframe. “Oh yeah. If Gus calls, just tell him I was balls-deep in your ass and that I’m on my way now.”

My cheeks flared and Wesley laughed. "Go!" I shouted, turning still redder.

"Love you."

"Love you too," I answered. "Don't forget; I'm going to that club meeting tonight."

"Oh yeah. The 'gay club.' Okay. Give me a call when you're done and I'll come and get you."

Wesley left and I heard the front door open and close. I fell asleep again and almost missed my first class. I got dressed and ran for the bus, catching it just in time. I went to class and to the library afterward. I usually went to the U-Mall before bio lab, but I wasn't quite ready to see Josh yet. What happened the other day seemed like a hazy memory, yet I was nervous to see him.

Wesley was the only person I had ever kissed. It was wrong of me to compare their kisses, but Wesley's was just…better. I waited for his kiss, anticipated it, fantasized about it, desired it. Josh's kiss was cold; I didn't like it and I didn't want it. I felt guilty thinking about it, but it made me realize how much I loved Wesley and how much I wanted to be with him.

I made it to class just as Professor Kitner was passing the exams out. Josh smiled and whispered "Hi" and I smiled back, feeling my cheeks turn bright red. I took the test as fast as possible, hoping to finish before Josh did. I turned in my exam and then went to the U-Mall to study until the club meeting started at 7:30.

"Toren! Welcome!" Professor Kitner greeted as I stepped into room 212.

I smiled and waved shyly. There were a lot of kids in the room and I felt my cheeks tinge. Girls and boys looked up at me and smiled or nodded until Josh stood up.

"Hey, Toren. C'mon, sit down," Josh said, touching my back.

I put my book bag down and wondered if anyone in the classroom knew that we had kissed. Josh sat down at the desk beside me, Professor Kitner grinned in my direction, and I felt my ears get hot. My stomach tightened and suddenly I wanted to leave. I took a deep breath and Professor Kitner started the meeting, drawing Josh's gaze away from me.

Professor Kitner was a strong speaker and active in LGBT affairs. He updated the group on various activities that we could participate in, on- and off-campus, as well as a larger, national picture of gay rights and same-sex marriage. He was very devoted and I admired that. I jotted down some information and meeting times that he suggested. He made me want to get involved.

Professor Kitner ended the meeting and thanked us for coming. I was glad that I went and I was excited to tell Mom about it. I called Wesley to let him know I was done and waited in front of the building. The weather was steadily growing colder and it was getting dark earlier and earlier.

"Hey. You need a ride?" Josh asked, stepping beside me.

"No! Um, no, thank you," I said, feeling my heart race.

Josh stepped closer to me and he turned his eyes to the side. I stepped back a little and hoped that I could send Josh on his way before Wesley showed up.

"Look, I'm sorry about the other day. I really didn't know you had a boyfriend."

"Oh, that's okay," I interrupted. Talking about it made it seem all the more embarrassing. I stared at the cement and shifted my weight from foot to foot.

"I just hope I didn't get you in trouble or anything. 'Cause your man seems…."

"Really, it's okay. We worked it out," I said and giggled awkwardly. I hoped Wesley would hurry up or take a long time; I couldn't decide which.

"Well, that's good for you, but bad for me, I guess," Josh said, staring at the ground. "You know, I really like you, Toren. Is there any chance for me at all?" He looked at me earnestly and I felt a slight pain in the pit of my stomach.

"I'm...I'm sorry," I whispered, unsure of what else to say.

Josh sighed and looked up at the dim horizon. He scratched the back of his head and smiled. "Oh well," he said and patted me hard on the back.

Wesley pulled up and my stomach dropped. I stepped forward but he was already out of the car.

"Hey, Tor. You ready?" He came around the car and stepped between Josh and me.

"Um, bye," I said, letting Wesley guide me to the car.

"Bye, Toren. See you next week," Josh said, waving and smiling. He stepped closer to Wesley and narrowed his eyes. "Better keep your eye on him. Toren deserves better, you know," he whispered, close to Wesley's ear, but loud enough that I could hear.

"What the hell did you just say?" Wesley shouted, turning quickly.

"What can I do? He's just too tempting," Josh said with a smirk and waved over his shoulder.

I watched him walk away and Wesley ran around to the driver's side. He slammed the door and gripped the steering wheel, gritting his teeth. I looked at Wesley and bit my lip. I didn't quite know what to say or do.

"Who the fuck does he think he is?" Wesley seethed.

"Wesley."

"Stay the hell away from him," Wesley ordered, glaring at me with furrowed brows.

"Wesley, I can't, exactly. He's my lab partner."

"Then get a new one."

"I can't do that now. But, it doesn't matter anyway."

"Like hell it doesn't."

“No. It doesn’t. You're the only one I want. You know that and I know that and I told Josh that. So, take me home and I’ll prove it,” I said, smiling faintly. I was trying really hard to be sexy.

“You might have to prove it a couple times,” Wesley growled, still angry about Josh, but then he grinned and drove home as fast as he could.

Chapter 31

"HI honey, I'm home! Take your pants off!" Wesley announced. He kissed my cheek as he passed me and put his lunch container in the sink.

"Heh. Welcome home. How was work?" He smelled like auto grease, sweat, and deodorant, a scent that was distinctly his.

"It was work." He stepped behind me and slid his arms around my waist. "How about you? Did you have a good day?" He nuzzled his chin against my neck and shoulder. His prickly stubble tickled my skin.

"Yeah, it was kinda slow though," I answered, slicing through a tomato and dicing it into small cubes.

"So, are you gonna take your pants off?"

I set the knife down on the cutting board and looked at Wesley sideways. "You know, your foreplay has gotten really lazy."

"I'm sorry," Wesley whispered, kissing my neck. "Please take your pants off?" His hands waited at the zipper of my jeans. He pressed his hips against my back and I felt him against my rear. He breathed heavily and I turned around in his arms.

"But, aren't you hungry?"

"Uh-huh. But, sex now, food later," he said, kissing me deeply and unzipping my pants.

"Wait! Wesley!" I protested halfheartedly since he already had his hand down the front of my boxers. My cheeks burned and I covered my mouth with my hand. "Not…not in here."

Wesley yanked my jeans down and took me in his hands. He stroked tenderly and my resistance melted. "But we've never done it in the kitchen," he said with a grin. "And besides, you already got pre-cum."

My body relaxed and then tensed up as he traced the head and the shaft with his agile tongue. He moved his hands around back and expertly tickled the sensitive flesh with his nimble fingers. I clenched my teeth and squeezed my eyes shut, feeling my orgasm course through my entire body.

I was overwhelmed and my knees buckled, but Wesley caught me against the counter. He looked in my eyes and smiled softly, kissing me lightly then deeply. He lowered his pants and tickled the solid shaft. I knelt down, licking enough to lubricate, then stood up and stepped out of my jeans and boxers.

Wesley slid his hands around the back of my thighs and pulled me into him, hard against his stomach. "Up you go," he whispered and lifted me up against the counter. I grasped the edge to keep my balance and Wesley stepped between my knees and pulled me forward to the edge of the counter. "Open your legs a little more," he said quietly and I obeyed, lifting my knees and wrapping my ankles around his waist.

He looked at me, straight in my eyes, and then pressed his way in. He always looked directly in my eyes just as was going to enter me and that expression was the sexiest I had ever seen. I liked making love with him face-to-face, just to see that look, even though it sometimes caused me hip and back strain. I wrapped my arms around his neck and pulled him closer, feeling his heat imprint inside me like a furnace.

He rocked his hips and I gasped with each thrust, taking him as deep as I could. He leaned forward and kissed me, taking me in his hand and rubbing the tip with his palm. I moaned and cried out, but Wesley quieted me with kisses. As he neared crisis, he closed his eyes and gritted his teeth.

"Wes…ley, I'm gonna…."

"It's okay. I gotta wash these anyway," he grunted, as he pushed into me to the root.

My back arched reflexively and I came hard on the front of his shirt. The milky white contrasted with the dark blue and I blushed down to my toes, feeling strangely embarrassed. Wesley came moments later, erupting inside me, pulling me close and hugging me tight.

When he withdrew, I felt loose and damp. I slid off the counter and Wesley caught me in his arms. He kissed me once, then again, and whispered, "I love you."

"I'm gonna go change. Why don't you clean up and I'll finish making dinner," he suggested, slapping my backside.

I nodded and went to the bathroom to wash up. Wesley flipped an omelet in the pan when I came back. He scooped it out of the skillet and gave it to me on a plate. I toasted some bread and we sat down on the sofa to eat and watch TV.

"Oh yeah, I almost forgot. Jeremy's having a Halloween party next Saturday. His folks are going out of town, so he's gonna have some people over," Wesley said, setting his empty plate down on the coffee table.

"That sounds like fun," I said, taking the last bite of my omelet. It was really good; Wesley always said that he couldn't cook, but he was really good at making breakfast foods. He wanted to get a charcoal grill because he said he could grill anything, but we didn't have the extra money yet.

"But there's a catch: he won't let us in unless we dress up."

I knew Wesley wasn't the type to dress up for Halloween, but I thought it would be fun. I had to think of a costume for him that he wouldn't object to. "Have you thought about what you wanna be?" I asked with a grin, secretly enjoying his discomfiture.

"No, but I thought about what I want you to be." I knew the look on his face too well. "Two words: French maid."

"One word: veto," I answered, rolling my eyes and shaking my head. I folded my arms on my chest resolutely.

"But, come on! You would look so good!"

"No chance. If you want a French maid so much, you dress up as one!"

"But I don't have the legs for it."

"And I do?" I argued. "Or have you forgotten that I'm a guy too?"

"That's what would make it so hot!"

I sighed and looked at Wesley right in his eyes. He knew he was defeated, but he was still trying. I closed my eyes and resigned myself to the fact that my boyfriend was a pervert. He was lucky he was so cute.

"No. No no no. But, how about this? You can be a dog and I'll be your master. You can get ears and a tail and those slippers that look like paws, oh, and a collar and leash. Then you just follow me around and obey my every command," I suggested, figuring that I should get him back for the French maid idea. But he actually seemed to be considering it.

"You be a cat and I'll be a dog," he offered, looking at me with a smile at the corner of his lips. I thought about dressing up like a pirate or Dracula, but this wasn't so bad; it might be fun. "You know, Catwoman; Halle Berry or Michelle Pfeiffer, I'll let you pick."

I looked at Wesley and pinched his cheeks hard. "Why do you always have to go there? You're such a pervert!"

"I was just kidding!" Wesley moaned, batting my hands away and rubbing his cheeks. "Ow."

"You deserve it, you big dummy."

"All right. We'll go as a cat and dog and you can be any cat you want," he conceded, threading his hand around my shoulder. "You can be whatever you want as long as you're with me."

Chapter 32

I WORE a black turtleneck, blue jeans, and black slippers that looked like paws. I had a long, black tail pinned to the back of my pants and black cat ears glued to a headband. I painted the tip of my nose black and drew four whiskers on both my cheeks. Wesley told me that I looked adorable, but I felt kinda silly.

Wesley, on the other hand, looked so cute. He had brown dog ears, a brown tail, and brown dog-paw slippers. He wore blue jeans, a brown long-sleeve shirt, and a red collar. I tried to persuade him into wearing a leash, but he wouldn't go for it. After much argument, he finally let me paint his nose and draw whiskers.

"Hi! Come on in," Jeremy said, opening the door wide. He had a patch over one eye, a black hat with a skull and crossbones, and a red and white striped shirt. He looked pretty cute too, with thick stubble covering his chin, and he even had a silver-painted plastic sword at his waist.

"Hey, Captain," Wesley said and held up a case of beer. Jeremy nodded and told him there was room in the fridge.

"What's up, Toren?" Jeremy smiled and patted my back. Wesley took the six-pack of beer that I was carrying and disappeared into the kitchen. "I'm so glad you guys could make it."

"Thanks. I'm glad we could come. Um, we had some leftover candy from last night, so I thought I'd bring it over," I said, holding up a plastic tub of mini candy bars. “We didn’t get as many trick-or-treaters as I thought we would.”

“Cool. Thanks,” he said and took the tub that I offered.

He closed the door behind me and I looked around the large house. There were about ten people already there, some that I recognized from high school but didn’t know. Jeremy walked toward the kitchen and Alycia came running out, the fringe of her costume flapping with her movements.

“Hi, Toren! Oh my God, you look so cute!” I could tell by the pitch of her voice that she was already drunk. I laughed and looked her over.

“You look really good,” I said.

“Thanks. Watch this!” She twisted her hips and waist back and forth to make the fringe spin out. She wore a headband with a feather, a long string of pearls with a knot in it, and a red, low-cut, fringy flapper dress. She looked cute and I could tell Jeremy thought so too by the way he glanced at her at every chance. “And know what? All this fringe is glued and stapled on! Mom helped me.”

“Stapled?” I asked. That was my sister: the ghetto Martha Stewart.

“Hey, Alycia!” Wesley called from the kitchen. He walked toward us carrying two beers. “You ran right past me in the kitchen,” he complained with a pout as he gave me one of the beers.

“Wes! I’m sorry. Maybe I didn't recognize you though!” she said, giving him a hug. Wesley stood next to me and Alycia looked us over. “You guys are so cute! A dog and a cat! That’s adorable!”

Wesley rolled his eyes and I elbowed him in the gut. We went into the kitchen where most of the people were. Many greeted Wesley familiarly and glanced at me awkwardly. Most of them were popular kids in high school and probably surprised to see me at one of their parties. Wesley introduced me without giving up our relationship, which I was glad he didn’t announce, although the matching costumes were a dead giveaway. However, he didn’t act any differently toward me and after a little while, I was sure everyone knew we were together. When they didn’t say anything or act strangely toward me, I began to feel much more comfortable, but that could have been because I was already starting my second beer.

"All right. Beer pong in the basement and boxhead at the kitchen table," Jeremy announced, waving over his head a case box with a hole cut out.

Wesley pushed me toward the kitchen table and took a seat. Jeremy and Alycia sat down and three others pulled chairs up to the table. Some people went down to the basement and the last few remained in the living room chatting.

"How do you play?" Alycia asked, sipping her beer.

"It's a dice game and it's a lot of fun. I'll teach the rules as we go," Jeremy said, picking up two dice and pushing a placemat to the center of the table. He gave a quick rundown of the game, the main point being if you rolled an 11 or 12, you were the boxhead, wore the box, and were at the mercy of everyone else. Each combination of dice had a different meaning, like making up a rule, giving away drinks, and something called a "waterfall."

"Basically, it's just a game to get you drunk faster," Wesley said, tipping back his beer and smiling. "And I'm gonna make sure you get sloshed."

"Oh, absolutely!" Alycia chimed in, nodding her head.

"Just hope you don't roll an 11 or 12 with these two," Jeremy said.

And with that warning, I rolled an 11 on my second turn. Anyone could tell me to drink at any time, for any reason. I was seriously screwed, but I was more worried about what Wesley might come up with if I had to do anything he said.

I was the boxhead for more than half the game and I lost track of how many beers I drank. I felt silly and light, like I was floating in water. Alycia was the next to roll a 12, so I had fun exacting my revenge, as did Wesley and especially Jeremy. After her third or fourth beer, we decided to take a break, at least to let Alycia and me recover a little.

Wesley went outside for a cigarette and, for some inexplicable reason, I decided to have another beer. There were only five beers left of the eighteen we brought and I really had no clue how many I had. I shrugged my shoulders with a grin and twisted the cap off.

"Hey, Toren. How you doing?" Jeremy asked, leaning into the refrigerator and taking out a beer.

"Pretty good," I tried to answer soberly, though I couldn't keep myself from grinning. "How are you?"

"Toasted," he responded happily and popped the top of his beer. "I think I might have to cut off Alycia pretty soon though."

"I know. She can be a handful even when she's stone-cold sober," I said, nodding my head.

"That's for sure," he agreed with a smile. "But she's so much fun. And so cute!" he added, his cheeks blushing lightly. He glanced down at the floor and turned the bottle around in his hands. "You know, I really like her," he said. "I know she just broke up with her boyfriend, but I'm pretty serious about her," he confided awkwardly.

It was kinda cute, hearing him nervously express his feelings. He was looking for my approval; after all, I was her older brother and he was her suitor. But he knew he already had my approval.

"I think she's serious about you too, but I think she's scared of moving too fast. Just go along at her pace," I said, taking a long sip of beer.

Jeremy's face brightened and he grinned. His mood was transparent, but I thought the alcohol might be to blame. He slapped my back and laughed.

"You're all right, Tor," he said, still slapping my back. "I mean it too. You and Wes are a perfect match. We grew up together, you know, and he's always been a moody bastard, but since you guys started going out, he's actually happy! So, just so you know, I'll always be cheering for you guys."

I blushed and looked at the bottle in my hands. "Th-thanks," I murmured, feeling my cheeks flare. It was an odd, but good, feeling, hearing Jeremy say that he'd be cheering for us. I smiled and felt a warmth in the pit of my stomach that I knew wasn't just the alcohol.

"Hey, Carroll! What's going on? I haven't seen you in forever!"

I looked up as I heard Wesley's last name and saw Alan Dunne walking in the front door, followed by Benny Wright.

"Alan, it has been a while, man. How you doing? S'up, Ben?" Wesley answered, bumping fists with Alan and nodding his head at Benny.

"Pretty good. Where've you been? I haven't seen you since graduation," Alan said, glancing around at the people in the living room.

"Hey, Wes! C'mon, let's play another game!" Alycia interrupted, walking up from nowhere. Alan's eyes widened as he looked her up and down and a smile crept across his lips. She coiled her arm around Wesley's and tugged impatiently.

"Well now, who's this?" Alan asked, glancing at Wesley, but quickly returning his attention to Alycia.

"Hi! I'm Alycia," she answered, dropping Wesley's arm, bowing slightly, and smiling broadly. She twisted her body so that the fringe of her dress spun out. I chuckled in spite of myself. She was always outgoing and friendly, but it was blatant when she was drunk.

"Not bad, man. Not bad at all," Alan said, smiling slyly at Wesley. My heart skipped when he thought Wesley and Alycia were together. "You had me so worried there for a while, especially with those rumors Jen's spreading around," Alan continued, looking Alycia over one more time.

I gritted my teeth just hearing Jen's name, but I forced myself to calm down. I took a long drink and turned the bottle around in my hands.

"What? What are you talking about?" Wesley asked, glancing at Alycia briefly. "Just what is Jen saying?"

"She's making shit up about you 'switching teams,' if you get me. I mean, you did start hanging out with that little queer all of a sudden. But, I can see you got your priorities straight," Alan explained with a laugh.

My stomach dropped. He was talking about me. No one had ever called me that before and it stuck in my ears. I gripped my hands tightly around the bottle and I could feel Jeremy glance at me.

"What? Who are you talking about?" Alycia asked, her chipper voice gaining an edge.

"You know, that little fag from school. I forgot his name."

"Toren?" Wesley said.

"Yeah, him. I don't know why…."

"You're really an asshole, aren't you?" Alycia said, her voice an octave deeper.

"What'd you say?" Alan asked, narrowing his eyes.

"Didn't know you were hard of hearing too. I said: you're an *ass*hole."

"Who the hell do you think you are, bitch?" Alan retorted.

"She's my boyfriend's sister, jackass," Wesley said, his voice deep and sharp. "And you better watch your fucking mouth," he warned, lifting his head and staring into Alan's eyes.

I swallowed hard and Jeremy left my side, walking up to Wesley, Alycia, and Alan. My stomach felt hollow as I watched from the kitchen, unable to will myself to take a step forward.

"You've gotta be fucking kidding me!" Alan said, shaking his head. He saw Jeremy walking toward him and held his hands up in inquiry. "Did you know about this?"

"Look, if you're gonna be a dick, why don't you just take off?" Jeremy said, standing next to Alycia and folding his arms on his chest.

Alan shook his head. "What the fuck? Am I supposed to believe you like guys now because some fag came on to you?"

Each time he said that word, my chest felt a little tighter. I swallowed hard and bit my lower lip, trying to keep my tears at bay. Wesley was standing up for me and I couldn't even bring myself to stand next to him. I felt like a coward; even Alycia and Jeremy were sticking up for me, but I couldn't do anything.

"I told you to watch your fucking mouth!" Wesley shouted, throwing his fist forward and hitting Alan squarely in the jaw.

Alan recoiled, covering his chin with his hand and looking at Wesley with angry eyes. "What the hell?"

"Why don't you just leave, Alan?" Jeremy said, stepping in front of Alycia in case Alan retaliated.

"Like I'd wanna hang out with a buncha fags," Alan said, still holding his chin and glaring at Wesley. He glanced at Jeremy then turned around and left, followed by Benny who never said a word the entire time.

Wesley shook his hand and stared at the door until Jeremy closed it. His eyes were narrow and angry and he gritted his teeth. Alycia touched his arm and he took a deep breath. He looked over his shoulder and found me still standing in the kitchen, gripping the beer bottle in my hands. He stepped past Alycia and Jeremy and walked over to me, his eyes never leaving mine.

I took a deep breath. He walked up and hugged me so tight I could feel his ribs pressing against my own. The other people at the party didn't matter; I clung to him and buried my face in the cradle of his neck and shoulder. It was the strangest sense of pride; he punched someone to defend me.

"I'm sorry. Are you okay?" he asked, lifting my head from his shoulder.

I nodded and smiled weakly. "How's your hand?" I asked, looking at his hand and rubbing my fingers over his knuckles.

I could feel eyes watching us, though people tried to pretend that they weren't paying attention. And I didn't mind sharing this moment of intimacy with them. I smiled at Wesley and he smiled back, taking the beer from my hands and finishing it in one gulp. Alycia and Jeremy came up to us and Jeremy apologized for Alan's stupidity. Alycia cursed him up one side and down the other and pretty soon, we were all laughing.

The night wore on and I wished that one of us were sober enough to drive because I really wanted to get home. The events of the evening, Wesley's unmitigated defense of me, and the alcohol had left me a little hot and bothered. But Alycia, Wesley, and I stayed the night at Jeremy's and we ended up playing beer pong until there wasn't any beer left. Fortunately, Wesley and I both had the next day off from work, because we didn't wake up until three the next afternoon. Tired and hung-over, we got fast food for dinner and were in bed again by eight.

Chapter 33

"THAT quiz totally sucked!" Mark complained, shaking his head and furrowing his brows. "How'd you do?"

"Pretty good, I think. I only got two wrong," I answered, following him out of the classroom.

"There were only two questions," Mark said, then grinned. He pulled at the shoulder strap of his book bag.

"I know. I'm just math-stupid," I conceded, buttoning my coat as we left the Sciences building.

Mark and I met in our pre-calc class. We gravitated toward each other, because we were both terrible at math and because he was gay too. It was sort of a "takes one to know one" situation and we became friends quickly.

"So, do you have any plans for Thanksgiving?" he asked. A cool breeze whipped through his brown hair and he glanced at me sideways.

"I'm not sure yet. I'm gonna go to my mom's and Wesley's welcome of course, but I kinda want him to go home for Thanksgiving. I mean, he hasn't really seen or talked to his parents since we moved in."

"That's too bad," Mark said quietly, staring at the ground. "It took a while, but Jared and I have finally figured out a family holiday schedule. We spend Thanksgiving with his family and Christmas Eve with mine. We sleep over, well, because my mom still likes to play Santa Claus," he confided, blushing lightly. "I mean, I'm twenty-four and I still get presents from Santa! Then, we spend Christmas morning with my family and the rest of the day with his. It took a couple years to get everything squared away, but we got it all worked out."

I smiled and imagined spending Christmas with Wesley's family and the thought sent chills down my spine. I was glad for Mark though. He was older and smarter than I was and he always seemed to inspire me. He was friends with Professor Kitner and an advocate of same-sex marriage. He and his boyfriend, Jared, wore matching rings so that the symbol of their bond was present; now they just needed the benefits opposite-sex couples enjoyed.

"I don't know if we'll be able to do that. Wesley's family.... Well, his parents objected to our relationship from the start. But my mom's really cool and pretty much thinks of Wesley as a second son," I said, shoving my hands in my coat pockets and smiling faintly.

"It's too bad about his family," Mark said, looking down and shaking his head.

I nodded and looked down the sidewalk. Several students were walking around campus, some wearing just sweatshirts and others wearing thick, winter coats. It was hard to tell what season it was by looking at all the different layers people were wearing. One of the kids wearing a sweatshirt looked like Wesley and I squinted my eyes for a better look. My heart started beating faster and a giant smile dawned on my face. It was him, and I waved and shouted his name. He smiled and walked toward me, then looked at Mark and lost his grin.

"Hi! What are you doing here?" I asked, feeling giddy through my whole body. Wesley looked really handsome and I was excited to show him off to Mark.

"I thought I'd see if you wanted to get lunch," Wesley said, glancing at Mark again with a sour look.

"Yeah, of course!" Wesley had never visited me at school and I was happy to see him. It was Monday, his day off, so I knew he made an effort to come see me. "Oh, I'm sorry!" I said, thudding my head with my palm and turning to Mark. "Mark, this is my boyfriend, Wesley.

Wesley, this is Mark." Mark extended his hand and Wesley shook it, his expression easing up with what looked like relief.

"It's nice to meet you. Toren talks about you all the time," Mark said with a smile and I felt myself blush. "I gotta get to my next class, so I'll see you Wednesday, Toren. It was nice meeting you, Wesley. Have a good lunch!" Mark said, stepping backward, turning and waving.

I waved goodbye to Mark, then looked at Wesley. "C'mon, let's go get lunch. My treat!" I said, taking Wesley's hand briefly. He followed and smiled back at me and we went to the cafeteria in the University Mall. There was a McDonald's, a Subway, and a Domino's and Wesley got a pizza and I got a sub. We shared our lunches, but Wesley wasn't eating very much. He seemed a little off; not exactly depressed, but definitely not himself. I asked him if something was bothering him, but he denied it, explaining that he was just tired. He had been busy at work the past couple of days, so I accepted his excuse without question. I told him about my math quiz and he said he would see if he could help. He was lucky; he could just read the textbook and understand it while I needed it spelled out for me. Wesley sipped his soda and sighed heavily.

"Are you sure you're okay?" I asked again, taking another slice of pizza. I couldn't shake the feeling that something was bothering him.

"Yeah, I'm just tired," he reiterated and sighed again.

"You're not acting like yourself. I want my old Wesley back," I said, brushing his hand on the table. He smiled, but it was like he was appeasing me. I glanced at the clock and looked at Wesley. I was disappointed that I had to go to class. "Thank you so much for coming to see me. It was the nicest present," I said, putting all the trash on the tray.

"No problem. I thought it would be fun to surprise you," he said, standing up and taking the tray.

We walked outside and Wesley walked with me to the liberal arts building. I took his hand and squeezed it quickly.

"Well, I gotta get to class. I should be home around five-thirty. So, I'll see you when I get home, okay? I love you," I said, smiling warmly and hoping that he would cheer up.

"All right. I'll see you later. Love you too." He waved over his shoulder and I watched him walk away.

I made a late dinner of chicken noodle soup for us because I thought that maybe Wesley was getting sick. But he had two bowls of soup and two slices of toast. We watched TV quietly, but Wesley didn't seem to be paying attention; his mind was somewhere else. I snuggled close to him on the sofa, resting my head against his shoulder. His arm was resting on the back of the sofa, but he didn't ruffle my hair or put his arm around my shoulders. I was pressed close to him, but he kept his gaze on the TV.

"Do you think we'll be together forever?" Wesley asked, out of the blue.

"I don't believe in forever," I answered devilishly, though it was true.

"Huh?"

I felt Wesley's body tense beside me and I pushed my head against his shoulder. "Forever is a long time. It's not even quantifiable. You can't promise something you don't know."

Wesley sighed. "I was hoping for something a little more reassuring."

"I think we'll be together as long as we both want to be. People change over time, but I think we'll be okay as long as we make each other happy," I said, hoping that reassured him.

"But you're already changing, aren't you?" Wesley whispered, nearly inaudibly.

"What?"

"You're already changing," he repeated. "You'll outgrow me one day. While you're going to school, meeting new people, and learning new things, I'll still be in the same place."

He continued staring at the TV with a blank look on his face. My stomach felt hollow. He didn't really feel that way, did he?

"What are you even talking about?" I asked, sitting up and looking into his eyes. He turned his gaze from the TV to the floor.

"Five years from now, you'll have your degree and a good job, and your life will be totally different from mine. You deserve someone who can keep up with you, who'll grow and change with you, someone smarter and more interesting than me. Someone who won't hold you back."

"What the hell are you talking about?" I shouted, jolting Wesley with the tone of my voice. It was the first time I ever raised my voice to him and my eyes teared up. "Who cares about the future? I wanna be with you now, but you sound like you wanna break up!"

Wesley stared at me for a long moment, then shook his head. "I don't want to break up. I wanna be with you forever, but I also want you to be happy and I don't want to hold you back. I can't help thinking about the future and my place in yours. You've got a ton to offer, Toren, and I just…."

I swallowed hard and wiped away the tears on my cheeks. I didn't understand what he was talking about and I didn't know what to say. I felt Wesley staring at me, but I couldn't look at him.

"Just forget it. Forget I said anything," Wesley murmured, furrowing his brows and standing up. "I'm just tired and my mind's not quite all there," he said with a forced laugh. "Want something to drink?"

I shook my head. I felt miserable inside and now Wesley was acting like nothing had happened. When he came back from the kitchen with a beer, he sat down with his arm around my shoulders. We watched TV quietly until I went to bed around eleven. Wesley said he was tired, but he didn't come to bed. I waited for him and realized I had trouble falling asleep without his arm draped over my waist. I had gotten so used to his warmth that my entire body felt cold without him. When he finally did come to bed, he lay down with his back to me. My heart hurt and I felt like he was out of reach, even though he was lying right next to me.

I GOT ready for school while Wesley slept. I felt awful and tired, but I went to school anyway. I didn't know how to talk to Wesley today.

When I said goodbye, he smiled and lifted his head from the pillow, told me to have a good day and that he loved me. He sounded normal, but he usually got up with me on his days off. We'd have breakfast together, then he'd take a nap while I was at school. Nothing was right this morning and the stress tightened knots in my stomach.

I went to my first class, but it was pointless; I couldn't concentrate on anything. Between classes, I went to the Mall and got a soda and a muffin. I sat down at an empty table and wondered how I went from feeling so happy yesterday afternoon to feeling so miserable today. I was so excited that Wesley came to visit me, but he didn't seem like himself yesterday afternoon either. I wondered what on earth was making him act so strange.

"Hey, Toren!" Josh shouted from across the cafeteria. "What's going on?" he asked when he neared my table.

I sighed quietly and forced a smile. "Nothing. How are you?"

"Pretty good. You ready for Bio?"

"Yeah, I guess." I sighed again. I sighed with every breath I took. I collected the muffin and straw wrapper and stood up. Josh followed me as I dumped it into the trash bin and walked to the side exit.

"Are you okay?" Josh asked, tilting his head to the side. "You seem kinda down today."

"Yeah, I'm fine," I said. "I'm just tired. And something's bothering Wesley, but he won't talk to me about it."

"Hmm. Wonder if he took what I said to heart," Josh mused aloud, looking up at the sky as we walked toward the sciences building.

"What do you mean?" I asked, following Josh's eyes to the light gray clouds overhead.

"I ran into him yesterday on campus. It was pretty funny; he looked so out of place here," Josh said, then looked at me. "Seriously, Toren, you need to leave that guy behind. He's just gonna hold you back."

"What?" I stopped and glared at Josh. "Just what the hell did you say to him?" My stomach tightened and I balled my hands into fists. Josh looked at me and seemed amused.

"I just told him the truth: that you deserved better. You're just limiting yourself by staying with him."

"Shut up! Just shut up! You don't know me, and you sure as hell don't know Wesley! He's a hell of a lot better than you could ever be! Don't you ever talk to him again!" I shouted. "Just leave us alone!" Josh's face contorted in a strange emotion mixed with surprise and I felt him staring holes into my back.

As I hurried to the bus stop, everything seemed to make sense in a disconnected way. Now I knew why Wesley seemed out of it. Josh had put salt in an already sensitive wound. Wesley was always insecure about his intelligence; his parents always told him that he wasn't as smart as his brother was and that he could never be as successful. Now, Josh told him that he wasn't smart enough to be with me. I wished the bus would get me home faster.

I opened the front door and shouted Wesley's name. He stood up, startled, from the sofa and looked at me. Tears began to fall from my eyes and I wiped them away.

"Wha…. I thought you were in class till six." Wesley said, surprised to see me and no doubt wondering about the tears in my eyes.

I stared at him for a moment, trying to think of something to say. My tears streamed down my cheeks and I ran in to him with my book bag still on my back. "You big…stupid…dummy!" I shouted, failing to express my feelings more accurately. "Why didn't you tell me you talked to Josh yesterday?" I asked, pulling my head back and looking up at Wesley. "Why do you believe what a jerk like that says? Why don't you believe me?"

Wesley stared at me bewildered for a moment, then put his hands on my shoulders. I felt calmer just with his touch. "I'm sorry. I just…. I don't know," Wesley mumbled awkwardly.

"When I say 'I love you,' I mean it! I don't want to be with anyone else. You're the only one that can make me happy. So why don't you believe me when I tell you? Do I not tell you enough? Or show you? I know you mean it when you say you love me, so how can I make you believe me?" I rambled, asking questions that I didn't even understand. I was making this his fault again, but I knew it was mine. I knew his insecurities and I did nothing to help make him stronger. "I'm sorry! I'm sorry, Wesley!"

"Toren, calm down," Wesley said, gripping my shoulders tighter. But I shook my head. Wesley felt bad yesterday and I only made him feel worse. "Toren, c'mon," he said, then slid his hands around my back and pulled me close. I felt his hand ruffle my hair and his fingertips between my shoulder blades. I could feel his ribs when he took a deep breath and I could hear my own heart beating.

"I'm sorry," I whimpered.

"For what? There's nothing for you to be sorry for."

"But, I knew. I knew something was bothering you and I didn't…."

"It's okay. I was just feeling sorry for myself and I took it out on you. I just…. I can't help but worry that I don't deserve to be with you," he whispered.

"Don't even say that! I don't deserve to be with you," I answered, lowering my eyes. "I love you so much it scares me sometimes. I don't know what I'd do without you."

"I feel the same way. It is kinda scary, but I do know that I wanna be with you. Forever. Regardless if you believe in it or not."

I smiled and laughed quietly. Now, forever didn't seem long enough. He kissed me sweetly on my lips and I closed my eyes and ran my fingers though his hair. His kiss became deeper and my body felt like it was melting.

"Why didn't you tell me you ran into Josh?" I asked, pulling back from his alluring lips.

"I don't know. It didn't seem important," he answered with a sigh.

"I was ready to punch him. Heh, I told him never to talk to you again," I confided, recalling my outburst. I felt a little embarrassed because I would have to see Josh on Thursday, but I meant every word I said. Wesley was a million times the man Josh could even dream of being.

"I wish I could tell him the same thing. I just can't wait for this semester to be over so you won't have to see that prick again," Wesley said, hugging me tightly, protectively.

I nuzzled my face against his chin and neck in agreement. But it didn't matter, because the cutest, smartest, funniest, sweetest guy in the whole world had his arms wrapped around me and I didn't have to share him with anyone. I didn't care if I was greedy; Wesley was mine and it was like no one else in the world existed.

Chapter 34

I GLANCED at my co-worker Jeanine, then at the man sitting on a stool in front of me. He had tattoos covering both arms and the back of his neck and a piercing in his eyebrow and lip. He was young, probably 24 or 25, and cute in an eclectic kind of way. He held my tongue out with a clamp, basically a pair of glorified tongs, and marked the middle of my tongue with blue ink.

"All right, you're gonna feel some pressure, but it shouldn't hurt and it'll be over in a sec, okay?" he said.

"O-pay," I managed, nodding slightly.

The man picked up a sterilized needle from a tray on the table beside him and I tried to swallow, unsuccessfully. He looked at me with the needle in his right hand and smiled.

"I'm gonna count to three and on three, I want you to exhale," he explained.

"O-pay," I answered, nodding again.

He counted slowly and I glanced at Jeanine and then balled my hands into fists. I exhaled deeply on three and the needle punctured my tongue quickly and cleanly. Fortunately, my tongue and jaw were numb and I only felt a lot of pressure and a dull ache. The man removed the piercing tool and screwed the ball onto the post of the stud. Carefully he removed the tongs and I pulled my tongue back into my mouth. He smiled again and handed me a small, round mirror. I stuck my tongue out, looked at the silver metal ball atop my tongue and grinned. Jeanine stood in front of me and nodded with a thumbs-up.

"It looks great, Tor!" she said and stuck out her own tongue. "Now we match!"

The man that did the piercing smiled lightly then explained how to care for and clean it, accompanied by a badly copied square of paper with the same information. I thanked him and gave him thirty dollars, twenty-five for the piercing and a five-dollar tip. Then Jeanine and I went out to her car.

"Let me see it again," she said, turning on the interior light after she started the car. I stuck my tongue out and she squealed the way only girls could. "That's so cool! And with your innocent face, no one would even suspect that you had your tongue pierced!"

I glanced at her sideways then laughed, picking up the grocery bag with the bottle of Biotene in it. I smiled, feeling the metal ball on the roof of my mouth. The numbness was fading and was replaced with a dull ache.

Jeanine drove me home and then asked to see it again as she idled in front of my apartment building. "It looks great, Toren. Wes's gonna love it, for sure," she said, nodding her head affirmatively.

"Thanks so much for going with me. And taking me," I said, laying the grocery bag on my lap.

"No problem! When do you work next?"

"Not 'til Friday," I answered. I only worked Fridays, Saturdays, and Sundays since I had school Monday through Thursday.

"Well, you should be pretty used to it by then. It might be uncomfortable sometimes, but just use the mouthwash three times a day, eat soft foods, and trust me, *no straws*!"

"Thanks so much for going with me," I said again and Jeanine shook her head. "I'll see you Friday."

"All right. Call if you have any questions or whatever."

I nodded, said goodbye, and shut the door. She left as I was walking up the stairs to the third floor. Wesley was home; I saw his car in the parking lot. The piercing was his birthday present and I knew there was no way to hide it from him for a week.

It had all started at work. Jeanine had laughed and I saw flash of silver in her mouth. As it turned out, she had her tongue pierced before we even met and I never noticed. I asked her why she had it and she answered that it was because it was neat…and her boyfriend loved it. Since I had been wracking my brain for a birthday present for Wesley, it seemed obvious. I asked Jeanine where she had it done and the conversation led to Wesley's birthday in a week. She explained that I should get it done soon if I wanted to "use" it on his birthday since it took about a week to heal and get used to. So after work, we went to a crumbling little storefront with a neon "tattoo" sign in the window. It was surprisingly clean and sterile inside despite its outward appearance. And now, I had a hole in my tongue.

"Hi, I'm home," I announced, walking in the front door. Wesley was in the kitchen, staring into the fridge.

"Hey, how ya doin'?" he asked, closing the refrigerator door.

"Pretty good. How are you? How was work?" I asked, dropping the bag with the mouthwash by the door.

"It was good. It was work," he answered. He was still wearing his navy work outfit so he must've just gotten home. I took off my coat and hung it on a hook by the front door. He opened the freezer door and looked inside. "Did you eat yet?"

"No, not yet. I'll make something for us," I answered, stepping into the kitchen.

"I thought you went out for dinner with that girl from work," he said, closing the freezer door.

I smiled in spite of myself, pushing the silver ball against the top of my mouth. "No, we did something else," I answered broadly.

"Like what? Anything I should be worried about?" he asked with a grin. He knew he could joke about cheating because I'd never do it—and because I was with a girl.

"Nope, just got your birthday present," I said.

Wesley's face lit up and he approached me with an excited smile. "What is it?"

"I can't tell you yet. Except if you try to kiss me," I said. The numbness in my tongue and jaw were gone and the pain was negligent unless I swallowed hard.

"Well, then, come here."

"No, you can't," I said, blocking his lips with my hands.

"What? I can't kiss you?"

"No, 'cause it'll hurt."

Wesley looked at me with a confused expression and I smiled. "Why will it hurt?"

"Because," I said, smiling shyly, "I got something for you." I blushed, sticking my tongue out. Wesley stared with wide eyes at the metal stud poked through my tongue. I pulled my tongue back in and giggled.

"Show me again," he said, stepping closer to me.

I stuck my tongue out again and quickly pulled it back in. My cheeks were red and I couldn't stop giggling playfully.

"You got that…for me?" Wesley asked, still with a look of confusion.

I widened my eyes at him. Could I actually be the more perverted one here? I smiled and bit my lip. "Think about it," I said, looking in Wesley's eyes and then dropping my gaze. "Just think about it lower."

Wesley's eyes rounded and a great smiled dawned on his face. "Are you serious?" I laughed at his elated outburst; this was the reaction I was expecting. "I can't believe it!" I giggled again as I blocked Wesley's lips. "What, I really can't kiss you?"

"No, it'll hurt. It takes about a week to heal, so that's why I had to get it today," I explained. Wesley gave me a mock pout and he looked so cute. "Well, maybe just a light kiss," I conceded. Wesley's lips touched mine gently and I closed my eyes. "Happy early birthday."

IT was November 9, Wesley's birthday, and I was on my way to Mom and Alycia's. I had thought about taking the day off work, but Wesley insisted on going in, so I decided not to request the day off. If I couldn't be with Wesley on his birthday, it was better to earn money.

I left work at 4:00 and got to Mom's place around 4:30. She wanted to help celebrate Wesley's birthday and bought all the ingredients for a delicious dinner that I was going to make. Alycia said she would take care of the cake.

I knocked and let myself in. Alycia greeted me at the door and Mom followed her. We said hello and hugged, then got down to business. Wesley got off work at 5:00 and if he didn't stop at home, he would arrive at around 5:15.

Mom bought chicken, pasta, Parmesan cheese, tomato sauce, salad stuff, and a French baguette. I was making from scratch an Italian meal that I found on the Internet and modified to Wesley's tastes. I was excited about it because I had never made it and Wesley ordered something like it in a restaurant once and really enjoyed it. From the pantry I got the apron, which I suspected hadn't been used since I left, and got to work.

Alycia was eager to show me the cake that she and Mom made for Wesley. It was a two-layer yellow cake with chocolate frosting. In the middle, written in white icing, was "Happy Birthday Wesley!" It also had the sugar-pressed decorations sold in stores that come packaged against stiff cardboard. Mom apologized for the yellow flowers around the side of the cake and the larger pink and yellow bouquet on top, below the writing. It was kinda girly, but it strangely suited Wesley, as Alycia pointed out.

Wesley arrived twenty minutes after 5:00 and we all jumped and shouted "Happy Birthday!" when he opened the door, even though it wasn't a surprise party. He smiled indulgently, expecting nothing less from my family and we paraded him in with smiles and shouts. Alycia and Mom got to him first and he hugged them, but smiled at me over their shoulders. He was still wearing his navy work clothes and I smiled with a naughty idea floating through my head.

"Man, what are you making? It smells so good in here!" Wesley said, after giving me a tight hug.

"Just wait and see. I hope you're gonna like it," I said, turning back to the kitchen. "It's just about ready."

Alycia set the table for four while Mom got drinks for us. Wesley went to the bathroom to wash up and then we sat down to eat. And it was a great meal, even with the risk of sounding arrogant. When Wesley went for his third helping, I knew it was a success. We took a long time eating, telling stories and making jokes. Then Alycia reminded us that we still had cake and ice cream to get to. Wesley smiled, blushed just a tinge, and I could tell he was really happy.

We decided to open gifts and allow our stomachs to settle before delving into cake and ice cream. Wesley and I sat on the sofa, Mom in the chair, and Alycia on the floor as Wesley started opening gifts. He started with a prettily wrapped box from Mom that contained two long-sleeved shirts. One was brown with thin blue and tan stripes and the other was solid blue with black sleeves. Both were very cute and very Wesley. Next, he opened a package from Alycia and, tearing off the paper eagerly, he found a kung fu movie and an action movie, both of which I had never heard of. Wesley thanked her giddily; apparently they had discussed their favorite movies at some time, which gave Alycia the inspiration. He opened the gift from me next, obviously not the one in my mouth, and was pleased to find an auto-fit wrench that adjusted at the push of a button. He thanked me with a kiss on the cheek and said he had wanted one for a long time. I thought it was kinda lame, but he seemed genuinely happy with it, so it was okay. Lastly, he opened another box from Mom, a large rectangular one with a red bow on top. Inside was a deep burgundy turtleneck sweater. I almost laughed, but I held it in. Most men could not pull off wearing any kind of turtleneck and shouldn't even try. Mom urged him to try it on and he relented, pulling the ribbed sweater over his head. I was wrong. He looked great in it. It wasn't a really long turtleneck that bunched up, but a little higher than a mock turtleneck and it really suited him. Even the resident fashion expert, Alycia, commented on how good he looked in it.

Wesley thanked us all with a hug and a kiss and we returned to the kitchen table to set the cake ablaze with nineteen candles. We crooned the happy birthday song, even though my family made it sound like a funeral dirge rather than a jaunty tune. Wesley blew out all the candles in one breath and winked at me and I felt certain that I knew what his wish was. He didn't say anything about the cake's decorations other than thank you until Alycia asked him how he liked the floral motif.

"I wasn't going to say anything," Wesley laughed, pulling extinguished candles from the cake. "It's cute, but it is a little girly."

"I know! That's why it's perfect!" Alycia said, sucking the chocolate frosting from the bottom of the candles.

"You're cruisin', kiddo."

Mom and I laughed at their banter and then took the cake to cut it up. I got four small plates and forks and Alycia got the ice cream. We sat around the table and enjoyed the special dessert that now read: Happy Bi Wes.

It was getting late and Mom and Alycia had work and school, respectively, so Wesley and I packed up his presents and half of the remaining cake and headed home. The light was blinking on the answering machine and, without thinking, I set the tinfoil-covered cake down and pressed the button. A mechanical voice announced that we had two messages and then Mrs. Carroll's voice came on, saying "Happy birthday, Wes." It wasn't a sad greeting, but it wasn't necessarily happy either. It was dismissive, like a formality. It sounded like the first call I got from Dad after the divorce: a little forced but with an "I'm not really sure what to say" tone. She asked Wesley to call her back and then said happy birthday again and the machine beeped.

"Heh, I'm surprised they remembered," Wesley said quietly, his mood darkening.

"Of course they would! It's your birthday!" I answered, trying to sound upbeat.

The machine stated the time of the second call and the quiet room was filled with a lively rendition of the birthday song in a duet. One voice was distinctively Scott's and the other voice must've belonged to his girlfriend, Michele. At the end of the song, Scott's loud voice boomed: "Happy birthday, little brother! Nineteen years old! Man, when did you get so old? I just wanted to let you know that we're thinking about you and that we love you. Happy birthday!"

I looked at Wesley and he was smiling. Scott's message stripped away the darkness from Mrs. Carroll's message and I was relieved. I wasn't going to misuse the timing of their calls and let Wesley remember his mother's message. I took his hands, leaned into him, and kissed him, rolling my pierced tongue between his lips.

"Oh, I kinda like that," he said, after I pulled my kiss away. "It's all healed then?"

"Yup," I answered. "I can't believe I waited a whole week before I could kiss you like that again."

"I know; it was a long week, but fortunately there were other things we could do," he said with a grin.

I kissed him again. "Well, now there's more stuff we can do. C'mon, I've been dying to try this out," I said, sticking my tongue out.

Chapter 35

“DO I really have to go?” Wesley asked, crossing his arms and pouting.

“Oh, c’mon. It’s only for a couple hours. It’ll be over before you know it,” I said, pulling on a pair of black socks. “Besides, you haven’t seen your parents since you moved out and it’ll be good to talk to them.”

“No it won’t. They’ll start bitching at me just like always.”

“You don’t know that for sure,” I said, getting a narrow glare from Wesley. “And your brother’ll be there too. You haven’t seen him since graduation,” I added, safely changing the direction of the conversation. “Don’t you want to know what his big announcement is?”

It took everything I had to convince Wesley to go home for Thanksgiving. Fortunately, Scott called the Monday before and told us he was coming home for the holiday and that he had a big announcement, but he wouldn’t say a word unless Wesley came to Thanksgiving dinner. He finally relented after a lot of coaxing, but he was still trying to get out of it.

I stood up from the bed and faced Wesley with a salacious grin. “C’mon. If you go, I’ll make it worth your while,” I propositioned, stepping closer and running a fingertip down his cheek to his lips. His resolve was already beginning to waver. “And, I’ll make sure to put this to good use,” I added, sticking out my pierced tongue.

Wesley sighed and kissed me. “You’re so unfair. You can’t use sex as a bargaining tool,” he complained.

"Sure I can, 'cause you're perpetually horny."

"So are you…."

"Yeah, but I can hold out longer than you," I said, giving him a light kiss.

He wound his arms around my waist and grinned. "Then, how about some motivation beforehand?" he asked, leaning in for another kiss.

"Hey, don't go getting all hard now," I said, stepping back. "We gotta get going. Mom's expecting me around two."

We drove to my Mom's and Wesley dropped in to say hi, and then went on his way. I sent him off with a good-luck kiss, but I had a strange feeling in the pit of my stomach as I watched him drive away. I felt nervous for him, but I hoped for the best.

A small turkey was already in the oven and I got the apron hanging in the pantry. I made stuffing and mashed potatoes from boxes and threw together a green bean casserole and then dinner was served. We even sat at the kitchen table to eat, discussing our Christmas wish lists.

Until six years ago, Thanksgiving was a big event gathering both sides of the family together. We always celebrated at our house and used the good china and cloth napkins, and had lit candles on the table. Dad would carve up a big turkey and save the wishbone for Alycia and me. Uncle Steve, Aunt Carolynn, Uncle Jack, and Grandpa would be glued to the TV watching football, Mom, Grandma, and Aunt Robin usually stayed in the kitchen, and Dad entertained all the kids. It was strange how distant those memories seemed to me now, like I was remembering a movie, not my life.

After dinner, Mom, Alycia, and I sat down on the sofa and watched movies, our new holiday tradition in the past six years. Mom made some chocolate pudding and we put in another movie.

Around eight, the phone rang and Alycia jumped to answer it. I knew it was Dad; he called every holiday to say hi. It seemed like a forced pleasantry, as if he could make up for leaving us with holiday telephone calls. But he did seem genuine and wanted to hear all about our lives since the last conversation. It was a sweet-tart feeling though; part of me forgave him, but the other part still hated him for breaking Mom's heart.

"Happy Thanksgiving! Yup, yup. I love you too. Here's Tor," Alycia said, handing me the phone.

I took a deep breath then smiled so that my voice would sound chipper. "Hi, Dad. Happy Thanksgiving."

"Hi, Toren! Happy Thanksgiving! How are you?"

"Pretty good. How about you?" I said, picturing my dad from a twelve-year-old's memory. Six years later, I was almost as tall as he was, but I remembered him towering over me. I also remembered medium brown hair and a muscular frame, but in recent pictures of him, I had noticed his hair had grayed a little and he had gained some weight. I supposed I would always remember him through a twelve-year-old's eyes.

"Doing good. So, how's school, college man?"

"I like it. I like my classes, except pre-calc, and I've got some really good professors. It sure beats high school, anyway," I answered, glancing at the TV. I remembered Dad's voice being deeper. "Oh yeah, thanks for the check for graduation," I said, though I sent him a thank-you card, in which Mom forced me to put a cap and gown photo.

"You earned it. I'm really proud of you, Tor. Have you thought of joining any clubs or school activities? You know, Mom and I were both on the newspaper in college. We had so much fun! You should…."

"Mom said the exact same thing," I said with a laugh. They really must have had fun together in college. Then I blushed thinking about Mom telling me to join the gay club.

"Well, we did have a lot of good times," Dad said, "but it doesn't have to be the newspaper. You could join a history club or something."

"Yeah, I'm looking into it for next semester."

"Good. You should really consider it. You'll have a lot of fun. Oh, I heard you got a job too. Where at?"

"Yeah. A place called the World Store."

"World Store? Oh, I love that place! They have so many great wines!" Dad said, very nearly squealing. There was a momentary silence and I blushed for him. "Um, well, in a couple years, you'll see what I mean," he added with an awkward laugh.

"I really like the place too."

"So, um, got any girlfriends?" Dad asked, lowering his voice an octave. Was he that concerned about coming off as gay to me? I nearly expected him to add "sport" or "champ" to the end of the question.

"No, no," I answered quietly, staring in my lap and feeling my face flare. I remembered Dad being an outdoorsy, hands-on type of guy, but with some effeminate qualities that he usually joked about. Did he always try to cover up "that side" of himself or did he just try to hide it from me?

"Well, it sure was good talking to you. Keep up the good work and remember to find out more about the history club, okay?" Dad said, segueing quickly to the end of the conversation. "Happy Thanksgiving, Tor. I love you."

"Happy Thanksgiving. I…love you too."

I handed the phone to Mom and she kicked her feet up and started chatting like a teenager. Alycia smiled slyly and sat down next to me on the sofa.

"So when are you gonna tell Dad?"

"I dunno. When I feel like it," I said, shrugging my shoulders before resting my chin in my palm. It wasn't like I hadn't thought about it, and I knew he'd accept it. I mean, I was preaching to the choir. But something always held me back.

"You gotta tell him!" Alycia urged with wide eyes. "Dad'd be so proud of you."

I shook my head dismissively and stayed quiet. I would tell Dad someday; I just didn't know when.

Alycia drove me home around nine and I found myself a little nervous to see Wesley. I hoped his day went well, but I had a strange feeling still. I fumbled getting the key in the lock with two bags of leftovers weighing down my arms. I pushed open the front door and caught it with my hip, holding it open. "Hi, I'm home! And I brought leftovers!" I shouted. The apartment was dimly lit and quiet. "Hello? Are you here?" I called out, setting the two plastic bags down on the kitchen counter. I peeked into the living room and saw Wesley sitting in the recliner holding a can of beer on the armrest. "Hi. What are you doing?" I asked, stepping in front of him with my hands on my hips.

"Nothing," Wesley answered, shrugging his shoulders. The TV was on but the sound was low and the light shadowed his face. There were six empty beer cans on the coffee table and Wesley finally looked up at me. "How was your Thanksgiving?" he asked, looking back at the quiet TV and taking a long drink of beer.

"It was good," I answered, stepping closer to Wesley. "How was yours? What was your brother's announcement?" My chest felt tighten and my stomach was tied in knots. I tried to sound upbeat, but I'd had a despairing premonition following me all day. I felt like I sent Wesley into the lion's den and it was foolish of me to think he would come out unharmed. But I tried to remain optimistic.

"He's getting married," Wesley said.

"Really? That's great!" I shouted, clapping my hands together. "He's getting…."

"We're not invited," he added and took another long drink.

My smile fell flat and I looked at Wesley blankly. "What? Why? What do you mean?"

Wesley finished the beer and tossed the can onto the coffee table with the others. He looked at the floor and shrugged his shoulders. Then he narrowed his eyes and gritted his teeth. "My parents don't want us making a 'mockery' of Scott's wedding."

I stared at Wesley, unsure if I should believe what I heard. "What? But…what do you mean?"

“My dad—my fucking dad—he heard me and Scott talking. Scott said he hoped you could get time off school to go and my dad heard and started yelling—fucking screaming. In front of everyone. Every word out of his mouth was fag-this and fag-that and so I told him to fuck off and I left,” Wesley explained, balling his hands into fists.

“What? Wesley,” I murmured, stepping closer. He sat still, staring into his lap, his brows furrowed, and then he shook his head.

“Fuck this. I’m sick of it. My fucking parents…. So I’m not going. Fuck it. I don’t care anymore,” Wesley said, holding his head up with his hand and shutting his eyes.

Tears brimmed and I reached down and petted Wesley’s head. “I’m sorry,” I whispered. “I’m so sorry.” I felt guilty, if I hadn’t forced him to go, this wouldn’t have happened.

“What are you apologizing for? It’s not your fault. It’s my fucking parents’,” he said through clenched teeth.

“But…I made you go, even though you didn’t want to.”

“No you didn’t. So don’t even think like that,” Wesley scolded, taking my hand and pulling me down on his lap. “If you can’t go, then I’m not going,” he said defiantly, wrapping his hands around my back and burying his face in my chest.

“Don’t say that,” I whispered, gently kissing the top of his head.

Wesley looked up at me quickly and shook his head. “No. I’ve made up my mind, Toren. If you can’t go, then I’m not going. There’s no room for argument here,” he said definitively, staring in my eyes.

“Wesley.”

“No. It’s my folks or us. That’s it,” he said, shaking his head. He rested his forehead on my chest again and I ran my fingers through his hair. “I’m just so fucking sick of this. Why won’t they get it? Why can’t they just be fucking happy for me?” he asked, his voice muffled by my chest.

"I'm sorry, Wesley. I'm so sorry. I'll never make you do anything like that again. I'll never make you do anything you don't want to do," I said, hugging his head tighter against my chest.

"I need another beer," Wesley muttered, pulling away from my embrace. I looked at the coffee table and the seven empty cans and shook my head. "C'mon, just let me drink tonight."

"You don't need it. Let's just go to bed and let this day be over," I said, cradling his face in my hands. Wesley looked at me with lonely eyes and I kissed him warmly. "C'mon. Let's just go to bed."

Chapter 36

IT was the middle of December and holiday season was in full swing. I was working extra hours at the store because we opened early and closed late to accommodate the Christmas rush. I was also preparing for the end of the school semester, writing papers and studying for exams. But my mind was a jumble. Ever since Thanksgiving, Wesley seemed a little distant. Scott called and apologized for their parents' outburst and Wesley was amicable, telling him not to worry about it. But I remembered the expression on his face that night and the way he clung to me like an abandoned puppy. I felt the wedge of his family's intolerance between us and it was overwhelming at times. With everything running through my mind, I couldn't concentrate on any one thing longer than ten minutes.

I looked at the kitchen table covered with books, papers, folders, and notebooks, and sighed. Wesley came up behind me and kissed the top of my head. He'd just stepped out of the shower and I breathed in the clean scent of soap and shampoo.

"What're you working on?" he asked, tugging on the towel draped around his neck.

"History."

"Still?"

"Yeah. But I just don't have any motivation right now. This paper's due on Monday, but I just can't get into it," I complained.

"Maybe you should take a break. We could go out and shoot some pool or something," Wesley suggested, opening the fridge and looking inside.

"Yeah, maybe you're right. Go clear my head and start fresh," I agreed, leaning back in the kitchen chair and glancing at Wesley. He had a can of soda in his hand and his eyes rounded.

"Seriously? You want to?" he asked, cautiously optimistic.

"Yeah. Besides, I wanna see Kate and Lissa. We haven't seen them in ages," I answered, charmed and amused by Wesley's excitement.

He put the can back in the fridge and pulled the towel from around his neck. "Cool! Let me go get dressed!"

We went to Cue and as we hoped and expected, Kate and Lissa were at a table in the back. They were smiling and laughing and so completely engrossed in each other that they didn't notice us until we were standing next to them.

"Holy crap! I don't believe it!" Kate shouted. "Where the hell have you guys been? We thought you died or moved to China or something!"

"Heh, nice to see you too," Wesley said with a grin.

"I'm serious! Where have you two been? We haven't seen you in forever!" Kate continued, furrowing her brows and standing with her hands on her hips.

"We've been around," Wesley said, taking off his jacket and holding his hand out to take mine too. "We just haven't gone out in a while since we got our own place. There hasn't been a need to," he added, with a lascivious grin in my direction.

"Oh yeah! That's another thing!" Kate complained, stepping to the side to let Wesley pass. He hung up our coats and patted Lissa on the back before returning to my side. "You guys moved out forever ago and you never invited us over!"

"I know, I know," I said with a laugh, holding my hands up as a sign of concession. "I promise we'll have you over real soon, okay?"

Kate folded her arms on her chest and pouted, then looked at me with a forgiving smile. "Promise?"

"I promise," I answered, drawing an X over my heart with my index finger.

"Man, you guys are so lucky. I wish I had my own place," Kate mused aloud. "I know! Let's get our own place after we graduate," she said, spinning around and facing Lissa with a childlike smile.

Lissa's eyes widened and her face reddened and she stared at Kate for a moment. "O…okay," she answered. She only said one word, but her expression spoke volumes.

Kate realized the weight of her question on their relationship and glanced at the floor with florid cheeks. Then she turned to Lissa again and smiled wickedly, trying to reduce the intimate tension and exhilaration of the moment. "Then, maybe, we can get that strap-on I've wanted for so long."

"What are you trying to say? My fingers and tongue aren't enough for you?" Lissa retorted quickly, and then held her breath. She bit her bottom lip in embarrassment and looked at the floor. "I-I didn't mean to say that…so loud."

Wesley and I looked at each other with amused astonishment. They'd only been dating a couple months, but they'd been friends for years. Lissa's unrequited love was finally returned and Kate learned exactly what love was and what it felt like. The girls smiled timidly at each other until Kate caught us spying on their intimate reflection. She latched onto Lissa's arm and tugged her forward.

"I know she looks all sweet and innocent, but she's really a pervert at heart," Kate announced with a grin, perhaps appreciatively. Lissa glanced up at us and turned an even brighter shade of red.

"Heh, sounds like someone else I know," Wesley said, bumping into me. He and Kate laughed while Lissa and I shared embarrassed shyness.

Kate pulled Lissa closer to us and then grinned with a sparkle in her eye. "I've been wanting to ask this for a while and since the subject came up," Kate prefaced, smiling salaciously, "what's it like? When it's two guys?"

"Oh, it's great! The best thing ever!" Wesley answered without the slightest bit of modesty.

I gaped at him and then glanced at Kate who smirked at me. "But…doesn't it hurt?"

I remained silent and slack-jawed and Wesley pulled me closer and smiled devilishly. "Well, yeah, it did at first, but it felt good too. Really good," he emphasized with a sly smile.

Kate and Lissa stared at us with wide eyes until Kate shook her head in disbelief. "What? No way! I thought for sure you would be the top!" Kate said loudly, looking at Wesley. "Are you serious?"

"Hey now, don't underestimate this guy," Wesley said, completely amused with himself.

The two girls exchanged glances between us and I took a deep breath. Even the tips of my ears felt red-hot. "No, it's not like that. It was only once. And to answer your question: yes, it did hurt. Like hell. But, it felt good too," I said shyly, unable to look up from the floor.

"See? I knew it!" Kate shouted giddily. "The idea of two guys together is so hot! Lissa thought that you would switch back and forth, but I knew Tor was the bottom," she said, laughing and relying on Lissa to hold her up.

"You mean you thought about it?" I blurted out, turning from bright red to hot pink.

"Of course! You guys are both so cute and it's a total turn-on when two good-looking guys get it on," Kate explained happily.

I was so embarrassed that I felt like I had the wind knocked out of me. Kate went on to say that some of her favorite books were gay erotica and that there was even a whole genre of Japanese comic books devoted to "boy-love," which she said was called *yaoi*. Wesley kept asking questions about the erotica and yaoi books and Kate said she would be happy to loan some to us.

Eventually, we got on to playing pool, though I couldn't look at Kate or Lissa without blushing for the rest of the night. But it was fun and heartwarming to see Kate and Lissa so happy together. It was obvious from their expressions, glances, and gestures that they were really in love with each other. It was silly, but I was prideful, and maybe a little arrogant, that I helped them get to where they were. Their relationship started as precipitously as Wesley's and mine. If Lissa hadn't made the first move, would they be together?

Wesley came up and hugged me from behind after the third game and I knew how lucky I was to have a man strong enough, brave enough, and confident enough to make the first move. I was indebted to him forever and I was just fine with that.

Chapter 37

"HEY, babe. I'm home," Wesley said, walking in the front door.

"Hi! How are you? How was work?" I asked, leaning back in the kitchen chair. I stretched my arms over my head and inadvertently yawned.

"Good. Busy as hell though," he answered, taking off his coat and hanging it on the hook behind the door. "At least it made the time go by fast. How about you? How was your psych final?" he asked and kissed the top of my head.

"I think I did pretty good," I answered, relaxing as he rubbed my shoulders.

I was almost done with finals; I just had my calc test left. I was sick of studying and with Christmas only three days away, I couldn't concentrate on anything.

"Have you eaten yet?" Wesley asked, opening two buttons of his navy work shirt.

"No, I was waiting for you," I said, looking back to my calc book on the kitchen table. "What do you want?"

"I don't know, but I'll make dinner. You just keep on studying," he said, opening the freezer and looking in.

"I thought maybe we could just get a pizza."

"I don't think I have any cash," he said, closing the freezer and pulling coins from his pocket. "Nope, just eighty-two cents."

"I've got cash," I said, staring blankly at the textbook.

"All right. Pepperoni okay?" he asked, picking up the phone and taking a pizza menu off the fridge.

I nodded and listened while Wesley ordered the pizza. It would take about twenty minutes so Wesley hopped in the shower while we waited. I yawned again and stared at my calc book; I couldn't concentrate anymore. I took several deep breaths and refocused my attentions to the matter at hand—but I needed to do some laundry tonight; I didn't think I had any clean work pants. I sighed as my mind wandered to everything except math.

Wesley got out of the shower and came into the living room without a shirt on. I was beginning to think he did that on purpose, knowing full well that I couldn't keep my eyes off his naked chest. But I took a deep breath and returned my gaze to the calc problems in front of me. The doorbell rang and Wesley happily answered it with a growling stomach and no shirt.

"Hi. How ya doin'? It'll be eleven sixty-four," the pizza-man greeted.

"Oh yeah," Wesley said, thumping his head. "Hey babe, you got the money?" Wesley called to me, feeling his empty pockets.

"Oh, here," I said, pulling a twenty from my pocket and handing it to the cute delivery boy. He looked at me, then at Wesley, and fumbled with the change as Wesley took the pizza into the kitchen. "Oh, six in change is enough," I added and got a five and a one in return.

Wesley was getting plates out and I went over and punched his arm. "Don't answer the door without a shirt! Now, go get dressed before you catch a cold," I scolded.

"Why? He was kinda cute. Do you think he would've went for it if I said I didn't have any money?" Wesley asked.

"You're mine and I wouldn't let you prostitute yourself for pizza. Now go put on a shirt," I said, pulling two slices onto a plate.

Wesley put on a T-shirt and we sat down at the kitchen table to eat. He looked over the problems I'd done, pulling the textbook closer as he ate his pizza. I watched him as he reviewed the chapter and I wondered again why he didn't want to go to college. He would be a great engineer and, with a degree, any car company would be lucky to have him. However, he was loyal to Gus and the shop and we already knew that Wesley would get fifty-percent ownership when Gus retired. I smiled and sipped my soda and realized again that I was in love with a truly remarkable man.

"Geez, I can't believe Christmas is only three days away," Wesley said, leaning back in the chair and patting his full belly.

"I know. This month has flown by," I agreed, picking up the empty plates and dropping them in the sink.

"So, did you get my Christmas present?"

"Yeah," I said, sitting down again and pulling my textbook closer. "And you're gonna love it!" I said, picking up my pencil and brushing my hand over my notebook. I was really excited about his gift; he didn't ask for it, but he had been dropping very subtle hints.

"What is it?" he asked plainly.

"I'm not telling," I answered, just as plainly.

"Do you have to work tomorrow?"

"Yeah, and on Christmas Eve 'til five. Well, we close at five. But, remember, we're going to my mom's around seven," I said, looking at the papers in front of me and trying to remember where I left off. Wesley nodded and I looked at him for a long moment. "Are you gonna drop by your parents' house on Christmas Eve?" I asked quietly, knowing I was treading dangerous waters.

Wesley looked at me sharply and furrowed his brows. "Why the hell would I do that?"

"Well, it's your first Christmas away from home, and I thought…."

"If I did, they would just yell that I wasn't their son, that I was a fag, and that everything's your fault. Why would I subject myself to that? Besides, my brother's not gonna be there, so…."

"Scott's not going?"

"No, he's spending Christmas with his girlfr—his fiancée's family."

"That's nice."

Wesley went to the bathroom and I refocused on studying with a lighter heart and a full stomach. I wrote down a sample problem in my notebook and tried solving it, looking back at the textbook every five seconds. Wesley returned and sat down at the table, holding his chin in his palm and staring at me. I got through one problem, but Wesley's deep brown eyes were distracting.

"Stop staring at me. Go away," I said after a few minutes. Wesley laughed. "I'm serious. I have to study. So, go away!"

"No. I don't wanna. Besides, you look really sexy when you're all focused and concentrating. It kinda turns me on. Why don't you take a break?" he said, smiling lasciviously at me.

"I can't. I really have to study. And if you're not going to help me, go away," I reiterated, trying my hardest not to meet Wesley's gaze.

"C'mon, just a short break. Say, ten minutes?"

I looked up and Wesley grinned at me. He took my breath away and I was already responding to his playful seduction. He stood up and kissed me, slipping his tongue between my lips, and what little resistance I had faded away immediately.

"Just ten minutes?" I asked, licking my lips.

"Promise," he said, looking into my eyes as he reached down and groped the front of my pants.

I stood up and followed Wesley into the bedroom, forgetting everything I had just studied as my blood drained downward. Wesley pulled his shirt over his head as he stepped past the threshold and my eyes lingered on his wide, smooth back. He turned and smiled at me as he dropped his shirt on the floor. I felt myself get harder as he pulled me in close and looked into my eyes for a long moment before kissing me slowly. His hands roamed down my chest and rubbed my nipples over the fabric of my shirt as he dropped his kiss to my chin and neck. He unzipped my pants, slid his hand inside my boxers, and stroked affectionately as he sucked on my neck. I opened his jeans and slid them down low on his hips, enough to grope freely inside his underwear. His lips returned to my mouth and we kissed softly, yet feverishly, until Wesley pulled away and squeezed his hand around me.

"I want you on top this time," he whispered throatily, hinting at a smile. I looked at him, feeling his firm grip, and I was unable to respond. "I was thinking about it, since we saw Kate and Lis the other night," he said, stepping back and pulling off his jeans. He sat back on the bed, reached for the bottle of lotion and tossed it to me. "C'mon. I want you to fuck me, Toren."

I took a deep breath, every atom in my body awake with lust. I stripped my clothes off and joined Wesley on the bed. He parted his knees for me and I flipped the top off the lotion, dribbling some on my fingers. He pushed himself toward me and lay back. With one hand on the inside of his thigh, I leaned down and met his large cock with my tongue. I slipped a finger beneath and easily found the awaiting orifice. I pushed one finger inside him as I slid my lips over the head and pressed my tongue against his sensitive flesh. I ground my fingers against his warm ring until I was able to press in two fingers past the second knuckle. I continued sucking him off until pre-cum coated my mouth and tonsils.

With his thighs blocking my peripheral vision, I looked up and Wesley's expression made me so hard it hurt. He looked at me with glassy eyes and he parted his moist lips as he gasped for breath. I pushed three fingers into his elastic hole and drowned myself in the musty smell of his balls. While I slurped and sucked them, I felt his hands in my hair.

"You're…you're gonna have to hurry," Wesley panted, lifting my head and looking into my eyes.

I glanced down at his large member, glistening with saliva and pre-cum, then back to his desperate, sexy face. I withdrew my fingers and stroked myself wet with lotion. Wesley lifted his backside up to me, his thighs rubbing against my hips and waist, and I held myself firm as I slowly pressed into him. A moan escaped his lips and his muscles tightened as I pushed farther into him. He spread his legs farther apart on both sides of me and I grasped his slippery cock with a firm grip and stroked back and forth, as I forced myself deeper. Wesley arched his back as I felt my balls slap against his warm flesh.

"F—uck! God, Toren!" Wesley shouted, squeezing his knees against my waist.

I nearly came just from the sound of his voice calling my name, but I renewed my effort, pulling back and thrusting forward again and again. Wesley panted beneath me and I felt like I was flying. This incredible feeling even tingled in my fingertips and toes.

"Tor…God! Tor, I'm coming!" Wesley panted as I moved above him.

"Me too. Wes…Wesley!" I shouted, nearly pulling out then driving into him again with a desperate, delirious fervor.

Wesley exploded, hitting my chest and stomach and I came hard inside his tender recesses until I collapsed on top of him. Panting and gasping, Wesley stroked his hand through my hair and I looked up timidly at his sexy face. I was still inside him and my cheeks reddened with embarrassment as I felt myself getting hard again.

"Can I?" I asked timidly. "Can I…one more time?"

"Yeah. Yeah, one more time," Wesley answered breathlessly.

I felt him harden against my stomach and he slipped his hand behind my neck and kissed me feverishly. I felt his cock rubbing against my stomach and I was instantly overcome by the sensation. Wesley wrapped his arms around my neck and I moved back and forth, feeling his heat and perspiring body sliding against mine. I was passionately overwhelmed, pumping inside him with unadulterated lust while Wesley bucked his hips into me. I tried to stave off my approaching climax until Wesley was near too. I looked into his eyes, he looked into mine, and then we climaxed together, draining ourselves of every ounce of love and desire within.

I flopped down atop him and breathed in his distinctive scent. I still had a fever behind my eyes, but my body was happily exhausted and Wesley drew his arms around me. We lay in bed for long minutes, savoring the memory and scent of sex until Wesley ran his hand through my hair. I looked up at him, biting my bottom lip, and then rolled off him onto my back.

"You did that on purpose," I said, staring at the ceiling.

"Did what?"

I closed my eyes, still feeling the heat emanating from my body. "You knew I wouldn't be able to stop after just ten minutes."

"Maybe," he answered with a chuckle in his voice.

"And I still have to study!" I complained, covering my eyes with my forearm. "You better take responsibility and help me."

"I know. I will," Wesley agreed, sitting up. "Get dressed. I'm gonna go wash up," he said, patting my hair and kissing my forehead. He slid to the side of the bed and grasped his lower back as he stood up. "Oh man, I'm gonna be walking like an old man tomorrow," he said, shuffling across the room to pick up his T-shirt and jeans before heading into the bathroom.

I watched him walk away, still with a hand on his back, and I suddenly felt really bashful. I got out of bed and got dressed, but stopped next to the bathroom. The door was open and I could hear water running in the sink. I leaned against the wall and blushed.

"Um, Wesley?"

"Yeah?"

"Did I do okay?" I asked quietly.

"What? I can't hear you," Wesley said, stepping into the doorframe with a washcloth in his hand.

"Was…was it okay? Did I do okay?" I asked again, feeling my ears burn.

"Why are you being so shy?" Wesley asked, a smile on his handsome face. "You were great. It felt amazing."

"But, I know I'm not as good as you. I mean, you have a certain…anatomical advantage. But, if I made you feel even half as good as you make me feel, then, I think I did okay," I confessed quietly, staring at the cream-colored carpet in the hallway.

Wesley stepped close to me and kissed my lips gently. "If I can make you feel even half as good as you make *me* feel, then…well, I think we're in a good place."

I smiled at his sweet, confident words and looked up at him. "I love you so, so much," I whispered.

"And I love you so, so much. Now, let's get to studying because I'm expecting a big reward when you pass," he said.

I kissed him again and nodded my head. "Deal."

Chapter 38

"WAKE up! Hey, wake up! It's Christmas!" Alycia shouted, pouncing on Wesley and me. "Come on! Let's go! Let's see what Santa brought!"

I rubbed my eyes and smiled. I was used to this; this was how she woke me up every Christmas morning. But Wesley lay still with his eyes wide open until an amused smile took over his face.

"What time is it?" I asked.

"It's almost nine. Now, come on! Let's go!" she said, grabbing onto our wrists and pulling. It was hard to believe she was sixteen years old.

"And what makes you think Santa would bring *you* anything?" I asked, pulling my hand away.

Alycia sat up on her knees between Wesley and me and placed her hands on her hips. "I've been good all year long! And besides, it's not like Santa would bring presents for a couple of homos!" she countered with a grin.

My mouth dropped open and Alycia giggled. "Get her!" I shouted and Wesley reacted quickly, pinning Alycia to the ground and tickling her mercilessly.

"I'm kidding!" she laughed breathlessly, squirming to get away. "I was kidding! I give!" she cried, laughing so hard her whole body shook. I let go of her arms and Wesley relented, letting her escape. She gasped for breath, still laughing, and stood up. "C'mon, it's Christmas!"

Wesley stood up and grabbed his blue jeans from my bed. I blushed looking at him in his T-shirt and boxers. I completely forgot about Alycia's Christmas morning ritual and didn't think about how Wesley always slept in his underwear. Fortunately, he wore a T-shirt to bed and boxers instead of boxer-briefs. Alycia didn't seem to notice and waited impatiently for us to follow her into the living room.

"Good morning! Merry Christmas!" Mom said, standing in her robe in front of the coffeemaker. "Did Santa visit?"

Alycia and I ran to our stockings, hanging in the living room, and sat down on the floor to look through our loot. I told Wesley to hurry up and get his stocking, threatening to claim what was inside. Wesley had the sweetest look on his face, astonishment and excitement, that he had his very own stocking in our family. He sat down on the floor next to me with his stocking in his lap, his name spelled out in glue and glitter. Alycia had told me the day before that it was actually Mom's idea to get Wesley a stocking and I flashed a happy, grateful smile in her direction.

An orange was stuffed in the toe of each of our stockings, a family tradition, and they were filled to the top with chocolates and candy. Also, each of us had a CD in our stocking: the new Clapton for Alycia, an old Pixies album for Wesley, and B.B. King's early recordings for me. Mom watched us with a nostalgic grin while she sipped her coffee.

"Okay, what should we do first? Presents or breakfast?" Mom asked, after getting a hug from each of us as our surrogate Santa.

"Presents! I wanna do presents!" Alycia shouted. "Presents presents presents!" She ran to the small Christmas tree and delivered the presents, singing the recipient's name and who it was from, and dancing around like a ten-year-old. Wesley sat in the armchair amidst the prettily wrapped gifts at his feet with a dumbfounded look on his face. Mom teased him about his astonished look and told him that he was part of our family and, of course, he'd be included in the gift exchange. I smiled and felt my chest tighten. I knew it was cliché, but this was the best gift I could ever ask for.

"Okay! Me first," Alycia announced, pulling a rectangular box onto her lap. She tore off the paper and held up a Persian-blue dress with a wide sash around the waist and a bodice that folded over the chest. It was beautiful and exactly her style and she thanked Mom happily while holding it up to her shoulders.

Mom was next in the circle and took a small box wrapped in red paper with a green ribbon. She already knew what it was; she got it every year. It was a bottle of perfume that she always got from Dad on Christmas. After their divorce, Alycia and I continued the tradition with mixed feelings, but Mom smiled and thanked us from the bottom of her heart. The only difference was that, this year, the gift tag read: From Wesley and Toren.

Wesley chose a rectangular clothes' box and unwrapped it carefully. Alycia chuckled as he folded the paper in halves and laid it down on the floor. Inside the box was a new pair of blue jeans that he desperately needed and a dark-orange, long-sleeved shirt. He blushed as he thanked Mom and Alycia giggled again.

At last, it was my turn and I opened a package elegantly dressed in cheesy cartoon elves decorating a huge Christmas tree. I smiled at Alycia as I crumpled up the paper; she always looked for one roll of exceedingly ugly gift wrap. I held up two DVDs and thanked her excessively; few people appreciated my love of kung fu movies. Wesley smiled and gave me a thumbs-up: *The Legend of the Drunken Master* and *The Defender*, two of our favorites.

We went around the circle, opening our gifts in turn, when Wesley pulled a long, thin box onto his lap.

"No! You can't open that one yet!" Alycia shouted.

Wesley looked up and then at the balls of crumpled paper on the floor. "But this is the last one," he said.

"Well, you still have a card," Alycia said, smirking at me.

"Oh," Wesley answered simply and picked up the forgotten card under some paper. He glanced at his name and the lopsided smiley face on the envelope and grinned at me. He pulled the card out and a sheet folded in quarters fell into his lap. He looked down and then read what I had written: "We can have it delivered any time. Merry Christmas! I love you! Love, Tor." He mouthed the word "delivered" with a confused look and opened the folded sheet of paper on his lap. His eyes grew big and his jaw dropped. "You gotta be kidding me," he mumbled, staring at the paper. "Are you for real?" he asked, tearing his eyes away to look at me for just a moment. "I can't believe it! This is awesome!"

"It has the charcoal/gas option and a side-burner," I said, beaming excitedly. I knew Wesley wanted a grill, but his hints were subtle.

"Thank you!" Wesley cried, toppling me over on the floor and hugging me so tightly that I couldn't breathe.

Mom and Alycia laughed and after Wesley calmed down a bit, I opened my last gift. Pulling off the solid green paper, I stared at the cell phone box on my lap in astonishment. I looked over the features: phone, camera, Internet. It was one of those phones that had everything.

"This…is so cool!" I stuttered excitedly and Wesley smiled proudly.

"Now you don't have to use pay phones and I can talk to you whenever I want."

"I love it! It's so cute too!"

"Lemme see," Alycia said, pulling the box away from me. "Oh wow! This thing has everything!"

"Well, it's not as cool as a grill, but…."

"No, it's better! I love it. Thank you," I said, touching Wesley's hand with a smile.

We cleaned up the living room, stuffing crumpled wrapping paper into a trash bag and putting our gifts into neat little piles. Alycia set the trash bag by the front door and I headed into the kitchen.

"All right, what do you want for breakfast?" I asked.

"Oh, don't worry about it, Tor. I bought some coffee cake and bagels," Mom said, sitting back down on the sofa and sipping her coffee.

"Even better," I said, and began to prepare breakfast.

We sat around and leisurely ate while talking about our presents and retelling old Christmas stories. We eventually got dressed in the early afternoon and broke out the Scrabble board, another family tradition since Dad left. It had been six years since he'd left and five years since we moved. I thought holidays would be difficult and sad because we didn't have any family nearby. But Alycia and I loved spending the holidays with Mom, just the three of us. Now we had Wesley to share these special times with and I couldn't keep myself from smiling.

Wesley complained the whole time we played Scrabble because he was in last place. He said he wasn't very good, but he did well—considering he was facing three serious Scrabble players. In the middle of the second game, the telephone rang and Alycia jumped to get it. She answered with a jaunty "Merry Christmas!" and we eavesdropped and continued playing while she talked to Dad. When it was her turn again, we waited as she told Dad about Jeremy, school, work, and the presents she got. Then she handed the phone to me with a happy grin. I talked to Dad while Scrabble continued, telling him about school and work and the gifts I received. It was nice to hear Dad's voice. Since I had been with Wesley, I realized how important family was. The bitter feelings I held toward him were beginning to dissolve and I began to feel proud that he was my father.

"Oh, come on! That's not even a word!" Alycia shouted, startling me.

"Yes it is!" Wesley answered, equally loud.

"Wow, sounds lively over there," Dad commented with a chuckle.

"Yeah, right! Pabst? What's it mean?" Alycia demanded.

"Um, yeah. Just another vicious game of Scrabble," I said with a laugh.

"It's a brand of beer!" Wesley answered, folding his arms on his chest defiantly.

"Is someone else there? I thought I heard another voice," Dad asked.

"Proper names don't count!" Alycia stated authoritatively.

"Ah, um…," I mumbled, hesitating and looking at the floor.

"Says who?" Wesley demanded.

"I see. So your mom finally found herself a boyfriend, huh?" Dad asked.

"Me and the rule book!" Alycia countered.

"Um, he's not Mom's boyfriend. He's actually, um, *my* boyfriend," I murmured, feeling my cheeks burn.

"Oh. *Oh*. Is that so?" Dad said. Somehow, I knew he was smiling. "Good for you, Tor. So tell me about him. What's his name?"

"Wesley," I answered, blushing even deeper. Mom, Alycia, and Wesley were staring at me with wide eyes. I felt my ears get hot and I looked away quickly.

"Oh, your roommate?" Dad asked, thinking for a moment. "Were you seeing each other before you moved in together?"

"Yeah."

"Sounds pretty serious. Good for you, Toren. You'll have to e-mail me a picture of the two of you."

"Yeah, I will. Definitely," I answered with a smile. I could feel everyone still staring at me and I turned my back to them.

"You sound really happy. And that makes me happy. So, e-mail me and tell me all about him, okay?"

"Yeah, I sure will. You wanna talk to Mom?"

"Yeah, put her on. Merry Christmas. I love you, Tor, and I'll be waiting for your e-mail!"

"Merry Christmas, Dad. I love you too," I answered and handed the phone to Mom.

"Did you just tell Dad?" Alycia asked eagerly, nearly tackling me.

"Yeah. I guess so," I said, glancing shyly at Wesley. He smiled warmly and gave me a tight hug and I felt really happy. Everyone who was important to me now knew about Wesley and me. It was a good feeling, a liberating feeling.

Alycia threw her hands up in celebration and grinned from ear to ear. "Good for you, big brother! Nothing says Merry Christmas like 'Hi, Dad! I'm gay!' "

WE spent the rest of the day playing games, talking, and laughing. We ate a delicious dinner and then watched *A Christmas Story*, the last of our family traditions. Wesley and I got home around 9:30, our arms full of boxes and bags.

"Don't forget to put the leftovers in the fridge," I said, dropping my load on the sofa.

"Yeah, yeah," he answered and I heard the refrigerator door open and close. "So, you ready for bed?" he asked, sticking his hands deep in his pockets.

"Nah. I'm not really sleepy yet," I answered, stacking up clothes boxes to take into the bedroom.

"Who said anything about sleeping?" he asked with his notorious grin. He laced his hands around my back and kissed me softly.

"All right, let's go," I agreed and licked his lips before leading him into the bedroom.

I sat Wesley down on the edge of the bed and he wrapped his arms around my waist as I took his face in my hands and kissed him. His hands dropped to my backside and I knelt down in front of him. He leaned back on his hands while I unzipped his pants. He was beginning to respond and I stroked the shaft and lowered my mouth to his tightening balls. Following the vein underneath with my tongue, I slipped the head between my lips, circling the slit with the tip of my tongue. I sucked hard and felt Wesley's body tremble when I swallowed him as far as I was able.

"Damn. I can't believe you actually got me a grill. That is just so cool! I'm so excited!" he breathed, closing his eyes.

I hesitated, and then pulled my lips away. "I'm sorry. Am I boring you?" I asked with a hint of a grin. "You're more excited about a grill," I said, flicking the tip with a moist finger, "than you are about me?"

"What? No. Not at all. I'm always hot for you," he said grinningly and gestured toward his lap as an invitation to continue.

I laughed and kissed the head where I had just flicked my finger. Grabbing hold of his balls and dropping my mouth, I began again where I had left off. Wesley moaned, but it didn't sound like genuine excitement.

"Ooh…charcoal/gas option…yeah," he murmured with a slight smirk.

"What? That's it!" I teased, standing up and pushing him back on the bed. I straddled his thighs and unzipped my pants.

"I was kidding!" he laughed, though he closely watched my hands.

"Just for that, you have to make me cum before you're allowed to."

"And how is that any different from any other time?" he smirked, reaching forward and kneading the tip in his palm.

He was right. I always went before him, except for the times when he was really horny or when we came together. Suddenly, Wesley sat up and pushed me down onto the bed on my back. He took hold of my jeans, yanked them down around my ankles, and parted my knees. He smiled as though a grand meal was set before him and he frigged me feverishly while he licked and sucked my balls into his warm mouth. My body felt slightly numb for a moment and then it felt like every erogenous zone on my body was suddenly linked and searing with pleasure. I catered to his every whim, pushing myself deeper into his mouth as he slipped a finger inside me. Already, I felt like I could cum, and with a great deal of restraint and conviction, I lifted Wesley's chin and he looked at me quizzically.

"I want us to go together."

"But you said I had to…."

"Oh, just get inside me!" I shouted desperately. My cheeks flared when I realized what I said and Wesley stared at me with wide eyes.

"God, you are just too cute," he said with a smile dawning on his face.

He pulled my jeans off and lifted my legs over his shoulders. He positioned himself with one hand and stared in my eyes as he pressed forward. My body accepted him eagerly and I gripped the corners of the pillow in my hands as he began to thrust. He closed one eye and clenched his teeth as he felt my muscles tighten around him, then he pushed forward again and I rocked against his passionate motions. He voiced a guttural moan and I knew he was close, and so was I. I whimpered his name, he grunted mine, and then we climaxed in unison, draining our bodies in a deluge of passion.

Atop me, Wesley heaved in air and I gasped for breath, joyfully crushed beneath him. After we caught our breaths, Wesley kissed me lightly and laid his head down on my chest.

"I can't believe you got me a grill."

Chapter 39

"HAPPY New Year, Toren!" Jeanine called as I pulled on my coat. "Wait a sec, I'm heading up," she added, stuffing a roll of quarters into her World Store apron.

We walked to the front of the store where she resumed her place behind the register, cracking open the quarters and dumping them in the till. She asked if I had anything planned and I told her that Wesley and I were invited to a party hosted by a friend of Kate's and Lissa's.

"Well, I'll see you next year," I said with a wave and stepped into the cold, evening air. It was a little past six o'clock and I debated whether or not I should stop and pick up something for dinner. The bus was running late, so I decided against it, and went home.

Wesley was sitting on the sofa with his feet on the coffee table, holding a beer on his stomach. "Hey, babe. How was work?"

"It was okay, but slow," I answered, taking off my coat and draping it over a chair at the kitchen table. "How about you?"

"The same. I only had two jobs today and they were both oil changes," he said, taking a drink and patting the cushion beside him.

I shook my head and went back to the kitchen. "Don't forget, we have that party tonight," I called from in front of the refrigerator. I popped the top on a can of soda and went back to the living room.

"Oh, yeah," Wesley answered drearily and tried to hide his obvious yawn. He dropped his head back on the sofa and sighed quietly.

"Don't you wanna go?" I asked.

"No, it's okay. We can go," he answered, staring at the ceiling with teary eyes from his yawn.

"That's not what I asked," I said with a smirk. "Do *you* want to go?"

"Not really," he answered with a coy smile.

I sat down next to him and put my feet up. "Honestly, I don't really wanna go either," I said, resting the soda on my belly. "I'd rather just stay home with you. But, you gotta call Kate and tell her we're not going."

Wesley looked at me blankly. "Kiss me," he said firmly. I leaned over and softly touched his lips. "Okay, get me the phone." I hopped up and retrieved the phone for him. "Oh, and we have to go shopping."

"For what?" I asked.

"Meat."

"Excuse me?"

"Meat," he said again. "'Cause I'm gonna make you the best dinner you ever had," he explained with a grin.

"Okay. Then I'm gonna go change and we can go," I said with a smile, then wiggled my butt at him before heading into the bedroom. I listened to him make excuses to Kate while I slipped on a long-sleeve shirt and blue jeans and folded my white work shirt and khaki pants. Then we got our coats and went to the grocery store.

We stood in front of the meat counter for about twenty minutes while Wesley debated over the perfect selection. Hamburgers were too casual, salmon steaks were too expensive, and he couldn't decide between pork chops, sirloin steaks, or strip steaks until the clerk at the counter recommended the strip. Then we picked up some fresh broccoli, red potatoes, and a bake-at-home French baguette.

When we got home, Wesley fired up the grill, running out onto the balcony without a coat to light the charcoal. I prepared the rest while we waited for the grill to heat up. Wesley tended to the steaks and I baked the bread, boiled the potatoes, and steamed the broccoli so that they would be done at the same time. Wesley set the table for two and we enjoyed a delicious, romantic dinner. Wesley wasn't joking when he said he could grill anything, and I was treated to a feast fit for a king.

After dinner, I started to wash the dishes, but I was so satisfactorily full that I didn't feel like it. Wesley scrubbed the grill immaculately clean with the utensils Alycia gave him for Christmas. I was happy that he liked the grill so much. He couldn't stop smiling all through dinner.

I sat down on the sofa and Wesley flopped down next to me with a mischievous grin. He pulled a joint out of his cigarette pack and asked if I wanted to celebrate. I nodded happily and we passed it back and forth until it was a fat roach that we set aside to finish at midnight. I felt light and silly and rested my hand on his thigh.

"You know what would be great now?" I asked. Wesley pressed his hand down on mine and smiled devilishly, but I giggled, pulled my hand away, and clapped once. "Kung fu!" I shouted.

Wesley scrunched up his face in disappointment, then nodded. "So what'll it be?"

"Bruce Lee. Or anything with Jackie Chan 'cause he's funny. But Jet Li's really cute…." I mused aloud.

"How about *Enter the Dragon*?" Wesley suggested.

"But we just watched that the other night. Let's watch *Rumble in the Bronx* or *Fists of Fury*," I said, nodding my head in agreement with myself.

The movie ended around 11:30 and we switched to a countdown special hosted by the eternally seventy, almost anachronistic Dick Clark. We fooled around during the show until there were about five minutes left. We each got a beer, put the roach in the bowl, and waited for the final ten seconds of the year. We counted down as the ball dropped and kissed and clinked beer bottles at midnight.

At 12:01, the phone rang and I nearly jumped out of my skin. A very inebriated Alycia shouted "Happy New Year!" in my ear and Wesley laughed because he could hear her from five feet away. She babbled happily and I could hear Jeremy in the background. Alycia rambled on about resolutions and good karma, then shouted "Happy New Year!" again and said goodbye. Wesley and I laughed and made our resolutions as we finished off the roach. Then I put in *Fists of Fury*, closed the blinds across the sliding door, and sat down, straddling Wesley's lap. I kissed him and pressed my hips against his.

"What's this? Are you hard already?" he asked playfully, sliding his hand around to my backside.

"Yeah, so why aren't you?" I said, resting my forearms on his shoulders.

"Kiss me again and you'll see," he answered, licking his lips.

I leaned into him and kissed him hard, grinding my hips in his lap. I closed my eyes and felt him respond as he'd promised. I slid my hands down his chest and unzipped his blue jeans. I pulled away from his kiss as I frigged him with one hand and he glanced down as he unbuttoned my pants. I pulled my jeans off awkwardly without leaving my place on Wesley's lap and guided his fingers between my thighs.

"You wanna do it out here?" he asked.

"Why do you think I closed the blinds?" I responded throatily and kissed him lightly.

"Are you gonna be okay without stuff?"

"Mm-hmm," I nodded, sitting up on my knees. I held him firm while I slowly impaled myself.

Wesley sucked in air sharply and scooted down on the couch. He ran his hands up my naked thighs, grabbing onto me with one hand and squeezing my balls with the other. I pumped up and down, alternating speed and angle until I was on the edge of climax. Wesley gripped the back of my head with one hand and kissed me deeply as I exploded in his embrace. He bucked his hips twice more and erupted inside me while Bruce Lee continued to fight his enemies against impossible odds.

Wesley looked down and touched the gooey front of his shirt and grinned accusingly at me. "I hope this doesn't stain," he said, caressing my cheek and kissing me softly.

Of course, he was wearing his new dark orange shirt Mom gave him for Christmas. I blushed, but gripped the hem and pulled the shirt over his head. He smiled handsomely, and a little bit devilishly, and kissed me until my entire body tingled.

"Let's go to bed," I whispered in his ear, sliding off his lap.

Wesley stared at me, his eyes glazed over with lust, as I stood up wearing only a long-sleeve shirt. I looked down at him with the same expression, at his naked chest and his jeans pulled low around his hips. He hurriedly followed me into the bedroom and tackled me on the bed, his hot fingertips touching me all over. He kicked his jeans off and flipped me onto my stomach and I climbed onto my knees with my backside high in the air. He frigged me with one hand and slid two fingers inside me while I ground against his knuckles. Wesley leaned over my back and licked the rim of my ear and I could feel his nipples brushing lightly across my shoulder blades.

"Hurry," I whimpered, my body on fire with a pleasing ache down below.

"Heh, I forgot how horny you get when you're stoned," Wesley chuckled, withdrawing his fingers.

He nudged playfully just to hear me moan pleadingly, and then with a strong thrust entered me wholly. I absentmindedly whispered "Thank you," and Wesley chuckled again, but then moaned salaciously when he felt me tighten around him. He held my hips in his strong hands and pulled me backward each time he pushed forward. I trembled beneath his hard frame, pleasure waving through my entire body, and he took me ravenously. He arched his back and climaxed while I spent at the same time. He took several deep breaths then pulled back, withdrawing slowly.

"I love seeing that," he murmured quietly, and even though it embarrassed me for him to watch, I arched my back so that he could see his semen leaking out of me. "I love you," he whispered, lying down on my back and nuzzling his chin in the cradle of my neck and shoulder. I turned my face to the side, my cheek brushing against his lips, and whispered back the same thing.

Chapter 40

"I HAVE to go to the bookstore. Wanna come?" I asked.

"The bookstore?" Wesley said, glancing up from the TV.

"Yeah, school starts next week," I said, retrieving my shoes from near the front door. Wesley nodded with a "now-I-remember" expression and crossed his feet on the coffee table. "Wanna come with me?" I asked again.

"Nah. I think I'll stay here, if you don't mind," he answered, resting his hands on his stomach.

I sat down on the sofa with my shoes on the floor and looked at Wesley. "Is your tummy still bothering you?"

"A little bit, but I'll be fine."

I slipped my shoes on and tied the laces. "Want me to get anything for you?"

"Yeah. Could you get some Tums or something?"

"Sure," I said, walking between Wesley and the TV and stopping. I looked at him with the best cutesy face I could come up with and swung my arms back and forth at my sides. "Can I take the car?" I asked sweetly with big eyes.

Wesley smiled, knowing I could manipulate him with that look. "Will you be all right by yourself?" He taught me how to drive a stick a few months before, but I'd never driven without him.

"I haven't stalled once the last few times you let me drive and I'll be really careful," I promised. Wesley's car was his baby and I wanted to assure him that he didn't need to worry. "Please?" I asked with pouty lips and upturned brows.

"How can I say no to that face?" he agreed with a light chuckle.

"Thank you!" I shouted, grabbing my coat from the back of a kitchen chair. I picked up Wesley's keys from the counter and pushed my hands through the sleeves of my jacket. "All right. I'll be back in a little while and I promise I'll be careful! Love you!" I said, heading out the front door.

I drove to the bookstore on campus. Even though school started next week, it wasn't very busy. I mulled around with my schedule in my hand, matching class numbers and sections, and picked out the books I needed. I had one text for chem, two for social psych, three for each history class, and two for English comp, and even though most of them were used, I still spent $250. I sighed as I handed my credit card to the clerk and he smiled knowingly at me.

I carried the two heavy bags to the car and was grateful I didn't have to take the bus. I stopped at a drug store and bought Tums and ice cream before heading home.

When I got back, Wesley was asleep on the sofa. I got a can of soda from the fridge and sat down next to him. Wesley was really cute when he was asleep. He slept with his lips slightly parted and he wrinkled up his nose regularly. I laced my hand with his on top of his stomach and smiled. He scrunched up his face and furrowed his brows and his hand felt clammy. I knew he wasn't feeling well the last couple of days, but he seemed a little feverish now. His body jerked and he shocked himself awake. He looked at me with sleepy, foggy eyes and managed a smile.

"You're back already?" he asked with a raspy voice.

"Yeah, safe and sound. But, are you okay? You look a little pale," I said, squeezing his hand.

"Yeah. My stomach's still bothering me, but I'll be fine," he answered, resting his head back on the sofa again.

“That’s what you said two days ago,” I countered and brought my hand up to his forehead. “Besides, you feel pretty warm. Have you taken anything?”

“I took some ibuprofen a while ago, but I don’t think it’s working. My stomach still hurts. Did you buy those Tums?” he asked, looking back at the TV.

“Maybe I should call my mom. This started about four days ago and hasn’t gotten any better,” I said, pursing my lips in thought.

“Nah, don’t worry about it. I’ll be fine. It just has to run its course.”

“Yeah, but I’m gonna call anyway. Maybe she can tell us what you can take so you’ll feel a little better,” I said, standing up to get the phone.

Wesley told me not to worry, but I called anyway. Mom was in the middle of her shift, so I left a message with the receptionist in the pediatrics department and Mom called me back half an hour later. I explained Wesley’s aches and pains and her tone startled me a little. She asked where the pain was and how bad it was, and asked about accompanying symptoms. She told me that it could just be the stomach flu but with the location of his stomach pain, it might be appendicitis. She recommended that Wesley keep taking ibuprofen and if the pain worsened, even the slightest, to head to the ER, just in case.

I began to worry a little more when she mentioned the emergency room and Wesley laughed when I told him what she said. We spent the rest of the day on the sofa and I gave him two ibuprofen tablets every four hours. He didn’t seem to be getting any better and he still felt feverish, but I reasoned that I did tend to worry too much. We went to bed around ten o’clock and Wesley fell asleep right away. I had to count sheep for a while, but I eventually fell asleep too.

Around one in the morning, I woke up and Wesley was sitting up in bed with both hands over his stomach. He was sweating and rocking back and forth slightly. My heart sank and I told him we were going to the hospital. Wesley declined, of course, trying to convince me, and himself, that he was feeling better.

“No. Get dressed because we’re going,” I demanded, getting out of bed and pulling on my blue jeans from the pile of dirty clothes.

"I told you, I'm fine. I'm not going to the hospital," he said, though his voice sounded weak.

"We're going."

"No, we're not."

We argued briefly and I sat down on the bed. I was fully dressed and Wesley was still under the covers in a T-shirt and boxers. I stared at him and he stubbornly glared back at me.

"Wesley, please," I begged, but he shook his head. "The pain has gotten worse, you can't sleep, and I think it's appendicitis. We have to go," I pleaded, but he refused again.

"Tor, I'll be fine. I just need to get some sleep. And you do too," he said. He was adamant and I knew I wouldn't be able to change his mind. He lay back down slowly, still holding his stomach.

"I'll get you some ibuprofen," I said quietly and got out of bed. Wesley nodded and closed his eyes. I went to the kitchen and got two pills and a glass of water. Wesley took them and I stepped out of my jeans beside the bed.

I tried to sleep, but I knew it was futile. I listened to Wesley's breathing when he dozed off occasionally, but he mostly twisted and turned in bed. An hour passed and Wesley sat up again, his hands over his stomach and his face scrunched up. I sat up and rubbed his back softly.

"Maybe…maybe I should go," he gasped.

I jumped out of bed and pulled my jeans up. I got a pair of blue jeans for Wesley and pulled the covers off, but when he tried to swing his legs to the side of the bed, a sudden pang made him recoil.

"Slowly, okay?" I said, touching his knee and helping him put his jeans on. He was in a lot more pain than he admitted to and I was angry with myself for not realizing how bad it was.

We got to the hospital around three a.m. and the ER was pretty empty. A nurse called for Wesley after about half an hour and led him to a small exam room. She took his temperature and blood pressure while he sat uncomfortably on the paper-covered table. We waited another ten minutes until the doctor showed up and asked what was wrong. Wesley explained his symptoms while I interjected regularly and the doctor asked Wesley to lie down. He pressed on his stomach and Wesley gritted his teeth in pain. Then the doctor calmly explained that he thought it was appendicitis and that Wesley needed a CT scan to confirm the diagnosis.

Wesley changed into a hospital gown and was taken to have the scan. I folded his clothes and waited in the small exam room, fidgeting nervously, until Wesley returned. He sat down beside me and took my hand, telling me not to worry. I kept my tears at bay, but I had to stare at my lap because if I looked at him, I knew I would start crying.

Minutes ticked by and at last, the doctor returned. He explained the results of the CT scan, confirmed the appendicitis, and told us that Wesley needed an emergency appendectomy. Wesley's hands tightened around mine and I felt tears slowly begin to well and overflow. Wesley was lucky, the doctor went on, that the appendix didn't rupture and that he was eligible for laparoscopic surgery, which consisted of four small incisions in the abdomen to remove the appendix. It was less invasive than the traditional procedure and greatly reduced the recovery time. The doctor had already spoken with the surgeon on duty and Wesley was scheduled for eight a.m.

"A nurse will be in shortly to give you some painkillers and a tranquilizer. Do you have any questions?" the doctor asked from the threshold. Wesley shook his head. "Well, take care. Someone from general surgery will come for you in a short while."

"Thank you, Doctor," I uttered weakly, smiling as best as I could manage.

The doctor nodded with a customer-service smile and walked away. I gripped Wesley's hand and he rested his head on my shoulder. He was more afraid than he was letting on and, of course, he wouldn't cry; he just clung to me for silent support and I wrapped my arms around him and kissed the top of his head. I tried to ease his worry, even making jokes about how cute he looked in a hospital gown, but neither of us was in the mood.

A nurse came in shortly with pills in a small plastic cup and some water. She smiled warmly and told us not to worry and then left with another hospitable smile. Then another nurse from general surgery came for Wesley and he waited patiently with a wheelchair. Wesley sat down and took my hand again.

"Don't worry. You're gonna be just fine," I told him with tears on my cheeks. "I'll be waiting for you when you get out."

"I'm not going to prison," Wesley said with a light smile. "But I'll be waiting for you."

"I love you," I whispered, leaning down and kissing him softly on the lips.

"I love you too. And don't worry," he said, smiling again.

I followed Wesley and the nurse out of the room and down the hall. Then the nurse paused and he pointed to the left.

"Follow this hall all the way down and make a right. The general surgery waiting room is right there. And don't worry, he's in good hands," the nurse said and smiled cordially.

Wesley held his clothes on his lap with one hand and waved to me with the other. I watched them until they turned the corner and then the weight of reality fell on my shoulders and I felt so heavy I could barely walk.

The waiting room was empty and I slumped down in a chair with my head in my hands. I hated that he was in so much pain and that he tried to hide it from me. I scolded myself for not making him go to the doctor sooner.

I wanted to call Mom and tell her what was going on, but I forgot my cell and I didn't have any change. I had to call Wesley's parents too. My stomach tightened with the thought, but they needed to know. I pulled my debit card from my wallet and found a pay phone in the main lobby. I dialed Wesley's old phone number and took a deep breath; I hadn't even thought of what I was going to say. After three rings, Mrs. Carroll answered.

"Hello?" she said, her voice a little rough from sleep.

"Um, hello? Mrs. Carroll?"

"This is," she answered, annoyed that a telemarketer was calling so early.

"Um, this is Toren Grey, Wesley's…."

"What?" she interjected with a tone of aggravation.

"I'm sorry to call, but…um, Wesley's in the hospital right now. He, um…."

"What?" she demanded again, this time in a panicked voice.

"He…he needs emergency surgery. He has appendicitis and…."

"Where? Where is he?" she asked.

"The University Hospital. He just went in for…."

"All right. I'll be right there," she said and hung up the phone.

I still had the receiver at my ear and the fear in her voice sank into me. I felt guilty all of a sudden, like I let this happen to Wesley, like this was my fault. My chest felt tight and I couldn't take deep breaths. She sounded so afraid. I hung up the phone and balled my hands into fists at my sides. Tears welled again and I blinked rapidly to keep them at bay.

I called Mom collect and started crying again before I could even say hello. I choked on my sobs and Mom guessed what had happened. She talked to me until I calmed down, and then said she would come up soon. I tried to tell her that I'd call her once Wesley was out of surgery and in a room, but Mom insisted on coming and I didn't argue. Then I went back to the waiting room and listened to the clock until Mr. and Mrs. Carroll arrived twenty minutes later.

They hurried into the waiting room and I stood up quickly. They stared at me silently and I didn't know what to say. I fidgeted my hands and Mr. Carroll glared at me.

"Where's Wes?" he demanded.

"He…he's in surgery now," I stuttered quietly.

"What's wrong? What happened?"

"He has appendicitis," I explained, staring at the floor. I reiterated everything the ER doctor told me and I started crying again.

They sat down across the waiting room from me and I heard them talking quietly but I couldn't understand anything they were saying. I sat in the wooden chair with the purple cushion with my knees together and my shoulders slumped, trying to take up as little room as possible, wishing I could disappear altogether. After a few minutes, Mr. Carroll went to the courtesy phone at the back desk. He spoke with someone but I only heard him mention Wesley's name. Then he and Mrs. Carroll excused themselves and I was left all alone again. I took a deep, unsteady breath and felt relief that they were gone. I held my head in my hands, closed my eyes, and waited.

Mom and Alycia startled me when they entered the waiting room. They both came even though I told them they didn't have to. Mom hugged me and Alycia rubbed my back and promised me that Wesley was going to be just fine. We sat down in the empty waiting room and Alycia grabbed a 500-piece puzzle from a nearby shelf.

Hours passed as we worked on the puzzle of an assortment of postage stamps. Mr. and Mrs. Carroll still hadn't come back. Alycia went to buy some sodas for us and we continued working on the puzzle.

"What time did Wes go in?" Mom asked, looking up at the clock.

"A little before eight," I answered, glancing up at the clock too. It was just past twelve-thirty.

"Hmm. He should be out of surgery by now. Recovery too," she thought aloud, counting back the hours. My stomach cringed and Mom patted my head. "Let me call. I'll see what's going on," she said.

Mom went to the courtesy phone and Alycia and I watched her. Her eyes widened, then narrowed, then she nodded her head.

"He's out of recovery. He's already in a room," she said.

We hurried and took the elevator to the sixth floor. I had to keep myself from running as we turned down the hall Wesley was on. My breathing sped up and my heart thumped against my rib cage. The door to room 612 was wide open and Mr. Carroll stood at the foot of the bed with his arms crossed. Mrs. Carroll stood beside Wesley and I inhaled deeply, realizing I had been holding my breath. His face brightened and he smiled at me.

"There you are! Where have you been?" Wesley asked in a rough and raspy voice.

He had dark rings under eyes, greasy, disheveled hair, and an IV in his left arm and I thought he looked more handsome than ever. I unconsciously pushed my way past Mrs. Carroll and Wesley held out his hand to me. Tears filled my eyes and my lips moved, but no sound came out.

"Hi. How are you?" I finally managed to say, taking Wesley's hand and squeezing it lightly.

Wesley closed his eyes and exhaled. "Really tired and a little achy, but a lot better than I was before," he said and smiled again. "How are you?"

"A lot better now," I answered honestly. Wesley closed his eyes again, but he kept hold of my hand. "Can…can I get you anything?"

"I'm really, really thirsty," he answered, licking his dry, chapped lips.

"Let me get you some ice chips," Mom said, smiling at Wesley.

"Hi, Amanda," Wesley murmured, opening his eyes. He seemed surprised but genuinely happy that Mom and Alycia came to see him. Alycia stepped forward after Mom left the room and Wesley blinked slowly but kept smiling. "Hey, little sister."

"Hi, big brother," Alycia said softly, patting his shoulder.

Wesley's parents stared with furrowed brows at the foot of the bed as we took over the room and Wesley's attention. Mr. Carroll folded his arms on his chest and looked out the door.

"You really had us worried for a second there," Alycia said with upturned brows. "I thought poor Toren was gonna have a heart attack," she confided with a smile and a glance in my direction.

Mom returned with a Styrofoam cup filled with ice chips and handed it to me. She leaned down and kissed Wesley's forehead and ruffled his hair. "I'm so glad you're okay," she whispered, then stepped back.

"Want some ice?" I asked.

Wesley opened his eyes and nodded. I gave him an ice chip and he sucked it between his dry lips with a grateful smile. "Oh man, ice is so good," he murmured, closing his eyes again. Alycia and Mom chuckled softly and I grinned lightly at them. "Gimme another one," he said, smacking his tongue against the roof of his mouth.

I held another ice chip to his lips and he caught my hand in his, sucked in the ice and kissed my fingertips. I blushed to my ears and Wesley chuckled quietly, laying his head back on the pillow. I closed my eyes and forced a smile, knowing Mr. and Mrs. Carroll were standing right behind me.

"So, where were you? I was waiting forever," Wesley asked, opening his eyes and looking at me. His voice was still quiet and raspy, but it lost its dry edge.

I shook my head side-to-side. "No one came to talk to me. I didn't even know you were out of surgery until my mom called and got your room number," I explained, squeezing his hand. As I spoke, I had a creeping suspicion, but I banished it from my mind.

"Huh, that's weird. I wonder why?" Wesley asked rhetorically, looking up at the ceiling. "But, you're here now, so I guess it doesn't matter," he added, smiling at me.

There was a knock at the door and a middle-aged woman in a knee-length white coat with black hair pulled taut in a bun stepped over the threshold smiling kindly. She had a stethoscope draped around her neck and hugged a large, metal clipboard to her chest.

"Hello, I'm Dr. Amani, Wesley's surgeon," she said in a thickly accented voice. She stepped into the room and made eye contact with each of us. "Wow, you've got a full house. Must be a pretty popular guy," she laughed, showing large, white teeth. She set her clipboard down on the bed table and felt for her stethoscope.

"Well, it's *supposed* to be family only," Mrs. Carroll remarked quietly, crossing her arms and shifting her stance.

Dr. Amani ignored her, or pretended not to hear, and the placed the wishbone end of the stethoscope in her ears. "How are you feeling?" she asked Wesley, tilting her head to the side.

"Tired," he answered, blinking slowly. "A little achy, but mostly tired."

Dr. Amani felt around Wesley's back and chest with the stethoscope, then pointed to his right side. "Can I take a look?" she asked, referring to Wesley's incisions. Wesley pulled up his gown beneath the knit blanket and Dr. Amani inspected the cuts. "On a scale of one to ten with ten being the worst, how's your pain?"

Wesley glanced at me and then at the doctor. "Probably a six. A five or a six, I think," he answered.

"Well, we can get you some more painkillers for that," Dr. Amani said, pulling Wesley's gown back down. "Your incisions look good. The surgery went very well and I expect you'll be back to normal in no time," she said with a friendly smile. "Now, you don't have stitches, but Steri-Strips that'll come off on their own in a few days. You're going to be tender on your right side and it's not uncommon to feel some pain in your shoulder. But, all in all, you're looking really good. We'll schedule a follow-up exam in two weeks, so until then, no work, no driving, no heavy lifting. We'll go over that again at your discharge as well as give you a prescription for oral painkillers. I recommend staying in bed, especially the first two days because you'll be pretty tired, and no sleeping on your stomach, only on your back and maybe a little on your left side. Just take it easy the next two weeks and your body will heal itself," Dr. Amani explained in a whirlwind of words. She picked up her clipboard and jotted some things down. "Do you have any questions?" Wesley looked at me, and then shook his head. "Well then, I'll send in a nurse for more Demerol and if you're feeling well enough, you may even be able to go home tonight."

Wesley smiled and bowed his head slightly. "Thank you very much, Dr. Amani," he said quietly and genuinely.

Dr. Amani smiled again, hooking her pen in the breast pocket of her white coat. "I'm glad I can help," she answered earnestly. "Take care and get well soon," she said, stepping backward and leaving the room, still with her pleasant smile.

Wesley rested his head back on the pillow and closed his eyes. He looked exhausted with dark circles under his eyes. He was so different from the usually bright and vibrant man that I fell in love with and it broke my heart to see him like this. Wesley gripped my hand and furrowed his brows. He opened his eyes and it took a moment for his vision to focus on his parents at the foot of the bed.

"What did you mean when you said 'family only'?" he asked quietly.

Mrs. Carroll glanced at me, and then shook her head. "It's nothing. Don't worry about it," she said dismissively, patting Wesley's toes over the knit blanket.

Wesley noticed her look in my direction and he tightened his grip around my hand and narrowed his eyes. "You meant Toren, didn't you?" he asked.

"Honey, it's all right, we just want what's best for you," she said, giving me a glare that might as well have been a knife in my heart.

"He *is* what's best for me," Wesley said violently, his pale face gaining color. "He was the only person I wanted to see when I woke up and you went out of your way to make sure he wasn't here! Did you actually tell the doctor not to talk to him?"

"Sweetheart, calm down…." Mrs. Carroll began, but Wesley interrupted her.

"I can't believe it! This is bullshit! Tor called you on his own even though I didn't want him to. In fact, I told him *not* to call you, and this is how you thank him? What the hell is wrong with you?"

I was taken aback by the strength in his voice. His face warmed to a reddish hue and he slammed his fist into the bed. He was taking deep breaths and I squeezed his hand.

"Wesley, calm down. It's okay." I whispered.

"No, it's not okay!" Wesley shouted. "I'm sick of the way they treat you."

"Wes, calm down," Mr. Carroll said stoically. His expression never changed and it was like he was blaming Wesley for being angry. Wesley looked down into his lap and went quiet; his grip loosened on my hand and he didn't say anything more.

"Why…why don't we go down to the cafeteria and get some lunch?" Mom suggested after a silent moment. "Wes really needs his rest right now, so let's give him some time to sleep."

Mom smiled awkwardly and Alycia picked up her purse from the floor. Mr. and Mrs. Carroll stared at Wesley, who didn't look up again, and then agreed. Mom and Alycia led the way out of the room, smiling at Wesley and telling him to get some sleep. Mrs. Carroll patted his leg over the blanket and followed Mr. Carroll out of the room after glaring at me again for a long moment. Wesley lifted his eyes to the door and then sighed with bated relief. He squeezed my hand and looked down into his lap again.

"You always do that," he said weakly, after everyone was gone.

"Do what?" I asked, turning to Wesley with upturned brows.

"Back down to my parents. You let them walk all over you and I'm sick of it," he said sullenly.

"I just thought that now wasn't the right time," I answered quietly.

"It's never the right time, but I'm sick of how they treat you."

"Wesley," I interrupted, tightening my grip around his hand. "They're never gonna accept me and I'm fine with that. Because you said you chose me. But I don't want you to cut all ties with your family. It's important to me. Besides, we don't see them all that often, so it's okay as long as you come home to me," I explained. It was honestly how I felt and I believed every word I said.

Wesley exhaled heavily through his nose and nodded. "All right, you win. But I still don't like the way they treat you. I just wish they would get it. I wish they would see that you really are what's best for me."

I leaned down and kissed Wesley on the lips, just a short kiss, but one that was filled with promises. Wesley finally smiled at me and sighed again. He laid his head back down and took some deep breaths.

"How are you feeling?" I asked, concerned that he wore himself out more from all the excitement.

"I forgot I was tired," he said with a sleepy laugh. "But, how are you? Are you feeling okay?"

"Yeah, I'm okay. Well, a lot better now," I acknowledged with a grin.

"Well, you look like hell."

"You're one to talk!" I said, lightly slapping Wesley's shoulder.

"You've gotta be tired though. Did you sleep any? Want me to scoot over?"

I kissed Wesley again and pulled a chair next to the bed. Wesley tried to stay awake, but his eyes kept shutting and he eventually drifted off. I watched quietly with a smile on my face. I was so grateful that he was okay; the thought of losing him scared me more than anything. He was still holding my hand and I squeezed it twice. I told him I loved him and then I fell asleep too.

Chapter 41

I HAD learned that clichés are often true; men do act like babies when they're sick, but Wesley acted like a six year-old without any toys.

He came home from the hospital the morning after his surgery. He stayed in bed and slept most of the day and I sat beside him, reading a book or doing puzzles. He didn't have much of an appetite, but he ate a little bit of soup and half a slice of bread. He took the prescription painkillers every four hours as directed and slept away the day while his body healed.

I called Gus at the shop and explained what had happened. His voice faltered when I told him Wesley had an emergency appendectomy and I clearly heard his relief when I said that Wesley was already home and on the mend. Gus wanted Wesley to take as much time as he needed because he would work his ass off once he got better. On the second day, Wesley spent most of his time in bed, but he sat up and talked and played games with me. He even sat on the sofa and watched TV while I made dinner. The third day was spent in the living room, curled up on the couch, watching movies and playing video games. He regained his appetite and ate larger portions of soup, sandwiches, and some of the lasagna that Gus's wife had made for us. By the fourth day, he was able to move around a little more freely, and he was getting restless.

"I'm bored," Wesley sighed, leaning back in bed and stretching his arms.

"So read a book or play a game," I suggested, dropping my T-shirt into the dirty clothes pile on the floor.

"Don't wanna," he answered, watching me closely as I pulled a white polo shirt over my head.

"Then watch a movie or something," I said, stepping into a pair of khaki pants. I took a pair of socks from the top drawer of the dresser and sat down on the edge of the bed.

"I'm not in the mood," he answered, sitting up and scooting closer to me. "C'mon, Tor, play with me."

"I can't. Today's the first day of school and then I have to work tonight," I explained calmly although Wesley was threading his arms around my waist. I had taken the past few days off work to take care of him and now I had both school and work.

"But I'm boooored!" Wesley complained, realizing his actions were futile.

"Alycia's coming over after school and if Jeremy's not working, I'm sure he'll come too. So, just be good until they get here. Now, I've gotta get going or I'm gonna be late," I said, standing up and then leaning down and kissing Wesley's forehead. "I love you and I'll see you tonight."

"Fine. Just leave me! Your poor boyfriend's just had surgery and now you're leaving him all alone. Poor me," Wesley whined, sticking out his bottom lip and pouting.

"I know, I'm so mean. But I'll make it up to you later. I love you!" I said, walking out of the bedroom.

"I love you too. And have a good first day of school," he called after me.

Chapter 42

I WAS frustrated. Beyond that even. It had been two weeks to the day since Wesley and I last had sex and at least another three days until we could again. It was strange; I had lived over eighteen years of my life never having sex and now I could barely function after a two-week dry spell! What was wrong with me? And Wesley didn't even seem bothered by it. He was feeling better, no longer taking the prescription painkillers, and his boredom and restlessness increased exponentially, but if he embroiled himself in an activity, he was fine. While I suffered from a twenty-four-hour headache and hard-on. It wasn't fair! And to make matters worse, Wesley strolled around in his boxers or without a shirt on knowing the exact effect it had on me.

But, it was partly my fault too. I knew Wesley couldn't indulge himself, so I had decided that I wouldn't either, but it was so hard! Quite literally. Even at work. The night before, I was straightening up the tableware aisle, started thinking about Wesley, and had to make a dash to the restroom. It was ridiculous, sitting on the closed toilet seat with clenched fists trying to talk myself down. I told myself that it wasn't fair; if Wesley couldn't then I shouldn't, and how much better it would be if I waited until we could satisfy our desires together. But thinking about that only exacerbated my situation and I had to make a choice: spend an hour trying to talk myself out of it or get it over with and get back to work. As embarrassing as it was, jerking off at work was better than being found grappling with an erection while still on the clock. I came in a wad of tissue, washed my hands, and went back to straightening tablecloths and napkins.

I got home around ten and Wesley greeted me happily while innocently playing video games. I felt so guilty that I couldn't even look at him. I made a snack and we watched TV before going to bed, finally letting sleep overwhelm the shame of ejaculating on company time.

The next day, I woke with morning wood so hard that it hurt while Wesley slept peacefully beside me. I slithered out of bed and went to the bathroom where I let the natural process of urine elimination take care of my erection. I sat down on the sofa and watched the morning news on a low volume until I heard Wesley rustling around in the bedroom. I thought about what to make for breakfast then went to say good morning.

"What—what are you doing?" I stammered as I stepped into the bedroom, seeing Wesley sitting up in bed with a flushed expression and his dick in his hand.

"Ah…oops. Busted," he said, staying his hand and grinning at me.

"Stop it! Don't do that!" I blurted out, hurrying to his bedside. I looked down at him and instantly felt my crotch stir in arousal. "You're not supposed to do that!" I shouted.

"What? Why not?" Wesley asked grinningly, cleverly sensing my line of thought.

"Be-because! The doctor said…."

"The doctor said no sex. She never said anything about masturbating," he explained candidly.

"But, that should be a given!" I complained, trying my best to avert my eyes from his lap.

"You really expect me to wait that long?" he asked, peering up at me from the tops of his eyes while he began stroking himself again.

"Well, yes! I mean, I didn't think you could and…."

Wesley rounded his eyes and looked at me squarely. "Do you mean you haven't this whole time?"

He stared at me without blinking. My face felt flush and I nodded my head slowly. "I just…. Well, I thought you couldn't, so I was waiting 'til you could," I said quietly, blushing deeper because I was lying. But how could I possibly tell him that I got so horny that I jerked off in the bathroom at work? At work!

"Oh man, you're a hell of a lot stronger than I am," he sighed wistfully, still with his stiff cock in hand. "Now I feel kinda guilty for all the times I've done it." I swallowed hard, feeling the twinge of guilt in the pit of my stomach for lying. But there was no way I could tell him the truth, and it was just once. "So how about I make it up to you," he offered with a sly grin, patting the bed. "I'll watch you. Besides, you can't keep that hard-on hidden from me," he said calmly with a wink and a glance at my crotch.

My throbbing erection was pleading with me and I felt my desire stirring in my stomach, my fingers, even the tips of my toes. Wesley stared seductively at me, licking his upper lip, while he kneaded the head of his cock in his palm. I watched with moist lips, mesmerized by his fingers in action, molesting his perfectly shaped organ. I had never wanted to suck a dick so badly in my entire life. My resolve evaporated and I sat down on the bed, unzipping my pants and exposing myself to Wesley's sparkling gaze. He reached forward, but I batted his hand away. If he touched me, there was no way I could resist the urge to fully impale myself on his rigid cock and have my way with him despite the injury it might cause him. No, we had to do it alone, together. I vigorously pumped my fist up and down, closing my eyes to the overwhelming sensation taking over my body. But I couldn't keep them shut long; I had to watch Wesley. I had to see his expression change from pleasure to climax, to see the way he handled himself, palming the tip and lubing the shaft with pre-cum while his other hand played with his balls. My own climax was near and I squirmed and bucked my hips in rhythm with my hand, fighting the aching desire to slip a finger inside my warm ring of muscle. I felt Wesley's eyes on me and the shame normally associated with masturbation only seemed to heighten my arriving orgasm. I exploded in a globular arch that landed in a sticky puddle on the bed and Wesley climaxed soon after, sitting up and aiming for the same spot. I heaved in air like I had just run a marathon and watched misty-eyed as Wesley drew a finger through the two small pools, mixing our semen together.

"I think that was the most erotic thing we've ever done," Wesley panted in satisfaction, with a smirk on his handsome face.

"Yeah," I whispered breathlessly, my grip finally loosening. I was hot all over and more in the mood now than I was ten minutes ago.

"You're still hard," Wesley said, directing his gaze into my lap with a half-smile on his face.

"So are you," I answered, glancing down at him and then looking away quickly, trying to stifle the enormous desire within me.

Wesley pushed the covers away and leaned back. He held his stiff prick in his hand and smiled in a come-hither manner. "Hop on," he said with a sweet, yet coarse voice. It was the tone of voice he used to turn me on, a throaty alto that was deep and animalistic.

I shook my head although I was unconvinced. I wanted it so badly that it felt like my blood was boiling, but I had to keep my wits; Wesley's health was more important than immediate gratification. "No," I said at length, shaking my head.

Wesley sat up and touched my face. "C'mon, babe. I know you want it, you know I want it, and besides, it's not like I'm gonna break."

I fixed my eyes with Wesley's, very nearly giving in, when I steeled my resolve and shook my head again. "No." I had to be direct and decisive or I would get lost in the fog of my passion. I leaned close, holding his stare, and spoke in a deeper voice. "Look, you *belong* to me, which means *this* belongs to me," I said, flicking the head of his cock with the tip of my finger. "And if you do anything to make me wait any longer than I absolutely have to, I'll never forgive you."

Wesley stared at me with wide eyes and his cheeks were tinted a little red. He let the weight of the words sink in and then he leaped forward, grasping me firmly in one hand while his other hand slipped around my waist.

"Oh man, now we gotta do it," he blurted out desperately, curving his hand around my backside and searching for the hole with his middle finger.

"Wesley, no!" I shouted, battling my fevered sensations, Wesley's moist lips, and his hot fingers. "Stop it! I said, no!" His passion ebbed at the forcefulness of my voice and he looked at me with puppy-dog eyes. "I'll just suck you off, okay?"

"But…but what about you? It's not fair if only I get off. You need it too," he answered blatantly.

He was right. Of course, he was right; I did need it. Looking up at him, his eyes hovering above my face, I caressed his cheek and let out a little sigh. "All right, but no penetration."

Wesley kissed me and I ravenously kissed him back. He rolled off me and onto his back. I turned and crawled on top of him, my knees on either side of his head. He didn't wait for me to get situated before he lifted his head to lick the oozing pre-cum. He slid one hand around my backside and forced his finger inside. I reacted so thoroughly to his salacious invasion that a desperate moan echoed against the bedroom walls. My legs trembled and nearly gave out before I could even lower my mouth enough to his eager shaft. I panted and rolled to my side.

"Can't…can't do it that way. My legs feel weak," I breathed, hearing Wesley chuckle with delight.

On our sides, with each other's thighs nestled around our heads, we sucked and touched and caressed and stroked and slurped in agonizing bliss that ended all too soon. We lay prone for a while, filtering the scent of sex, sweat, and semen though our wide-awake senses. I touched my sticky lips, still aching for more, my backside disappointed with the limited thrill of Wesley's finger. But I made up my mind. I rolled to my back and twisted around, lying beside Wesley and his cute grin.

"No more. Not 'til Monday when the doctor says you're okay," I declared boldly, hoping my body would live up to my celibate decree.

"What? But that's three days away!" Wesley complained, staring at the ceiling.

"I know, but you can do it. Because, if we don't, I might break you in the meantime," I said honestly.

"That might not be so bad," he said with a smirk, raising an eyebrow at me.

"No, three days is nothing compared to another two weeks—or longer," I said, sitting up and looking around the room with glassy eyes. It was gonna be a rough three days, but we had to persevere. Just three more days.

AND it was the longest three days of my life.

I drove Wesley to his appointment on Monday morning at 11:00. I sat in the waiting room and flipped through an old *Newsweek*. Wesley finally appeared after a long twenty minutes. I set the magazine down and Wesley was smiling broadly.

"I'm A-OK. Everything's in the right place and working as it should be," he said cheerfully, chuckling softly at my loud sigh of relief. "Let's go. Gimme the keys," he added, patting my back.

I happily, yet regretfully, handed over his keys. I had gotten used to having the car and I was sad to go back to walking and riding the bus, but it was all well worth it.

Wesley turned over the engine and backed out of the parking spot. "Ah, I missed driving," he sighed nostalgically, as if it had been years since he was behind the wheel.

I gazed at the rolling scenery then turned to Wesley with a happy expression. "Do you wanna go out for lunch? In celebration?" I asked and then touched my lips in thought. "Or we could swing by the store and get something really good for dinner?"

Wesley glanced at me sideways with a puzzled expression I couldn't figure out. He looked back at the road. "Maybe later," he said, chewing on his thumbnail.

"Why? Since we're out, we might as well stop…."

"We can't right now. There are things I have to do first," he said, looking at me with a grin.

"What?" I asked, innocently walking into his trap, though I should've known better by now.

"Like take you home and fuck you up, down, and sideways," he answered, like it was the most obvious thing in the world.

I blushed to the tips of my ears, but nodded with a smile. My passion briefly ebbed in the anticipation of a healthy checkup, but now it was back with a vengeance. There was no more waiting or holding back anymore. Suddenly, Wesley couldn't drive fast enough.

Barely inside the front door, Wesley turned and pulled me into his arms. He slammed the door shut and pulled my coat off. He kissed me as he took off his own jacket and let it drop to the floor.

"Wait. Wait," I murmured, reluctantly pulling away from his warm lips. Wesley looked at me with a "now what?" expression and I smiled and patted his cold cheek. "I have to go to the bathroom. So just go to the bedroom and wait for me."

I used the bathroom and zipped up my blue jeans, but left the button undone. What was the point? I washed my hands and glanced in the mirror. My cheeks were still red from the blustery cold outside.

I was expecting Wesley to be completely naked in some embarrassing, sexy pose, but when I stepped in the room, he was sitting on the edge of the bed, fully clothed, with his elbows resting on his knees and his fingertips touching. He looked up at me and I felt a shock of shyness overwhelm me. He was really handsome: brown eyes in a strong face, dark glossy hair, and supple pink lips. I swallowed hard, overcome with a sudden nervousness, like it was our first time all over again.

"C'mere," Wesley said in a deep, throaty tone and already I felt myself react to the sound of his voice.

I walked over to him and he slid his hands around my back, pulling me closer and leaning his head against my stomach. I looked down and ran my fingers through his hair.

"I missed you," he said quietly, his voice muffled. He pressed his hands against the small of my back. "You don't know how hard it was, not to touch you when you were lying right next to me."

I lifted his head in my hands and looked into his deep eyes. I kissed him lightly and smiled. "I do know how hard it was," I answered, kissing him softly again. "I missed you too. So don't make me wait anymore."

I kissed him deeply, sliding my hand around to the back of his head. He returned my eager kiss and gripped the back of my shirt in his large, strong hands. It had only been two weeks but it felt like so much longer. He excited me like no one else and I could feel his pulse through my entire body. He inched back on the bed and pulled me down to straddle his thighs. Our lips never parted and his cool, hard hands warmed my skin and everywhere he touched me felt like a flame was lit. He lifted my shirt over my head and looked down at my chest and erect nipples. He circled the firm buds with his fingertips and I brought his mouth back to my lips while grinding my hips against his.

We kissed like we were starved for it. He kept one hand on my chest and smoothed his other hand between my shoulder blades as I unzipped his pants and rummaged around like a kid looking for the prize in a box of cereal. Wesley followed my cue and lowered my jeans enough to get his hand inside. I wriggled on his lap with the sensation of his touch and Wesley pulled away from my kiss long enough to grin at me. He glanced down and took me in his hand and then scooted closer. He stroked both of us in one large hand and I joined my hand in the mutual masturbation, turned on beyond expression. I licked and nibbled his lips while rocking my hips against our moving hands and Wesley firmly grasped my backside in his free hand.

I came quickly and Wesley followed within seconds. I gasped for breath, resting my forehead against Wesley's and kissing him intermittently. We rested long enough to catch our breath and then kissed long again, like lovers parted for years.

"Take off your shirt," I said quietly, gazing down at his chest. He obeyed silently, smirking, knowing my fascination with his chest and the way he took off his shirt. I watched slack-jawed as he pulled his shirt over his head, then off his arms, and he chuckled at my gaping stare. I didn't know why, but it was the sexiest thing I'd ever seen.

"You ready?" he asked, noticing the erection that he was fully responsible for.

I nodded and stepped off the bed. I let my jeans drop to the floor while Wesley pulled his jeans off and tossed them aside. He got up on his knees and stretched his hand out to my face. His fingers were hot on my cheeks and I turned my head, drawing two fingers into my mouth and sucking on them. He pulled his hand back and replaced it with a warm kiss, pulling me down on the bed.

"Wait. Wait. We have to take it slow, so you don't hurt yourself," I said, looking down at his stomach and the four small cuts. The one by his belly button had bruised, but the others only had scabs over the incisions. I crawled over him and straddled his thighs, pushing him back on the bed.

Wesley gazed at me with glassy eyes, pushing his hand under the hem of my shirt, and I reached to the nightstand for the tube of lotion.

"Get me ready," I said, pressing the tube in his hand. I raised my hips and Wesley flipped the top and squeezed some of the lube over his fingers. "Better use more than usual since it's been a while," I said, leaning over him to part my legs more. Wesley took that as an invitation and kissed me wantonly as he pushed his hand between my thighs and circled the ring with his greased finger. My entire body tensed and I tried not to rock against his fingers. As much I preferred the real thing over being fingered, it was enough to almost make me cum and I had to concentrate to keep that from happening. I kissed Wesley and then leaned back, easing myself down slowly and with a little discomfort. I squeezed my eyes shut and my legs trembled as I impaled myself. Wesley kept one hand behind me, bracing me as I brought my backside down on him until I felt his balls. He slipped his hand to the front and grasped onto me and I moved up and down in rhythm with his slow strokes. I gasped for breath as I began to thrust my hips in earnest and I glimpsed Wesley's wild, sexy face in the throes of passion. I bit my lip hard, drawing a small amount of blood, and the metallic taste on my tongue aroused me even more.

"Oh God, Wesley!" I cried, pressing my hands down on his chest for leverage as I bounced on his lap.

Wesley grunted feverishly and looked in my eyes as he shot into me like a volcano, and seconds later, I climaxed in his hand with a cry and a whimper. I settled my body down against Wesley's, gasping and panting, and holding my breath long enough to give him a short kiss.

We remained as we were, locked in the closest union, savoring the tingling dissipation of orgasm in our bodies. Wesley ran a hand through my hair to the back of my neck, around my ear and then followed my jawline until he cupped my florid cheek in his palm. He looked long into my eyes and a small smile turned his lips.

"I love you," he said quietly, plainly, like it was the most obvious thing in the world.

"I love you too," I answered with a shy smile that made my chest burn with indescribable happiness.

"Tor, kiss me," he murmured, still touching my cheek.

I leaned close and kissed him lightly, barely touching our lips. Another kiss and then a third before our tongues met lasciviously in a long, deep kiss that made my toes tingle. I felt a stirring below me and pulled away from his alluring lips.

"Again? Already?" I asked with a smirk. I was partly surprised and impressed, but mostly turned on.

Wesley looked me over with lustful eyes and rubbed his hands up and down my thighs. "I've had to wait two weeks. Do you really need to ask?"

Chapter 43

WESLEY sat on the sofa watching TV with his feet up on the coffee table. I sneaked up behind him and blew lightly in his ear. He batted his hand at the sensation and I giggled, giving up my presence.

"Mornin'," he said, looking up at me.

"Morning, my ass. It's past noon," I answered, leaning to kiss him upside-down. "Why didn't you wake me up?"

"You were sleeping so good. Besides, I just got up too," he said, crossing his ankles.

I leaned my elbows down on the back of the sofa and stared at Wesley's profile. He really was handsome, even with his hair pointing in every direction (and not on purpose). "Anything you wanna tell me?" I mused aloud with a smirk on my lips.

"Can't think of anything," Wesley said, scratching his head. "Happy Monday?"

"Anything else?" I asked, bouncing my knees into the back of the sofa.

"Hmm. It snowed a little last night," he said, suppressing a grin. He glanced back at me and smiled, showing his teeth. "I'll say it if you kiss me." I leaned down and pecked his cheek, his stubble tickling my lips. Wesley looked at me with a frown, and then grasped the back of my neck with his large hand. "Happy birthday, Tor," he said and kissed me ravenously. He let go of my lips and then my neck, and sat up straight on the sofa. "Want some breakfast?"

"No!" I shouted, lifting my hands over my head. "Presents! I want my present!"

Wesley laughed like he was choking and then nodded. "All right, all right. Man, you and Alycia really are related," he said, standing up. He went to the closet by the front door and pulled down a small box wrapped in balloon paper from the top shelf. An envelope was taped to the top and had my name written on it in Wesley's distinctive print. "Happy birthday," he said and handed it to me.

I flopped down on the sofa and ripped the paper off a DVD collection of Bruce Lee movies. I smiled happily and appreciatively as I leaned over and kissed Wesley. "Thank you! I love it! Let's watch 'em now!" I said eagerly.

"What about the card?" Wesley asked, accepting my kiss while picking up the envelope from the floor and pulling it from the wrapping paper.

I blushed lightly and opened the business-size envelope. I pulled out a sheet of cardstock cut to the size of the envelope and smiled at the bright colors and the clip art of a bouquet of balloons, a birthday cake, and even a clown. In the upper-left corner "One Day Only!" was printed in yellow and red ink. "Birthday Coupon: I will do anything you say on Monday, January 25th" was printed in the center and at the bottom in a smaller font: "Excludes windows and laundry. Other restrictions may apply. See issuer for details."

I looked up at Wesley, on the verge of tears, because this birthday coupon was so ridiculously cute. Just the fact that he took the time to make up this cheesy yet adorable card was so sickeningly sweet that I hugged him so tight I could feel his ribs.

"It—it's so cute!" I finally managed to say, nearly squealing. Wesley recognized my excitement for what it was and blushed. I never thought it was in his disposition to do something this sappy and it made him all the cuter. "I love it! Thank you," I cooed, hugging him again and planting kisses on his lips, which only embarrassed him more.

"So, um, you want breakfast?" he asked, standing up with flushed cheeks.

I looked up at him and fluttered the coupon against my lips. "No, not right now," I said, glancing up and down his figure. "I want something better." I held up the coupon and smiled lasciviously. "Strip."

Wesley's eyes widened and a smile turned the corner of his mouth. He looked me over and nodded, then walked to the middle of the living room. He gathered up his shirt at the waist and pulled it over his head and off his arms. My pulse sped up and my body began to warm outward from the pit of my stomach. He dropped his shirt on the floor and began to unbutton his pants. I bit my bottom lip as I watched him unzip and lower his jeans to the floor. He was wearing black boxer-briefs and I gasped at the sight of his stomach and the sparse trail of hairs that disappeared beneath his underwear. He was hard and stretching the cotton fabric to its limit and he pushed his thumbs down into the elastic waistband.

"Wait," I murmured with glassy, lustful eyes. Wesley looked at me and grinned. "I want you to kiss me."

He stepped over his shirt and blue jeans and bent over me with his hand on the back of the couch. He touched my lips and leaned down, kissing me softly and sweetly. I closed my eyes and felt Wesley's hand drop to my neck and then my chest. His hand glided lightly over my lap and I twitched from the delicate sensation. Wesley pulled his hand and his lips away.

"Anything else you want me to do?" he asked with a smirk.

In a state of dazed arousal, I could only nod. Wesley took my hand and led me to the bedroom when I realized I still had the coupon in my hand. I wrapped my arms around his neck and tapped the top of his head with the cardstock.

"I didn't really need this, did I?" I asked smugly. Wesley chuckled and shook his head. "That's all right, because I'm probably gonna need it later," I said, setting the coupon down on the bedside table.

WE spent the majority of the day in bed and on the sofa. Dad called for his annual "happy birthday" conversation and I talked to him for longer than any previous call. Wesley made dinner, grilling hamburgers and making macaroni and cheese. I skipped school and seduced him back to bed around 7:00.

"There's something I have to tell you, but I'm not sure if you're gonna be happy about it or pissed off," I prefaced, staring at the ceiling. I was holding Wesley in my arms and tousling his hair with my fingers.

"That's an interesting way to start a conversation," Wesley said, pushing the back of his head into my shoulder to look up at me.

"Yeah, well…." I hesitated, looking back up to the ceiling. "I got an e-mail from your brother the other day."

"Oh yeah? What'd he have to say?"

"It was about the wedding," I answered, feeling Wesley's body get tense against mine.

"Heh, I should've known," Wesley said in a derisive tone.

I expected this reaction. We had argued about the wedding situation since the beginning of the year. He sounded like a broken record: "If you're not going, I'm not going." He was just being stubborn. Scott wanted Wesley to be his best man and without him, Scott wouldn't have one. They were both stubborn.

"So what'd he have to say this time?" Wesley asked, brushing his fingertips along my forearm.

"He sent a confirmation for plane tickets and booked and paid for a hotel from Thursday to Monday," I said, nervously awaiting his reaction.

"He what?" Wesley said, rolling onto his stomach. "Why the hell did he…? That moron!" he stuttered, thumping his forehead with the butt of his hand. "He knows! I've told him!" he shouted, slamming his fist into the pillow. "That idiot. If he wants to waste his money, that's fine, but…."

"You're not listening," I interjected firmly, after allowing him to rant a moment. "I said plane tickets, plural. One for you and one for me,"

I explained calmly, sitting up and pulling the sheet over my lap. Wesley looked at me blankly and blinked his eyes. "Scott wants you to be there. He wants us to be there; no matter what your parents think. You're his best man, Wesley. You have to go."

He mulled this over in his mind and then looked at me with serious eyes. "So, you're going?"

"Only if you are."

"Damn it. This means I have to take more time off work," he muttered, flopping onto the bed. "Gus's gonna kill me."

I leaned down on Wesley's back, brushing my cheek against his shoulder blade. His muscles flexed and his body was warm. I hugged him tightly and kissed the back of his neck.

"Gus already knows about the wedding, right? So I'm sure he already knew you would need time off. Just talk to him tomorrow. It'll work out," I said, sliding my hand down his back and beneath the sheet. I fondled his backside and he glanced at me over his shoulder.

"You sure are persuasive," he said, sitting up and pinning me down on the bed. He kissed me deeply, moving his hands over my torso. "Will you turn around for me?" he asked in a husky voice.

I licked his lips before crawling onto my hands and knees. The sheet slipped down and uncovered my bare ass to Wesley's delight. He pressed and fondled my flesh lovingly, cherishingly, and I begged him to touch me. His hands drove me wild because I felt his strength in his palms and fingertips. He pushed his way in, rocking me to and fro with his thrusts. A fever spread through me and I moaned in pleasure, echoing his lusty murmurs. He pumped my backside until I came, gushing in exhilarated bliss, and exploded moments later.

The bed was warm and the room was quiet except for our gasps. I lay down in the white mess, careless of the stickiness, and sighed delightedly. It was almost eight o'clock, just about the time that break would be over if I had gone to class. I smiled devilishly; there was something fun about having sex when I knew I should be doing something else. The salacious demon in me was getting louder and more demanding and since I trusted Wesley with my life, I tried to satisfy the lascivious, little monster.

"Can I tie you up?" I whispered almost inaudibly, feeling my cheeks burn with the quiet question.

"What'd you just say?" Wesley asked, turning to his side and making the bed squeak.

"N-nothing," I stuttered, surprised that he heard me. "I didn't say anything."

"Yes, you did! You just asked if you could tie me up," he answered, sitting up to look at my face.

"No…no, I didn't," I murmured, my entire body blushing. I covered my face with my hands and turned my head further to the side.

"Yes, you did! I heard you!" He grabbed my wrists, pulling my hands away from my face, then grinned and leaned close. "If you want to, I'll let you." I bit my lip and found the courage to look into his eyes. He smiled as if he knew a secret then looked around the room. "But we don't have any rope or anything we can use."

"We…we can probably use long-sleeved shirts," I suggested, sitting up and looking down in my lap. The mere conversation was making me hard.

Wesley stared at me a moment with searching eyes. "You've thought about this, haven't you?" he asked with a smirk.

I blushed deeply, and then hopped out of bed. All I had to say was "Yes, I think about it a lot," but I was too embarrassed. Yet, I could stand stark naked in front of him with cum smeared across my stomach and dripping down my inner thighs.

I rummaged through the hamper and found two long-sleeved shirts. Wesley asked for one and we tied one sleeve of each shirt to the bed frame. Then Wesley jumped on the bed and stretched his arms out. I hesitated and looked at his face. It felt like we were at a precipice of perviness and ready to jump.

"Are you sure you wanna do this?" I asked.

"Oh yeah, I'm sure," he answered with a grin and nodded down at his erection.

I climbed on the bed, tied one sleeve around his right wrist, and asked if it was too tight. Wesley shook his head and I crawled over him and bound his left wrist with the other shirt sleeve. Then I straddled his stomach and looked at him. With his arms stretched to the corners of the bed, he was completely under my control, vulnerable to my every whim. I sucked in air sharply and bit my bottom lip. The cup that held my desire was overflowing.

I leaned down and kissed him savagely, gliding my hands down his muscular arms. I was strangely aware of the absence of his touch, but it seemed to excite me even more. I left his mouth and kissed his neck, Adam's apple, and collarbones while my hands roamed freely across his bare torso. I laved his nipples with my pierced tongue, sucking and nibbling, feeling Wesley's eyes watching me closely. I got up on all fours and moved backward, allowing my lips and tongue to rediscover every inch of his warm, perspiring body. Down to his calves and ankles, I caressed and rubbed, then moved back up again. He was oozing pre-cum and I slid my fingers over his stiff shaft and sucked on the two low-hanging appendages. I glanced up at Wesley's face and his expression was the sexiest I'd ever seen. Bringing my lips to his favorite spot, I licked the tip and brushed my fingers along the flesh of his inner thighs. He lifted his hips, pushing himself deeper into my mouth while allowing my wet fingers to explore the pliable ring of muscle. Wesley pushed his head back into the pillow and moaned in short, quaking gasps. I swallowed him deep and rimmed the hole with one finger while I massaged his balls with my other hand. His body shook and he called my name as he erupted in my mouth. Tears collected in the corners of his eyes and he slumped heavily into the mattress. I lay atop him and gave him light kisses while he returned to his senses. Finally, Wesley opened his eyes and looked at me with a grateful smile.

"God…damn," he panted, pulling his hands up before remembering they were tied firmly in place.

"Don't think we're done yet," I said with a grin, lifting myself up on all fours again. "You can get it up for me again, right?" I asked, touching myself with long, slow strokes.

Wesley's eyes glided over my frame and settled on my throbbing erection. He knew he was responsible for the state I was in and, like a good man, found himself capable of satisfying me.

I kissed him deeply and pushed my hand between my thighs, fingering the moist hole in heady preparation. I sat up on my knees and inched back until I felt him nudging against my backside. I slowly took him in until his balls met with my flesh. He watched me with glassy eyes while he pumped his hips into me and I whimpered in short, quiet gasps.

"Tor, Tor, untie me," he said, pulling his hands forward and stretching the cotton shirts tied to the bed frame.

I nodded with a sense of relief and leaned forward, loosening the knot around his wrist. He pulled his hand free and frantically helped me liberate his other hand. He sat up quickly, rocking me against his cock, hips, and thighs and I was instantly aroused by the touch of his hard hands. He held me desperately, pumping into me feverishly with quick, strong thrusts. We climaxed in delirious unison, achieving heights of pleasure that were almost godly.

We fell to the mattress, panting and gasping in silence for a full five minutes. No words needed to be spoken and our warm, sticky bodies clung to each other as if our very molecules were making love.

Chapter 44

"WES! Wes, over here!" Scott shouted, waving his hand over his head.

Wesley looked up and smiled when he saw his brother. It was a heart-warming reunion and I stood at their sides with a dopey grin on my face. A young woman with dark brown hair looked at me and smiled. Scott slapped Wesley's back and then faced me with the same excitement.

"Toren! Wow, this is so great! I'm so glad you guys came!" Scott shouted, throwing his arms around my shoulders and patting my back. "I can't believe it! How was your flight?" he asked, stepping back and bumping into the dark-haired girl.

"Man, you are such a spaz," Wesley said, shaking his head. I laughed, but it was true; I would never have expected such a reaction from a big, tall, muscular man. But Wesley had a similar quality; he was always so cool and calm, but he sometimes got overly excited about certain things.

"Ahem?" the woman said, coughing into her fist melodramatically then smiling at Scott.

"Oh yeah! This is my future wife, Michele," Scott stated beamingly, putting his arm around her shoulders. "And this is my little brother Wesley and his boyfriend Toren."

She smiled largely, showing her perfect white teeth, and stepped forward. "It's so nice to finally meet you," she squealed, taking both of Wesley's hands in hers. "I'm so glad you guys could make it! Scott's been so worried that you wouldn't come," she continued, turning to me and shaking my hands. "Plus, I've been dying to meet you two. Scott's already told me so much about you."

Wesley smiled and I blushed. I hadn't seen Scott since the graduation and he and Wesley seemed to look more similar than before. Scott slapped Wesley's arm and started walking away, waving his hand for us to follow.

"C'mon, let's go get your bags and then we're going out for dinner," Scott stated, glancing over his shoulder.

"Wait a sec…," Wesley started, catching up with his brother, but Scott turned quickly and cut him off.

"I'm going to spoil you for once. So just shut up and say thank you, you little brat," Scott said, using his big-brother trump card. Wesley rolled his eyes and Michele and I smiled in amusement.

We only had one large suitcase that I borrowed from Mom. We picked that up and then the four of us went out to Scott's car in a distant parking lot. Wesley eyed it interestedly; it was a newer Mustang and he was happily impressed. He looked over everything as we drove to a Chinese restaurant close to the hotel where we were staying.

Scott and Michele were a perfect couple. They smiled and laughed together with their whole hearts and I wondered if Wesley and I looked like that together. Scott and Wesley caught up on the past few months and argued again about the expense of the plane tickets and hotel. I also learned that both Scott and Michele graduated from college in December and I slapped Wesley's shoulder for not telling me.

"Well, congratulations, even if it is a little late. If I knew," I emphasized, looking at Wesley, "we would've sent you a gift."

"Don't worry about it," Scott said cordially. "So, how's school going for you?"

"Really good," I answered, nodding my head. "I'm still taking a lot of gen ed classes, but I'm taking two history classes that I really like."

"After next year, you'll really be able to focus on your major. And you won't have to bother with any more bio classes," Scott laughed, taking a long drink of his beer.

My eyes widened, my face turned beet red, and I slapped Wesley's arm again. "You told him?" I asked in a loud, outraged whisper.

"It was too funny not to share," Wesley answered, patting my leg under the table.

"That's because it didn't happen to *you.* Sheesh, is there anyone you *didn't* tell?" I said embarrassedly, folding my arms across my chest. "You forgot to tell me your brother graduated from college, but you remember to tell him that?"

"C'mon, Toren. It really *is* funny, and besides, I'm sure you're not the only one that's happened to," Michele said, trying to comfort me, but it only embarrassed me more that she knew too. "We've all had our share of embarrassing experiences," she said, glancing at Scott. "I was still living with my parents when we got engaged and one afternoon—yes, you guessed it—my *dad* walked in on us," she confided blushingly. "Talk about mortifying!"

I laughed and her disclosure did make me feel a little better.

"The thing that gets me, though," Scott added with a laugh, "is they're still letting me marry her."

"It's probably only because I was on top," Michele countered quickly.

We finished dinner and started talking about the wedding. Tomorrow, after the rehearsal dinner, Wesley would go rent a tux. The wedding was Saturday at four o'clock with the reception immediately following. Wesley would need to leave early and Scott spoke with a friend to come pick me up before the ceremony if I didn't want to hang out at the church.

The check came and Wesley grudgingly let Scott pay. We stopped at a convenience store and bought a case of beer, some soda, and snacks, before heading to the hotel. Scott and Michele helped us to our room and then left a little while later. I took my suit from the suitcase and hung it in the bathroom to pull out the wrinkles. Then I called my mom to let her know we arrived safely. Wesley filled the bathroom sink with ice and put the beer bottles in to keep them cold. We drank the rest of the evening and went to bed around midnight, tipsy and tired.

IT was a beautiful day. The sky was partly cloudy, but rays of sunshine broke through and bathed everything in golden light. Wesley got dressed and he looked incredibly handsome in his tuxedo, with his hair slicked back. One of Scott's ushers came to pick up Wesley about three hours before the wedding for pictures, but I decided to stay at the hotel because Mr. and Mrs. Carroll were going to be there, and I didn't know if they even knew I was here. Half an hour before the ceremony, a friend of Scott's came to pick me up.

The church was pretty and old. Families and friends mulled around, happily chatting before the ceremony. I strolled around the church, making sure I was any place Mr. and Mrs. Carroll were not.

As four o'clock neared, the church began to fill with people. I waited until Mr. and Mrs. Carroll sat down in the first pew on the right side. I slipped into the fourth row at the end because all the aisle seats were taken.

The minister quieted the crowd and Scott stood in front of the altar with his hands folded. He looked very handsome with a graceful elegance and my heart swelled with happiness for him. The minister said a few words and then the ushers and bridesmaids came down the aisle with smiles and bouquets. Wesley and Emily, Michele's younger sister, walked down the aisle and took their places. Wesley patted Scott's back and smiled genuinely at him, and butterflies flitted in my stomach. Then the "Wedding March" began and Michele and her father started down the aisle. She looked beautiful, and I glanced at Scott, who was taking deep breaths with glassy eyes. At the altar, Michele's father hugged her and placed her hand in Scott's.

The ceremony was beautiful, touching, and even humorous at times. When Scott and Michele were exchanging their vows, Wesley found me in the audience and smiled warmly. I mouthed the words "I love you" and his eyes widened, his face turned red, and he quickly looked to the front again.

At the end of the ceremony, Scott and Michele joined for a sweet, gentle kiss and faced the congregation. "I happily present Mr. and Mrs. Carroll," the minister said joyfully and the small church erupted with applause. Scott and Michele beamed as they walked down the aisle together as husband and wife.

I was given a ride to the reception hall by the same friend of Scott's that picked me up and we took our seats. I was at a table with Scott and Michele's friends, only a few years older than me, and I felt comfortable there. When I introduced myself, I was surprised that they had already heard about me. They told me how happy Scott was that Wesley and I came and about how he was so worried. I felt happy and confident; I knew just how much Scott wanted Wesley, both of us, to share in the celebration.

The wedding party arrived a little before six o'clock and everyone in the reception hall clapped and whistled at the newlyweds' arrival. Wesley sat at the head table for dinner and gave me reassuring smiles all the way through. The meal was often interrupted with the clinking glasses of toasts, usually initiated by the guests at my table.

After dinner, the DJ began spinning in earnest and the open bar was constantly busy. Wesley met up with me and we watched from the side for the first dance and the father-daughter dance. Then the dance floor was overrun with Michele and Scott's friends and family. Wesley went to get us some drinks from the bar and I sat down, watching the excitement from the sidelines.

"You got a hell of a lot of nerve showing up here," Mr. Carroll's voice thundered above me. I looked up and saw Wesley's father standing in front of me with his arms crossed. "Just what the hell are you trying to do?"

I swallowed hard and stared at the tall man towering over me. Everything had gone so well today that I nearly forgot the threat the man imposed. My eyes teared up and I wished with all my heart that Wesley would come back.

"I asked you a question. What are you doing here? Why the hell are you doing this?" Mr. Carroll demanded, his voice even more severe. At last, Wesley came back and I breathed a sigh of relief, but Mr. Carroll redirected his anger at Wesley. "Just what the hell are you trying to prove? What is wrong with you? I told you not to bring him," he said, sneering at me. "Just the sight of him is disgusting! You had no right…."

"Shut up," Wesley said, his voice edged with anger. "What the hell is wrong with you? If you don't like it, just ignore us. Better yet, don't even talk to us. Go to hell," Wesley growled, taking my hand and turning his back to his father.

Mr. Carroll slapped our hands apart and stepped into Wesley's face. He was at least six inches taller, but Wesley stared up at him defiantly.

"You think this is funny? I *told* you not to bring that little faggot here," Mr. Carroll snapped.

Wesley's eyes sparked and he pushed his dad back. "Don't you fucking say that! Don't you ever say that!" Wesley shouted.

Mrs. Carroll and Scott stepped in at the same time, restraining Mr. Carroll and Wesley, respectively.

"What the hell is wrong with you?" Scott shouted, staring at his father. "I wanted them here, so if you've got a problem with it, come to me!"

"Scott!" Mrs. Carroll interrupted, surprised by her elder son's outburst. Perhaps she was expecting this confrontation with Wesley, but not with Scott. She looked around embarrassedly; the argument between Mr. Carroll and me had turned into a spectacle. Michele was standing by Scott and even her parents were in the near background.

Mr. Carroll turned on me again with fire in his eyes. "This is all your fault!" he shouted. "Get the hell out of here!"

"Shut the fuck up!" Wesley yelled, stepping in front of me.

I had never heard his voice so rabid before and it scared me. I was a fool to think I could come to the wedding without something happening. Wesley always defended me and now Scott and even Michele were lending me their support.

"I love him," I said, stepping next to Wesley. "I don't care what you think, but I love Wesley with my whole heart and there is nothing you can do to change that," I said in a surprisingly firm voice. Wesley looked at me and I narrowed my eyes at Mr. Carroll. "And it's not your choice anyway. You can say whatever you want, but I'll never stop loving him. And by the way, we're gay. We're not faggots; we're gay."

Mr. Carroll looked at me with a bewildered expression. He probably wasn't expecting a queer to stand up for himself. But his anger redoubled and he started shouting, screaming at me. But Scott stepped forward and held up his hand.

"Go home, Dad. If this is the way you're gonna act, I don't want you here," Scott said darkly, shaking his head. Mr. Carroll began to rant again, but Scott cut him off. "I said, go home. I don't want you here."

Mr. Carroll stared at Scott, then Wesley, then me. He turned on his heel and shook his head. "I thought I raised you better than this," he said as one last jeer.

"Yeah, we have to thank Mom that we didn't turn out like you," Scott replied, stealing the last word.

Mrs. Carroll followed her husband out of the reception hall and Scott turned to me with an apologetic expression. Wesley sat down in a chair and breathed like he had been holding his breath. The DJ was still playing music, there were people on the dance floor, and I felt relieved that it wasn't as big a spectacle as I thought it was. Michele's parents stepped back and returned to their friends with smiles. Me, Wesley, Scott, and Michele stood together.

"Jesus Christ, I'm so sorry," Scott said, shaking his head ashamedly. "I…I don't know what to say, except I'm sorry."

I touched Scott's shoulder and smiled gratefully. "It's okay. Don't worry about it. If anything, thank you for defending us," I said.

Scott excused himself and I pulled a chair next to Wesley and rubbed his back. He had downed both the beers he brought for us. Tears were at the edges of his eyes and I ruffled his hair and kissed his forehead.

"I'm sorry, Tor. I'm so sorry," Wesley said quietly, staring at the ground. "I've never actually wanted to kill anyone before."

"Don't talk like that," I said, rubbing his back again. I smiled and laughed softly. "You said it yourself; you can't choose your family. But you chose me and I chose you. And I would again and again and again."

Wesley finally looked up at me with a smile, when Scott tapped me on the shoulder. He was smiling ear-to-ear and held his hand out to me. The song "Hero" by Mariah Carey started playing. "May I have this dance?"

Scott grabbed my hand and pulled me onto the dance floor. He locked his arm around my back, held my hand up, and swayed me to and fro across the hardwood floor. I couldn't help but laugh and I glanced at Wesley, watching us with a blank, open-mouthed stare. Michele grabbed one of her bridesmaids and began dancing, and then their friends paired up with same-sex partners and filled up the dance floor. I looked at Wesley again and he was laughing. The tension in the pit of my stomach broke and I hugged Scott.

"Thank you," I said, with tears rimming my eyes.

"Thank you," Scott answered. "It took some huge fucking balls to stand up to my dad like that. And thank you, too, for making my brother so happy."

I smiled timidly and Scott waved to Wesley to come over. Wesley cut in and wrapped his arms around me. I felt like crying, but instead I laughed when I saw Scott dancing with Michele's father.

"I love you. So much," Wesley said and kissed me simply on the lips.

He smiled and my world was bright again, so I kissed him. "Thank you for loving me."

J. M. COLAIL currently lives in a suburb of Detroit with her dog, Maizy. She graduated from the University of Michigan-Dearborn with a bachelor's in anthropology. She loves reading and writing and works at a bookstore, which is bad for her wallet. She is looking for the perfect girl to make all her dreams come true but having fun while she does it.

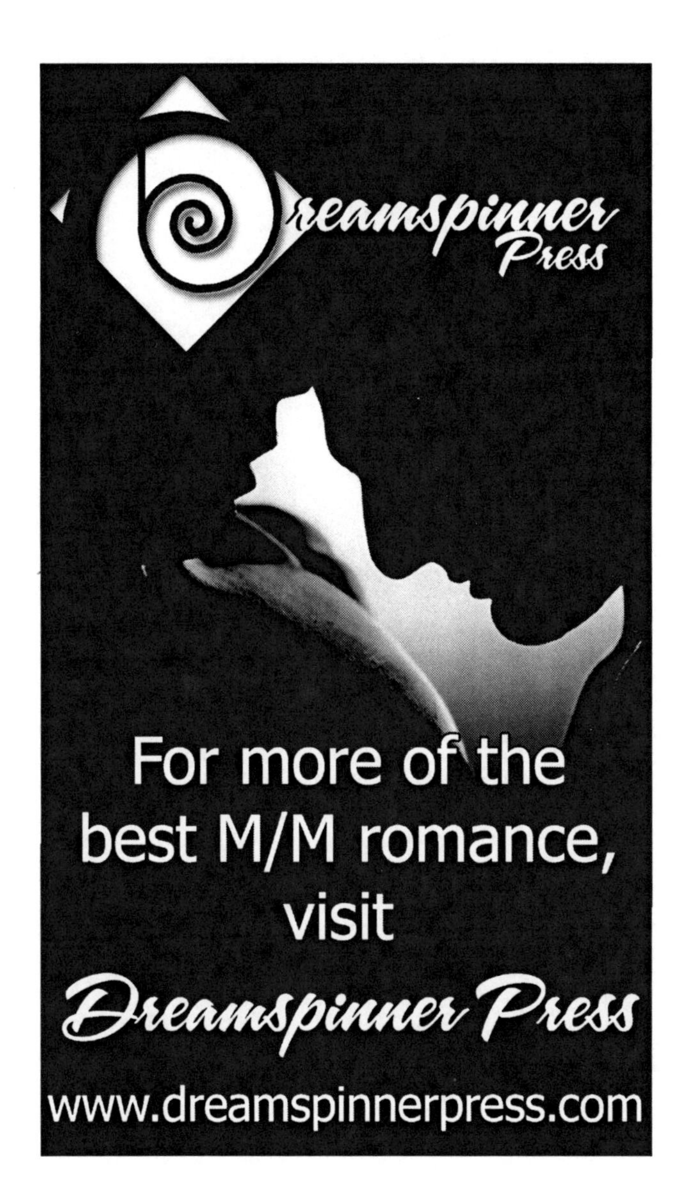
Dreamspinner Press
For more of the best M/M romance, visit
Dreamspinner Press
www.dreamspinnerpress.com

Printed in the United States
148478LV00008B/78/P

9 781935 192473